PLAYERS CLUB

MERCY

USA TODAY BESTSELLING AUTHOR

SARA CATE

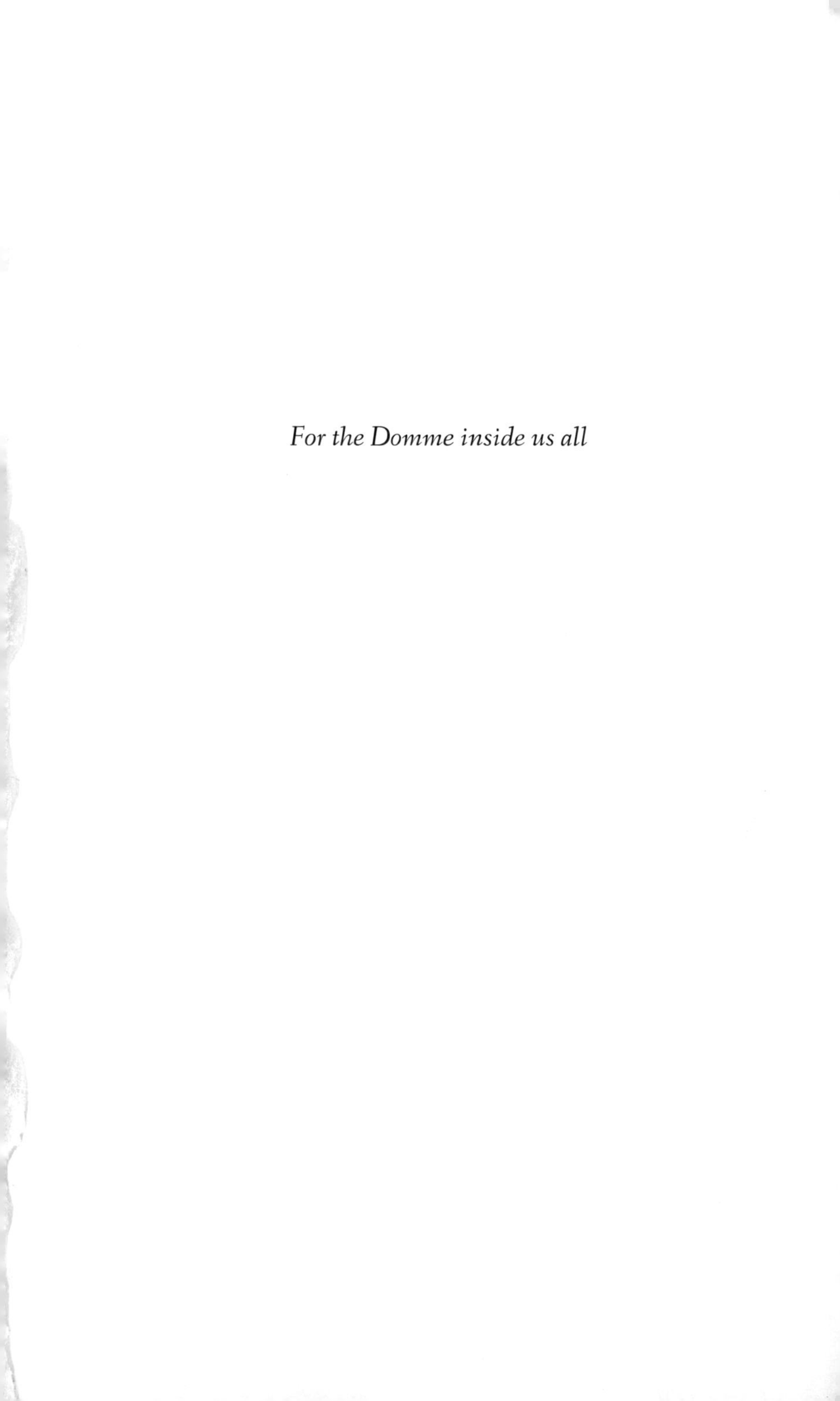

For the Domme inside us all

Content warning

Dear readers,

This book ended up being a touch darker than the other books in series. It revolves around a man with pent up emotions, not equipped to deal with big feelings properly. Inside these pages, you will find a bit of violence and sexual degradation. You will also find healing and overcoming a harmful upbringing.

Naturally, there is the heavy presence of BDSM. It's meant to inspire you, but should not be used as a guidebook or manual for healthy sexual relationships. With the help of someone with more experience than me, I've done my best to portray the lifestyle in a safe, sane, and consensual manner, but please remember to do your own research before embarking on anything new or potentially dangerous.

Have fun and enjoy!

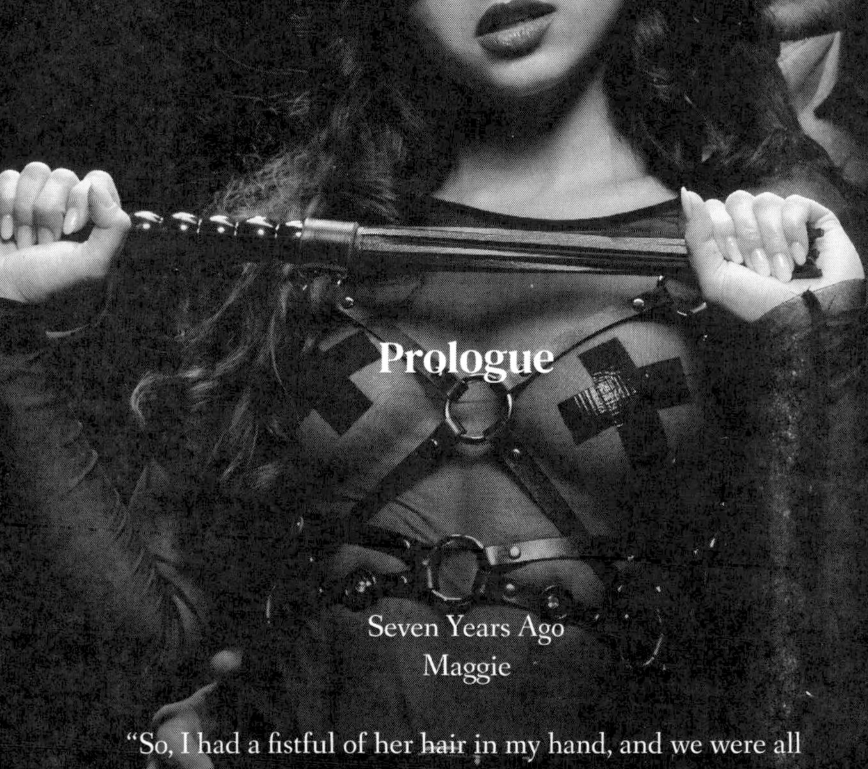

Prologue

Seven Years Ago
Maggie

"So, I had a fistful of her hair in my hand, and we were all in the moment when I looked her right in the eye and said, 'Suck my cock like a good little girl.' The next thing I knew, she reared back her fist and clocked me straight in the face."

I nearly choke on my Chardonnay. Across the table, my friend, Emerson, entertains us with his most recent bedroom trauma. It's always something with these guys. Every Thursday, we meet up for drinks and everyone shares some outlandish sexcapade story to regale us with while I sit silently at the end and wonder how the hell I got here.

While the men all react with winces and curses, I quietly find the words to add to the conversation.

"I don't think she liked that," I say with forced laughter, and naturally, they think I'm joking, responding with their own sarcastic replies.

"You think?" Emerson shoots back with a pained smile, using his beer like an ice pack against his bruised face.

I met Emerson a few years ago when I organized an event for his failed startup. After that, he started working for this company and begged me to join him. Unlike most men I work with, Emerson doesn't see my assertiveness as a threat. He seems to appreciate me for all the things that others like to berate me for having.

I'm a control freak. I'm great at both delegating and giving orders. And I don't let others push me around or make me feel stupid. Which is exactly why I took the job with Emerson.

Do I despise the company we work for? Absolutely. It's a mess, unorganized, corrupt, and run by complete imbeciles.

But I love working with these three. Emerson, Garrett, and Hunter are rare. They don't talk over me or belittle my ideas. They actually listen to me, and as is apparent tonight, they treat me like a friend. Even though I can't exactly join in on their crazy sex stories.

I mean...they're three single men in their prime. I can't exactly say I'm surprised.

"I thought we were getting along great," Emerson says, looking genuinely despondent after his failed attempt to be the slightest bit adventurous in the bedroom. "She seemed kinky enough, and she definitely appeared into it, but I guess I was wrong. Not a fan of a little sexy degradation, apparently."

I take a sip of my wine without responding to that last comment. Maybe I should explain to Emerson that not all women like to be degraded. There's a good chance she's been humiliated so much she's grown a defense to it. Or I could let Emerson in on the little secret that women 'appear into it' more often than they actually are.

In this case, I bet she *was* into it. Emerson is handsome and confident and is probably great in bed. But if a man ever grabbed my hair and spoke to me like that, I'd slug him in the face too.

"Fuck, man," Garrett says with a scowl. "It's bullshit that there isn't a way to match people up by the kinky shit they like to do in the bedroom."

As the guys laugh at him, I stare in contemplation.

"I'm fucking serious. How nice would it be if you could meet up with someone who likes the same weird shit you do? You wouldn't have to hide it or be embarrassed by the kinks that get your panties wet."

This time I do laugh because this whole thing with Emerson could have been avoided with a simple conversation with his partner, and the fact that Garrett seriously thinks an app will solve that problem for him is laughable. *Men.*

"You're fucking crazy, Garrett," Hunter says with his girlfriend, Isabel, by his side.

"I am not," Garrett argues. "Who here doesn't have some freaky bedroom desires you've always wanted to do but are too afraid to ask? I mean, obviously, Emerson isn't afraid to ask."

There's more laughter and jeering, teasing Garrett because they take everything he says as a joke. And I guess, so do I because what he's proposing is easy to imagine—from a man's perspective. No shame. No fear. No creepy assholes waiting to take advantage of you. In a perfect world, an app like this would be awesome. But we don't live in a perfect world, and Garrett has no clue what it would be like for women.

"Come on. I'm serious," Garrett replies. "Out of all the shit you've done, what is the one thing you wish you could ask for? You know you have something. So let's hear it."

"You first," I say, knocking the ball back in his court.

"Fine." After straightening his spine, and mustering his courage, he announces, "I like to watch."

I resist the urge to roll my eyes. Of course, he does. No one can be surprised by that. But the guys still show their interest and I sit back and smile. When it comes around to Hunter, he deflects, naturally. But it's the demure redhead on his right that proudly announces her taste for group activities, which *really* stirs up the conversation. I give her props for owning up to that.

But when their eyes all fall on me, I shake my head vehemently.

"Don't look at me," I announce.

"Come on, Mags," Hunter says with a smile.

"I don't have a kink. I'm completely vanilla."

Garrett narrows his eyes at me, and I bite my bottom lip to hold back my bashful smile. "It's always the quiet ones."

"What?" I laugh.

"I bet you're the kinkiest person at this table," he jokes, and I let out a loud laugh.

I wish he was right.

A couple hours later, we're in the parking lot saying our goodbyes. Emerson walks me to my car, like he does every week, and as I pull my keys out of my purse, he lets out a laugh.

"Garrett has some crazy ideas," he says.

"He does," I reply, thinking nothing of it.

"This one could actually work, though. Don't you think?"

As we reach my car, I stare up at him. "No, I don't think it would."

His face falls. "Why not?"

"Because I don't know a single woman who would feel comfortable giving away that information without it feeling exploitative. The minute we admit we're the least bit kinky, men take it as a personal invitation to overstep."

"What if we vetted our members? Put safety protocols in place. Made it more welcoming to women."

I tilt my head and shrug. "I don't know. I guess I'm not the best person to ask. I'm not as...sex-driven as you guys are."

"Well, I wouldn't do it without you," he replies, and my lips tighten into a thin smile at that. I believe him, and I don't know what Emerson sees in me that no one else does, but my world would be a better place if more men could have an ounce of the respect he does.

"Then, I guess it's a good thing it's just a crazy idea," I joke as I unlock my car and pull open the driver's side door.

"It doesn't have to be," he adds, and I pause. Slowly, I turn toward him with a bad feeling in my gut.

"You're not serious."

"Maggie, let's be honest. The company we work for has three months *at best*. I don't want to just move on to another shitty entertainment company that doesn't have new ideas. I'm ready for *our* ideas. I think the four of us can do something amazing."

I squint at him. "You've been collecting us for a business, haven't you? This whole time I thought we were friends," I joke. He laughs with a devilish smile.

"You love me," he says with a cheesy smile.

"No, I don't," I reply, tossing my purse in the passenger seat. After I climb in and start my car, Emerson leans over, staring at me with a shameless grin.

"Say you'll help me. I'm serious, Maggie. I think this could be amazing, and I can't do it without you."

The fight in me dissipates as I let out a sigh. What are my choices? I know he's right about the company going under; it's already happening. And if I don't move on with Emerson, then I'll be forced to go back into event planning or working for some asshole who thinks I'm nothing more than his secretary, programmed to take orders and get coffee. I refuse to go back to that.

Looking up at him with a stern expression, I relent. "Fine, but we have to make it inviting for women. Not like some shady hookup app."

He slaps my car with a smile. "Of course. Whatever you say."

"It has to be a no-judgment zone for *everyone*. And safety is the top priority."

"I agree," he replies with a serious expression.

"I don't know how you're going to keep members safe without a physical location to let them meet at, though."

I mean it as a rhetorical point, but Emerson's eyes suddenly light up and that uneasy feeling returns.

"*That* is a great idea."

"No," I respond quickly.

"Yes," he argues, "we already have experience running clubs and events."

"So now you want to open a club for people to...meet at and, what? Have sex?"

He smiles wickedly and I want to slam my face against the steering wheel. "Emerson, we cannot open a sex club."

"Why not?"

"Because...I'm not...I can't. It's..." I'm stammering, and he's staring at me, waiting for me to give him just one valid reason for why this is a bad idea, but the truth is, I don't have one. All I have is voices in my head telling me that sex is shameful and wrong, and even if my rational brain can admit how ridiculous that is, indoctrination runs deep.

"Think about it," he replies.

"I will."

"Because it would be a mess without you."

"I know it would." I laugh.

With that, he closes my door and watches as I pull out of the parking lot and onto the road home. On my drive, I laugh again at his insane ideas. If Emerson thinks I'm the kind of woman to run a sex club, he is crazy.

Either he doesn't know me at all...or I don't.

Rule #1: Wizards are dickheads.

Beau

"The sorcerer casts a Ray of Sickness. Roll a constitution check."

"What the hell does that mean?" I snap.

"Roll the dice." So I do, and the players around the table wince in unison when it rolls to a stop.

"What the fuck does that mean?" I ask again.

"It means you're dead," the freckle-faced asshole sitting across from me says with a smug grin.

"What the fuck?" I toss down my character sheet as I glower at him, and I swear I see him flinch.

"Beau..." Sophie groans next to me in warning.

"What? That's not fair. This guy literally makes up the rules and just decides that his stupid wizard kills my barbarian? This game is bullshit." Trying to snatch the booklet out of his hand, I feel Sophie's hand on my arm, so I pause. I look over at her, pink-faced, embarrassed by my outburst, so I quickly sit back down and let it go. Feeling all the players' eyes on us, I decide to cool off.

With a grimace directed at the wizard, I bite my tongue. As much as I hate this stupid, fucking game, I do like being able to bring Soph, and if I act like an actual barbarian, she'll find someone else to drive her to D&D night.

Since I'm now technically dead, it means I get to sit back and do nothing while she continues the campaign. It's fucking boring, but it goes by quickly, and within an hour, we're done, and we can finally leave.

As we're packing up, I notice that fuck face wizard staring at Sophie a little too long. "Let's get out of here," I grumble as I tug her toward the door of the comic book shop.

"Bye, guys," she says and they reply in unison.

"Bye, Sophie," the kid calls after her.

Once we're in the car, I sense her glaring at me. Finally, she breaks the silence. "Now I remember why I used to hate you."

What the fuck? "You used to hate me?" I scoff.

"Well, you did cheat on my sister and treat her like shit, so...yeah."

"Ouch," I reply. "But wait...why do you hate me now?"

"Oh, I don't know...maybe because you embarrass me in front of my friends and only care about yourself." Glancing over at her, I do feel a hint of remorse.

"Why do you care about those nerds?"

"Those are my friends, Beau. And if you haven't noticed...I am also a nerd."

"But like a cool nerd," I reply, smiling at her. She rolls her eyes at me and stares back down at her phone.

When Sophie's sister, my ex, started dating my dad a year ago...it was fucking awkward as hell. Made even worse by the fact that I was pretty sure Charlie's mom and sister hated my guts. So I've been doing everything I can to make things less awkward. Which has basically turned into me being a fifteen-year-old girl's chauffeur and D&D partner.

"I don't like that wizard kid. He's not your friend, right?"

Her head snaps up in my direction. "Kyle? Yeah...I mean, no. He's not my friend, friend, but I sort of know him from school. Why?"

My jaw drops as we pull up to a red light and I stare at her in shock. "Holy shit...do you have a crush on that wizard?"

"No!" she shrieks.

"You do," I reply with a smile.

Her expression turns sour as she shoots me one of those sassy head tilt glares. "Even if I did, you're the last person on earth I would talk to about it."

"Why? I give great dating advice."

She laughs. "Your ex-girlfriend is now dating your dad, so..."

"Ouch again. You're being mean tonight."

"Well, it's true."

It still feels like an insult, no matter how true it is, but I don't tell her that part. Instead, I continue driving, trying to look as unaffected as possible.

I'm not bitter about Charlie and my dad anymore. I'm over it. I don't care. It's not like I thought Charlie was the fucking love of my life or anything. We broke up. She was too needy and wanted way too much from me...which I guess, looking back, was literally the bare minimum but that's why I've said *fuck off* to dating all together. No matter what I do, it's not enough, and I can't keep anyone happy. And vice versa. No one holds my attention or makes me want to give them more.

Charlie is just better suited for my dad, and I'm happy for them. They can continue doing whatever the fuck it is they do at that weird club of his, and I can show up to Taco Tuesday every week with a smile on my face and it's fine.

It's fine.

"So are you going to talk to him?" I ask as we pull into Sophie's neighborhood. "The wizard, I mean."

"Probably not," she replies, clearly forgetting that she just said I was the last person on earth she'd talk to about this.

"Why not?" My defensive instincts flex inside me, but I keep my cool. Sophie is as tough as nails, and I know she wants me to treat her like every other girl, but I can't help but feel a little extra protective of her. It's hard enough being a teenager these days, but then those fucking transphobes out there want to make it especially rough on her.

"Because I don't want a boyfriend," she replies in a flat tone as she types out a text on her phone. I furrow my brow at her, readying to ask my next question, which she clearly anticipates because she looks up and answers it before I get the chance. "And no, I don't want a girlfriend either, if that's what you were going to ask."

It was.

"I just don't want anything right now. My best friend, Chloe, has a boyfriend and it seems like a pain in the ass. So much work and stress."

A laugh trickles its way out of my chest. "Smart choice." I mean, if anyone knows what it's like to be a pain in the ass boyfriend, more stress and work than I'm worth, it's me.

As I pull up to her house, she starts to reach for the door handle, but I stop her. "You know, I think it's smart that you avoid that drama. But if that little wizard fucker gives you any trouble, I'll kick his ass."

She smiles as she shakes her head at me. "I know you think you're being chivalrous, and I appreciate you looking out for me, but beating up jerks isn't going to make anything better."

"It'll make me feel better," I joke.

"Exactly. You want to beat up guys who pick on me because it makes *you* feel better."

"Well, what do you want, Smurf?" I ask, even though most of the blue in her hair has grown out. Nicknames are just hard to shake, I guess.

She lets out a sigh. "First of all, someone who will take me to D&D night without cussing out the Dungeon Master."

"He killed me!"

"You got yourself killed with those reckless moves," she argues. "Which I clearly warned you against, but you're a barbarian through and through. *Destroy, smash, kill,*" she says, obviously mocking me.

"I thought that was the point."

"You obviously need more guidance. What you need is a girlfriend who you'll actually listen to for once. Find her and bring *her* to D&D night."

I arch a brow in her direction. Not likely.

When she sees my reluctant response to that idea, she laughs and opens the car door. "Or keep being the same self-centered barbarian who gets himself killed each week."

"Does that mean I'm invited back next Friday?" I ask.

After climbing out, she peers back in with a smile and

a roll of her eyes. "You don't have to, you know. I can get a ride with a friend or something."

"What kind of older brother would I be if I let you go to D&D night without me?"

"Technically...I'm closer to being your step-aunt."

"Never say that again," I reply dryly. "Besides, as much as the wizard prick pisses me off, I like going with you. You make me look cool, Smurf."

She laughs and shakes her head again. "Thanks, Beau. I'll see you next week."

"See you next week," I say as she closes the door and walks up to the house.

Driving home, I consider that maybe I *should* let someone else drive Sophie. I mean, I started taking her as a favor to Charlie, but I don't owe her any favors anymore.

Rule #2: Sometimes you just have to smile and lie.

Maggie

"I'm an idiot." Standing in the middle of the two-story entryway of a completely empty home that now belongs to me, I hear the delicate echo of my voice bouncing off the hardwood floor—that could use some work—and empty walls—that could use some fresh paint. "I'm an idiot!" I yell, this time enjoying the way my voice reverberates through the huge empty space.

My eighty-pound Great Dane, Ringo, comes galloping back into the room after giving our new house a thorough sniffing. He seems a good deal less worried about the move, especially since this one comes with a yard he can enjoy.

My heels click against the floor as I make my way toward the kitchen in the back. Dropping the deed of the house on the quartz countertop—which seems to be in pretty good shape, thank God—I try my best to see potential and not rust, dust, and grime.

What on earth did I get myself into? Why does a single woman in her thirties need a giant house? Just because Emerson Grant owns a thirty-four-hundred square foot Spanish colonial does not mean I should, too. Yet, somehow, here I stand, keys in hand.

Why shouldn't I have a big house? Just because I'm single doesn't mean I don't deserve it. I can afford it. My last house was fine, but the guest bedroom did double as my office, which was less than convenient when I had Hunter living in it for two months.

So now I have a guest suite and an office, and I deserve that, dammit.

A car door closes outside, followed a few moments later by a gentle knock on the door.

"Come in!" I call because I know it's one of the guys. Turning from the kitchen, I'm relieved to see Hunter walk through the door in a pair of gym shorts and a T-shirt. Ringo greets him with a familiar nuzzle against his side, which Hunter rewards with a scratch behind the ears. I wouldn't say Hunter and I were all that close before but after he spent his period of soul-searching and coming out in my house, we grew a lot closer.

Which means he instantly reads the expression of regret and remorse on my face before the door even closes.

"Oh no..." he says as he crosses the space and swallows me up in his arms. "Don't cry, Mags."

"I'm not crying. I'm just feeling sorry for myself."

"Why? Because you bought a beautiful house?"

"No. Because I bought a giant fixer-upper on a whim and now I have to figure out how to fill it."

"You mean with a husband and kids?" he asks, pulling away.

"God, no!" I reply, shoving him in the chest. "Not all women need a husband—"

"It was a joke!" he says with a laugh. "I was trying to lighten the mood. I know you meant furniture."

Giving him a skeptical glare, I pull away and lean against the counter. "Speaking of kids, how's Isabel?"

"Ready to pop and hating life."

"I bet. When is she due?"

"Four more months, but the doctor said she probably won't make it that long."

I screw up my face in disgust. The last time I saw Isabel, she already looked ready to burst, and she has to get all the way through summer like that. But I mean...she was glowing, I guess. I just hope for her sake those babies are Hunter's and not Drake's. No one should have to endure birthing that giant Viking's spawn, let alone two of them at the same time.

"Are you nervous?" I ask.

"About being a father? Incredibly. But not about the baby stuff. I'm more worried about when they get older. What if they hate me? What if they resent us? I see what Emerson goes through with Beau and that's the shit that scares me."

I nod. I can completely understand that fear. Emerson is the only one of us to have raised a kid so far, and that's been a rocky relationship at best. Beau wasn't a fan of his father owning a sex club and spent six months not talking to him as punishment, meaning we never heard the end of it from Emerson during that time. Then to pour salt on the wound, Emerson went and snatched up Beau's ex-girlfriend for himself. Now, those two are like the spokesmen for strained father-son relationships.

So yeah...if that's the best example Hunter has of fatherhood, I don't blame him for feeling a bit nervous.

"Well, I'm willing to bet your kids won't be entitled, self-absorbed, spoiled brats. So I wouldn't worry too much about it."

"Ouch!" he replies with a laugh.

"Did I say that out loud?" I add with a mischievous grin.

Both of us are still laughing when the front door opens again. This time it's Garrett, who doesn't knock, of course.

"What did I miss?" he asks.

"Oh nothing," Hunter says, clearly not letting Garrett know that we're currently roasting his best friend's son. Not that Garrett wouldn't have some fuel to throw on that fire.

He whistles as he walks through the house, checking it out as he does. "Nice place, Mags."

I shrug and try to force a smile. "Thanks. It's going to be a lot of work."

"Well, if anyone can handle the work, it's you."

Can I, though? The guys all seem to think I just *love* hard work. As if just because I *can* handle it all automatically means I want to.

"You guys really don't have to do this. I could have easily hired a moving company."

"Now, where's the fun in that?" Garrett replies with a laugh. "Besides, it keeps us humble. Especially since you think we're all a bunch of arrogant assholes."

"I never said that!" I say, slapping him on the shoulder.

"When was the last time Emerson Grant even got his hands dirty?" Hunter jokes. "This will be good for him."

Shaking my head, I laugh.

Hunter looks down at his phone, clearly reading a message. "Drake is almost here with the moving truck."

And just then, the door opens again. We all stare in surprise as Emerson walks in, casually dressed as if he's about to help unload a moving truck—which is exactly what he's about to do.

"I didn't even know he owned a T-shirt," Hunter mumbles.

"Are those...sneakers?" Garrett asks.

"Leave him alone, guys," I say. "He clearly didn't want to get his Armani dirty."

He pauses at the door with a scowl. "Ha ha. Very funny."

Our laughter is suddenly cut short by an unexpected guest following Emerson through the front door. Looking hesitant and disgruntled, Beau stands in the entryway of my new house, giving us an awkward wave.

"I figured we could use some help," Emerson says, gesturing to his son.

"And someone under thirty," Garrett adds.

I'm standing here speechless because it must be at least five years since I've seen Emerson's son, and I certainly don't remember him looking like this. Broad shoulders, thick arms, and golden tan skin.

The room is swallowed up in tension when I realize I should probably be the one to say something.

"Of course!" I stammer. "Thanks for coming, Beau."

"You're welcome," he mutters uncomfortably.

"I haven't seen you in years. I hardly recognized you," I reply, and he gives me a tense smile. I sound so old, hearing myself say that, but it's true. I remember Beau as a bratty seventeen-year-old, not a full-grown man.

When I notice Emerson looking around, I tense, praying that he doesn't notice the scuffed floorboards and dripping faucet. Not that I bought this million-dollar home to impress him, but I do feel the self-inflicted scorn of having a house not quite as nice as his. Especially when we carry the same job title and take home the same salary.

I almost wish he would sneer at the little details that only I notice. But, of course, he doesn't. Instead, he smiles, approaching me with arms wide, and presses a friendly kiss to my cheek. "The house is beautiful, Maggie. Congratulations."

It's hard enough to compete with Mr. Perfect himself when he's rich and smart and in control and basically has the world kneeling at his feet without effort. The real cherry on the sundae is the fact that Emerson Grant has never treated me poorly in all of our time working together. But maybe that's why it hurts so much that he doesn't see—or rather, acknowledge—how unbalanced the dynamic is between us.

We run different races to cross the same finish line.

"Thanks, Emerson," I mumble with a smile as he pulls away.

Outside a loud horn honks twice, which means Drake is out there parking a truck holding everything I own.

"He's here," Hunter announces, leading the pack out the front door.

Emerson lingers with me for a moment, studying my face with concern. "Everything all right?"

I fake a smile and nod.

But inside I'm thinking, no. Everything is not all right. I just bought a house I don't need that's going to require a lot of work I definitely don't want, and I did all of this to prove that I'm just as successful as him when, deep down, I'm probably using this house to cover up something that I haven't had enough therapy to identify yet.

And to top it all off, I haven't been properly laid in almost two years, and I've given up on dating altogether because, no matter where I look, the only men interested in me are boring, middle-aged divorcees with giant egos and tiny penises.

I'm not afraid of spending my life alone. I actually like being alone, but I'm tired of being unfulfilled and I'm terrified the best years of my life are behind me, and unlike being a sexy rich man in his forties, I'm a thirty-four-year-old workaholic woman that never gets to play the starring role in anyone's fantasy.

So on top of probably living and dying alone, I'm also doomed to spend my years having sex alone too.

"Yep. I'm great," I lie with a smile, and he buys it. Throwing an arm around my shoulders, he drags me toward the door, where he helps me and four other guys unload everything I own into this giant emotional Band-Aid of a house.

And I really wish I could hate him, but he makes it so freaking impossible to do so.

Rule #3: Wine and friends is a dangerous combination.

Maggie

Two hours later, the six of us are sitting on my still plastic-covered sectional, exhausted from unloading the truck, when a car horn blares outside.

"The girls are here," Hunter announces as he lifts a cold beer up to his lips.

"The girls?" I ask.

"Yep. They wanted us to let them know when we're done so they can surprise you," Garrett replies.

"No..." I say carefully.

Emerson laughs. Maybe he's the only one who picks up on it, but I don't do so well with the girls. I work with men. I've always worked with men and I'm used to them. It's easier this way, and I *love* the girls, I really do, but they are exhausting in the best way possible.

But still...exhausting.

"Housewarming party!" Mia exclaims as she bursts

through the door with a stack of pizza boxes in her hands, and as much as I'd like to tell them I'm too sweaty and exhausted for company—not to mention everything I own is in boxes—their energy is too infectious to ignore. Oh, to be twenty-two again.

Charlie follows behind Mia with a box of wine and a package of plastic cups.

And behind her, Isabel waddles in, looking far too sexy in those yoga pants to be pregnant. Meanwhile, I'm a hot mess.

"You guys did not need to do this," I say as I stand up, greeting the girls with a hug. The four of us head into the kitchen, leaving the guys in the living room, and Mia wastes no time cracking open the wine.

While they busy themselves with small talk and dishing out food and drinks, I settle into the corner of my kitchen, checking my work email, just in case anything has popped up today. The guys keep to themselves in the living room as the girls go on and on, mostly talking about Isabel, who is now resting her forearms on the kitchen island and letting her belly hang, looking relieved from the weight off her legs.

"Oh my gosh, Isabel, let me get you a chair!" I say, jumping away from the corner.

"I'm fine, really," she argues, but I wave her off as I rush into the dining room. It's littered with boxes, but the chairs are stacked along the wall, just out of reach. If I lean over this wall of boxes, I can probably hoist one of the chairs off the pile. But as I stretch, nearly toppling over, I feel my shorts riding up my backside and the cool air from the air conditioner brushing against the lower side of my ass.

"Need some help?" a deep voice asks, making me

scream as I lose my balance and fall head first into the pile of boxes. Just before I'm completely vertical and upside down, I feel a pair of firm hands latch onto my hips, pulling me back up until I'm pressed against a solid wall of warm muscle.

"Are you okay?" he asks, his cool and slightly unfamiliar voice just next to my ear. As I turn my head, staring directly into the piercing eyes of Beau Grant, I let the mortification wash over me.

It couldn't have been Drake. Or Hunter or Garrett, or even Emerson. It had to be Beau.

"I'm fine. Thank you," I say, trying to jerk away from his hold, his hands still gripping my hips. When he finally backs away, I swear my internal temperature is about a hundred degrees too hot.

"Can I help you get something?" he asks with a slight smirk on his face, and I glance around his large frame, hoping no one else just saw Emerson's son in a very precarious position behind me, probably looking like he was trying to hump me into a pile of boxes.

"Um...yeah. That chair for Isabel, please."

He nods. "Yes, ma'am." Then I watch as he deftly reaches over the mess and grabs a chair. His shirt rides up enough to reveal a peek of sharp ab muscles, and a delicate tuft of dark hair shows through as he does.

What the fuck, Maggie? I scold myself as I force my eyes away.

With his large hand tightly gripping the leg of the chair, he carries it over my head and sets it on the floor in front of me.

"Thank you," I mumble as I pick it up and take it into the kitchen. As I disappear through the doorway, I feel Beau's eyes linger until I'm out of sight.

"Okay, Maggie, we have to know," Charlie says enthusiastically as I re-enter the kitchen, setting the chair down for Isabel.

I pause, staring at her skeptically.

"Have to know what?"

"When on earth we're going to see you with a hottie of your own!" Mia finishes for her.

"Oh." I shake my head as I reach for a plastic cup to fill it with red wine. "I am just fine. I don't need to settle down with anyone."

"We're not talking about settling down," Charlie replies, lowering her voice. "We're talking about getting laid, Maggie."

I nearly spit out my Merlot. "Again...I am just fine."

"Liar," Isabel replies, muttering into a bottle of water.

I scoff at her. "Traitor."

"It's true, though," she continues. "I've known you for years, and I've never seen you with anyone. What is going on? Do you have a secret lover?"

"Ooh," Mia replies, moving closer.

I respond with a laugh. "The only lover I have is handheld and doesn't care if I have makeup on or if I shaved."

"We need to get you hooked up with someone," Charlie replies. "What's your type?"

"Again...handheld," I reply, taking another drink.

Mia squints her eyes as she stares at me, and I start to get the ominous feeling that she's plotting something I won't like.

"What?" I ask.

"What were the results of your kink quiz?"

Dread settles in my belly. That stupid kink quiz. I didn't take it seven years ago when Hunter developed it for the app, and I'm not taking it now. I don't need some stupid Cosmo personality quiz to tell me what I'll like in the bedroom. And it certainly won't make some perfect man miraculously land on my doorstep.

Owning a sex club was a big enough step for me. No one seemed to understand just how out of my element I was at the club when it first opened. Sex wasn't something I was used to seeing so freely. It was hard enough just hearing the guys talk about it so much. So while the three of them have been off having their fun at Salacious, I've spent the last year flustered, overwhelmed, and terrified.

Am I going to lie and pretend nothing has affected me in my time at Salacious? No, obviously some things have been more resounding than others. Watching Madame Kink dominate in the voyeur rooms. Letting my imagination get away from me when stocking the bondage room. Hearing what comes out of the punishment room.

But every time I was even caught staring for the slightest moment or spent too long in the voyeur hallway, the shame would creep in, and I couldn't brave the nerve to go back.

I can own a sex club. I just can't handle being there.

"Um..." I mumble.

"You've taken the quiz, haven't you?" Charlie asks.

"What if I'm just vanilla and proud?" I reply.

Mia scoffs. "No way."

"Well, there's only one way to find out." Charlie puts out her hand as if she's waiting for me to hand her something, but I stare in confusion. "Your phone, please."

"No way," I reply.

"Oh, come on. We've all taken it," she argues. "And nothing on that list could be crazier than anything we've done. Isabel is getting railed by two guys at once. I've been auctioned off at Salacious in my underwear, and Mia...well, Mia clearly has no shame."

"Nope," Mia replies proudly, and I laugh. For a girl who literally uses masturbation as a performance piece, she's the last person I would ever feel embarrassed around.

It's obvious they're not going to give up, so with a sigh, I hand over my phone to Charlie.

She's quick to pull open the Salacious app, which has barely been touched in years. I downloaded it when we launched, but I never actually used it. The purpose of the app is to match up users based on a special form of compatibility—their kinks. So voyeurs and exhibitionists. Doms and subs. Sadists and masochists. And absolutely none of it interests me, so I never bothered checking it out.

"Okay, question number one—" Charlie starts, but I hold up a hand.

"Wait. I need more wine."

"We should make it a drinking game! Every time she answers no, we drink," Mia adds with a wicked smile.

"You'll die of alcohol poisoning," I reply.

The girls laugh as I open the spout on the box of wine, letting it fill my cup more than halfway. "All right, go."

"Would you consider yourself spontaneous?"

"No," I reply as we take a drink.

"Do you like to test your own limits and boundaries?"

"No." *Drink.*

"Are you a rule breaker?"

"No." *Drink again.* "See. I told you."

"Does the idea of inflicting pain on others excite you?"

My mouth forms the word *no*, but I hesitate for a moment too long.

"Oh..." Mia jokes when she notices me pausing.

"Should I put down *maybe*?" Charlie asks.

The wine is making my brain fuzzy, but the more I think about it, the idea of marking someone up just to see them in pain is...intoxicating. Is that the same as excited?

"Um...sure. Put *maybe*."

Mia is currently staring at me with her bottom lip pinched between her teeth as if she knows something I don't.

Charlie rolls through a lot of questions that get a very hard *no*. Would I let someone lick my feet? Would I enjoy being someone's pet? Would I be willing to hand over complete control of my life to my partner?

No. No. Absolutely not.

Pretty sure, the three of us are properly drunk, giggling our way through the questions to the point where Isabel has to take over reading them because Charlie is three sheets to the wind.

"Does the idea of withholding your partner's pleasure turn you on?"

"What the hell does that mean?" I reply with a drunk giggle.

"It means not letting him come!" Mia replies a little too loudly.

"Shhhh," I say, glancing toward the living room where the guys are mostly ignoring us and having a conversation of their own. A small part of me is dying to know what they're talking about. Are they discussing the club without me? I should really go in there and see what I'm missing, but when a pair of ocean eyes glance up in my direction, a playful smirk on his face, I pop my head back into the kitchen to avoid his disarming gaze. God, I hope he can't hear what we're talking about in here.

"Maggie...answer the question."

"Um...not letting him come? Is that really so fun?" I ask.

"Hell yeah it is. I've done it a few times. It's fun," Mia replies with a shrug as if it's nothing. "Use him to get yourself off and then just torture him until he's begging you to let him finish."

I wince, not exactly enjoying the image of her and Garrett together, but I'm not going to lie...the idea is enticing.

"I mean...how many times do they get off without letting us get off," I say and then promptly shut my mouth. I did not mean to say that out loud.

"We really need to find you better men than you've been with," Isabel replies with an expression of pity on her face.

"That's what we're doing. Come on, Maggie. Answer the question!" Charlie barks.

"Yes! Okay...yes. That does sort of...turn me on."

The three of them break out in excited giggles as my cheeks heat up to the point of scorching. I can't believe I just admitted that.

Suddenly, the questions get a little easier to answer, especially when I'm not sober enough to put too much thought into them. They just fly out of my mouth without hesitation.

Would you like to share your partner with others? No.

Would you like to treat your partner like a slave? Maybe.

Do you prefer to have control and know what's coming in the bedroom? Yes.

Would you like to be addressed by a proper title during sex? Maybe.

Would you prefer a partner to be younger or older than you? *Is that really a question?*

Younger.

The wine is gone by the time Isabel reaches the end of the quiz and the results begin to generate. We're waiting on bated breath for the results, and when her eyebrows dance upward in surprise, I nearly scream.

"What is it?"

"Maggie...you're a—"

"What are you girls doing in here?" Emerson asks as he walks into the kitchen, and I snatch my phone out of Isabel's hand so fast it's nearly violent.

"Oh, nothing..." Charlie responds with a tight-lipped smile on her face as she moves to her man's side. He lifts a brow as he looks down at her.

"Are you drunk?" he asks.

Her cheeks turn pink. "Maybe."

He gives her a quick pat on the butt and she yelps with a laugh as she buries her face into his chest. His lips press against the top of her head, and I feel the need to look away. Their constant public displays always make me uncomfortable. I mean, they're a cute couple and it's clear they're ridiculously crazy about each other, but I always feel like I'm intruding on their privacy when they touch each other in our company.

As my eyes quickly dance away from their cuddling, I find *him* staring at me again. Beau is watching from the living room, but instead of focusing on his dad and ex-girlfriend, he's looking at *me*. Our gazes meet for only a moment before I glance away, but it makes me wonder if seeing them touching is even harder for him.

One by one, everyone starts to pair up and meander their way to the door. Isabel nestles under Hunter's arm as they both follow behind Drake. Mia clings to Garrett, who is whispering something in her ear that I really don't want to know, judging by the flirty grin on her face. And Emerson guides Charlie out toward the door with a comforting touch on her back.

"Have fun with those results," she says to me before disappearing out the door.

"What results?" Emerson asks, but I only shake my head, shoving him away.

"None of your business," I mutter.

When I turn to find Beau lingering alone, I give him a polite smile. "Thanks again for your help."

"No problem."

With an awkward glance in my direction, he follows his dad out the door and I close it gently behind him. Once my house is empty and I'm alone, I bolt back into the kitchen where my phone is resting face down on the countertop.

Quickly, I pick it up and open the app to see my quiz results.

A laugh bursts out of my mouth as I stare at the screen.

Dominant, Master/Mistress, Brat Tamer.

I cackle even louder at that last one. Oh my God, this quiz is a joke! This is what we're selling to our customers? How ridiculous.

First of all, I am *no* Domme. Can you even imagine me in black leather with a whip like I'm freaking Madame Kink? Not even close.

And Brat Tamer is just comical. As if I don't get called the babysitter enough, now even my own kinks want me to be the nanny.

Without another thought, I close out the app, quickly clean up the kitchen, and stare at the mess of boxes and projects around my new house. What am I thinking? Getting myself involved with someone through the app is the last thing I need right now. I clearly have my work cut out for me with this house.

And I certainly don't need some brat to tame.

Rule #4: Self-absorbed assholes don't get happy endings.

Beau

"Where are you going?" My mother's voice stops me as I pause with one foot out the door.

"Lunch with Dad," I answer slowly, waiting for the inevitable hiss or scoff at the mention of my father. She'd never miss the opportunity to cut him down.

"What does he want now?" she replies with a huff.

There it is.

"Just to hang out, I think."

She laughs, scrolling through her phone, not even looking up while she talks to me.

"Not with your father. Emerson always wants something."

With a roll of my eyes, I bite my tongue. Getting between my parents is tempting, but I think I'd rather drag my face across concrete. Well, not exactly between *them*. Emerson will occasionally ask how my mom is, but that's it. She, on the other hand, talks shit about him like she's giving a TED talk, and I mostly nod along as if I agree. I don't buy into her lies as much as I used to.

Would it be so hard for her to look up at me, tell me to drive safe, wish me a good day or ask how I'm feeling? Apparently, because all I hear as I pocket my keys and open the front door is, "Tell him I said hi." Which is obviously a joke. My mother wears her bitterness like an armor against my father...who frankly couldn't care less. And when she found out about him and Charlie... suddenly her arsenal of spite was overflowing.

I just try not to stick around long enough to hear any of it. The sooner I can save up for my own place the better. It's like I'm being slowly poisoned in that house, and I don't know how much longer I can breathe in those noxious fumes before I turn petty and bitter too.

Of course, saving up would be a lot easier if I could hold on to a job, but evidently taking off too many nights to drive your pseudo-little sister (or what was it? Step-aunt?) to her D&D night will inevitably end in your employer asking you not to return to work.

I wasn't cut out for working in a kitchen anyway. Or landscaping. Or a coffee shop.

Movement out of the corner of my eye stops me in my tracks as I walk out across the yard to the driveway. There's someone on the other side of my car, and when I hear the sound of an aluminum can hit the pavement, I take off in a sprint to see what the fuck it is.

"Hey!" I yell when I spot a man bolting down the drive toward the road, and just as I take off to chase him, I'm stopped in my tracks by red spray paint all over the side of my car.

GET OUT PERVERT.

What. The. Fuck? Pervert? Is this some kind of sick prank?

Then it only takes a moment before realization dawns. As I spin away from the car, I look to the house and notice something taped to the front door that I didn't see when I walked out. It's a printed article from some online website with a picture of my dad's club in black and white on the top. I snatch the paper down as I read the headline: *A perverted establishment in Briar Point: citizens petition to have heinous club closed down.*

I guess someone did a quick Google search of Emerson Grant and came up with this address. My dad can't still be listed as the owner.

"Wrong house, dumbass!" I yell, although the guy is long gone. "Fucking great..." I mutter, inspecting the damage to my car. There's no way in hell I'm driving anywhere with this. But if I leave it here and have my dad come pick me up, my mother will have the good fortune of holding it over his head for the next ten years.

Grabbing a roll of duct tape out of the garage, I work swiftly to cover as much of the paint as I can, but I quickly run out and it's not nearly enough. Anyone can still easily read the slur scribbled across the side.

Fucking wonderful.

I grit my teeth as I climb in the car, throwing the crumpled-up article on the passenger seat. Then I start the car and pull out of the driveway with *PERVERT* still mostly visible on the passenger side. It's a good thing my dad doesn't live far.

"Beau, I'm so sorry," he stammers as he assesses the damages. We're standing in his garage, where he has plenty of space to hide my sweet new paint job while we both stare at it. "You can borrow my car until we get this fixed."

My teeth are clenched as I avoid eye contact.

"We've been receiving baseless threats from these people for a couple weeks now. I had no idea they'd stoop to vandalism. You know, we should really file a police report."

"Just fix it," I grumble, looking away.

"I'm sorry, Beau."

"Yeah, you said that already. It's fine. Let's just go get something to eat."

He clears his throat as he clicks the unlock button on his car, and we both climb in. Once I fasten my seat belt, I ask, "Why would they come to Mom's house anyway?"

He shrugs. "I don't know. That's weird, but I'll take care of it."

As we drive to our favorite burger joint, I notice him tensing in the driver's seat. Something is definitely up. I study him as we park, order from the waitress, and eat our food. He's being a little quieter than normal, and appears slightly uncomfortable. Maybe it's just the spray paint incident that has him acting weird.

But when the meal is done and he doesn't move to leave, my suspicions are confirmed.

"Beau, I have something to tell you, and I'm not sure how you're going to take it."

Oh shit.

"What?"

"I want to ask Charlie to marry me."

I'm not sure if the sound that comes out of my mouth

has a name, but it's somewhere between a choke and a laugh, and it has me nearly spitting out my drink in the process.

"You're joking," I snap after I have composed myself.

The stern expression on his face says he's not.

"You're fucking forty-one. She's twenty-two."

"Keep your voice down," he scolds, and I roll my eyes.

"I'm serious. Why on earth would you two get married?"

His brow furrows as he sits up a little straighter. "Because we love each other."

"You really think she'll say yes? She has her whole life ahead of her."

"Yes, I think she will say yes, and I have my whole life ahead of me too, Beau."

"Well, not nearly as much!"

He lets out a heavy sigh, clearly brushing off the insults I'm hurling at him, but he never responds with the rise I expect. Instead, he just pushes his shoulders back and waits. I can't believe what I'm hearing. It's like a joke that's gone too far. I got over the fact that they were screwing, and I learned to accept that they were living together, but I expected it to end any day now. This weird little fling of theirs can't last forever.

"You're not going to have kids, are you?" I ask, racking my brain to remember if Charlie ever mentioned wanting them when we were together.

"No. We're not going to have kids."

"Then, what's the point?" I ask.

"The point is that we want to make a commitment to each other. Someday, you'll meet someone you want that with."

"Not likely. I mean, it's only been a year. How do you know in ten years she'll still want you?"

He leans forward, letting his features soften as he scrutinizes me for a moment. "Not all marriages end in divorce, Beau. Not all relationships are bad. Some couples don't work and some just do. Even if you think they don't make sense or they come from different places or are different ages, when you meet someone that wants what you want, it just fits. Someone who makes being you a little easier. When you find that person, you'll know."

Right about now, I could throw something unfairly cruel his way, something about how I thought I had that with Charlie, but I've spent long enough making my dad pay for what happened with my ex-girlfriend. It never changed a damn thing anyway. So, this time, I don't say a word.

But I do wish I could tell him that whatever the hell he's talking about just isn't in the cards for me. Because every girl I date never fits. They either want what I can't give or give me what I don't want. There is no compatibility with other people when you're a self-absorbed asshole only looking out for yourself—or so I've been told.

"I hope you know I'm telling you this because I wouldn't do it without your approval."

"Bullshit," I bark back. He's lying, and I know it. "You want my approval, sure, but you would do it anyway."

His mouth turns up in a small smile as he shrugs. "I do want your approval, though."

"I don't care. I really don't. I think you're crazy and probably a little stupid for expecting someone like Charlie to commit the rest of her life to you, but I'm not gonna stop you. It's your funeral."

He laughs. "Technically, it's a wedding, but thanks."

We fill the silence with small talk, and he seems a little more relaxed now, as if he just needed to get that part off his chest. I still can't picture him up at the altar with Charlie, but I'm going to choose not to think about it anymore.

Rule #5: You're kinkier than you think.

Beau

Someone nudges my arm, and my eyes pop open. I'm staring up at the popcorn ceiling of Dash and Brody's apartment. I must have nodded off after those hits off the joint. I lost count of how many times it made its rounds.

Brody's offering me another, but I shake my head. Why couldn't the asshole just let me sleep?

With a shrug, he puts the joint between his lips and turns his attention back to the video game he's playing with Dash. There's another guy over here that I've only met a couple times, and he's browsing his phone on the recliner, his presence making me uncomfortable. I hate when they bring new people over. I miss when it was just us three.

Well, technically it was four before Peyton went and got *engaged*. Jesus. Are we at that age already? I'm only twenty-two, and he's only a year older than me. I'm nowhere fucking near ready to even think about that shit.

And to think Charlie is about to get engaged. If we hadn't broken up, would I be ready to propose? The idea seems insane to me. I mean...what's the fucking rush?

"Hey Victor," Dash says to the guy on the recliner. "You want in?" he asks, holding up the controller.

"No thanks, man. I'm chatting with some chick on this app."

"Like a hookup app?" I ask. When he glances up at me, I sense a little pretentiousness on his face. As if he's so much more mature than me.

"No," he replies with a smug grin. "It's more than that. It...uh...matches you up with other people who like the same sex stuff you like."

I freeze, my eyes laser-focused on the coffee table, afraid that if I move, I'll give everything away. Yeah, I know that app. I know it really fucking well.

"What?" Dash blurts out with a laugh.

"Yeah, it's called *Salacious*. You take this kink quiz and based on the results—"

"Are you guys hungry?" I interject. "I'm going to order some pizza."

Brody stares at Victor. "Like...what kind of sex stuff?"

Victor turns his phone toward the guys, and I have to look away. "This chick I'm talking to wants a guy to degrade her and shit."

"What?"

"Holy shit," the guys reply.

"Sounds fucked up," I mutter, rising from the couch and heading to the kitchen to escape the conversation. I don't offer up the information to my friends about my dad's company, and I certainly don't delve into the relationship between him and Charlie. I keep my shit private.

I watch from the tiny kitchen as the guys abandon their video game to pull out their phones, both downloading the app like it's fucking Candy Crush or something, and the sight of it grates on my nerves.

Maybe they'd think my dad was some kind of hero for owning a sex club and a kink matchup app, but I know they'd look at me differently if I told them.

"Beau, do you have this app?" Dash asks, his eyes glued to the screen.

"Nah," I reply, fishing a beer out of the fridge, "not really into that kinky shit."

The guys laugh, and I clench my teeth. "Did you not hear the part about the girl Vic is talking to who wants him to call her a dirty slut and shit?"

"Excuse me for not wanting to call a chick names while I'm fucking her," I mumble.

"Dude, it's so hot though. I get laid so much more with this app. All I have to do is agree to whatever freaky shit they're into."

I pause, the beer bottle lifted halfway to my lips. And right at this very moment, I decide I hate this douchebag. With his stupid blazer and leather shoes and cocky attitude. But I especially hate him because even I know, what he's saying is fucked up. He's clearly abusing the app.

"Isn't the whole point of it to match people up who like the same things? Not just give you the keys to the kingdom so you can get more willing pussy?"

All three of them look up at me like I just started spouting Latin.

"So you have heard of it," Victor replies, his brows folding inward.

"No. I mean...yeah, I've heard of it, but my point is...I think the purpose of it is pretty clear."

"Yeah," he says with a tilt of his head, "the purpose is to help these bitches get all their freaky needs met, and to put me in contact with them." He laughs, looking down at Dash and Brody who both join in, and I'm suddenly so irrationally pissed off and I don't even know why.

"It's not a fucking joke!" I bellow, and all three of them shut up.

"Jesus, Beau. Relax." Brody is staring at me with confusion written all over his face, and honestly, I'm fucking confused too. I'm not sure where that came from, but I do know that I need to get the fuck out of here.

"I'm gonna go," I mutter as I set the beer on the table and fish my phone out of my pocket.

"I thought you were crashing here," Dash replies.

"Not tonight, man. Thanks though. I'll just grab a ride." As I pull the door open, I feel a hand on my arm. It's Dash, and when I spin around, I'm met with his concerned expression.

"You sure you're okay? We were just messing around. We didn't mean anything by it."

I shrug. "Dude, I'm just in a weird headspace today. I think I just need to go home."

"You wanna take a joint with you?"

I can't help but smile. Out of all of my friends, Dash is definitely the most empathetic. Through every job loss and breakup, he's been the only one who actually listened while the other guys figured beer and weed would do the trick. At least Dash offers his friendship *and* weed.

"No thanks, man. Have a good night."

With that, I head out of the apartment and make my way down to my dad's car. I drove here, but I'm still too high to get behind the wheel. It's only a mile and a half anyway. And the weather isn't bad for late April.

So I take off down the busy road toward my mom's house.

Maybe a long walk will help clear my head, so I can understand why the hell I got so worked up about that fucking app. I'm not exactly sure why, but for some reason, the first step in chilling the fuck out seems to be looking it up in the App Store.

It has almost a million reviews. And pretty good ones too. Which I assume at first are just a bunch of jerks like Victor, who think it's a hookup app of the kinky variety.

But they're not.

Finally! An app that normalizes healthy kinks.

Not your average hookup app. This one actually values kink-positive lifestyles!

I had no idea I even had a kink. Thank you, Salacious! Best sex of my life.

"Jesus," I mutter. People really will post anything on the Internet.

It's ultimately curiosity that gets the best of me and has me hitting the download button. I mean...just because I'm looking at it doesn't mean I'm going to turn into some kinky freak like my dad.

As I reach the crosswalk, I open the newly downloaded app and follow a few prompts like age, sexual preference, location. After crossing the street, I open it back up to find myself at the beginning of a quiz.

No, fuck this. I can't take this quiz.

Clicking off my phone, I shove it into my pocket and walk into the gas station on the corner to get myself something to drink. But the entire time I'm standing at the soda fountain, I'm thinking about that quiz. I bet if I took it, it would tell me I'm just safely classified as a normal guy with healthy sexual cravings.

If it's a legit quiz, that's exactly what it's going to say. I mean, who needs an app to tell them what their sexual preferences are? Shouldn't people just know what they want?

After paying for my soda and walking back out to the road, I open the app again. My high has worn off enough that I can focus a little clearer on the questions now. And I decide to take the stupid quiz because I have nothing better to do and I'd like to prove them wrong. Who, I don't even know.

Do you consider your taste in sex normal? Duh. Yes.

You are good at making decisions. Agree or disagree. Um...not exactly a sex question, but I guess if I had to choose, it would be disagree.

Does it bother you to be seen naked or seen pleasuring yourself? What the fuck? I mean...bother me? I don't love the idea, but it doesn't bother me. So, no.

Are you interested in having sex with multiple partners? At once? No.

You use sex as a form of escapism. Agree or disagree.

My fingers pause over the screen for a moment. Why are they asking me this? Who doesn't use sex to escape? *Yes.*

Do you tend to find sexual partners you consider out of your league? Sure. Again...who doesn't?

The next round of questions sounds more like actual sex questions. And I find myself flying through them, sure as hell that I'm not answering anything out of the ordinary. These are things *everyone* wants.

So when the screen starts generating the results, just as I turn onto the street to my mother' house, I'm wearing a smug smile. But when the screen pops up with a list of kinks, I freeze in my tracks.

Experimental.

Brat.

Submissive.

I read the last one a few times because I'm worried I'm still high and confusing that word with another one. *Submissive.*

Then I let out a hearty laugh, standing under the street light. Submissive? This stupid quiz is a joke. Even if this is my "kink," it doesn't mean I have any desire to be bossed around by a lady in black leather. Just because some people like this stuff doesn't mean it's for everyone.

Those kinky bastards can have all the fun they want, but I'll stick to regular sex. It does the job just fine. With a swipe, I close out the app and pick up my walk again.

But as I'm opening up Instagram, a notification pops up on my screen, and I come to a standstill.

One new match in your area.

What the hell does that mean? Against my better judgment, I click the notification. It flashes to the app again, but now I'm staring at a profile. There's no picture, and the profile name is nothing but a jumble of numbers and letters. The only things it says are Female and kinks: *Dominant, Master/Mistress, Brat Tamer.*

That's it. For all I know this lady could really be an eighty-year-old dude, who may or may not be a serial killer using the app to lure in unsuspecting submissives. Never in a hundred years would I ever message this person or agree to meet them. And especially not just because an app says we like the same stuff in the bedroom based off some internet quiz.

But even after I swipe the app closed, I can't stop thinking about it. I'm just too curious to let it go. It would be so easy to contact that profile. Start up a conversation. Meet up and know for sure if the whole thing is bullshit or not. But, of course, I'm not going to.

Like I said, they're probably a creepy serial killer.

But...maybe they're not.

Rule #6: Don't flirt with internet strangers during the staff meeting.

Maggie

Garrett: The PR team needs the social media passwords again.

Hunter: Did you get the email I forwarded from the Dev team?

Mia: The decorations I ordered for Masquerade night weren't signed for and now they're stuck at the post office. Help!

Emerson: I need you to sit in on the staff meeting at noon.

"Ugh!" I toss my phone against the pillow. I'm literally standing in my towel with wet hair dripping all over my hardwood floor, checking messages that can all wait. Ringo lifts his head in concern after my little outburst, but quickly decides it's not important and goes back to his nap.

In a rush, I pull clothes from my box-covered walk-in closet. There is no time for blow drying today, so I quickly run my fingers through my hair, mess it up a bit and hope for the best. As I stand in front of the mirror in my bra and underwear, I mentally scold myself for the weird bulges on either side of my hips and the stupid cellulite riddling my thighs. In the corner of my room, my exercise bike does more good as a laundry hanger and dust collector, taunting me with broken promises to finally get in shape, so maybe someday I can walk around in tight clothing with half the confidence of Mia or Eden.

Instead, I pick on myself in the bathroom, pinching the weird poochy underside of my stomach.

My phone is buzzing from my bed as I get dressed and throw on a thin layer of makeup and some eyeliner. When I finally pick it up from where I hurled it, I'm surprised to see that the notification is not from someone at the club, hounding me for favors, but from the Salacious app.

One new match in your area.

Uh...delete. My finger hovers over the app to decline it, but I suddenly find myself opening the notification instead. Call it curiosity or stubbornness, but I just want to see it before I erase it.

It opens to a mostly blank profile. The name is generic, to protect the identity. And the About Me section just says, *this is stupid.* Which isn't surprising since the age and gender show: *Male,* 22.

Great, another grown man who needs babysitting.

"Hard pass," I mutter as I carry my phone into the

kitchen, answering emails and messages while simultaneously making myself a cup of coffee.

To Garrett: For the hundredth time, the passwords are in the drive.

To Hunter: Yes, and I already responded. It's taken care of.

To Mia: I'll stop at the post office on my way to the club.

To Emerson: Yes, sir. ;)

I'm smiling to myself as I mix in my hazelnut creamer and snap the lid on my overused travel mug. Then for some reason, I open the Salacious app again. It's true what they say—a workaholic with nothing to do will find something to do. And while this isn't really work, I busy my mind with scrolling through the matches sent to me. Mostly men, some with very thick profiles full of details about their lives and sexual preferences. It's Cringe City in these match results. The more they tell me about themselves, the less interested I am.

Which is probably why I end up on the new guy again. A little mystery is sexier than too much information, I guess. Suddenly I find myself clicking on the *Message* button.

Me: Why is it stupid?

I say in response to his profile page.

I hit send without much thought. I have absolutely no

intention of seeing this through, but for some reason, I want to mess with him. There's something less intimidating about speaking to a guy, not even in the same generation as me, who takes this even less seriously than I do.

Also...and this is a big part of it...he matched with a *certified* Madame/Domme/Brat Tamer, which means his results came up as the opposite—submissive and/or brat.

I laugh to myself as I slip on my heels and gather up my stuff—laptop, phone, sunglasses—tossing them all in my bag. *Certified Madame.* Hilarious. I should really email the Dev team and let them know their algorithm is drunk.

My phone buzzes as I haul everything out to the car. I'm not sure why I feel almost disappointed that it's not *Mr. Stupid.* Instead, it's *Mr. Boss Man* responding to me saying, *yes, sir,* in our messages, just to tease him for all of his Dom-ness.

Emerson: Very funny. Knock it off.

Emerson: And thanks a million. You're the best.

As I drop into the driver's seat, I read his text and try, once again, to hate him. But it's hard when he hurls compliments my way like their spears meant to break my cold, uncaring armor. And it's working. Asshole.

The staff meeting is a bore. We have a floor crew now, managers and team leaders to keep the ship running tight, but Emerson insists that one of us sit in on them. It's usually Garrett, but he sees his therapist on Tuesdays.

Mia is leading the conversation regarding the event this coming weekend, and I'm mindlessly scrolling through my phone. There's really no reason for me to be here.

New message: Because I don't need an app to tell me what I like.

I freeze, staring down at the new message in the notification bar at the top of my screen. It takes me far too long to make sense of it, finally realizing it's from the Salacious app. Before it disappears, I click on the pop-up.

It's *Mr. Stupid*—a name I've given him, regarding his lame one-liner profile. With a roll of my eyes, I type up my response.

And yet, you took the quiz.

To prove how wrong it is.

Oh yeah? How wrong is it?

I'm teasing him. I don't know why I even bother. This guy is clearly not worth the time, but I'm bored. In the meeting, I mean.

Okay, let me guess. It told you you're a bossy Dom right?

Technically it's Domme, but yes.

So, that makes me a sub?

You tell me.
You're the one who took the quiz.
Are you saying it's wrong?

Fuck yes, it's wrong.

How do you know?

Because I don't want to be whipped by a woman in black leather.

Sounds like you haven't tried it.

Is that what you do?

Ha. No. I'm as new to this as you are.

But I mean...is that what you want to do?

Leather is hot and uncomfortable.
And I'm not sure how well I could handle a whip.

So you think the quiz is bullshit too.

I don't know.
Something in our answers must
have gotten us these results.

What if we're just normal people who don't have kinks?

People with kinks are normal.

You know what I mean.

What is normal though? Vanilla?

Yeah.

Did you get vanilla as one of your quiz results? Because it was definitely an option.

You cornered me into that.

I GIGGLE, AND I NOTICE THAT THE ROOM AROUND ME is quiet, so I look up to find Mia staring at me with the same look teachers give when they're waiting for you to stop talking in class.

"Care to join us?"

I bite my lip. "Sorry, I'm paying attention."

She's fighting a smile as she glances down at my phone. "We're basically done. Did you have anything to add?"

"Nope. If you guys need anything, you know how to reach me."

With that, everyone starts to disperse, but I feel Mia watching me, and I already know she's going to be harassing me for information. As predicted, she rushes to my side the moment the staff is mostly gone.

"Did you get matched? What did the results say? I mean...I have my theories."

I hold my phone against my chest. "It's nothing. No matches. And what are your theories?" I ask out of curiosity.

"Based on the way you answered those questions the other night, you've got some inner FemDom kink, which means there's a guy out there just waiting to kiss your boots."

I push off the bar I'm leaning against and head toward the shared office, eager to get as far away from this conversation as I can. "Nope. I can't talk about this. I don't even own boots."

"Oh, come on!" Mia whines, following close behind me.

"It's too weird!"

"Don't bc a hypocrite. It is not weird."

"For me, it is."

"Okay fine," she replies, rushing to my side. "We don't have to talk about it, but just tell me if my theory is right."

I pause, pressing my lips together as I turn toward her. "You won't tell anyone?"

She holds up a hand as if taking an oath. "Promise."

"Yes. Your theory is correct."

She squeals, covering her mouth.

"Shhh..."

When she finally stops making noises of excitement like the bouncy twenty-three-year-old she is, I roll my eyes and head toward the office. "Don't you dare say a word, Mia!"

"I won't," she calls back. "But I bet that within six months, you'll be the kinkiest person in this club!"

With a groan, I close myself in the office, hoping to God no one heard that last part. As I drop everything on my desk, I let out a heavy sigh.

I hate attention. And I really hate feeling like people are laughing at me or that I'm the odd one out, so I've spent the last ten years drawing as little attention to myself as possible. But now that the girls have gotten me to take this stupid quiz, I have a very bad feeling that it's going to get out and I'll be the laughing stock of Salacious.

My phone vibrates, and I pick it up to find I have three missed messages from Mr. Stupid.

Why can't I just be a vanilla guy? What's so wrong with that?
Technically my results are Experimental, Submissive, Brat. Which sounds a little vague, don't you think?
What about you?

I stare at the screen. What started as me teasing him has turned into something else. A real conversation. And I know where real conversations go. Soon we're talking about ourselves, and using the promise of anonymity as a safety net to expose our deepest secrets, and then what?

Then he finds out that I'm too old for him, nothing like the hot young girls he could probably get, and it will end with disappointment. Best to get it out of the way now.

I'm thirty-four.

That's what your quiz results told you?

No.
I'm telling you now, since I didn't put it in my bio.
I'm thirty-four, and I see you're twenty-two.
So maybe before this conversation goes any further, we should just get that out of the way.

K

K?

Yeah. K.
So, what did your quiz results say?

Well, that's not the response I was expecting.

Domme, Mistress, Brat tamer

Wow.
You sound scary.

LOL. I'm literally the least scary person ever.

Nice on the outside.
Fucking terrifying on the inside.

I laugh, hating the way my cheeks are burning with a blush. I'm wasting so much of my time flirting with this complete stranger, which is stupid. My to-do list is a mile long. I don't have time for this.

I think you like the idea of me being terrifying.

Yeah, maybe I do.

You know what that means, right?
You might be more submissive than you think.

Haha. Nice try.
I was just saying it's hot that you have a hidden kinky side.

Would it be as hot to you if my hidden kinky side liked to be tied up and treated like a slave?

You're trying to make me admit that my quiz results were right. I'm not going to do it.
And no. I think the fact that you're sweet on the outside and a scary domme on the inside is especially hot. Something about how unexpected it is.

You don't even know me.

True. But I'm using my imagination.

Okay. And what are you imagining?

Hmm...

I'm picturing you in a cardigan. Button-up blouse. Tight pants in a fun color, like orange or purple. You like your clothes, but they don't show off your body well. And it's a great body.

I bet you work a lot. You love your job. You're in management or something where you're in charge...obviously.

And I bet you don't have sex nearly as much as you should.

I force myself to swallow. Looking down at my outfit, I start to wonder how much I could have possibly given away in our limited conversation, but then I realize that was a generic answer.

You got all that from my blank profile?

Was I right?

I'm wearing a dress today. It's black.

I smile to myself as I add the next part.

My cardigan is red.

I was close.

I don't wear clothes that show off my body
because clothes were made to cover your body,
not "show it off."
I do work a lot, and I do love my job.
I own a company, actually.

What about the last part?
The part about sex.

SOMETHING BETWEEN MY LEGS TINGLES AT THE thought.

I'm not answering that.

Haha, so that's a yes.

I mean...I'm on this app.
I feel like that should say enough.

Well, I'm on the app, and I get laid plenty.

. . .

I LET OUT A GROAN. JUST LIKE THAT I'M REMINDED that he's twenty-two. He ruined it with one line.

I'm sure you do. Lots of vanilla sex. There's nothing wrong with that.

Aren't you going to tell me how you imagine me?

I TAKE A MOMENT TO THINK. I DON'T WANT TO BE cruel, but what I imagine might not come across as complimentary. But if I couldn't scare him away with my age, maybe I can scare him away with the truth.

I imagine you're just as good looking as you think you are. You have no problem getting girls, but you do have a problem with finding satisfaction, which is why you're on this app. I think you've been lied to by so much toxic masculinity in your short, sweet life that you believe real men have to be dominant, so you won't let yourself accept the truth that you're really submissive, and the idea of a woman taking control over you secretly turns you on.

THERE'S NO RESPONSE. AT FIRST, I FEEL BAD, BUT IF the truth is too much for him, then so am I.

With that, I close the app and get back to work. At least, I try to. But it's hard to focus. I fight the temptation to message him back. But then I remind myself I don't need another man to babysit.

Rule #7: Don't make it awkward.

Beau

"What about this?" I ask, turning the tablet toward Sophie.

"Holy shit. You're getting good."

"Sophie!" Gwen snaps. "You better watch your mouth or I'm going to take that iPad away."

She responds to her mother with a roll of her eyes, and I stifle a laugh. Across the table, Charlie does her best to look innocent, but we all know she's the one enabling Sophie's cussing.

My dad is sitting next to Charlie with his hand on the back of her chair, but I turn my eyes away from them, glancing down at my tablet, where I've been working on this sketch for over a week now.

Sophie was the one to inspire me to buy a tablet with a drawing pen. She always brings hers on our weekly family dinner outings, and I found it intriguing how easily she can come up with these sketches, so I picked up a used one for myself. I was never much into art, but I find drawing on the tablet strangely addicting.

When I glance up, I see my dad watching me with curiosity. He's trying to peek at the drawing, which is lame, so I click out of the app before he can see it. It's just something inspired by a video-game character: a bulky female soldier covered in blood-spattered armor and a machine gun arm.

See what I mean? Lame.

"What are you working on?" he asks.

"Nothing."

"It didn't look like nothing," he replies.

"It's badass," Sophie replies, making Gwen wince. "Show him."

I let out a sigh. I know he's just trying to show interest in my hobbies, but my default is, and always has been, to shut him out. But since Sophie's pushing, I open up the app and turn the tablet toward my dad.

"Oh wow," Charlie replies while my dad simply smiles.

"It's good," he says. "I didn't know you were such a good artist."

My jaw clicks as I squeeze my molars together. "I'm not. It's just a stupid sketch."

Just then, the waitress brings out our food, and I slip my tablet onto my lap as we dig in. The entire time I eat my steak fajitas, I'm thinking about what the mystery Domme wrote today about being so ingrained with masculinity that I'm afraid of being submissive. It's been killing me that I haven't responded, but what the fuck am I supposed to say to that?

You're right. I must have been lied to my entire life. Please fix me, Mistress.

But, at the same time, I'm not going to argue with her. Yeah, she's probably right, but you know what? That's just the world we live in. Men have to be tough, dominant, in control. I mean, look at my fucking father. He wouldn't kneel for anyone, and because of that, his masculinity is safely intact. He can sleep well at night, knowing he's properly *being a man*. It's not *toxic* masculinity when it comes to him, it's just a shit-ton of it.

And he has a woman who loves him for it.

Then my mind goes back to the lady in my chat. And I'll admit, there's something very liberating about the idea of *not* having to be so in control. I never seem to get it right anyway. She admitted that she's new to this too, but how nice would it be to be with a woman who knows what she wants and takes all the guesswork out of it for me?

All the black leather and whips aside, it sounds...hot.

Different, but hot.

"Do you need anything for the party on Friday?" Gwen asks, once we've all finished with our meals.

My dad looks up and takes Charlie's hand in his. I find my eyes transfixed on the giant diamond on her left hand. He really wasted no time in asking her or planning an engagement party. If they keep going at this rate, they'll be married by Sunday.

With a smile, he shakes his head. "No. Thank you, though."

"It's really casual," Charlie adds. "Just some drinks and hors d'oeuvres."

He's spinning her ring between his fingers, and my jaw clenches. Instead of joining the conversation, I pick up my iPad and start doodling again. This whole thing is so fucking awkward, and I don't know if the fact that no one acknowledges how weird it is makes me more angry or thankful.

It was Charlie's mom who started inviting me out for family dinners, and at first, I appreciated the thought. Over the past year, I've slowly started to win over Sophie, but being around Charlie and my dad never really got any less weird. I just keep waiting for them to decide their relationship is ridiculous and break up.

But that dumb rock on her hand and the even dumber smile on his face say otherwise.

Lying in bed, later that night, I can't stop thinking about the Domme. Even after deciding I didn't *hate* what she said, I still haven't quite worked up a response. And maybe I never will. She's just a random woman on the internet I chatted with for a couple hours today. And there are a hundred other locals to scroll through, who would probably be happy to tell me the exact same thing.

But there's something...fuck, what's the opposite of intimidating? Unintimidating? Yeah, I guess there's something unintimidating about her also being new to this.

God, what am I even saying? I am *not* interested in getting into anything kinky. Everything she said about me being as good looking as I think I am and getting pussy regularly was accurate.

But so was the part about not being satisfied.

But only *a little* unsatisfied. Sex is still sex. Even when it's bad, it's still good.

And that's really what this is about, isn't it? Sex.

Neither of us are looking for a relationship or to be a part of the lifestyle. We're just looking for sex compatibility.

In that case...why not? Why not just message her back, maybe meet up once or twice. Let it go where it wants to go and hey, if she wants to be a little bossy in the sack, then I'm down for that. I'd let an older woman ride me like a bull. Who the fuck wouldn't?

Not to mention, I have a point to make here. She thinks I'm brainwashed into believing I can't be the brat she needs to tame, well then, I'll show her.

With my tablet in my lap, I open a new sketch. Then I let my fingers go wherever they want, and before I know it, I'm sketching a woman. Curvy hips, thick thighs, mousy brown hair, and round glasses perched on her face. I literally have no idea what this lady looks like, but in my imagination, this is her. I even draw on the black dress and red cardigan.

Then I pick up my phone and type up a message before I can change my mind.

You're wrong.

It doesn't take long before she replies.

Am I?

Yes.

You think I'm too stubborn to accept a woman being in control. But I can.

Is that so?

Don't believe me?

Not really.

So, let me prove it.

This time, there's a long pause before she says anything else.

My age doesn't bother you?

You're thirty-four, not eighty.
Stop trying to make it a problem.

I'm not sure I'm ready for a real date.

I'm not talking about a date.
I'm talking about fucking. Just a hookup.
You'll be in control.
You can tell me to do whatever you want.
Use me.
You want me to lick your pussy for two hours straight, I will.
You want to strap me to your bed and ride my dick like a bicycle, you can.

Okay, stop.

Why? Does talking about sex make you uncomfortable?

A little.

You need to get over that.
Come on.
Tell me right now what you would do to me.

No.

Why?

Because I don't know you.

So.
I just told you I'd lick your pussy.
It's not that hard. Come on.
If you could have your way with me right now,
what would you do?

The typing bubbles bounce for a few minutes before she finally responds.

I hate being on top. And I don't really want you to lick my you-know-what *for two hours.*

I smile. There's something about this woman I like. And I might be crazy for trying to meet up with her and willingly let her do what she wants with me when I haven't even met her, but I can't help it. She intrigues me.

Okay. So what do you like?

I don't know.

Sounds like you just haven't been with the right guy.
Give me a chance.
I'm literally giving you my body so you can use it to get off.

Why would you do that?

Chances are I'm going to enjoy it.
And I'd like to prove a point.
And maybe experiment a little.

Okay, I have an idea.

I'm listening.

There's a sex club. Salacious.

My fingers freeze over the screen. Oh god, please don't suggest we go there. This woman has no idea my dad is the owner, and she's never going to find out.

I know it sounds crazy, but they have a masquerade night once a week. You don't have to be a member to go. It's like an open house. We could meet there. And if we want...we can rent a room.

Do you go there?

No.
I just saw the announcement.

When is it?

Friday night.

Fuck. My dad's engagement party.

What time?

Late. Ten?

Surely, I can sneak out of the party by then. Fuck, am I really considering this? Going to his fucking sex club?

Yes, but it's not in support of him or the club. It's just to meet this lady and hopefully get laid. Like an ironic form of rebellion.

I'm in. Friday at ten.
Until then I want you to think about what you want.
Watch some porn to get some ideas.
Text me when you think of something.

For a guy who was so sure this was all fake, you sure do seem eager now.

I smile.

Yeah, I guess I am eager.
I'd like to see what the fuss is all about.

Okay, don't chicken out.

Trust me. I won't.

Rule #8: Watch porn...for research.

Maggie

I've lost my damn mind. That's the only explanation for this. Why on earth would I agree to meet a twenty-two-year-old *at the club*, with plans to have sex and dominate him?

Certifiable. This is insane.

And yet...he's messaged me every day since the first one. We agreed not to use real names, and we won't share photos. He says the mystery makes it easier, and I agree. So tomorrow night when we meet, he will have on a black mask with an 's' marked in black light paint for sub. I will have a 'D' on mine for Domme. It was my idea, and I admit, it's not very creative, but I'm not going for creative right now. I'm going for clarity and assurance. I need to be sure I'm walking into a private room with the right guy.

It works out perfectly that we're doing this on Friday because all of the owners will be at Emerson and Charlie's engagement party. We have this masquerade event every week, and the floor managers are ready to handle everything, so no one will suspect that I'm me. I should be able to blend in easily with the crowd.

I can walk in as Maggie, the owner, slip on my mask, and find my mystery man.

God, this is crazy.

But I do think about what he said, about telling him what I want. It would be easy to play it off as shy or ignore the question, but this is literally about me being in control, so I guess I better figure it out.

I also listened to what he suggested, which is why I'm lying on my couch, in my partially unpacked house at three p.m. on a Thursday, scrolling through a porn site. I see porn as a necessary evil. I don't objectively enjoy it or like it, but for a woman with little time on her hands, I do appreciate how effectively it gets the job done.

I don't have time to waste, trying to use my stunted imagination to get off.

But I'm not scrolling the site today for that reason. No, today is strictly for research. Because if I'm going to do this, and go in there ready to wield control, then I better be prepared. My stomach clenches at the thought of being in the middle of a scene and completely at a loss for the words or commands. I can only imagine how mortifying and awkward that would be for him.

Unfortunately, I'm not finding anything on the site that gets me excited. I tried looking up Domme videos, but it just gave me more anxiety. These women are all confident and sure of what they want.

All I know is that I want to be in control—I just don't know what turns me on.

Finally, I land on a video that is more artful than vulgar, a welcome sight for my overstimulated brain. There is no black leather or whips. No in-your-face genitalia. Just a woman, sitting on a desk, with a man kneeling between her legs. He's not touching her, but she's gently patting his head, running her fingers through his long hair. Something about it is intriguing—a man willingly giving over control.

I watch the video as she guides him around the room like a pet, bends him over the desk, spanks him with a paddle while reciting forms of degradation in a tone that sounds more fit for praise.

Then to my utter surprise, she pulls a strap-on out of the desk and begins clasping it into place. My eyes widen as I swipe the app closed.

No. No way.

Quickly, I stand up from the couch, leaving my phone on the cushion as I go to my wine cooler to pour a glass of chilled Pinot Grigio and do my best to ignore the tingling arousal between my thighs. *That* can't possibly be what turns me on.

Watching porn is a lot like opening a bottle of wine. Once you've popped that cork, you have to just see it through and drink the whole thing. Can't let it go to waste. Or at least that's the justification in my mind when I return to my couch.

I'm already aroused...so I might as well finish the job.

Lying back down on the pillows, I open the site again and the video picks up where it left off. He's still bent over the desk when she starts prepping and probing him with lube, and I have to keep looking away.

What is wrong with me? In the club, I've watched so much sex, of various types, so why is this so hard to absorb? Pegging is nothing new to me, but suddenly I'm putting myself in her shoes—or heels, I guess—and it's hitting me differently. As if my brain is telling me I should feel bad for how turned on I am right now.

When the woman slides into him from behind, I bite my bottom lip, without tearing my eyes away. She looks amazing as she thrusts her hips against his backside. So powerful and in control, and judging by the euphoric expression on his face and the way he's moaning, I'd say he seems to be loving it too.

The next thing I know, I'm slipping my hand into my loose shorts to ease the burning ache building there. I don't make it half as long as they do, and I'm tensing into my own orgasm just as they change positions, him sprawled on the surface of the desk for her, so they can gaze into each other's eyes.

It's erotic and exciting at the same time, and I take that vision with me for the rest of the day. I would have never watched this before. But now it's taken on a new meaning. Instead of just watching her, I'm imagining how it would feel to *be* her.

And I love it.

Mr. Stupid: How's the research going?

TERRIBLE, I REPLY. I'M PRETTY SURE HE'S NOT READY for me to tell him I'd like to peg him on our first date. And aside from the student-teacher video I watched yesterday, I haven't found anything I'd feel comfortable doing with him tonight.

If you want to cancel, I understand.

Do you want to cancel?

No.

Then, I'll see you tonight.

I'm standing in my closet, my lunch threatening to come back up as I stare down at his last message. I've never been so nervous in my life.

There's a part of me that's tempted to cancel the whole thing and just return to the safety of my normal, boring life. But once I close this door, I'm never opening it again.

Then there's a part of me, a voice growing stronger every day that feels almost as if it's bullying me into this. A fiercer, more confident version of myself I've learned to suffocate and ignore in order to play the role, get the job, not anger anyone or create any conflict. She's clawing her way out of my psyche, and I'm too intrigued by what this new feeling promises that I can't quiet her now.

Pocketing my phone, I find the sleek black dress hidden at the back of my closet. It's one of those items I bought for an occasion that never existed. It's low-cut, tight around my waist, and short enough that if I drop anything on the floor tonight, it's going to have to stay there because there will be *no* bending over—well, not for that reason at least.

No. *No.* I am not sleeping with the mystery man tonight. I know he probably thinks he's about to get laid, but I need to take things slow. It's just a meeting to see if this is something we want to pursue or not.

I grab the dress, a pair of black stilettos, and pack a quick bag for the masquerade event before rushing out the door to get to Emerson and Charlie's engagement party.

Parking down the street, I walk up to Emerson's immaculate two-story home in my modest flats, knee-length skirt, and polka-dot blouse. It's a far cry from the black mini and stilettos currently waiting their turn in the trunk of my car.

"I look like a virgin," I mutter to myself as I walk up the long driveway toward the courtyard before the front door.

"Are you?" a dark voice says from the corner behind me. A scream bursts from my chest as I jump what feels like three feet into the air.

Spinning around with my hand clamped to my chest, I stare in shock at an amused-looking Beau. "Sorry. Didn't mean to scare you."

"And standing in the corner of the courtyard, answering questions I mumble to myself, isn't supposed to be scary?"

He laughs again. "I couldn't help myself."

"Well, you should try," I respond, sounding more disgruntled than I am. "What are you doing out here anyway?"

He shrugs. "Just not ready to go in."

I turn to face the door, hearing the music and voices of the party on the other side. And sympathy drowns out my annoyance. This can't be an easy situation for him. Surely, everyone will be looking his way tonight, watching for his reaction, waiting to see him blow up or act out.

I'm a little surprised he's even here, to be honest. I don't know if I could do it if I were him. But Emerson either coerced him into coming or he's just trying to be supportive for his dad's sake. Either way, I feel bad leaving him out here alone.

"To be honest, I hate parties," I say, pausing in the courtyard, only a few feet from him. "I obviously never know how to dress." I gesture down at my outfit.

His crooked smirk sends a flood of butterflies to my belly. How dare he be so charming when he's clearly supposed to be a self-centered prick?

"You do look like a virgin," he replies, and the butterflies dissipate just like that.

"Wow, thanks."

"Well, you are walking into a party full of sex club owners."

"*I'm* one of those owners, remember?" I reply, furrowing my brow at him.

"Yeah, and I'm only messing with you."

With a snarky response readying itself on my tongue, I pause as I blankly stare at him. Of course he was only joking, so why did I have to go and get so defensive, as if he was actually insulting me? Suddenly, I feel like a bitch.

"Why don't you just walk in with me? That way you don't have to go in alone and if you want, you can stick by my side."

He looks momentarily surprised by my offer. There's a gentle crease between his brows as the warm summer wind blows through the courtyard, ruffling the brown locks of hair hanging over his forehead. It's no secret that Beau is gorgeous in those fitted jeans and a tight polo shirt that shows off the impeccable shape of his muscled shoulders, but he knows how gorgeous he is and that's what kills his appeal. If only he finished off the look with a touch of humility, he'd be a ten.

"Yeah, sure. Thanks," he mumbles as he pushes away from the wall. "I'm not staying long anyway."

Me either, I think, but I don't say it out loud. I'm sort of hoping I can just slink out undetected.

With Emerson's son on my right, I open the door to the party and walk inside.

Rule #9: Get into trouble as often as you can—trouble is half the fun.

Beau

Is it nine thirty yet? The clock is taunting me, moving slower than it should as I stand on the sidelines of the party with the remnants of a warm, half-empty beer in my hand. Every once in a while, I catch people looking at me, people I've never met, who probably heard about me through gossip or rumors. There's a good chance half the people here just came to get a front-row seat to the biggest live-action soap opera story in Briar Point.

Millionaire club owner steals girl from his own son.

Well, that's probably how they saw it. The details are irrelevant, like the fact that Charlie and I broke up months before she started banging my dad. They'll soak up the scandalous stuff, though, like little drama sponges.

Did you hear Beau cheated on her, so to get back at him, she slept with his dad?

Did you hear Beau hasn't had a serious relationship since?

No one wants to date the off-brand Emerson Grant.

"You all right?" Maggie asks, and I look up from the spot on the floor I was blankly staring at to avoid eye contact.

"No. This party is fucking boring."

"No one is forcing you to be here," she replies in that slightly sweet, bossy tone. It's funny to me how someone so nice-looking can also be so strict and a little bitchy. Not that I don't like Maggie. I find her fascinating, in a non-sexual, un-intimidating sort of way. I bet if she stopped dressing like a frumpy virgin and actually let her badass side out, she'd be pretty hot.

I am tempted to leave early, but it's only eight, and I'd rather just kill time here because I'm sure as hell not going home, where I know my mother is waiting to talk massive amounts of shit about my dad and this whole engagement.

"I know that."

Suddenly, we're ambushed by a man in a tight blue suit, who approaches us with an inquisitive expression. I'm caught off guard, just staring at him as he smiles at Maggie.

"Fitz, I didn't know you were here," she says in a businessy tone, unlike the way she was just talking to me.

When she reaches out a hand, he shakes it, and I find my eyes trailing to the place where their palms touch. It's a formal greeting, but something territorial in me stirs at the sight.

As they break their handshake, he reaches his hand toward me. "Is this your boyfriend?"

"What?" I snap, flinching. "No."

Her firm grip latches onto the back of my arm like a claw as she composes her response much more politely than I did. "Actually, this is Emerson's son, Beau Grant."

His eyebrows rise upward in surprise as he surveys

me, his eyes raking over my casual polo shirt and jeans, and I clench my jaw as he does.

"Beau, this is Xander Fitzgerald, the club's attorney."

"Please, call me Fitz." His hand is still outstretched as he waits for me to shake it, but there's just something about this guy I don't like. I can see why he works with my dad. He looks just like him, but with more fashion sense and richer taste. Another guy with too much confidence and swagger who wants to make me look like a fool.

Maggie's claws tighten, so I quickly reach out to shake his hand. "Nice to meet you," I say through gritted teeth.

He smiles proudly as if he finds this amusing. "I see a lot of your dad in you," he replies, and my eyes squint, refusing to show the faintest sign of interest in his opinion.

"Oh yeah? So you're saying I look like a smug asshole?"

"Beau," Maggie snaps.

Fitz lets out a howling laugh. "Yep, that's it."

A gentle smirk tugs on my lips as he lets go of my hand, but Maggie's death grip on my tricep doesn't ease up in the slightest.

"I've known your dad a long time, long enough to know he's not going to get any less smug now."

Okay, maybe this guy isn't so bad.

"But he never had a sharp tongue like you. Hold on to that. It's going to get you in trouble, but trouble is half the fun."

"Says the lawyer who loves trouble," Maggie retorts proudly.

Fitz responds with another laugh. Then he looks at me as he says, "This one's been trying to put me out of my job for over a decade now. Trouble is my livelihood, Mags."

She rolls her eyes playfully. "Yeah, I know it is, but it also takes years off my life every time you come around."

"Well, things seem to be running smoothly at the club, so hopefully, you won't be seeing me for a while."

She lets out a heavy breath. "Don't get too excited. Those protestors are back. They posted some bullshit article online and the *Briar Point Journal* actually picked this one up."

"They printed it?" he replies, sounding astounded.

"Not exactly. But they've called twice. Might as well get your pen handy. We're going to need it."

My attention is glued to their conversation, but I choose to keep the little spray paint incident to myself, not wanting to draw even more attention to myself.

"I'm ready. The legality is ironclad, Maggie. The most important thing is that we don't engage with them. But you guys know that, so don't worry."

She takes in a long sigh, nodding her head as if she's trying to build up her own confidence. "I'm trying, Fitz. I'm trying."

He gives her a reassuring wink and pat on the shoulder, but when I shuffle my feet, clearly not part of this conversation, he turns toward me. "So, what about you, Mr. Grant? When are you going to join the family business?"

I screw my face up in disgust. "Gross."

He laughs again. "Okay, I take it back. You are nothing like your father."

"Thank God for that." As I look away from Fitz, I feel Maggie's eyes on my face, and I don't like the look of concern in her features. Like I'm a disappointment for shaming my dad's business, again.

I feel the disappointment, like knives. And I don't like it. Not at all.

When I glance down at my phone for the hundredth time tonight and see it's nine thirty-seven, I say a silent prayer of thanks. The partygoers are starting to get tipsy anyway, which means people are getting loose and obnoxious, and for a pretty formal party, it's not as entertaining as you'd think. I lost track of Maggie about fifteen minutes ago, and I feel too exposed alone.

Just as I start to slip toward the door, I hear the cling of a spoon against glass. The party silences, making my exit a little too obvious. I freeze midstep and turn around to find my dad and Charlie standing at the front of the room, near the entrance to his office. She's nestled against his side with a bright, beaming smile on her face.

"Charlotte and I would just like to thank you all for coming out to celebrate our engagement."

I silently shuffle toward the edge of the party, trying to hide myself behind a large potted plant by the window. I scan the crowd again, looking for the familiar brown-haired woman who stood by my side all night. It's weird that Maggie is suddenly my security blanket, but this would just be a hell of a lot less awkward if she was next to me.

"I'm not really the type of man to boast about his love life, but I feel the constant need to brag about how lucky I am to have this woman in my life."

Give me a fucking break.

I roll my eyes. I can hold my tongue and watch what I say, but I can't be held accountable for what my face does.

"Oh my God, Emerson, stop," Charlie replies, hiding her smile in his chest, her left hand lifting to cover her face and showing off the giant diamond on her ring finger. I force in a deep breath. *Just get this over with already so I can leave.*

The exit is clear across the room, so any hope of getting out of here now is gone.

"I've never met a woman so brave and kind and funny and perfect." Then he looks down at her, their eyes locked in a private expression that feels far too intimate for this public setting as he whispers, "You are perfect."

And I fight the urge to vomit.

She smiles back up at him, and I tear my eyes away to see everyone else in the room gazing at them with loving expressions, as if they're watching the greatest thing they've ever seen.

Almost everyone here is coupled up and they're all clinging to each other as if watching my dad with his twenty-two-year-old fiancée is somehow reviving their own love lives.

"I'm sorry for being so cheesy," he says with a laugh, and the crowd responds with their own chuckles. "But I feel incredibly lucky tonight to have the woman I love and all of my friends here. I don't know how I got so lucky to have found you."

"Ha!"

I'm the only one who laughs at that. Loudly.

Suddenly, all eyes are on me at the back of the room. I bite my bottom lip as I try to fade further into the wall, and I can't possibly bear looking up at Charlie or my dad, so I freeze in my awkwardness until they finally all tear their eyes away.

Fuck my life.

"I'll stop talking for tonight. Thank you all again for coming."

With that, the room breaks out in applause, and I take it as my sign to hightail my ass out of that party. If anyone bothers following me, I'm too far gone by the time they have a chance to catch me.

Rule #10: Some mysteries should remain mysteries.

Maggie

I slip through the back door of the club undetected and head straight for the shared office, where I know none of my colleagues will be waiting for me.

This is by far the craziest thing I've ever done.

With shaky hands, I open my bag and start pulling out the clothes I brought, including the white feathery masquerade mask.

God, what if someone that works here recognizes me?

Oh well. They won't dare say a word or I'll have them fired on the spot.

Okay, that's a little harsh, but I'm still fairly confident they won't say anything, so I'm safe. We all have a mutual, unspoken agreement that everyone's sex lives are private and discretion is gold-plated.

Shedding the stupid virgin skirt and blouse, I stand in my thin, lace thong and satin bra, quickly slipping the black dress over my body. My cleavage immediately pops out of the top, but instead of tucking it back in like I would have done before, I shimmy it out a little bit more.

Using my phone's camera as a mirror, I apply some red lipstick and thick eyeliner. Then, I brush back my bangs, pinning them down as I tease my hair into a sexy tight ponytail.

As I slip the white mask over my face, I realize that this feels a little like transforming into an entirely different person. My dominant alter ego. Because I certainly don't feel anything like myself at the moment.

And I like it.

I duck my head out the door to make sure no one sees me coming out of the office like this, and when the hallway is clear, I slide out and close it behind me. In a scurry, I rush toward the service entrance that leads to the main room.

Once I enter the frenzy of the masquerade party, I pause. The room is full, the lights dimmer than normal, and bright-colored strobe lights illuminate the crowd. On the stage, the DJ is playing, and for the most part, it resembles a regular nightclub more than a sex club. The only difference being that everyone here tonight is in disguise.

My feet are glued in place as I marvel at the sight of Salacious from this angle. Not that I haven't stood in this exact spot or been to an event of ours before, but I've never been here as a member. I've never stood in this room, nervous to be meeting someone soon with the promise of something intimate and exhilarating.

It's terrifying. How do people do this all the time? Put themselves in such a vulnerable position? Open themselves up to rejection and heartbreak? Isn't it easier to just avoid it altogether? Stay home. Stay alone.

As I slowly meander through the crowd, feeling the eyes of those around me slowly examining me, I stare back at each one, looking for that glowing green *s* that should be written on his mask.

It's so crowded, I have to squeeze through the mass of bodies, getting a little frustrated by how impossible this feels. An older man with gray in his short beard steps in front of me, and I quickly try to move around him.

"Can I buy you a drink?" he shouts into my ear over the sound of the music.

I quickly shake my head. "I'm meeting someone. Thanks, though!"

With a shrug, he moves aside, clearly looking for his next target somewhere behind me. I shouldn't be here, and that thought alone has my lunch threatening to return. I'm an *owner*. I feel as if I'm exploiting my company for my own personal gain, and although it shouldn't, it has me swallowing down some mild discomfort. I know I shouldn't feel this way. My partners use the club all the time, so why do I feel guilty?

Minutes go by and there's no sign of him.

Glancing down at my watch on my second turn of the room, I see that it's almost ten twenty, and he's clearly not here. Which means he's not coming. I should have expected as much. He was probably just messing with me the whole time. With no intention to actually see this through, he was just a young guy on an app, having a little fun with a desperate lady over a decade older than him.

I need a drink, but I'm too nervous to go to the bar and order one because Geo is bartending tonight, and I'm not quite confident enough that he wouldn't recognize me in this disguise. I'm now lingering uncomfortably alone on the outskirts of the room, watching the entrance like a hawk. When the second guy of the night offers to buy me one, I shake my head again—even though I really want one.

Just as I'm about to give up on this whole dumb idea and pack away all of this Domme talk into a suitcase that I'll bury forever, I glance up to see a very tall man in all black walk through the curtain and enter the masses.

My heart hammers in my chest, and I force myself to swallow as I spot the shiny letter on the outside corner of his black mask. He's beautifully tan and slender, brown hair slicked back, and he's wringing his hands together as if he's nervous. Standing near the edge of the throng, he lets his eyes scan the room, and I wait in silence near the border as they finally land on me.

His hands freeze as his gaze rakes over my body, all the way down and back up again. His Adam's apple bounces as he swallows, and he licks his lips, delicately making his way over to me.

Oh my God, this is happening. Oh my God, this is happening.

No turning back now.

I lift a hand to wave awkwardly, and before I know it, he's standing only inches away. It's so loud in here that when he opens his full lips to greet me, I don't even hear his voice, but I make out the word, *hi*.

I'm staring at his eyes, or what little I can make out through the mask. His is black with intricate metal-like designs that reach up to cover his forehead and descend low enough that I can only see the bottom half of his mouth.

He reaches out, softly touching the side of my white

mask with tall feathers covering the top of my face. As he delicately traces the *D* I scribbled on the side with the black light paint in the office, a shiver runs up my spine. And he's not even touching me yet.

When he leans down, pressing his face close to my ear, I forget to breathe.

"Sorry I'm late," he says, loud enough for me to hear but gentle enough not to shout in my ear.

"I didn't think you were coming," I reply back, clinging to his tall frame to keep from tumbling over.

"I wouldn't miss this. I've been looking forward to it all week, and now that I see you, I'm so glad I'm here."

My mouth goes dry. Then his hand wraps around my waist, a large palm at the small of my back. And when his fingers skate over my soft rolls, I tense. But instead of pulling away, he squeezes, letting my body press tightly against his.

"Are you nervous?" he asks.

"Yes," I answer without hesitation.

"Don't be. I'm yours tonight, remember?"

I've forgotten how to breathe.

"I don't know if I'm ready for this," I mutter, distantly remembering that I was supposed to turn down sex tonight, but that idea is crumbing like sand through my fingers.

"I'm ready for whatever you are."

As he pulls back and stares down at me, I try my hardest to breathe normally, but he's so perfect and beautiful. And even though I can't see most of his face, it's just this...aura of him that is intoxicating, and I want so badly to make him mine. Make him do whatever I want. Use him, claim him, show him off, keep him.

Wow, this is going to my head too fast.

But it's only because he's literally telling me to, and I feel his sincerity. Like he won't challenge me or take control from me. And maybe I'm making this assumption too fast, but everything about the way he's standing here now, staring down at me with a smirk and a willingness in his eyes says...this guy wants to be my fuck boy, and God help me...I want to let him.

"We should get a room." It's not until the words are out of my mouth that I realize I was the one who uttered them. His smile intensifies, and I quickly add, "To talk, I mean."

With a wicked grin half hiding under that mask, he reaches for my hand. "Lead the way, ma'am."

I pull in a heavy inhale, loving the way that phrase sounds coming from him. And I don't waste any time. As I drag him away from the crowd and toward the hallway on the opposite side of the voyeur rooms, I see a green light above door number twelve—the dark room. Not exactly what I wanted, but it's the only one available at the moment, and I can't take the risk of going to the front desk to be put on the wait list for another.

I pull the master keycard out of my bra and glance back at my man—oh my God, another burst of shock runs through me. He's really here. But he's not looking at me, he's glancing around the hallway, clearly trying to soak up the experience of being at his first sex club. It's cute to see how curious he is.

When the door clicks open, he turns his attention toward me and smiles.

"You can just walk right into these rooms?"

"Um...yeah, sort of. Come on." I divert the conversation, so I don't have to explain why it was so easy for me to get into this room.

As we enter the pitch-black space, the green lines shine brightly, displaying where the furniture is so no one gets hurt. I feel him tense behind me as the door closes.

"Where are the lights?" he whispers, his hands clinging to my waist.

"It's a dark room."

"Oh," he replies. "So I can't look at you?"

He crowds me from behind, his hard body pressed against my *less hard* backside. Okay, it's more than less hard, it's downright pillowy. But he doesn't seem to mind.

"Maybe this will be better. We can just talk and..."

His hands dance their way over my ass and then up to circle around to my front, grazing over my breasts. "And what?" he whispers. The music is still loud in here, but not nearly as loud as the main hall filled with people.

"And touch," I say with a slight whimper.

With him subtly squeezing my breasts, I nearly lose the ability to stand. They haven't been felt in so long, and even through my dress, they are loving it. I lean my weight against him, and when his mouth reaches the apex of my neck and shoulder, I realize he's taken his mask off.

His warm, wet mouth caresses its way up my neck toward my ear. "Does this feel good?"

Another firm squeeze of my breasts. "Yes," I murmur.

"What else do you want me to do? You're in charge, remember?"

I swallow. He smells so good and his touch is muddling every clear thought in my head. We just met ten seconds ago. This is all happening too fast, and I literally just said we came in here to talk, but right now, he's offering his hands up at my disposal and my body is too hungry for his caress to listen to my brain at the moment.

"Lift my dress," I reply, my tone coming out more assertive than breathy.

"Yes, ma'am."

"We're moving too fast," I whisper as his hands reach down, tugging the hem up above my hips.

"Do you want to stop? You're in control."

Fuck no, I don't want to stop. I want to keep surging down this river to see where it leads, but it's just as terrifying as it is exciting.

"No, don't stop."

He lets out a groan as I touch the top of his hand, guiding it slowly toward the spot between my legs. Even though I'm a tall woman, I still only come up to just under his chin, so as he folds over me to caress my now soaked panties, I feel the rock hard and impressively large bulge of his cock against my back, causing arousal to pulse through me like lightning.

I guide his fingers to my clit, hovering my hand over his as he explores this sensitive part of me. Large fingers stroke circles before running farther down, feeling the moisture pooling there.

"You're so wet," he mutters raspily against my ear. "You're enjoying this. So tell me what to do next."

I shut off the cognitive function of my brain and let the sensations and cravings of my body guide me.

"Make me come," I reply in a breathy command.

With the hand not holding his, I reach up and find the back of his head, gripping his hair in my fist, tugging him even closer. The power in my hands is intoxicating.

"How should I do that?"

"With your fingers. Slip them inside me. Fuck me with them."

Who am I?

A subtle, rumbling growl vibrates from his body to mine as he springs into action, sliding his hand down the front of my panties and plunging one finger inside me. I cry out, a desperate sounding moan. It's been too long since I've been touched, and it's never felt like this.

"Turn to face me," I say.

Keeping his finger inside me, he spins me around until I'm facing him, and with two steps, he presses me hard against the wall, his frame crowding me into the tight space.

The movement of his finger doesn't stop, and it is just enough to drive me wild. I want him to fuck me, but I don't want to go too far right now. I want to savor this, enjoy the small things until we gradually make them big things.

"Kiss me," I say, and without missing a beat, his mouth is on mine. His lips are so soft and sweet, a little facial hair around his mouth enough to add to the friction without being distracting. Our tongues tangle, the chemistry between us so nuclear, I'm afraid I might actually die from the intensity of it.

He rips my mask off, without me having to tell him to, and then deepens our kiss. His finger is moving faster, and my breathing is erratic. When he adds a second finger, using his thumb to add pressure to my clit, I feel my climax creeping closer.

"I want to hear you come," he whispers against my mouth.

I couldn't keep in my noises at this point if I wanted to. I'm panting, moaning, trying to find room in my lungs for oxygen as I gasp for air.

"Don't stop," I plead. Lifting a leg to give him better access, I grab the back of his head again, squeezing a handful of his hair so he feels my pleasure with a sting of pain.

"Yes, ma'am."

When I feel my orgasm coming, I reach down, slamming his hand against me and using his palm pressed tightly to my clit to ride out the sensation. With my head hanging back, his mouth is on my neck as pleasure assaults every nerve ending in my body. It pulses and pulses until I'm left with nothing but tingles and breathlessness.

And as an owner of a sex club, I'm not proud to admit this part, but that was the first orgasm I've ever had in public. Even worse, it's the first one I've ever had in the company of another person.

Not that I'm about to tell him that.

But still...it was amazing. Easily, the best of my life.

As I start to come down, his hand still buried in my panties, two fingers stuffed inside me and his mouth near my throat, I smile.

"That was amazing," he says, his deep voice vibrating against my neck.

"Don't move for a minute," I reply, wanting to ease myself down from this moment.

"Yes, ma'am."

My eyes pop open, not that I can see anything, but I play his words over and over in my head because it sounded too familiar for my comfort. And not just because he's said it at least five other times in the last fifteen minutes, but because it reminds me of someone else.

I rack my brain for a moment, feeling a little unsettled as he squeezes me closer, clearly not noticing my sudden discomfort.

Where did I just hear that? It was somewhat recent, so I replay the last few days in my memory: moving, unpacking, the party.

Finally, it hits me, and at first, I feel relieved. It was just Beau. He said that to me on the night of my impromptu housewarming.

Still frozen in place, I run through a quick list of facts about my mystery man, searching for at least one that will relieve me of this paranoia and confirm that Beau and my mystery man are two different people. He's twenty-two. He's new to kink. He's local.

But Beau's at the party. He was at the party when I left.

Although he was late meeting me here.

"Okay, pull out," I whisper in a rush, and he quickly takes his hand from between my legs.

"Are you okay?" he asks, and the blood drains from my face. When you're not expecting it, it's easy to trick your brain into thinking there's nothing to worry about. But the minute I hear his voice, a voice I've listened to all night, I hear exactly who it is.

Shoving my hand over my mouth, I muffle my own ear-piercing scream.

Rule #11: If you're not good with words, actions will do.

Beau

"What? What's wrong?" I snap, quickly backing up as if I've hurt her somehow.

I can't say I've ever had this response after giving a woman an orgasm. Definitely not what I was going for.

She fumbles along the wall like she's trying to find something. Without warning, the lights in the room turn on, blinding me as I slam my eyes shut and cover them with my hands.

"Oh no, no, no, no," she mumbles, and I struggle to peel open my eyes in the now bright room. The moment they adjust, I quickly slam them shut again.

"What the fuck!"

Why is Maggie here? Why is Maggie standing against the wall with her dress hiked up around her hips? Did I just...

Holy shit.

My mind is scrambling for answers while she

continues on her dramatic rambling and overall freaking out. It's obvious I'm not who she expected either.

"I was supposed to meet a girl I found on the app," I mutter.

"Beau, that was me!" she snaps, clearly irritated by how long this is taking my slow brain to comprehend.

"No. It couldn't be."

When I open my eyes again, her dress is back down covering her panties, and she's pacing the room in a frenzy. "It was a mistake. I didn't *know*! There was no way I could have known."

"Maggie, calm down."

She freezes and glares at me with wide eyes and a wild look of panic on her face. "Calm down?"

"Yes, calm down. So...we know each other. Big deal. We're both adults. And we didn't even have sex."

The intensity of her expression does not waver for a drawn-out moment before she finally scoffs and shakes her head. "I keep forgetting you're only twenty-two."

"Hey," I reply. I'm not exactly sure what that was supposed to imply, but it felt a lot like she used my age as an insult.

"Beau, we don't just *know each other*. Your dad is my friend—my *good* friend. And colleague, and if he knew I had you here in his club—" She looks pained as she covers her face with her hands, dropping onto the bed.

I don't talk for a while, not sure what to say, but definitely feeling a sense of disappointment. Not disappointed because my mystery woman is Maggie—not disappointed by that at all, actually—but more so because everything we had planned is basically nixed now. My dream woman, ready to boss me around and take control, is no more.

Well, technically, she's sitting right in front of me, but she's having a full-blown crisis at the moment, and I don't see her getting over it anytime soon.

"Do you want me to leave?" I ask reluctantly, because I don't really know what else to say at this point.

"Yes, please. But keep your mask on."

I watch her carefully as I slip the black ribbon over the back of my head, and I hate that we're ending it this way. It doesn't feel right. One minute I had my fingers inside her, and now I'm being sent away.

"Beau..." she says, calling after me as I open the door. When I look back, she continues, "No one can know about this."

With a nod, I reply, "I know." And just like that, I disappear into the dim hallway. Music is still blaring from the main room along with the low chatter of voices, and I make my way toward the exit. I know we can't continue what we were doing, but I don't like walking away from her, not like this. Not after what we just did.

I take that uneasy feeling with me all the way home. Even as I crawl into bed, artfully dodging my mother's prodding questions by sneaking in through the patio instead of the main entrance, I'm still thinking about Maggie.

Lying in bed, I replay the way it felt, not just physically. Although her body was incredible—soft and warm and so pliant, like putty in my hands. But there was something about surrendering myself to her commands. I didn't even get off, but I was never thinking about my pleasure. I was too focused on hers. And that's not something I've ever really experienced before.

Her sexy commands echo in my mind. *Lift my dress. Kiss me. Make me come.*

God, that was hot and not in a way I'm familiar with. It wasn't hot in the *jack off to the memory* sort of way, but when I was touching her, I felt invigorated and alive, warm tingles covering every inch of my body. My brain was off and the only signal it was receiving was *us*—our chemistry and the intensity between us.

Oh well.

I can find another one like her. There was a giant list of names to scroll through. And maybe I will. Maybe they'll go easy on me and let me learn on them while they learn on me. Surely, there has to be someone else.

As I start to drift off, I keep coming back to the same idea. *I don't want to find someone else.* Now that the shock has worn off, I see Maggie in a different light. That low-cut neckline with that fucking phenomenal cleavage. Her hips filling out the dress and the way she felt pressed against my cock.

It was not the same woman who showed up to my dad's party, looking like a virgin. Knowing Maggie has a sexy, dark side makes it that much hotter. I've never imagined what she might taste like before, but I sure as fuck am now. I want to know the sounds she makes while I tongue-fuck her. I wonder what she would make me do, how she would use me to get herself off. I imagine her tying me up, hurting me, *praising* me.

Now these are thoughts to jack off to.

But for some reason, I don't. I could easily reach under the sheets and relieve the pressure that's been building since I saw her across the room tonight, but I don't want to. A quiet voice inside is keeping me from my favorite indulgence. And it's a voice I want to obey.

The next morning, I'm in my car sitting outside Maggie's house with the sole purpose of apologizing since she's not responding to my messages on the Salacious app. My guess is that she deleted it. But I can't just leave things the way we did last night.

As I walk up the drive toward the front door, I keep rehearsing my apology. Even though I know there is so much more I want to say. I'm not even sure why I think I need to apologize, but something along the lines of 'I'm sorry that happened and I hope you're okay' sounds good enough.

But to be clear, I'm not entirely sorry it happened. It was still hot as fuck, and I can't get the memory of her tight pussy pulsing around my fingers out of my head.

I'm still thinking about it as I press the doorbell and *still* thinking about it when she opens the door, staring at me in shock.

"Beau," she says sternly. Her giant gray dog stands calmly by her side, but she quickly sends him away, and he listens, obediently taking his place on the couch.

After last night, I'm seeing Maggie very differently, my eyes studying her as if this is the first time we've met. Never before noticing the sharp line of her lips, the sexy button shape of her nose, the innocence of her large blue eyes, the delicate softness of her pale skin. My eyes trail down to the spot just below her throat, that little divot between her collarbones, and my fingers itch to reach out and touch it.

Instead, I force myself to swallow and look up at her. "I just came to apologize for last night."

"Last night didn't happen," she replies with confidence.

And for some reason that bothers me. Sure, it'd be

easy to pretend the whole thing was just a glitch in the matrix and we can go back to our normal lives, but with the way I can't get her out of my head, that's going to be easier said than done.

I don't like her pretending it didn't happen. I don't like knowing it's that easy for her to forget.

When my gaze connects with hers, intensity burns between us, and it's so strange to feel a fire where there was none before—at least not before last night.

"But it did happen," I reply in a low mumble.

"According to us, sure. But as far as everyone else is concerned, *nothing* happened."

"Okay," I say, feeling somewhat defeated. I should just leave it at that. I apologized, sort of. Now I need to let it go.

But I can't.

"Well, according to *us*," I say, emphasizing that word, "it was pretty fucking amazing."

She tenses, her eyes starting to gloss as if she's lost in the memory. God, I want to kiss her again. Just for fun. Just because it feels like something I'm not supposed to do and I like the idea of rebelling, especially where my father is involved—seeing as how he's the only reason Maggie feels compelled to push me away.

So, I pounce.

Closing the distance between us, I take her by the neck and crash our mouths together, slipping my tongue between her lips as she shoves against my chest. I don't stop as we shuffle backward, and I slam the door behind me, pinning her against the wall the same way I did last night.

Soon, her fight turns into surrender and she relaxes into my arms, letting me explore her mouth again. Her hums and moans remind me of last night, and I love how vocal she is, urging me on with every little sound.

"Wait, Beau," she gasps. "Stop."

With one last nibble of her bottom lip, I pull away breathlessly, and we freeze there for a moment, both of us gasping for air. I wait for her to speak again because I frankly have no clue what to say. I thought I came here to apologize, but I'd rather slip back into her panties, if we're being honest.

"You shouldn't have done that," she says, and I'm already leaning back in again as I reply.

"Then punish me for it."

I notice a shudder in her breath as those words travel to her ears. Just as my lips are about to find hers again, she shoves me back. "No, Beau, I'm serious. We can't do this."

"Why not?"

"Because your father is my friend and business partner. And I've known you since you were a kid." She shivers, a pained expression crossing her face.

"I'm not a kid anymore, though."

"It doesn't matter," she replies. "It's just...not right."

I can't keep the smile off my face as I step closer, resting an arm against the wall above her head. "Something about it being against the rules makes me want to do it that much more."

I lower my mouth closer to hers. Before our lips touch, she slips out of my hold and spins me until it's *my* back against the wall. With her hand pressing firmly on my chest, she stares up at me.

"That's because you're a brat, Beau." She closes in, her breath landing against my lips.

"I can live with that," I reply, just before taking her mouth in another harsh kiss. Our lips tangle as she hums again, latching her hand around the back of my neck. My cock throbs behind my jeans, and I grab her hips, grinding her against me, wanting her to feel what she's doing to me.

"God, this is so bad," she whimpers. And I get a thrill just from the way she tries to fight this decision.

"Can I touch you again?" I whisper against her neck. "I can't stop thinking about your perfect little cunt."

"Yes," she replies without hesitation.

I quickly lift her pencil skirt and find the apex of her thighs with my fingers, running them along the soaked fabric of her panties. She hums in response, the sound of her pleasure sending a wave of pride through me.

Maybe it's because she's so vocal or because she gives off this authoritative energy, but I'm suddenly so turned on by the idea of pleasing her. I'm dying to make her come again. To my disappointment, she stops me before I have the chance.

"No, no, no," she stammers, shoving away from me again. In a rush, she walks farther into her house, pacing again in that erratic and panicked way she was last night. "I should say no to this. I should be the mature adult here and just say no. Oh God, how can I look Emerson in the eyes after this?"

Slowly, I follow behind her, my heart pounding wildly in my chest. I've never felt so desperate for someone in my life. And I could argue with her, tell her exactly why she should do this, but I've never been all that great with words.

So I use actions instead.

With her back to me, still in a state of panic and her chest heaving from the intensity of our kiss, I keep my eyes on her as I slowly lower to my knees.

"Maggie."

When she finally turns around to face me, she lets out the tiniest gasp. Her gaze sweeps over my body appreciatively. She clearly likes to see me this way, even if she tries to hide it. "What are you doing?"

"If you don't want me to touch you, I won't. If you do want me to touch you, I will."

Her lips are parted as she stares at me, and I can practically see the ideas brewing behind those eyes.

"You told me I couldn't be submissive, remember? That I was too stubborn. Well, here you go. I'm being submissive."

"To get laid," she replies, making it sound like an accusation.

"I just told you. You're in charge. If you don't want to have sex, then we won't have sex. But...we both found something on that app that made us curious enough to get into this mess. It'd be a waste to let that go now."

"Beau..." she says with gentleness. There's something about the way she says my name that sends a wave of pleasure down my spine. Even when she does it with impatience or as a warning. "But you hate kink. You didn't talk to your father for six months because he owned a sex club, and now you want me to be your Domme. This is all built on trust, and I don't know if I can trust you."

"You can trust me," I argue. "I don't understand this any more than you, but all I know is that I want to see this through—with you."

Since I see her about to argue again, and I'm learning that she is beyond persistent, I decide to throw in a pity plea.

"I suck with women, Maggie. I never say the right thing. Never do the right thing. Never react the way they want and I'm just fucking lost. At least with you, if I fuck up, you can punish me for it. Otherwise, I'm here to do exactly what you want. Maybe I'll learn how to be less of an asshole to women. Maybe with your help, I won't end up alone."

Her shoulders soften. "Oh, God, Beau… Am I seriously considering this?"

I watch as she covers her face with her hands, clearly grappling with her morality in this situation. Finally, she lifts her hands away and stares at me. "All right. Fine. We can learn together, but it's strictly a learning experience."

I smile, but she quickly adds, "Absolutely no sex."

"Yes, ma'am," I respond, feeling a little hopeful that that rule will eventually change.

"And no one can know about this. No one."

"I won't tell a soul."

With a tense expression, she stares at me. "We'll have to go over some rules and limits. If we're going to do this, we have to do it right."

I smile, and I see the way it almost makes her break. But before letting hers slip through, she looks away. "Just get off the floor."

Obediently, I stand.

"I'm going to hire you to help me out around the house, painting and repairs. If anyone asks."

I nod.

"You'll start tomorrow. Nine a.m."

Biting my bottom lip, I nod again. As much as I'd love to be back to where we were a minute ago, with my hand up her skirt, this is almost more exciting—the unknown waiting around the corner.

With that, I turn and head toward the front door, barely able to contain my grin now. But just as my hand finds the knob, she throws in one more command.

"Oh, and, Beau..."

I turn toward her expectantly.

"No coming until I tell you to."

My brow furrows. "What?"

Closing the distance between us, she steps closer. Only a few feet away, she adds, "You heard me. I don't want you masturbating or touching yourself at all tonight. And I'll know if you do."

The blood in my veins suddenly feels like lava. "How will you know?"

"Because this is based on trust, and if we're going to do this, then you can't lie to me."

"Is this a punishment?" I ask.

"No. It's dominance. This is what you're signing up for. But if you're good tomorrow, maybe you'll get a reward."

My eyebrows shoot up. "But I thought you said—"

"No sex." Then she shrugs. "But there are other things."

My mouth is hanging open as she reaches around me to pull open the front door. She's making it very fucking hard to leave now. And maybe with any other woman, I would just take control. Carry her to the bedroom and make her come so many times, she changes her mind. But that's not what we're doing here. And that's not the point.

Somehow, I think this is better.

"See you tomorrow, Beau."

With a forced gulp, I stare at her face as I reply, "Yes, ma'am."

Rule #12: When you're unsure, consult the professionals.

Maggie

I need help. I have no clue what I've gotten myself into or what to do next.

I've been around the community enough that I know the basics—it must be safe, sane, and consensual. But beyond that...I'm lost.

Lucky for me, I know exactly who can help.

Eden St. Claire is sitting across from me at one of the VIP tables upstairs, and since it's still early in the night, it's quiet. In about two hours, having a conversation at this table will be difficult, considering the people behind the curtain next to us will be in full orgy mode.

"This isn't business-related, is it?" she asks, sipping on her martini.

I force myself to swallow. "Not exactly."

That makes her smile as she leans forward. She's in a sleek black dress that is surprisingly buttoned all the way up to her neck. And I nearly die with envy at how much sexuality she can exude without even trying.

"Tell me everything," she replies with a gentle sincerity that calms me. It's what I love about Eden. She is open and approachable, so nothing is intimidating about coming to her and asking questions about the lifestyle.

"I took the kink quiz," I say, and her interest suddenly piques.

"Let me guess. It told you you're a Domme."

My eyes widen. "How did you know?"

"Maggie, I've been watching you for the past year and I see how much you require control. You handle everything on your own, instead of delegating to anyone else. You're not spontaneous in the least, and for a long time, I just assumed you were vanilla. And if you were having sex, it was probably unfulfilling and unsatisfying."

My jaw hangs open. Does everyone around here know more about me than I do myself?

"That's incredible," I whisper.

She laughs, taking another drink. "It could be my circus act. Guessing people's kinks based on their personalities."

While that is impressive, I've seen Madame Kink in action through the voyeur hall enough to know that probably wouldn't be her only circus trick.

"So, technically, my results were Domme, Mistress, Brat Tamer," I say, suddenly wishing I brought a pen and paper to take actual notes.

"Oh, Brat Tamer. I can see that one, and I love it."

"Eden...I have no clue how to do any of this."

When she reaches out a hand and places it over mine, it's immediately calming. "Okay, first of all, relax. It shouldn't be work. It's supposed to be fun."

Air leaves my lungs in a rush as I nod. "Okay, okay. I know."

"You do know how to have fun, right?"

I respond with a sarcastic glare. She lets out a clipped laugh.

"So...have you found someone willing to play with you?"

And I'm tense again.

"Yes," I reply tightly.

This response surprises her. "Oh. Well...that's great. Someone new to kink too?"

"Yes..."

She can obviously sense my hesitation. "Maggie, relax."

"I'm trying, but this stuff scares the hell out of me, and he's so eager, and I love the idea of having fun with him, but what if I fuck it up? What if I hurt him? Or he doesn't like it? Or—"

"Here, take this." She's putting her drink in my hands, and the next thing I know, I'm sipping down straight vodka. My cough feels like fire as I hand it back to her.

"Okay, first of all, you're too worried about his expectations. His safety...sure. That's important, but you're too codependent in your sexuality. You've trained yourself to believe that your pleasure relies on theirs. You've been trained to be a people pleaser and a service lover. But what you need is to be dominant and take your pleasure without obligation to anyone else."

"Well, I want him to enjoy it," I argue.

"But that's the point, Maggie. It's not about him, not really. If he's a real sub, serving you is what he wants, no matter what that means. It's not selfish. It's literally what the entire dynamic is all about. Stop worrying about what *he* wants. What do *you* want?"

"That's the problem, Eden. I literally don't know. I feel broken."

She opens her mouth to reply with a look of sympathy on her face when a familiar voice pops up behind me.

"What are you guys talking about?" Charlie hops into the seat next to me, and my cheeks burn with embarrassment. God, how much did she hear?

Eden doesn't reply, just stares blankly ahead, waiting for me to take the lead on that question.

"Umm..."

Realization dawns on Charlie's face. Then she gasps. "Wait, is this about the quiz you took last week?"

My face falls as her smile only grows. "Did you find someone?" she asks with even more eagerness.

I drop my face into my hands, without responding to her.

"You know...Charlotte might be a good person to talk to. From the sub's perspective."

"Oh yeah," Charlie replies. "Ask me anything."

I let out a groan. If only they knew the truth. Charlotte is literally the last person I could imagine talking to about this. Considering the submissive in question is her ex-boyfriend. Oh, and her Dom's son.

Talk about complicated.

"Maggie is struggling with what to do with her guy. She's too worried about him not liking it," Eden answers for me.

"Well, whatever is on the checklist is fair game," Charlie replies. "Emerson and I try stuff all the time, and some of it is great, but sometimes, it's too weird and I don't like it."

I groan again. I don't know if I can listen to this, but

also...my curiosity is piqued. "It doesn't make you mad, to do stuff for him?" I ask.

She tilts her head to the side as if this question is crazy. "No. It doesn't make me mad. It makes me...happy in a weird way. I can't explain it, but pleasing him pleases me."

"Does he ever let you have control?" I ask, suddenly full of questions.

Her mouth lifts into a coy smile as she fights a blush. "Sometimes."

I lean forward. I couldn't imagine Emerson submitting if I tried, and I'm trying. "Really?"

"Yeah. It's good to switch it up from time to time. To get the other person's perspective. It's weird but fun."

God, I can't believe I'm about to ask this. I just need to pretend these are two random people I don't know very well as I say, "What sort of stuff do you do when you're... in charge?"

Their eyes light up simultaneously. "Anything I want. I'll blindfold him, tie him up, tease him until he's begging for mercy—but not literally because that's our safe word."

"Mercy is your safe word?"

She nods. "Yep. It's easy to remember."

I swallow uncomfortably. "Have you ever had to use it?"

Her lips tighten as she shakes her head. "But Emerson trusts that I would if I needed to."

"The trust goes both ways," Eden adds. "You have to trust your sub as much as they have to be able to trust you."

"And what about...punishment?" I ask, which makes Charlotte shake her head with a sweet smile.

"Maggie, I'm a good girl. I don't get punished."

Eden laughs. "Bullshit."

"It's true!" Charlie replies, nudging Eden playfully on the shoulder. "I spent enough time pissing off ex-boyfriends. I don't like to be *reprimanded,*" she replies, and I swallow down the discomfort building in my throat. I have a feeling I know exactly which ex-boyfriend she's referring to.

"Well, Maggie has herself a brat."

"Oh," Charlotte says with interest, "I have to admit, that sounds fun. I can think of a few guys I'd like to punish." She and Eden laugh while I dig my fingernails into my thigh to keep from cracking under the pressure of this conversation. *Oh, if they only knew.*

"Do you tell him if you don't like something?" I ask, changing the subject.

"Oh, sure. We'll talk about it after, and sometimes I cross it off the list," she says.

"I need a list."

"Here," she replies eagerly, taking out her phone, "let me send you the one we use. It's long, but it covers everything."

Reaching across the table, I grab Eden's martini glass and force the rest of it down, just as my phone pings. It's a text message from Charlie with a link to a BDSM checklist, and my stomach turns.

I'm definitely not going to tell Beau where I got this.

I'm sending you homework.

I TYPE WITH A SMILE. IT'S PAST THREE IN THE morning and Ringo is snoring by my feet as I lie in bed to see if Beau is still awake. The three dots start to bounce, which means he's up, so I wait for his reply.

Teacher/student role-play? That's hot.

A laugh escapes my lips as I type back to him.

This is real homework.

Like reading or something?

It's a checklist.

I drop the link Charlie sent me into our chat then press send. After a few minutes, he responds.

Oh.

I furrow my brow in concern.

What's wrong?

Nothing. I've seen this before.

Where?

I'm feeling strangely curious and a little wary.

Doesn't matter. I'll fill it out.

A few minutes later, he sends another message.

I don't know what half of this stuff is.

Well, then look it up.
You have to use it to tell me what you do and don't want to do.
It has to be completed before we do anything.

Electrocution?
Mummification!?
What the fuck.

Don't kink shame.
Just cross it off if you aren't interested in trying it.

I do not want you to electrocute me.

Noted.

You would, wouldn't you?

Only if you let me.
And if you deserved it.

What would I have to do to get you to electrocute me?

Okay, first of all, you're being dramatic.
It's a little shock, not an electric chair.

And I think the punishment should fit the crime.

What does that mean?

It means you'd have to do something really bad to get punished like that.

Define really bad.

Lie to me.
Masturbate after I told you not to.
Disobey me.

The last one was hard to type out. This is still all so weird to me, and I can't believe I'm doing this. But the thrill running through me right now is exhilarating, and I can't remember the last time I was this excited.

Does that turn you on? Punishing me?

Heat blossoms in my belly.

Yes.
Does it turn you on?

Yes.
Makes me want to be bad.
What would you do if I jerked off right now?

My mouth goes dry. What is this man doing to me? Suddenly I'm reminded of the vision of Beau on his knees this morning and how enticing that image was. A tall, beautiful man submitting to *me*.

Then I remember what Eden said today. He *wants* to bring me pleasure. Even if that means letting me hurt him, torture him, punish him, and use him. What he wants is to give me what I want. It's almost too foreign to comprehend.

I'd have no choice but to lock up your

cock in a cage until you learn.

A cage?!

Yep. Look it up.

I'm grinning ear to ear as I wait. And just as expected, a moment later he texts back.

You're crazy.
I'm a little scared of you right now.

Good. Then maybe you'll behave.

Maybe. ;)

Do your homework.
I'll see you in the morning.
No jerking off.

Yes, ma'am.

The instant serotonin boost I get whenever he says that to me is like a hit of something potent and intoxicating. As I put my phone on the charger and roll over to fall asleep, I remember what Eden said tonight at the club—this is supposed to be fun.

I just need to stop worrying about the expectations and my preconceived notions, and let the amazing chemistry we have lead the way. It doesn't need to be so scary.

And with what I have in mind for him tomorrow, I'm going to have to work up the guts to go through with it. I'm crossing a major line, but it's not one we haven't already crossed. I said no sex, and I'm sticking to that. Sex complicates things, and things are too complicated as it is.

But I also said there are other things we can do that don't include sex, and I intend to use them all.

Emerson would have my head if he knew what I had planned for his son, but with his track record, he really has no room to talk.

Rule #13: If you don't take it seriously, you will be punished.

Beau

I feel like I'm in school. A kinky sex school with a teacher who looks even more nervous than me.

I filled out the checklist on a scale of one to five for each item. They were mostly zeroes and fives, and I was a little surprised by how many of them involved my pain or me being fucked by something. Or at least that's what I assumed. When it asked about fisting, I sort of figured I would be the one being fisted, which for the record, was a zero.

Plugs and beads? One.

The reason I'm here is to prove to her I'm not afraid of being submissive, so I'm not going to shy away from the good stuff now.

I didn't tell Maggie about how I saw this list on my father's desk once, not knowing then that it was more than likely my ex-girlfriend who filled it out. I didn't want to drag the past and all of that awkwardness into this thing Maggie and I have. The past belongs in the past.

I'm sitting on her kitchen counter next to a stack of unopened boxes while she looks through the list, chewing on her inner lip. Finally, she sets the packet down on the counter and glares at me.

"What?" I ask.

"Are you taking this seriously?"

My face screws up in confusion. "What? Yes!"

She picks the paper back up. "Okay, so you *love* the idea of flogging and choking?"

I shrug. "I'm game."

"Beau," she says, sounding exasperated. Then she pinches the bridge of her nose as she continues, "If I'm going to be the one making you do these things, I need to know what you're comfortable with. None of this is worth humiliating or hurting you."

"If I don't like it, I'll tell you to stop."

She sets the paper back down. "That reminds me—we need a safe word.

"I can't just say stop?"

"No," she replies. "Well, technically yes, you can, but in some scenarios, that's not enough, so the safe word is necessary."

"Okay..." I say. Reaching down, I scratch the giant gray dog nudging my leg for attention, and he jumps up, putting his massive paws on the counter, nearly matching me in height. "How about Ringo?"

"Absolutely not. We are not using my dog's name as our safe word. Ringo, down!" she snaps, and the dog immediately obeys, dropping down to the floor. I continue to scratch his head when I look up at Maggie. She's wearing an uneasy expression. "Mercy."

"Excuse me?" I ask.

"Mercy...will be our safe word. Can you remember that?"

I nod. "I guess."

When I look up at her again, I notice something is different. Her shoulders are pressed back further than normal and she's keeping her expression more guarded. She looks more confident today.

"We have to go over a few rules too," she adds.

"Okay." I stop petting Ringo to give Maggie my full attention. Soon, he loses interest and disappears into the living room.

Maggie scratches the back of her neck before quickly composing herself. "I don't want you seeing anyone else while we do this. Even if we don't have sex, it's important to me that this is exclusive."

My brow furrows. I wasn't getting laid much anyway, and I sort of figured I'd be spending all of my free time—which is all of my time lately—here with her.

"Okay," I reply, but she quickly cuts me off.

"Yes, ma'am," she snaps. "You'll address me as ma'am, and as long as you're at my house in this setting, then you can assume we're in a scene."

"A scene?"

"Yes, that's what it's called...when I'm your Domme and you're my sub."

"Yes, ma'am."

She's getting stern and serious, and I notice the way it has my skin prickling with excitement and a smile fighting its way onto my face, but I manage to keep a serious expression.

"Get down," she barks in command, much like she did to her dog. I slip off the counter to stand in front of her.

With one small step, she's standing closer to me. I don't kneel or bow or anything because she hasn't really told me to, so I just stand here and wait.

"Last rule is...no one can know about this. No one. Don't tell your friends or anyone online. Understand?"

"Yes, ma'am."

I wasn't planning on telling anyone anyway. My friends clearly wouldn't understand after the way they reacted to the app the other day. I'm not using this like a quick pussy scheme like they did.

With another step, she's now only an inch away from me, and I get a whiff of the coconut scent of her hair and the subtle hints of her perfume. Seeing her so close in the daylight, I notice the hazy freckles across her nose. I want to brush the overgrown bangs out of her face. Instead, I wait patiently.

After a heavy breath, as if she's preparing herself, she reaches out and lays a hand over my chest.

"I want you to know that as long as you're here as my sub, I'm going to control everything you do. As long as it's within the parameters of that list, I'm going to make you do whatever I want. You should *want* this. If at any time you stop wanting this, I need you to communicate with me."

Her eyes are focused on my chest where her hand rests, and I wonder if she can feel the way my heart rate has sped up. When she lifts her eyes to my face, I'm pretty sure it stops. Because the next words out of her mouth nearly knock me out.

"I'm going to use you, Beau. In fact, when you're here, you're not Beau anymore. We are not friends or lovers or acquaintances. You are my property to do whatever I want with, and if you deserve it, I'll punish you. It will hurt, and I'll try to make sure you don't enjoy it. But if you earn it, I'll reward you, and I'll make sure you do like it."

Her large blue eyes are on my face, and I have to remind myself to breathe.

"Yes, ma'am," I whisper.

"Good."

Then her hand trails down, over my chest and stomach, stopping when her fingers brush the elastic band of my shorts.

"So, what about last night? Were you good or bad?"

I know she's referring to her instructions not to masturbate, and I feel a sense of pride swell in my chest because I really did make it all night, and it wasn't easy. After our texting and browsing through that spreadsheet, it was tempting. But I kept my hands off my dick.

"I was good," I reply proudly.

Her eyes scrutinize my face. "Good."

Suddenly, her hand drifts lower over my shorts until she's rubbing her palm over my cock, making it jump behind the fabric. I suck in a breath as she strokes, making me hard in record time.

With her eyes on my face, she stops her stroking and reaches for the waistband. I'm frozen in place, silently begging her to touch me, as she reaches her hand into my shorts and wraps her warm fingers around my hard length.

"Oh fuck," I mutter in a breath.

"Is this a good reward?" she whispers.

Fighting to keep my eyes open as she moves her hand over my now throbbing dick, I nod. "Yes, ma'am."

"Good boy," she replies, and I never thought I'd like to hear those words so much, but I swear my legs almost give out under me. "What about this?"

I swear I'm seeing shit as she slowly lowers to her knees in front of me.

What is happening right now? Did I fall and hit my head? Am I hallucinating?

Staring up at me, she pulls my shorts down far enough that my cock pops out and points directly at her face. She looks at it, and I notice the way she pauses. Is she *admiring* my dick?

Then, I swear I see stars when she reaches her tongue out toward me, running the soft, wet surface from the base to the tip.

"Holy shit," I growl, drawing the words out.

The next thing I know, her lips are open wide and she's pulling my cock into her mouth. Suddenly, I'm painfully aware of how long it's been since I came. This won't take me long at all, but I wish I could savor it for a little longer because the vision of this woman, who I *thought* was so sweet and innocent, swallowing me down her throat like dick is her favorite meal is doing me in fast.

Her head is bobbing up and down, coating me in saliva, humming and moaning when I feel my balls start to clench and the head of my dick tighten.

"Fuck, I'm gonna come," I gasp, gripping the counter tightly. God, yes, I will be so fucking good for her if this is the reward I get every time. So fucking good.

Just as I'm about to lose it, she pops her mouth off my cock, a string of saliva hanging from her lips. I let out a pained gasp as I stare down at her. The orgasm eases off before it ever had a chance to start, and I gape down, waiting for her to put her mouth back on me.

Slowly, she brings her tongue back, letting it run the length of my cock. It's not enough to make me come, but it still feels fucking good. Her soft lips press kisses around my shaft as I edge closer to the pleasure I was ready to dive into a second ago.

Then I feel her fingers brushing my balls, and I tense, a small yelp escaping my lips in surprise as she tugs on them gently. My body is buzzing with excitement when she finally lets me slide down her throat again—a delicate mixture of pleasure and pain.

"God, yes," I groan. With her massaging my balls and sucking my cock, I'm definitely about to come. The climax is building, just within reach, and I close my eyes, ready to blow my load when the soft grip on my ball sac becomes a harsh tug.

"What the fuck," I cry out, and the orgasm disappears again, a little faster this time.

When I stare down at her, she smiles a wicked, evil grin.

Oh, I get what's going on here. She's fucking with me. And I'm about to give her hell, but then her mouth is back, and I let it go.

"Please don't stop," I beg as she sucks hard on the head of my cock, sending me in a whirlwind of sensation. Her hand is still on my sac, but at least she's being nice and not tugging on it anymore.

But when I feel a stray finger start to massage my taint, I nearly catapult off the counter.

"Maggie...I mean, ma'am." She's sucking the life out of my dick and massaging the space between my balls and ass, but she's not letting me come, and I'm about to lose my fucking mind.

"Please, please, please don't stop," I beg, slightly thrusting my hips forward to meet her mouth. And just like before, the head of my dick tightens, my balls lift, my body tenses, and I know this is finally it. I can see heaven before me, ready to let it engulf me. My feet almost lift off the floor. My spine straightens, and my skin pricks with anticipation.

But then it's just...gone.

"No..." I say with a groan as I stare back down at her.

To my utter horror, she lifts the waistband and tucks my poor, aching dick back into my shorts.

"I—I didn't come," I stammer—as if she couldn't tell.

She stands up and places her hand on my chest. "Coming wasn't your reward. You'll have to do more for that."

"What?" I'm gaping at her in horror.

"A little discipline is good for you, Beau. I'm doing this so you understand just how serious I am. You don't come unless I tell you to. And you have to ask politely every single time. Is that clear?"

My mouth is hanging open, and my body is locked up in a vise grip. I'm angry and worked up and I want to tell her to fuck off and let me come, but at the same time...this is the most I've felt in a long time. Even if it is anger. At least it's something.

Through gritted teeth, I obstinately mutter, "Yes, ma'am."

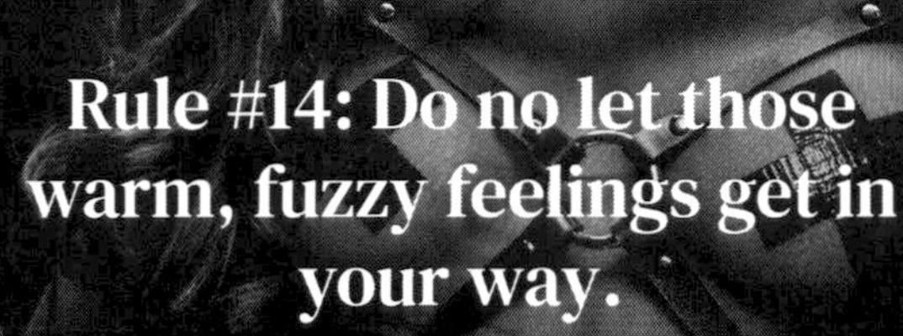

Rule #14: Do no let those warm, fuzzy feelings get in your way.

Maggie

I can't believe I just did that. Oh my God, I cannot believe *I just did that.*

I'm headed to my office—the only room I've gotten even remotely set up, leaving him alone in the kitchen with his neglected hard-on.

I hear him hot on my tail before I even have a chance to sit down. My hands are still shaking and there is a pool of arousal in my panties that I'm opting to ignore at the moment.

I'm over the fact that Beau is a lot younger than me. Hell, I'm already mostly over the fact that he's Emerson's son. But seeing his cock today, feeling the heavy weight of it against my tongue, made me realize that he is just another man, with the biggest dick I've ever seen. No wonder Beau has been wreaking havoc with that smug ego of his—he's been carrying *that* thing around this whole time.

It makes sense now why Charlie stayed with him as long as she did.

"Wait, wait, wait," he calls out from the hallway as he follows me into my office. "What do I have to do to get that reward?"

I look up and force my shoulders back. The way he's standing right now, chest puffed and face fit with a scowl, is telling me that he's trying to fight me for control. With any other man, I'd probably give it to him. I'd relinquish whatever it is he's demanding to avoid confrontation, but not this time.

This time, I'm in control, and if there's going to be a power struggle between us, I'm going to win.

I give him a scornful glare. "You have a lot to learn. I'll admit, we both do. But you're not addressing me properly and the way you're talking to me right now is disrespectful. I'm starting to think you want a situation that means easy orgasms for you and a chance to say you're being kinky, without actually putting the effort in."

I see his lips tighten and his breath shudder out of him.

"I'm not in it for easy orgasms, but can I at least know the rules? I was good. I did what you said, and I didn't jack off. So what do I get for that?"

I cross my arms as I lean against my desk. Then I remember that Beau agreed to this because he wants to know how to keep the woman he's with happy. He has no plans to be a lifelong submissive. He's not here for the lifestyle.

Does that make his intentions wrong? I can still help him, but it's harder to commit when he's doing this without the desire to do this long term.

"Why do you think I asked you not to come?" I ask with a gentleness in my voice.

He shrugs. "To control me?"

"Yes. So why did you agree to it?"

"Because I want the reward. I thought—" His voice trails off, as if he's just realized something, and I feel a sense of pride as I watch him figure it out. "Oh fuck."

"Go ahead..."

"There are no rewards, are there? Letting you control me *is* the reward. Making you happy...is the reward."

A gentle smile pulls on the side of my lips. "Imagine that I'm your girlfriend, Beau. And I need something from you...a phone call or a moment of your time. Do you do it because you want to get off?"

He winces, as if he's just realized that's exactly why he would have done it.

"Your girlfriend isn't your Domme or your Madame, Beau, but I bet every single one of them just wanted to feel as if your motivations were about more than getting your dick wet."

There's a flash of something stubborn and willful on his face, and I think for a moment that he's going to quit. He could. It would be easy to walk right out that door and forget this whole arrangement, but he doesn't. The stubborn look is gone and immediately replaced by something more compliant.

"Yes, ma'am."

I smile, biting my lower lip as I admire the way he looks at the moment, when he's all in and not holding back. Somehow he's better-looking than when he's being a cocky jerk. Because at the moment, he's mine.

"As far as what you're supposed to do, don't worry

about that. I will tell you what to do. You don't need to think or worry. Just obey."

He nods.

"Now, get on your knees," I say in command.

Without a word, he drops to the floor. And if I thought he looked beautiful a moment ago as he submitted to me verbally, it doesn't hold a candle to the way he looks when he's kneeling for me. And it's not so much about the warmth in my belly or the moisture in my panties, but something else.

A tenderness. The all-consuming desire in my chest to protect him, nurture him, keep him.

Make him mine.

"Crawl to me," I say. Our eyes are locked on each other as he presses his hands to the floor and moves toward me. With a hint of hesitation, he creeps toward me in a position that *should* be humiliating, but is somehow sensual and sublime. My breathing slows as he crosses the space at a delicate, easy pace, stopping when he's at my feet.

"Kneel. Sit back on your feet with your hands in your lap. Eyes on the floor."

He pauses, and for the first time, I see his struggle to obey. For a second, I think maybe I was right. No matter how submissive Beau is deep down, maybe he's too ingrained with the idea that men can't be submissive, that he'll fight this command.

But then he surprises me. He obeys without a fight, settling into position. Once his head is bent, I give in to the urge to touch him, running my fingers through his hair and along the back of his neck, over each vertebrae until they disappear into his shirt.

"This is how I want you when you come over. I'll get

you something to kneel on, but consider this your default position. And you'll stay like this until I tell you what to do."

"Yes, ma'am."

"Okay, now stand up and look at me."

When he does, and I'm staring up into his vivid blue eyes, there is less fire in them. And I don't quite know how I feel about that.

"How did that feel?" I ask.

His head bounces in a subtle nod. "It was good. Easy."

"You should do some research when you get home. I'll send you some websites and blogs that are good for beginners. I want you to read them a little each day."

As I speak, I can see his gaze travel from my eyes to my lips then down to my neck and back up to my eyes.

"What are you doing?" I ask.

He swallows. "I want to touch you. I think I'm going to hate this if I can't touch you."

A laugh bubbles up from my chest, and maybe it's because it sounds more like a joke than a real complaint. But when I see his face freeze, I realize he's being serious. "Why do you want to touch me?"

His brow scrunches in confusion. "Is that a trick question?" When I don't respond, he continues, "You just sucked my dick in your kitchen, and now we're going to act like it was nothing." He voices his complaints, his tone rising in volume. My eyes pop open in surprise as he adds, "I'm thinking about sex the entire time we're together, and I can't explain *why*, but I just want to fucking touch you."

Then for some reason, I decide to play with him. "What if I never let you come? Would you still want to touch me?"

"Yes," he answers without hesitation.

Shit, now I want to give in. I want to let him touch every square inch of me. Let him do whatever he wants. If he wants to fuck me, lick me, kiss me, whatever, I'd let him. But I have to stop myself because this isn't about what *he* wants. And I can't let him have what he wants or I'm going to spoil him. And all this will be for nothing.

"Well, the good news is that you will get rewards, but *not* for every time you obey me. And not right now."

His jaw clenches as disappointment washes over him. Even though I just told him he would get rewarded eventually, apparently Beau likes instant gratification. He clearly has a lot to learn.

For now, I have actual business to settle.

"Okay, we're out of the scene now," I say as I pull myself away from him and round my desk to sit in the chair. On my computer, I pull up the mile-long to-do list. "Because I have something to talk to you about. Well, an offer really."

When he stares at me in confusion, I point to the extra chair. "Sit down."

He obviously likes taking orders because he does.

"I know you're out of a job, and I could actually use some help around here, so I want to offer it to you. Would you be willing to do some *actual* work for me? Painting, unpacking, maybe some light handiwork."

"As your sub," he replies, and it almost sounds like a statement instead of a question.

"No. I'll pay you."

"Why can't I be both? I mean at the same time."

"I'm confused," I reply. "You want to stay in your sub role while doing work at my house?"

It takes him a moment to reply, and I see the hesitation before he does. I'm reminded of how vulnerable and new this is for Beau, and I honestly think if anyone else was in the room, he would deny it to the death. But he'll be vulnerable with me, which means he trusts me.

And I love that more than I probably should.

"I still have to pay you, Beau. But I want to be clear, it's for your work around the house, not for everything else."

"Would I live here with you?"

"What?" I snap in surprise. "No! We can't live together."

I swear I see disappointment wash over him.

"Do you...want to stay here?"

His expression is unreadable. It's blank yet guarded, and I pause for a moment, trying to decipher what's happening. Before he can answer, I take the choice from him.

"You know you're always free to stay here. For whatever reason."

"Okay," he mumbles.

That tender spot in my chest aches again. He has the ability to look so cocky one minute and then innocent and desperate the next. As if he needs something he's too afraid to ask for. Like a puppy that's been kicked one too many times.

I wish I knew what it is he needs, but now, all I can offer him is exactly what he came here for. And I wish what I needed at the moment was an orgasm or something more fun, but sadly, what I really need is some help around this house.

"There are six boxes in the kitchen that need unpacking. Do your best to guess where everything goes, and if you don't know, set it aside, and we'll go through it later.

Break down the empty boxes and stack them in the garage. When you're done, come kneel by my desk. Understood?"

"Yes, ma'am," he replies, a gentle smile playing on his lips. Then he rises from the chair and disappears down the hall. I'm staring for a moment at the spot where he just sat, trying to figure out this weird, tender feeling in my chest when he lets his guard down around me.

Most men I work with don't show a lot of emotion. I'm not used to seeing the facade crack like that, but there's something about seeing it with Beau that I didn't expect. The sexual chemistry between us is distracting, but I cannot let myself get emotionally attached in this situation.

This is just an arrangement to him, and we can't let it escape the confines of this house. We have no future, no relationship, no connection other than the ones we need to serve our roles. That tender feeling will just have to go away because I'm not entertaining that idea at all. I can't.

Rule #15: Once a dick, always a dick.

Beau

"Fuck," I mutter, sucking in a breath through clenched teeth as I slam my laptop closed. I'm not going to make it. Even after that cruel, unfinished blow job, Maggie sent me home without an orgasm.

After I unpacked the kitchen, I came back to her office and knelt next to her like she told me to. Minute after minute, she ignored me, typing on her laptop and making phone calls. With every passing second, I grew more and more irritable, struggling to stay still until, at one point, she set a *fucking* cup of tea on my head.

I fumed while it wobbled, warm against my scalp.

Finally, when I'd had enough, I quietly mumbled, "Fuck this, Maggie."

And for that...I got punished.

I had my safe word. I knew my way out. If I wasn't digging the scene, I could have said *mercy* and been done. Instead, I got a disappointed glare and another menial task while she ignored me.

No blow job or hand job or make-out session. I didn't even get to see her pussy. Nothing.

She just made me dinner, forced me to eat, and sent me home with strict instructions to do my research and keep my hands off my dick.

Which leads me to this little dilemma. It's kinda hard to research BDSM with a poor, neglected cock and a pair of swollen nuts in need of release.

It's been four days. Four fucking days, and I can't remember the last time I went two days without jacking off since puberty.

And what's really fucking stupid is how ridiculously good every brush of my cock feels. It makes me wonder... how would it feel after a week? Two weeks? A month? The right breeze would make me come at that point, and I bet it would feel like heaven.

Carefully, I open my laptop again and try reading through another blog post about things Dommes and their submissives can do together, but my brain literally cannot focus. All I keep seeing is the image of Maggie while I stared up at her from the floor, looking so much more confident and sexy than normal.

I wonder if she can see how much she changes when she fills that role. How surprising it is to see her facade transition from overstimulated and distracted to confident and collected. It's addicting. And it's the only reason I'm still playing along. I can't get enough of this new version of her, and I feel like if I quit now, that version will disappear forever, and it would be my fault.

Tossing my laptop aside and giving up on the research for tonight, I find what's left of a joint in my desk drawer and open my bedroom window to light up.

Just as the hazy calm of my high settles over me like a

warm blanket, I see my phone screen light up. There's only one person I want it to be, so I dive over to my bed to grab it.

But it's not Maggie.

It's from the *one* person I don't want it to be—Charlie.

I'm in the neighborhood. Can I swing by to talk to you?

"What the fuck?" I mutter quietly to myself.

Why?

I have something to ask and I don't want to do it over the phone.

Sure, I guess.

Just meet me out front.

I reply with a simple *K*.

I know why she won't come inside, and I can't say I blame her. Charlie has only met my mother a couple of times, and it wasn't a pleasant experience for her. I'd avoid her, too, if I could.

Five minutes later, I'm sitting on the low wall around the garden up front as Charlie pulls up. When she gets out of the car, I immediately realize this might be the first time she and I have been alone since she officially started dating my dad. Although she's not the same person she was back then.

When we dated, Charlie was walking chaos. Her mood, her style, her personality. All of it was on a whim, as if she woke up a different person every day, and no matter how hard I tried to predict what she wanted or who I was dating, she changed.

But as she gets out of the car tonight, I do something I haven't done in a very long time. I think back to when we first met and how hard I fell for her big, bright smile and infectious personality. I thought she was a beacon, and if I just followed her lead, I would have it all figured out. It didn't take long before we both realized that neither of us had it figured out and it was clear she thought she could follow *my* lead. Which is why we were a mess.

"Hi," she says with an awkward wave. Oh, so she can tell how weird this is too. Good. It's not just me, then.

"Hi," I reply grimly.

"I'll make this short, but I just wanted to come over to ask you to please just go easy on your dad."

"What?" I must be really high because I swear she just asked *me* to go easy on *him*.

"You heard me, Beau. Your little outburst at the party has been bugging him for the past two days. I know this is hard on you, but you've had your chance to get over it. Don't ruin this for him now."

A laugh escapes my lips, and yeah...I'm high as fuck, so it doesn't stop. It turns into cheek-burning giggles, and I have to wipe the tears away from my eyes. When I do, I see Charlie glaring back at me.

"Are you high?" she asks with accusation.

"Yes, but that's none of your business. You're not my girlfriend anymore."

She rolls her eyes, and I know, deep down, I'm acting like a child, but it's my default. Don't men mature slower anyway? Or something like that?

"Unless you want to play my stepmom now?" I ask, laughing again.

"What are you doing, Beau?" Her tone is so serious it kills my buzz.

"Why do you care, Charlie? Or should I say...Charlotte?" I ask, mocking my dad's stoic tone when he calls her that. "What's wrong? I wasn't bossy enough for you? I didn't make you kneel and treat you like a dog and call you a good girl enough?" My tone is full of humor, but my words aren't funny. I know that. I'm immature and high, not stupid.

Her arms are crossed, and I sense something in her facial expression change, a hint of hurt coloring her features.

"I don't understand you," she replies sadly. "What do you get from hurting me? And not just tonight...but our entire relationship? You always tried to bring me down. It's not about how your dad treats me. It's how he values me. You can dress that up in any kink you want, but that's all I ever wanted. I wish you could find that, Beau."

As she turns to get back into her car, I feel the need to have the last word. And it doesn't even make sense, at least not to her. So I don't know why I feel the need to shout it. But I do.

"I'm nothing like you, Charlie," I say, but she doesn't respond. She looks like a wounded puppy in a rush to return to her owner, who will no doubt pat her head and make her feel all the warm gooey things I can't.

But before she leaves, she stops and stares at me over the top of her car.

"It would be amazing if you could just surprise me, Beau. You wouldn't believe how much he wants you there, even if he knows you'll make him regret it. He loves you so much, and I'll never hold a bigger place in his heart. That belongs to you, and you don't even want it."

With that, she slips into the driver's seat and backs out of the driveway. I sit out here for a long time after she's gone, replaying every stupid word I uttered as I slowly start to sober up. And the only thing I realize, as I start to head up toward the house, is that I am *nothing* like Charlie. She is perfect and obedient and she loves to be told so.

As for me, I am what I am. An insensitive asshole. An arrogant prick. A disobedient brat.

So, as I shut myself into my bedroom, I do the first thing that comes to mind. I shed my clothes and climb into bed, eagerly stroking my dick to life. But I'm not just going to break the rules tonight. I'm going to earn every stupid punishment in the book—just to prove how *not* like Charlie I am. I hope Maggie turns my ass black and blue for this. I hope she makes me balance her tea cup on my head until my kneecaps bleed. I hope she edges me until I pass out. I don't care. Because any punishment is better than being some rich prick's perfect little doll.

Feeling angry and obstinate, I open up my phone camera in the dim light of my room and I aim it directly at my swollen cock. Then I stroke it with purpose. I don't need porn tonight. I just need to think about all the ways Maggie is going to make me pay for this tomorrow.

And I capture the entire thing on camera as I shoot my load all over my hand and belly, groaning and cursing the entire way through.

Then, without a single caption or word, I put it in a text and send it over.

Rule #16: If they want to come...make them come.

Maggie

"So it's between Phoenix and Sacramento," Garrett says, chewing on the end of his pen.

"I think I can talk the owner at Fire Palace down, if I give them what they're asking for," Emerson replies from the head of the table.

"That club cannot stay the way it is right now if we want to put Salacious's name on it," Hunter adds, and even I hear the tension in his voice.

"We can't afford to build from the ground up in a new city," I say, and they all nod in agreement. "And if we can't make Phoenix work, then we have to take the foreclosed property in Sacramento."

Emerson looks unhappy with this decision as his brow furrows, and I don't blame him. The closed-down club is too seedy and not in the right area for our new location, but we can't keep waiting to make this move. It's now or never.

"Let me make a call to Phoenix and see if I can strike

a better deal," Emerson replies, and I nod in agreement, because if anyone can do it, it's him.

"If that doesn't work, take Garrett and I'm sure the two of you can sweet talk 'em," I add with a smile, and Garrett loves that idea, pointing at me with his chewed-up pen and a mischievous grin.

"They have a stage," Hunter throws in with a wiggle of his brows, which makes me laugh and Garrett flinch.

The guys fall into a non-work conversation, just as I feel my phone buzz in my lap. I look down to see a text from Beau—titled in my phone as just *s*.

It's almost ten at night, and I haven't seen him since his little tantrum this afternoon, and I can't help but grin as I swipe open the message. My eyes widen in surprise when I'm suddenly looking at his engorged cock in the dark and his hand stroking it angrily.

"Here you go, ma'am. This one's for you," he says in the video.

He moans loudly over the sound of his slick hand moving over his cock, and I fumble to close the message, suddenly registering how loud that was. I'm clutching my now silent phone in my lap as I gape up at the people in the room. Hunter, Garrett, and Emerson are all staring at me with interest, and my cheeks feel downright nuclear from embarrassment.

"What was that, Maggie?" Garrett asks with a smirk.

Oh my God. Did Emerson recognize Beau's voice? Fuck, fuck, fuck.

Judging by the amused expression he's wearing, I'm going to say no. He didn't, but still…I just played a video of his son jacking off on my phone, two feet away from him.

"None of your business," I snap, and they share a little chuckle before resuming their conversation.

I'm going to kill Beau for that. Of course he had no idea I was going to be in a meeting with his dad when I opened it, but he still shouldn't send me videos like that—

It takes me far too long to register what he just sent me. He was...jacking off. I didn't get to the end, but with the way he was working himself, I'm pretty sure he was sharing the proof that he disobeyed my orders and just came.

What the hell?

I start to panic. I clearly don't know what I'm doing if I can't handle one bratty twenty-two-year-old. He's out of control and doesn't listen to me. What if I don't have the backbone to do this?

"Are we done?" I ask, interrupting their conversation again.

Emerson nods. "Yeah, I'll keep you updated on Phoenix tomorrow. Get some rest, Mags."

"Thanks," I reply as I grab my things and dash out of the office. In a mad rush, I head out to the club through the voyeur hall, but I only make it halfway down before I see who I'm looking for.

Behind the glass of room number three, Eden is in black lingerie, straddling a man currently tied to the platform by his wrists and ankles. He's also blindfolded and gagged, letting out a scream as she drips hot wax on his chest.

Pausing in the hallway, I watch her tease and taunt him with the pain of the wax and the pleasure of slow strokes of his cock. She's so calm and in control, a look of satisfaction on her face with every whimper and squeal that he makes through the gag.

When she glances up and catches my eye through the glass, I give her a small wave. As she smiles at me, she gestures down at the bench in front of the window for viewers, and I consider taking the seat. I wish I could, but what if someone we know comes out here and sees me watching the scene with interest.

It's easier for the others—Mia and Charlie and Eden. I'm sure none of them grew up in the same conservative home I did. They are so open with their sexuality, and it's such a foreign concept to me.

When Eden gets the man on her table to the brink of his orgasm, only to pull back and make him squirm with need, I swallow down the rising discomfort of being so aroused in public.

I can't do this.

Waving again to Eden, I quickly disappear down the hall and out to the main floor. I don't stop until I get to the bar, where I ask Geo to fix me my usual, a glass of chilled Chardonnay.

It's nearly gone when Eden finally emerges from the voyeur hall, this time dressed and slightly red in the face.

"You should have stayed," she says a little too loudly. "The sounds that man made when he finally got to come were amazing."

"Shhh..." I reply as I take her by the back of the arm and guide her to a more discreet table at the club. It's still not private enough, but it will do for now because I'm in crisis mode.

"Eden, I can't just stand around and watch."

"Why not?" she asks.

"Because that's not who I am and everyone knows it."

Disappointment flashes across her face, and I know

it's not the right response, but what other answer can I give? It's true.

"That's not the point right now. I have a problem," I say, leaning over the table and moving closer to her.

"What is it?" she asks.

I explain to her everything between me and my sub so far, the blow job and the kneeling and how it was going so well at first—leaving out his name, obviously.

"So I told him *no* masturbating and the next thing I know, he's sending me a video of him jacking off until he came."

"Oh..." she says with a naughty grin, "Maggie, you have a real brat on your hands."

I don't know why she's smiling because I'm panicking. "I have no control over him, Eden. He doesn't listen to me, and I don't think he even likes doing this. What do I do?"

She leans back and furrows her brow at me. "Maggie, he *wants* you to punish him. That's what you have to do."

"What if he still doesn't listen to me? Wasn't this supposed to be about what I want?"

"Don't you want to punish him?" she asks.

Oh, do I ever.

"Yes, very much."

"So, that's what you have to do. He's literally asking for it."

"Okay, so give me some ideas," I ask, leaning in.

She looks contemplative for a moment.

"You could bring him to the club and show him the cane."

My eyes widen. "Baby steps, Eden. I'm not ready for that."

"Okay, okay," she replies. "Well...you could either

edge him to the point of misery. You could keep him tortured for hours. Or..."

Her eyes light up as she gets an idea, and I'm not gonna lie, I'm a little scared.

"Come with me," she says, snatching me by the hand and dragging me across the club toward the small shop on the other side. I keep glancing around skeptically, afraid one of the guys will see me with her and start asking questions.

"I know you guys have it..." she says as she browses the selection of high-end sex toys in the glass case. "There it is!"

When I glance down at what she's pointing at, my cheeks start to pale. "You want me to wear a butt plug to punish him?"

She knocks my shoulder with a delicate laugh. "It's not for you, babe."

As Monica, the young clerk who mans our shop, approaches, I quickly turn away as if I'm not shopping for myself. Eden points out what she wants and shoves it into my hands. I'm staring down at the clear plastic box holding the black silicone plug.

Beau is not going to go for this. It's too soon, isn't it?

"Wait...how is this punishment?"

She takes the box and flips it over to show me the underside. "It's remote-controlled and connects to your phone. Put this in him and tease him with it all day long. If your brat wants to come, you can use this thing to make him come so much, he'll never want to come again."

I bite my bottom lip as I imagine his torment. I'm so distracted that I don't even bother being embarrassed when I tell Monica to charge it to my account.

After thanking Eden, I slip the plug into my purse as I

head toward the door. Before I leave the parking lot, I write a text response to Beau.

I hope that was worth it.

A moment later he responds.

Do your best, ma'am.

I can't stop smiling as I drive home, climb into bed, and for the first time in a long time, I'm excited for tomorrow and it has nothing to do with work.

Rule #17: Fuck around and find out.

Beau

This morning I got a text.

> *The door code is 1025. Let yourself in and take off everything but your underwear. Be in position in my office at 9:00am on the dot. I'm taking Ringo for a walk. Don't be late.*

There's a black cushion on the floor in the entryway of her house when I let myself in.

Is it weird how much I love it when she gets bossy? Probably not, since that's what I'm here for, right? But fuck, it turns me on when she packs away that sweet and timid version of herself and really lets the bossy bitch take over. It's hot as fuck.

Even I know I shouldn't be too excited today. I'm aware that I'm in for it. I wouldn't have done what I did if I didn't know I'd pay for it. I just wish I knew what the punishment would be. Does she have a paddle and whip around here somewhere? Will she make me hold tea on my head again for an hour? I hope not. Is it wishful thinking to hope for another torturous blow job? Probably.

The house is quiet when I let myself in. It's weird not to have that big gray monster greeting me at the door when I close it behind me. I glance down at my phone and notice I only have four minutes to get in position, so I quickly tear off my shirt and shorts and slip off my shoes, leaving it all in a pile on the floor as I grab the pillow and run to her office.

Of course, she's late. Nine o'clock comes and goes, and it's not until 9:07, according to the clock on the wall, when I hear the front door open. She's talking sweetly to Ringo as I hear her take off his leash and feed him a treat from the jar in the kitchen. He finds me before her, greeting me with a kiss on the nose before she follows behind him, barking a command for him to go lie down, which he does.

Then, she mostly ignores me. Walking to her desk, she only impatiently mutters, "Do not leave your clothes on the floor in my house. Fold them and place them on the guest bed from now on."

"Yes, ma'am," I mumble, still staring at the floor.

She ignores me for a while longer, typing away at her computer while I wait. If this is my punishment today, I'm gonna be pissed.

Finally, she calls my name. "Beau, come here."

Biting my bottom lip, I get up from the floor and walk over to her desk. She's still in her chair as she stares at me with an expression of anger and mischief. Oh, for fuck's sake, please have something good in mind. I don't know if

I can take another day of being furniture or her house bitch. I need to *feel* something.

"Did you have fun last night?" she asks.

Technically, no. Charlie's little visit pissed me off and the orgasm I had wasn't even worth it. It was rushed and unsatisfying. And I almost lie, but then I remember we're supposed to be building trust. I mean, that's why I sent her the video. I could have lied. But I wanted her to know how bad I was...for reasons I don't even understand.

"No, ma'am."

"Then, why did you do it?" she asks curiously.

"I don't know. Because I'm bad, I guess."

Her brow furrows as she studies me. "You're not bad, Beau. But you do have to be punished."

I nod, clenching my jaw as I wait for what comes next.

Make it good, make it good, make it good.

"I was thinking...since you want to come so much, I figured I would give you exactly what you want."

Wait, what?

Is it weird that I don't want her to go easy on me? If she thinks making me come is a punishment, I'll be disappointed.

"So, I bought you something to wear while you work today."

There's a clear box on her desk, and inside the box is something matte black and small with a cone-like shape and a flat-base bottom. Is that...a butt plug?

I force down a gulp. What the fuck did I get myself into?

"Have you ever had anything in your ass, Beau?"

"No, ma'am," I stammer, my mouth going dry.

She reaches into the top drawer of her desk and pulls out a small, clear bottle of lube. She then proceeds to cover the black silicone as she speaks. My eyes are transfixed on the thing in her hands, unable to focus on what she's saying.

I'm standing in silence, but inside, I'm screaming.

"I have everything set up for you to paint the dining room for me today. The paint, supplies, rollers, and everything else is already in there for you. I picked a nice *cream* color for the space."

She looks up at me expectedly. "Briefs down and bend over."

Fuck.

I stand here for too long staring at her. The look on my face is probably screaming for mercy, but until I say it out loud, it means nothing.

"I can't do this," I reply.

Her head tilts in surprise and she waits a beat before responding. "Yes, you can. I'm not taking away your right to come anymore. In fact, today you can come as much as you want. Isn't that what you wanted?"

"I didn't expect this," I say, gesturing to the toy.

"Well, what did you expect, Beau?"

"I don't know," I argue. "Tie me up and smack me around a little. Maybe do that...electric shock thing?"

Finally, she stands, and even though she doesn't reach my height, she gives me a powerful glare and takes a disarming stance, making me feel like shit for arguing with her. Fuck, I *want* to listen. I do. But what she's telling me to do right now...it's fucking scary.

"You fucked up, Beau. Last night, last week, last year. And you want to keep fucking up, but you don't want to pay the price. I'm telling you exactly what you need to do. Do you trust me?"

My breath is shaky as I stare at her. "Yes, of course I do."

"Then, bend over."

Still, I hesitate.

This time in a softer tone, she adds, "Or say the word, and we can stop, but I know you can handle this. Show me."

I'm doing this for a reason. I literally asked for this. So, what am I so fucking afraid of? There has to be some payoff at the end of this, right? Some good to come out of it. Because I know what she's saying is true. I've lived all twenty-two years of my pathetic life without consequences. My mother couldn't care enough to hold me accountable for anything and my fucking dad would turn the world inside out before he'd expect me to own up to my own shit. Everyone seems to think I don't know that, but I do.

And maybe that's why I've resented him for so long.

I'm not sure why *that's* the thought that changes my mind, but the next thing I know, my elbows are on her desk and my briefs are down by my knees.

"Relax," she says in a soothing command, and I do, resting my forehead against my arms. When I feel the soft, lubricated silicone of the plug, I tense. "I said relax," she adds, this time with more conviction.

"I'm trying," I reply through clenched teeth.

She takes her sweet time, working it in and out just an inch at a time, adding lube and prepping my hole in a somewhat humiliating position. The entire time, she rubs my back and thighs and is surprisingly gentle, although I know this is supposed to be a punishment.

"You're doing great, Beau," she whispers, bending over with her mouth near my ear. Her tone is kinder now and less authoritative, which seeps into my muscles like warm water.

Finally, after what feels like forever, when I'm sagging against the desk in a pliant mess, she makes me take a deep breath and works the plug fully in, feeling foreign and wrong and burning, but only for a minute. When it's finally settled in place, I stand up and immediately hunch back over.

"Oh fuck," I grunt. It feels like pressure on my balls from the *inside*. Not entirely a bad thing, but definitely new and very fucking unexpected.

Maggie lets out a little chuckle. "Feel a little foreign?"

"Yep," I grunt.

"Wait until you feel it hit your prostate."

I groan again.

"All right. Stand up. Get to work."

I turn my head in her direction, a bead of sweat forming on my forehead. "Like this?"

With a tilt of her head, she smiles. "Of course not. Pull your underwear up first."

A rumble courses through my chest as I force myself to stand again, wincing at the new sensation of this thing inside me. I gently pull up my briefs, afraid to move too fast. I'm so aware of the foreign object lodged against my prostate, I don't know how the fuck I'm supposed to get anything done. Let alone paint a fucking room.

With my first step, I wince again. But I force myself to take another and another until I reach her office door. My cock is hardening behind the black fabric, and suddenly, I remember she said I could come as much as I want.

Turning back to her, I ask, "So I can just...masturbate with this thing in and I won't get in trouble?"

"That's right," she replies with a nod of her head.

"Oh!" Her face lights up as she grabs her phone. "I almost forgot to tell you about this part. It has an app on my phone."

"An app?" I'm almost too afraid to hear the rest, although I can guess what's coming next.

"You can try to prepare yourself for what the intense pulsing vibrations will feel like for the first time in your ass, but it's really impossible until you experience it." As her finger touches the screen of her phone, an extreme buzzing assaults my body, from the base of my spine to the tip of my dick, and I nearly lose my balance and fall to the floor.

"What the fuck!" I bellow.

After a second, it's gone. And in its wake is this strange sudden urge to come.

"Try not to make a mess," she adds, before setting her phone down and turning back to her computer. "You don't need to ask permission to come today. It's the only exception."

Okay, I see where this is going. I know what she's doing, but how bad could it really be? My punishment is orgasms? I can take that. She's clearly underestimated how much I love to come.

It takes less than an hour before I realize I was the one who did the underestimating. As I try to pour paint into the tray, it buzzes again, longer this time, and I nearly lose half the bucket on the plastic tarp. I fall to my knees, landing in cream-colored paint as the first almost orgasm hits me.

I don't bother keeping my voice down either. It's intense and euphoric, but not entirely a real orgasm. I don't really come either. It's more like...pre-cum. And instead of easing off like a regular climax, it just sort of comes and goes like a spasm.

After it subsides, I pick up the paint brush, do my best to clean up my mess and get back to work. Honestly, it's not so bad. If it was in a better scenario, like actual sex, I might actually like it. I can definitely handle it as punishment.

Sometimes the vibrations are short and pulsing and sometimes they're longer and intense. I get that little lightning-burst orgasm every time, but it's never enough.

When she hits me for the twentieth time in less than an hour, I can't take it anymore. In desperation, I drop the brushes and wrap my paint-splattered hand around my cock and stroke until I come for real, filling my palm and finally feeling a moment of relief from an *actual* orgasm.

But it doesn't last long. Before I even get a chance to breathe, she hits me again, and it's an unwelcome, torturous feeling. My orgasm relieved the arousal, but my dick is still hard, and there's still this thing in my ass reminding me that my punishment is far from over.

As I'm edging the floorboards, she does it again. I grind my hand against my cock and suffer through a mini orgasm that feels a lot like dry heaving. My body convulses, and my ass clenches around the plug, but the pleasure is sorely lacking.

And again, when I'm rolling paint on the big wall for the first time. This time coming without even touching myself.

And again, when I'm refilling the tray, making yet another mess. I land in a heap on the floor afterward.

I didn't know pleasure could be painful. But with each intense stimulation, my body aches and my head starts to pound.

If she's trying to make me hate orgasms, I'm afraid I just might by the end of the day.

After I wash my hands, I get back to work, picking up the roller and finishing the big wall. A few minutes go by without any vibration and I try to enjoy the reprieve. I even pour the paint without making a mess. My dick is starting to deflate, but as soon as I start on the next wall, it's back.

"Fucking stop!" I yell, feeling my knees buckle and sweat start to bead again on the back of my neck. But she doesn't stop. If anything, she only makes it worse.

Once again, I reach into my briefs and stroke my aching cock. This orgasm is even worse. Weak and unfulfilling. But it gives me a short moment of relief before she's at it again.

I'm covered in paint, my underwear are stained with the cum I couldn't catch, and my body aches worse than I've ever felt it ache before. I've completely lost track of how many times I've come. Some of them I think I masturbated and some I didn't. They all just sort of blend together.

Was jacking off last night worth it? Fuck no.

But I take my punishment in stride. There's something strangely gratifying that comes with getting what you deserve. Because, once I've paid the price, I don't have to live with the guilt anymore.

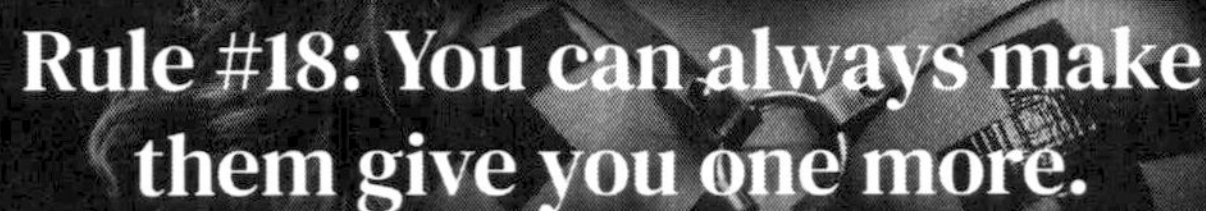

Rule #18: You can always make them give you one more.

Maggie

"I'm done." His small, raspy voice draws my attention to the doorway, and I look up to find Beau, looking ragged and miserable. His face appears a bit clammy and his hair is sweat-soaked. There's paint everywhere, and I bet if I took one look in his underwear, I know I'd find it cum-stained.

Was I too harsh? He looks so hurt and sad, and as much as I loved punishing him, I hate to see him like this.

Okay...I sort of like seeing him like this. It's the remorse in his expression I especially enjoy.

"Did you clean everything up?" I ask.

He nods weakly. "Yes, ma'am."

"Good." I stand from my desk and lead the way to the dining room to inspect his work. And much to my surprise, it looks great. By some miracle, there's not a drop of paint on the floorboards or hardwood.

I give him a proud smile. "You did great, Beau. I'm proud of you."

His face doesn't seem all that receptive to my praise. He's staring at me with a sullen, tired expression. And I bet more than anything, he just wants me to take the plug out.

As my eyes dance downward, I notice he's still half-hard behind his briefs. It's been a while since I buzzed him, so he's finally getting a little break, but he's not done. Stepping toward him, I hook my finger under the elastic band and pull his underwear back to look down at his deflating cock. As predicted, he's been leaking in his underwear all day.

I really did torture him.

"Take these off," I tell him, and he looks confused for a moment. He's probably hoping I don't try to get him aroused right now. I can't imagine he'll want to come again for the next week. Slowly, he peels the underwear off and holds them in his hands. Standing fully naked in front of me, I let my eyes soak up the tan surface of his body, toned and muscular with a patch of dark hair leading down to his cock.

For the first time, I really let myself get excited about having some fun with Beau...or rather, Beau's body. It's a foreign idea, to be allowed to *use* someone's body for your own pleasure, but this is the dynamic and that's what he wants. He literally told me so.

But now that I see him, and really admire him, I'm thinking of all the ways I can enjoy him, as if he was mine.

Dragging myself out of the fantasy, I grab his underwear from his hands.

"I'll wash these for you," I say, glancing up into his

eyes. "I want you to go upstairs and get into the shower and wash up. I'll be up in a moment."

"What about the—" he asks.

"Leave it in," I reply.

He nods with a defeated grimace as he heads toward the stairs, looking almost too exhausted to walk. Once he's gone, I throw his underwear in with another load of laundry and start the machine. Then I grab my phone from my office and head upstairs.

I find him leaning his forehead against the wall of the shower, and I watch him through the steamy glass as I turn up the vibration on his plug to low. He jumps and groans in response.

"Come on, Maggie. Please," he begs, sounding pathetic.

I love the sound of him begging.

"I think you can give me one more," I say as I slowly unbutton my blouse. Getting undressed, I watch him run a tired hand over his cock, noticing the way his arm almost gives out from exhaustion. Once I'm down to just my bra and panties, I open the glass door and stand at the entrance of the shower, getting a fine mist of warm water on my skin.

He stops his stroking when our eyes meet.

"Go ahead. Let me watch."

With our eyes locked and his nostrils flaring with his uneven breaths, he picks up his movements again. His expression morphs from pain to pleasure and misery, but he's clearly struggling to reach his last climax.

"Come here," I say, and he stills his hand as he steps toward me.

With the smell of soap on his skin, he stands just a few inches away from me, the cool air from the open shower door creating goosebumps on his skin. When he drops his hand from his cock, I reach down and wrap my own around it. He visibly reacts to my touch with a wince, and I start stroking at the same fast pace that he was. He moans as I pull one last orgasm out of his racked body. I love watching his face as blissful agony washes over him.

My gaze trails down to my hand when he gets close, and I watch with interest as he comes, shooting a small, sad spurt of cum from his cock. It lands on the shower floor between us.

I notice the tremor in his legs, so I rest a hand on his hip and give him a reassuring squeeze. His eyes find mine again, and they're pleading for mercy.

"Turn around," I whisper.

With relief on his face, he spins and places his forearms against the wall. Gently, I work the plug out of his ass and notice the way his body seems to melt once it's gone. I leave the still vibrating toy on the floor of the shower to take care of later, but for now, I focus on him.

When he turns back to face me, I rub my thumb over his cheek. Then, I spin the dial on the faucet to turn the water off and grab the giant fluffy towel hanging on the rack.

He steps out and reaches for the towel, but I hold it out of his grasp. "I'll do it."

His eyes don't leave my face as I pat his body dry, taking care of his tired arms and legs, and trying to memorize every inch of his skin as I do. He's staring at me with confusion as I towel him off.

"Is it over?" he asks.

I'm kneeling at his feet, drying off his knees down to his toes. "Yes, it's over," I reply.

When I stand back up, his gaze is more intense, and I pause as I stare into his sky blue eyes.

"Am I forgiven?"

My posture relaxes as I let out a sigh. "Yes, Beau. You're forgiven."

His expression of misery slightly changes with that response, as if he's miserable *and* relieved at the same time.

"I'm going to get you some water. You can lie in my bed and rest until your underwear are out of the dryer."

"Yes, ma'am," he replies, followed by a hearty yawn.

Grabbing my phone off the counter, I turn off the vibration and close out the app. By the time I come back upstairs with his water, he's drifting off. Lying on top of the covers, the towel is draped over his midsection, so I gently lift it away and toss it on the unused exercise bike to dry. Then I pull a thick blanket from the basket in the corner and lay it over him.

"Sit up. Drink something."

With a sigh, he scoots up the pillow and takes the water from my hand.

"How are you feeling?" I ask.

He shrugs in response. "Good." And I expect that to be it, but he seems almost in a daze as he continues, "I mean...it sucked, but I did it. And I feel better now. Like I...made you proud."

I bite back my smile. "You did make me proud."

He passes me back the water, and I place it on the nightstand. Then I set a sandwich on his lap. "Eat."

I didn't give him any breaks today, so I know he's starving. As he picks it up and takes a bite, I stroke his wet hair out of his face. I want to say something, but the words get caught on my tongue. I'm not so good at the praise stuff, but I'm dying to tell Beau just how *not bad* he is. As much as I was punishing him, I think he was really punishing himself.

I just don't think we're there yet. I can be firm, and I can wield control, but I'm struggling with the softer things. And I desperately want to be softer for him.

Instead, I settle next to him on the bed, so at least I'm near him. We're not exactly in the scene anymore, so it would be weird for me to touch him, no matter how much I want to.

When he's finished his sandwich, I take his plate and go down to the kitchen. By the time I return, he's out cold. For some reason, I find myself standing here for far too long, watching him sleep.

I really didn't think he would go through with that today. I saw the power battle coming, but I figured he'd safe-word his way out of the punishment. To be honest, I don't even know where we'd go from there.

But he did it. He suffered through my cruel torture, and with minimal complaining. It's weird that I'm so proud of him for this, but I am.

I took him to his limit today. I pushed him past his comfort zone, and I think he found out something about himself in the process. I know I did.

I learned that I *love* making Beau pay for his misbehavior.

And I love the idea of taking care of him afterward.

This is more of that stupid tenderness talking, and I need to be very careful here. I could see myself falling for the one person I shouldn't, especially since there is no way in hell Beau would ever feel the same way.

Rule #19: Don't flirt with other women in front of your Domme.

Beau

"Aren't bridal showers supposed to be only for women?" I whisper to Maggie with a grimace.

She and I are, once again, stationed outside the throng of people, this time along the fence line of my dad's pristinely landscaped backyard. Somewhere in the middle, Charlie is gleefully unwrapping presents she doesn't need, while my father stands in the crowd watching with a smug grin.

"Well, Emerson and Charlie don't do things the old-fashioned way," she replies quietly.

"Sounds like an excuse to have another stupid party."

She laughs, picking at the vegetables on her tiny party plate. "Maybe it is."

I glance sideways at her. It's weird being out together like this, although we had no trouble hanging out at the last party. The urge to call her *ma'am* and do what she says is still there, but for now, we're just unlikely friends.

As far as our *other* weird relationship, I've noticed recently that Maggie's been holding back. I don't know if she's nervous or afraid, but something is keeping her from doing what she really wants with me. It's been almost two weeks since the Orgasm 500, and she's been taking it easy on me ever since.

Not to mention...it's also been two weeks since I came at all. I didn't even know this was possible, but every night she sends me home, telling me I'm not allowed to come, and every day I follow her rules. She's training me—I know. It's discipline, something I desperately need, so I'm not putting up a fight about it, but I can feel the tension between us growing. And I'm ready for what comes next.

I haven't seen a glimpse of her body at all. I expected there to be a lot more finger-fucking and face-riding, but what am I going to do? I'm the sub. I can't suggest anything or force her to do it.

For the most part, I like this whole submissive thing a lot more than I expected. I'm sleeping better than usual. I don't feel so stressed all the time anymore.

Every morning, I show up at her house, and I do exactly what she tells me to. Usually, it's work around the house, but if I had one complaint...it's that there's not enough sexy stuff.

I just wish I knew how to change that. I feel like we just need something to ignite the spark.

"I assume you'll behave this time," she says, meeting my gaze.

My face morphs into one of shock. "I always behave at parties."

She laughs. "I heard all about your little outburst at the engagement party."

I scoff with a roll of my eyes. "Come on, it was not an outburst. I just laughed a little, that's all."

"Yeah, at the *worst* time."

She's not wrong, so I don't bother arguing with her. "I'll behave," I reply in a low whisper.

"Good boy," she says under her breath, and we both fight back our laughter.

When no one's looking, she reaches over and snatches a piece of cheese from my plate.

"Excuse me, ma'am," I reply quietly with a joking tone, "get your own."

She's wearing an adorable grin as she pops the Brie in her mouth and chases it with a sip of wine.

"Okay, seriously, we should both mingle so it doesn't look suspicious."

My shoulders deflate as I glance around the yard, absolutely no one of interest sticking out to me. "I don't want to. I hung out with you at the last party."

"Exactly," she replies. "It's starting to look like something is going on between us."

"Something *is* going on between us," I reply, and that makes her pause, glaring at me with intensity. I can't tell if that made her nervous or mad. Since I'm not looking for any more punishment right now, I hold my hands up in surrender. "Yes, ma'am."

With that, I reluctantly leave her standing against the fence and make my way over to the food table. My dad clearly didn't invite any relatives, not that I would want to talk to any of them anyway. And since he's too engrossed in watching his bride-to-be get spoiled rotten, I do a solo meander around the crowd. I wave at Sophie, who is sitting next to her mom, helping take photos and looking as if she's being held hostage. She looks as desperate to ditch this soiree as I am.

Maybe once this present business is through, she and I can escape. I'm sure she'd rather check out the new merch at the comic book store than be here. I realize I've barely seen her since I started working at Maggie's. Apparently, she got a new ride to D&D night...and I can't say I'm surprised. I just hope it's not that wizard dickhead.

"Beau?" A feminine voice says from behind me, and I turn to face a woman about my age with long brown hair and a loose-fitting dress.

I smile politely at her, and although she looks mildly familiar, I couldn't place her face if you held a knife to my throat.

"You don't remember me, do you?" She smiles brightly, showing off white teeth and fluttering her thick lashes.

"I'm sorry..." I reply apologetically.

"It's okay. I'm Charlie's cousin. We met once at her birthday party when you two were dating."

"Oh yeah. Courtney?" I ask.

"Caitlin."

"Shit. I'm sorry," I say with a laugh. "It's been a long time."

She giggles, tilting her head and jutting her hip out as she bites her lip. "So how have you been?"

"Um..." I scratch the back of my neck. How the fuck do I answer that?

"I'm sorry...stupid question." Her smile dissipates as her eyes dance their way over to Charlie and my dad.

"Yeah," I reply awkwardly.

"That must have been hard to get used to."

"A little." I force a playful laugh as I shuffle my feet.

"Are you still working at the coffee shop?" she asks, gracefully changing the subject.

"Fuck no." That was, like...four jobs ago, but I don't include that part. "I mean...no, I'm working as a handyman at the moment."

"Oh, that's good!" she says with enthusiasm.

"What about you?" I ask because it sounds like the right thing to say to further the conversation.

"I'm still working at the gym, although my boyfriend and I broke up. You met him at that party too."

"Oh," I say, my brow furrowing as I try to remember. But nothing is coming up. There's a good chance I was high.

When I glance up, she's staring at me with a loaded gaze. I swallow as I realize she's flirting with me. And she probably shared that part about her breaking up with her boyfriend for a reason.

I force a smile as I stare at her, realizing this is exactly the kind of girl I might have tried to hook up with. It would have been easy, too. A quick hookup and maybe a little fling, but it would have inevitably ended in an ugly breakup and her hating my guts.

"Are you...seeing anyone?" she asks, casually sipping on her drink.

"Um...no," I stammer, because, technically, no one is supposed to know about me and Maggie.

All of a sudden, I look up and find Maggie's blue eyes in the crowd. She's staring at me, but clearly trying not to be obvious about it. As she glances away, I wish she would just look at me again because I clearly do not know how I'm supposed to act right now.

Then I get a wicked idea. I am a brat, after all.

Knowing Maggie is watching, I look back at Caitlin with a smoldering, half-smile that she immediately matches with her own.

"So...you work at a gym, huh? I bet you get hit on all the time." I shoot her a subtle wink, and she lets out a loud giggle that I know can be heard all the way across the yard. In my periphery, I notice Maggie's head snap up, staring in our direction.

"I do not," Caitlin replies with a laugh.

"No? I don't believe it."

"You're bad," she says, blushing as she curls her hair behind her ear.

While Caitlin goes into some story about the gym, I stop paying attention, glancing at Maggie every chance I get. She's deep in conversation with someone I don't know, her fingers delicately resting on her lips as she smiles at them, and I can tell how restless she is. Her eyes dance back and forth between me and the person talking to her.

I want to send her over the edge, so when Caitlin finishes her story, lifting her drink to her lips, I reach out and brush her hair out of her face, turning on the charm with my eyes. She pauses, gazing up at my face as she bites her bottom lip.

"Want to get out of here? Go for a walk or something?" she asks.

Out of the corner of my eye, I see Maggie moving across the yard in a fury toward the house, and as she disappears through the door, I turn back toward Caitlin.

"I'm sorry. Will you excuse me?"

I don't even bother waiting for her response before I'm rushing after Maggie. The house is quiet when I close the door behind me, and I bolt through the kitchen toward the bathroom. Before I even get a chance to look for her, I feel a tight grip around my forearm, as I'm being hauled into the bathroom, the door slamming behind me.

She presses her hand against my chest and shoves me against the wall. She's pissed and it gives me a strange sense of satisfaction knowing I got her attention.

"Who was that?"

"What?" I ask.

"Who were you talking to?"

"Charlie's cousin. She remembered me," I whisper.

Her hand is firm against my chest and in the private space, I'm desperate to touch her. One kiss, one touch, or anything I can get. We only have a minute before we have to go back to the party or risk being found together, which makes this moment even more charged.

"What does she want, Beau?"

I lean in, desperate to kiss her.

"I don't know, and I don't care," I reply, trying to pull her closer. "Why? Are you jealous, ma'am?"

She shoves me harder against the wall and attacks my lips with hers. It's the exact response I was hoping for. I devour her kiss in this quiet stolen moment, hungry for her touch. It's not long enough because her hand travels upward, encircling my neck as she shoves me back again.

"I am not jealous because *nothing* will happen with her," she says possessively, and I grin down at her.

"Yes, ma'am," I reply.

"You're mine, Beau Grant. Do you hear me?" She's leaning in, about to press her mouth to mine again.

I bring her closer, feeling her breath against my lips as I reply, "Yes, ma'am."

"Now kiss me again." She gasps before our mouths

are fused, and I'm licking my way in until our tongues are tangled and we're both left panting and hungry for more. Seeing me talking to someone else was apparently the trigger to getting her to finally break her calm composure, and I love it.

"Can we get out of here, please?" I ask as our mouths finally part.

"Yes," she whispers. Then with a tight grip on my scalp, she painfully tilts my head back, and I wince. "Do not talk to her again. Meet me out front in fifteen minutes."

"Okay, okay," I mutter, and she tugs harder.

I suck in a breath through my teeth as she presses her lips to my neck. "Try that again."

"Yes, ma'am," I stammer with a smile.

But she doesn't let go. Instead, she creeps up on her toes, her mouth next to my ear. "I think I like hurting you, Beau."

Even though my head is screaming in pain and I can't move my neck, I manage to smile anyway. "So take me home and hurt me some more."

"Oh, I'm going to do something else to you."

A door closes somewhere in the house, and we break apart in a rush. She adjusts her clothes as she leaves me standing there, and I'm left with an aching hard-on as she quickly whispers, "Fifteen minutes."

Rule #20: Rules are made to be broken.

Maggie

I won't get the sight of him reaching out and touching her out of my head anytime soon. And I definitely won't forget the way it made me feel.

She was beautiful. Young. Fit.

And he was *flirting* with her.

Whether he knew it or not, that smile of his is more powerful than he realizes. With one lopsided grin, Beau can make a woman forget her own name. Forget she has a boyfriend. Or convictions.

Pure, unfiltered Beau eye contact is potent.

And, for a moment, as I stood with Garrett and Mia, I considered that this was the end of *us*—whatever that means. I made it very clear that we were exclusive, but if someone younger and prettier catches his eye and he wants out, then it's over. Why would he want to come home with me when she so clearly gave him *fuck me* eyes for fifteen minutes straight?

But he's not walking through her front door right now—he's walking through *mine*.

And he has no idea what he's in for.

The electricity between us is palpable. And my emotions are warring between heady lust and brutal jealousy. I want to hurt him and fuck his brains out at the same time. I have every intention of making this both bliss and agony.

Once we're inside, he reaches for me, but I place a firm hand on his chest, stopping him. I feel his heart racing under my palm.

"Go up to my bedroom and wait for me *in position.* I want you naked by the time I come up there."

There's a subtle twitch in his lips as he fights the urge to smile. Instead, he tilts his head. "Yes, ma'am."

I watch from the foyer as he jogs excitedly up the stairs, and I shove away that stupid tender feeling that creeps up whenever I'm around him. Once he's gone, I go into the bathroom and do some quick freshening up. Really, I just want to give him enough time to get in position. For some reason, it just feels easier to get into the Domme mindset when he's already submissive. If we had fumbled up the stairs in the same frenzy we felt at the party, I'm afraid I would have never gained control.

As I stand in front of the mirror, I look at myself for a long moment. Pushing my shoulders back and licking my lips, I try to make myself look the way I feel on the inside—sexual, confident, seductive.

I pull my blouse over my head and unfasten my skirt, letting it fall to the floor. Underneath, I'm wearing a white padded bra that shows a bit of cleavage and a matching white thong. I desperately need to buy some better lingerie.

After giving myself a quick *I can do this* pep talk, I head upstairs. What I find as I turn the corner into my bedroom has me feeling weak in the knees.

Beau, in all his tan, muscled beauty, is kneeling on the carpet in my bedroom, naked from head to toe, his cock hanging hard and heavy against his thigh. His head is bowed, letting a wisp of brown hair fall over his eyes as he stares obediently at the floor.

My mouth goes dry and my heartbeat picks up speed, hammering in my chest. I pause as I realize the possibilities that are within my grasp at this very moment. He's giving himself to me. To use and do whatever I want with his body.

Do I deserve this?

Am I good enough for him?

I catch a glimpse of myself in the full-length mirror across the room, and I see the same self-deprecating, fearful, shy woman I just saw downstairs and for all of my life.

But that's *not* who I am. That's just a role I play, a form I've fit myself into.

I am the woman in the masquerade mask that night at the club, about to meet a total stranger.

I'm the woman Beau wants. I own a goddamn *sex club*, for fuck's sake.

I am his Domme.

With my eyes on the mirror, I stand taller and take a deep breath. Then, I cross the room, stroking his head as I pass him, headed toward the dresser, where I open the top drawer to find a silk scarf. I toss it on the bed before sitting on the edge and calling to him.

"Crawl to me."

Without looking up, he does, a little faster than last time and clearly eager for what's to come.

When he kneels between my legs, I lift my foot and drag the top slowly across his abdomen, over every hard ridge of muscle, before resting it on his shoulder. My leg falls open, and he tries to keep his eyes down but quickly loses the fight as he drags them up. With his gaze right at the level of my open thighs, he stares longingly at the spot between my legs.

"Seeing you on the floor like that does things to me," I tell him, and he glances up to my face. There is a wanton need in his eyes and I feel it too. Every bit of it. And I want to prolong this, tease him with it, make it last forever until it's so explosive, it takes us both out.

"Knowing you're *mine* and no one else's...it makes me wet for you, Beau."

He licks his lips as he looks back down at my core.

"Do you want to see it?" I ask.

"Yes, ma'am."

"Do you want to *taste* it?"

His lips are parted as he nods. "Fuck yes, ma'am."

Reaching down, I grab him by the hair again, tilting his face up toward me. "Do you deserve that?"

He nods.

"After you flirted with that girl?" I ask with attitude.

"I did it to get your attention," he admits, and I smile at his honesty.

"You wanted to make me jealous?"

"Yes, ma'am."

"Why?" I ask, feeling a little confused.

After thinking about it for a moment, he shrugs. "Because I'm a brat."

"*My* brat," I add.

"Yes, your brat."

"Tell me you're mine."

"I'm yours," he answers without hesitation.

"Good boy," I reply as I bring his face down, closer to the heat growing between my thighs. "Take these off and see for yourself."

Eagerly, he wraps his fingers around the elastic of my thong and I use the leverage against his shoulder to lift up enough to let him drag them down my legs.

With my hand still gripping his hair, I shift myself closer to the edge as I pull his face right where I want it.

"Go ahead, have a taste," I say, and I swear I hear the faintest growl rumble through his body. I lose my breath as he lets his tongue hang over his lower lip and drags it hungrily through my folds, going all the way up to my clit, where he latches his lips, sucking as he lets out a long moan.

I can't help the soft whimper that escapes my lips, but when he starts to take over, I pull him away.

"I said *a taste*."

He stares up at me with a mischievous expression, a hint of a smile and hooded eyes. I admire for a moment how well he fits this role, how perfect he is when he obeys.

"You're going to use that mouth of yours to make me come, but first, I want to hear you say it again. Tell me who you belong to."

His grin is almost wolfish as he replies, "I'm yours."

"Good. Now, don't come up for air until I pull you up, understand?"

"Yes, ma'am," he whispers.

Tightening my grip on his hair, I shove his face back between my legs and the growl he lets out this time is not subtle. I gasp loudly as he devours me, the coarse texture of his facial hair tickling my clit as he licks his way inside me. My eyes don't leave him for a second, watching him lap and suck every moist and throbbing inch of me, until I'm left panting and gasping for air.

My legs hang over his shoulders as I press his face even closer, grinding myself against him. I've never been so brazenly open with my orgasms before. In fact, before Beau, I was never bold enough to make it happen around others. And I certainly never held anyone's face between my legs until I saw stars.

I gasp as I lean back on one hand, still watching where he devours me. He is relentless and not bothering for air.

"Don't stop," I cry out, my muscles tensing as I feel every inch of me start to tingle with anticipation. "God, I'm gonna come. Don't stop," I shout.

He goes harder, sucking my clit between his lips until my orgasm slams into me, pulling me under the waves. I stop breathing, letting out one last yelp of pleasure before I'm drowning in it.

As soon as I've recovered, I tear his face away, and I find him gasping, lips wet and red. Dragging him upward, I pull his mouth to mine, running my tongue over his bottom lip. He groans again as I kiss him, letting my free hand drift over his heart, so I can feel it thundering behind his rib cage.

Then, I drift my hand lower until I find his cock. He whimpers into my mouth as I wrap my fingers around him and give him a gentle tug. Running my fingers over the head, I find him dripping pre-cum, and I wipe it away with my thumb before lifting it to his mouth.

"Open," I say, after ending our kiss. He hesitates for a moment before obeying.

With his intense crystalline eyes on my face, I drag

my wet finger over his waiting tongue. He doesn't react, only closes his mouth and licks his lips.

God, he's so fucking good at this.

My core flutters with arousal again.

"Did that taste good?" I ask.

"Mh-hm," he replies, and I give him a scornful glare. Then I tug painfully on his scalp again.

"Where are your manners?"

"Yes, ma'am," he says, wincing in pain. I finally let go of his hair, and push him into an upright, standing position in front of me.

"Good." I stroke him, admiring his hard, impressive length, the red tip growing harder with each pass of my hand. Using the other, I reach under him and cup his balls, massaging them in my palm as I watch his reaction. "You don't come until I say you do."

He watches with his mouth hanging open as I pull his cock to my mouth, lapping up another drop of pre-cum on the tip. Swirling my tongue around the head, I listen to the sounds he makes, groaning and gasping as I tease him.

When I suck him into my mouth, he lets out a heady moan, and I purposely draw him closer to his climax. Sucking hard and moving quickly, I bring him all the way to the brink.

"Fuck, fuck, fuck," he stammers as he tries to pull away.

Just before I know he's about to lose it, I take my mouth away and pull gently on his balls, bringing him just enough pain to stop the orgasm.

When I look up at him, he stares down with wide eyes, racked with chills running all the way up his spine and making him shudder.

This is going to be fun.

"Lie down," I command, letting go of him and moving to stand. As I unclasp my bra, he hops up on the bed, lying on his back as he waits. I pick up the scarf I placed there earlier and climb onto the bed to straddle him.

"Wrists together over your head."

He quickly obeys as he watches me climb over him to tie his wrists in a simple knot. My platform bed doesn't have bed posts to bind him to, so cuffed above his head will have to do for now. But as I stare down at him bound and at my mercy, I'm considering buying a new bed for this purpose.

As I tie his wrists, my breasts hang in his face and I notice him watching them as if he wants a taste.

"Go ahead," I say, and with that, he doesn't hesitate to latch his mouth around one side, sucking the sensitive bud between his teeth. I feel his hips rise as if his cock is searching for me.

Rules are going to be broken today, and I don't even care anymore. We're too far gone now.

"Bite it, just a little," I say, and he does, adding enough pressure to make my core light up with arousal again.

I whimper and he thrusts his hips up once more, grinding his aching erection against me. As much as I want to let him have what he wants, I'm not quite done with his punishment yet.

The more I draw this out, the better. Eventually, I will let Beau come, but not before I torture him a little more first.

Rule #21: The reward is usually worth the wait.

Beau

I've never been more turned on in my life. I'll admit, at first, it was hard to fight the urge to throw her down and fuck her hard until I came, but finding the patience to wait and the faith to put the control in her hands is paying off in a big way.

Her mouth is wrapped around my cock again. My hands are restrained over my head as she kneels between my legs and brings me to the brink once more. But I'm not allowed to come. No matter how good she makes it and how much I want to, I won't break this rule.

Because I don't want punishment today—I want the reward.

But it's not easy. She's making it hard on purpose, literally. Even the way she plays with my balls, massaging them gently as she sucks on the tip of my cock, drives me absolutely insane.

All sense of manners and decorum are out the

window. Fuck *ma'am* and being quiet and obedient. I'm writhing, sweating, cursing, and begging.

"Maggie," I groan. "You are fucking killing me."

She pops her mouth off, and I lie my head back, gasping in relief. "Did you just call me Maggie?" she asks.

In a desperate huff, I apologize. "I'm sorry. Ma'am. Mistress. Madame, whatever you want me to call you. Can I just come, please?"

Her smile is wicked as she climbs back up my body. Her warm cunt runs along the length of my cock, grinding herself against me.

"Tsk, tsk, tsk," she replies as she reaches over me and opens her bedside drawer. "I was about to let you come too. But for that...I think you should have to watch me again."

When she sits up, holding a white massage wand, I groan, slamming the back of my head against the pillow to express my frustration. As she pushes a button, it whirs to life, buzzing quietly. She drags it across my chest, the vibration giving me goosebumps. With my hands tied above me, I have to just lie here and watch as she drags it to her clit, letting out a sweet moan as she does.

Biting my lip, I watch her tremble. I can feel the buzz rumble through her body into mine. Then she lifts the wand and reaches it behind her to press it softly against my inner thighs. I jump as she teases it closer to the base of my cock. The urge to come gets unbearable before she pulls it away and rests it against her clit again.

As she grinds herself against me and the wand at the same time, I can't tear my eyes away. In just two weeks, Maggie has changed so much. The first time we chatted, she seemed so shy about sex, and now look at her. Edging me to the point of pain and making me watch as she draws out her own orgasm while straddling my tortured dick.

With a gasping squeal, she comes. I feel her thighs clench around me and her pussy pulse along my shaft. My dick twitches as I watch her. It's an exquisite sight, but I swear to God, if this woman doesn't let me come too, I might lose my fucking mind.

"Do you want your turn now?" she asks with a smile, dropping the vibrator on the mattress as she starts to come down, her chest heaving from the exertion.

I nod enthusiastically. "Yes, ma'am."

"I want to hear you beg for it," she whispers against my face.

"Please, ma'am. Please, I'm begging you. I'll be good. I just want to come."

"And where do you want to come? In my mouth? On my face?" She runs her tongue along the length of my cheek before whispering in my ear, "Or deep inside me?"

Fuck, I'm going to lose it. A long, rumbling groan aches against my throat as it makes its way out.

"Wherever you want. I'll do whatever you want."

"Like such a good boy," she replies. I watch as she reaches back, and when I feel her hand wrap around my dick, I nearly lose it again. The head of my cock nudges against the warmth of her wet cunt, and I hold my breath, afraid she's just teasing me again.

"Look at me, Beau," she says in a raspy, lust-filled tone.

As our eyes meet, she slowly settles her weight. And as her pussy swallows my cock, I lose the ability to breathe. Before I know it, she is fully seated and we are joined, completely.

I am inside her, and it's never struck me so powerfully as it does in this moment with her.

I have no control, no ability to move or thrust, and not because she has me restrained, but because she is in charge. And I wouldn't dare move without permission.

Right about now, I'm very fucking grateful that she made me get tested and is on the pill, so we don't have to keep anything between us. Having her skin to skin is like heaven.

"Don't you dare come, until I say." Her voice is strained, her cheeks flushed with arousal as she gently lifts up and lowers herself.

It's too much, too intense, too perfect, and I'm afraid that I can't control myself anymore. There's no way I'll be able to stop myself if I have to come.

Especially as she finds her still swollen clit with her hand, running soft circles around the sensitive bud as she starts to grind her hips back and forth, chasing her pleasure, again. With her head hanging back, she moves in a beautiful rhythm, as if she's riding an invisible wave, everything in sync—her hand, her hips, her breathing.

"Tell me who this cock belongs to," she barks out a command.

"Yours," I grunt, "it's all yours."

And I'm struck speechless as I watch her slowly unfold for the third time, piece by piece. It's so fucking stunning, I almost forget about my own orgasm. My hands are still bound over my head, and I love the feeling of being this thing she's using to make herself come. I'd give her my body every chance I get if this is what I get to experience every time.

She's perfect.

Her thrusts pick up speed and intensity until she

finally tenses, her spine curling as she lets out a long, high-pitched moan. The tightening pulse of her pussy around my cock sends me over the edge.

"Fuck, ma'am, please...I'm gonna—"

"Come, Beau. Do it now," she cries out in the throes of her own climax, and I've never been more relieved in my life. I completely let go. My body takes over, and I'm blinded by an unstoppable train of ecstasy as my cock jolts and releases inside her. The sounds we're making mingle in one perfect cacophony of carnal sex and pleasure.

An orgasm has never felt so good in all my life. Two weeks of agony were worth this thirty seconds of heaven, easily.

When her body is spent, she collapses on top of me, pressing her face against my chest, and I lift my bound wrists over her head to hold her closer. I don't know if we're still in the *scene* or if this is just us...or if there is any difference anymore.

All I know is that I am hers—in all the ways.

And I did not see that coming.

Her head is resting on my chest, her soft brown hair fanned out against my neck, and I'm fighting the urge to fall asleep.

"We broke the rules," she whispers.

"Technically, *you* did. I can't be punished for that."

She laughs. "I do love punishing you, but you're right. That was my fault." She lifts her head and gazes up at me. Her hair is tousled and her makeup is smudged under her eyes. Everything about her is raw and real, and I can't help myself as I pull her face toward mine to kiss her swollen lips.

As our mouths part, I whisper, "That was no one's fault. That was amazing."

"It was," she replies, dropping her head on the pillow next to me. "It was kind of a first for me."

My brow furrows as I lift up and gaze at her in shock. "What? Maggie...were you a vir—"

She responds with a laugh, pressing her hand to my mouth as she blushes. "No, no, no. I just meant it was the first time I've ever really...came during sex."

The shock doesn't really go away with this explanation. "Are you serious?"

With tight lips, she nods. "Unfortunately, yes."

Her head settles against the pillow as we stare at each other.

"I never had the guts to take what I wanted before." There's a softness in her eyes, and I run my fingers along her arm as I think about all the times she was fucked by some random asshole, who couldn't bother to make sure she at least climaxed.

Fuck, how many times have *I* been that asshole?

"How is that even possible?"

"Ugh..." She lets out an exasperated sigh. "I don't know. I just thought that's the way it was supposed to be. I never thought I'd become...this."

"But I mean...look at you now."

She blushes, holding her cheeks. "I've never been like this. I'm a little embarrassed by how...vulgar that was." She looks adorable as she tries to hide her face, pretending she didn't just let her inner vixen out.

"I'm so confused," I whisper as I rest my head on the pillow and stare at her.

"I grew up in a pretty conservative community. From the minute I started middle school, I remember everyone, my parents, teachers, friends telling me how harmful sex would be to me. How it would ruin me. That girls who had a lot of sex were...somehow tarnished. That losing my virginity meant being impure and somehow less of the person I was before. So I saved myself for a really long time because I believed them."

"That's fucking crazy," I mutter, brushing the hair out of her face as I rest on my elbow.

"I know that *now*, but when you grow up with that mindset, it literally strips away all of the power a woman can have and replaces it with shame. So that when I did start doing it, I didn't bother trying to enjoy it or find what I liked. And, after a while, I just stopped caring about sex altogether."

As her eyes find mine, the moment grows heavy, and I can't tell if I'm sad for her or pissed at the assholes who did this to her...or determined to give her as many orgasms as physically possible to make up for what she's lost.

"So...how the hell did you end up owning a sex club?"

She smiles. "Your dad."

My face morphs into a grimace as I let out a groan.

"You asked."

Then realization dawns as the blood drains out of my face. As my eyes widen, I stare at her in terror. "Oh my God, Maggie...please tell me you two haven't..."

"No!" she squeals. "God, no. That's not what I meant."

"Then what did you mean?"

With a laugh, she continues, "Your dad was the one who got me the job at the company we used to work for. And when it went under, I was going to fall back on event planning, but he begged me to start Salacious with him. I tried to decline the job so many times. I wasn't cut out for kink and sex, and I tried to tell him that, but he—being your dad—wouldn't take no for an answer. He made me believe I was worth more than an employee, that I should be the owner, and honestly, no one had ever told me that before."

I roll onto my back and stare at the ceiling, a feeling of unwelcome guilt settling in my mind. I remember when my dad started the company. I was in high school. And I remember thinking how cool he was.

Until it became more than an app, and I learned that my dad was a deviant, pervert, and creep—as my mother put it.

The irony is not lost on me. Maggie was raised in a purity culture and I was raised in...almost the opposite, and yet, we ended up in similar situations. All of the lies they fed her, my mother was feeding me the same.

"You weren't ever embarrassed?" I ask. "To own a sex club."

Her hand rests on my chest as she lets out a sigh. "No. I felt like I was taking back something that was stolen from me. And I wasn't going to let them shame me anymore."

Like the way I shamed him.

I don't react, staring at the ceiling. And before long, she picks up on my thought process.

"What are you thinking about?"

"People judge what they don't understand," I say. "And that's not an excuse. It's just a fact."

She nods before reaching up and pulling my face toward her. "Do you understand now?"

As I stare into her blue eyes, I realize that what

started as a dare between us has changed into something more. It's not just the best sex of my life, but the deepest connection I've ever felt too. But do I really understand? No. There is still so much I can't grasp.

"I'm getting there."

She gives me a small smile before leaning forward and pressing her lips to mine.

"Me too," she replies, before resting her head on my chest again.

Rule #22: If he wants to worship you, let him.

Maggie

"You didn't sleep with him, did you?" my mother harps from the front seat of the car.

"No!" I snap in response, immediately cowering when I feel her harsh glare on my face through the rearview mirror. "We're just friends. I lost track of time!" Which is a lie.

I know what my mother saw when she caught me climbing out of the passenger seat of the quarterback's car after the football game, where his hand was under my skirt, feeling me up through my underwear. He was begging me to touch him, but I was too shy to do anything more than rub the hard bulge through his football pants.

He's two grades above me and easily the most handsome boy I've ever known. I wish we were more than friends, but after tonight, when my mother came looking for me, screaming through the parking lot because I didn't come home on time, I'm pretty sure he'll never call me again.

I can still feel his forbidden touch between my legs, and I'm choking on my shame as she pulls over on the side of the road. She looks exasperated, fighting between angry and scared. Flipping on the light on the roof of the car, she grabs a piece of paper from the passenger seat and turns to show it to me.

"What's that?" I ask meekly.

"This is your heart," she replies, and my brows knit together. Then, she violently rips off a large corner of the paper. "This is your heart after you've had sex. You give a little piece away every time." When she rips it again, I flinch. And again and again and again until there's nothing left but a shred of white, crinkled paper.

"Save yourself, Maggie. Save yourself for someone who truly matters."

I'M STANDING IN SALACIOUS'S SMALL SEX SHOP AS the memory of that night replays in my head, realizing now how long I let those lies infiltrate my mind. And just how warped my views on sex are because of it. I doubt Eden or Mia had to listen to that or grow up believing that sex would do nothing but ruin them. No wonder I can't walk around the club without feeling embarrassed or ashamed.

What happened with Beau last night certainly didn't hurt me. I don't feel any less *me* because of it. In fact, I feel more like myself than ever.

My fingers glide over the glass of the display case as I smile. The assortment of items displayed inside all promise something different. Pain, control, excitement, pleasure. I've never taken the time to really look at them before. They always held promises for someone else, but never for me. And now...I see them all differently.

I can imagine striking Beau's flawless skin with the assortment of floggers. How he'd look strapped to my bed with the sleek black ropes hanging along the back wall. I even consider taking one of the modern cock cages for the days when he deserves it. I love the image of him wearing it and hating me for it.

But my eyes keep coming back to a certain display of items kept securely in the case by the front of the small store. Items that promise something I'm stupid to wish for —commitment. The Salacious store only carries a small variety of collars, and they are all perfectly minimal. Simple, sleek, and more inviting than I ever realized.

Yesterday, he promised me he was mine. But that was just something we said in the *scene*, whatever that means. Our relationship is still neatly tucked inside this Domme/sub dynamic, but even I'm struggling to see the blurred lines. Beau is mine in every way that matters, but for how long? And how much is he really giving me?

We never take our relationship outside of my house. I won't meet his friends and we can't go on dates. There is no future, only secrets.

So, how *mine* is he, really?

And why do I care? This was just supposed to be an experiment. It *still is* an experiment. I'm sure to him, that's all I am. And I hate my stupid heart for getting soft on him and even daring to imagine more.

Now that I've helped him find his submissive side, he'll be a better boyfriend for someone else. Someone like that beautiful girl he spoke to yesterday.

And I'll be free to find another sub, maybe one more suitable in age, and someone I can be with in the open. It will just be better that way...and surely, the agony of even imagining that will fade with time.

"We got Phoenix," a deep voice jolts me from my internal reckoning. In a rush, I spin toward Emerson, who's leaning against the same glass case I am, but instead of looking down at the collars I'm currently imagining his son wearing, he's staring at me.

"What?" I ask.

"I'm about to close the Phoenix deal. I need you to sit in on the call with me."

I should be more excited about this, but even work has felt menial and bleak lately.

"Um, yeah. That's amazing. Sure," I stammer.

He stares at me for a moment, his brow furrowing, and I know Emerson well enough to know that means he's about to bring up something important.

"Maggie, this might sound forward, but..."

My temperature rises instantly, and I feel myself start to panic before he even gets the rest of his question out.

"I'd like you to consider running it."

Wait. What?

My mouth falls open as I stare at him dumbfounded.

"I know. It's a big decision, and you just bought that house, but it could be something temporary until we find someone more suitable to manage it, and then we can handle the ownership remotely. But with Garrett on the mend and Hunter, Drake, and Isabel expecting..."

"You want me to move to Phoenix?"

"It's just an idea. Like I said, something temporary."

"Because I don't have a spouse or child, you mean. So it would just be easier for me." There's a hint of hostility in my tone and he picks up on it immediately.

"Because you're a smart business woman," he replies.

"Business *owner*," I snap back, and he looks offended. I wish I could take it back, and I hate how defensive I feel, but the smallest mention of moving has me in fight or flight mode. And, apparently, I already have my punching gloves on.

If I leave Briar Point, I have to leave Beau. I know we're not built for forever, but I'm not ready to stamp an expiration date on us just yet.

"Did I do something wrong?" Emerson asks with concern written all over his face.

I let out a huff and squeeze my eyes shut. "No. I'm sorry. It's just...I don't know."

"You know I would never use your gender in any of our business matters. Have I done that to you before?"

When I open my eyes, I almost pity him. Because, of course, he doesn't see that. How could he? Emerson has no idea what it's like to be the only woman in a world of men, and all things considered, he's one of the good ones. But treating me like he treats everyone else doesn't mean things have been equal for me.

"Of course not, Emerson. I didn't mean that. I'll give it some thought, okay? I promise."

His face is still stoically serious as he leans in. "You could run the whole thing yourself, Maggie. Make it the way you want it. I wouldn't offer that to just anyone."

I swallow down the pride hearing that makes me feel, but it's not that easy for me. But, instead of arguing with him, I tuck the idea away for the moment and nod my head in agreement. "Thank you."

After a tense smile, he glances down at the case we're hovering over. When his eyes trail up to my face, a spark of mischief hinting there, I blush and glance away.

"Shopping for anyone in particular?" he asks.

"I was doing inventory," I lie, and he laughs in response, which means he reads right through it.

"Okay." Then he stares down at the collars before subtly adding, "I've heard the snapping buckles are more comfortable than the others."

My cheeks start to heat up with embarrassment. I can't talk about this with him, for multiple reasons. The first and biggest one being that his *son* would be wearing it for me. Then, there's the discomfort of me being too reserved in general to discuss it so openly.

"I'm doing inventory—"

"I don't mean to pry," he says, interrupting me. "But I heard you ladies talking in the kitchen that night, and I know you took the quiz. I know you well enough to guess what the results were. And I'm just offering it to you without obligation, but if you ever need advice—"

"I don't," I snap. "Thank you, though."

"Don't feel bad, Maggie. You've got this." He rests a reassuring hand on my back and I force a smile.

For a moment, I almost wish I could talk to him about this. Emerson has been my closest friend for over a decade and up until now, work has been the only thing we have in common.

Then, with a wicked grin, he adds, "Get the black one. He'll love it." And once again, my cheeks flush and my eyes widen, and I try to hide my discomfort. God, if he only knew what he was suggesting...

With that, he stands up and adjusts his suit. "The call with the Phoenix owners is in an hour. I can't do it without you."

I smile. "Relax, little boy. I'll be there."

With a wink, he turns and walks away. My smile fades as I glance back down at the collars. It was a short-lived dream. If I'm moving to Arizona anytime soon, I can't give Beau the commitment this would symbolize.

So maybe an expiration date is exactly what we need. If there is a deadline, then my heart will know better than to get attached. Once I leave, this is over.

THE MEETING WITH PHOENIX RUNS LONGER THAN I expected, and it's well past seven when I finally leave the club. I haven't seen Beau all day, and that shouldn't be as weird as it feels. The rain is coming down in sheets when I run out to my car. The moment I'm safely tucked inside the driver's seat, I pull out my phone.

I'm sorry I worked late today, I say in a text.

We still communicate through the app because it's more discreet this way. A moment later, he responds, *I don't like you driving in this.*

I smile at his sweet concern. More and more every day, I lose sight of the spoiled, selfish man I thought I knew and love this new version of Beau, who shows more compassion than I thought possible.

I'll be careful.
Can you come over? I'll pick you up.

A moment later, he responds.

Isn't that a little suspicious?

It is. If his mother saw him getting into my car, the whole town would know by morning.

You're right. I'll see you in the morning.

No, I'm coming. I'll drive safe.

See you in fifteen.

It's very hard not to speed home, but I keep my promise and drive slowly. Knowing I'll see him soon, be able to touch him, to kiss him, to have him completely to myself is so enticing that it's hard to be patient.

A part of me doesn't want to do the Domme/sub thing tonight. I just want to be with him. But does he want to be with me without that? I'm still so unsure if all of this is real or just a continuous scene we're playing.

I pull my car into the garage, and before I shut it behind me, I see his car pull into the spot next to mine. But it's not the same electric sports car he's been driving. It's an older sedan.

"Where's your car?" I ask as he climbs out.

"This is mine. I was just driving my dad's for a while," he responds.

"Why?"

As he looks back at his car with a contemplative look, I wonder if there's something he's keeping from me. Finally, when he looks back at me, tight-lipped and nervous, he explains, "Someone vandalized it. Wrote pervert all over the side. So my dad had it repainted."

I gasp. "Pervert? Why would someone..." And before I can even get to the end of that question, it all comes together. "It was about the club."

He shrugs. "They must have thought it was Emerson Grant's car. And house."

"Your house got vandalized too?"

"Not really. It was just a threat, but I don't think they have the guts to do anything about it."

Why didn't Emerson tell us about this? We all know that these conservative trolls in Briar Point have a problem with the club and want to have it removed, but I didn't know they were out vandalizing his family's property. And knowing Beau is involved...turns my stomach.

Emerson is ashamed. Not of the club but for putting his son in danger. If I know him like I think I do, he's keeping this to himself because he's too afraid to admit it.

"If it happens again, call the police. Don't engage with them. Understand?"

"Yes, ma'am," he replies with a soft smile.

I press my hand against his chest as I stare into his eyes. "No, Beau. I'm serious. Promise me you won't mess with these people and you'll call the police next time."

His smile fades as he studies my face, clearly caught off guard by my sincerity. "I promise," he whispers.

The rain pours outside as we stand a few inches apart in this delicate moment. His eyes on me and mine on him, unspoken words hanging in the air between us. I know they won't be spoken, not yet.

"Do you mind if we don't...play the Domme thing tonight?" I ask.

He reaches up to brush a strand of wet hair out of my face. I let out a shaky breath as he touches me.

"Whatever you want. Does this mean I can kiss you without needing permission first?"

My heart skips a beat in my chest. "Yes."

Leaning forward, he softly pulls my lips toward his, tracing the shape of them with his tongue before sliding into my mouth to find my own. I don't push or demand control, but we dance a fine line of dominance, each of us giving and taking and meeting somewhere in the middle.

With a couple steps, he has me pressed against the side of my car. His hands lift the back of my shirt as my skin presses up against the cool, wet glass. I shiver as his fingers explore my body, but as I feel his touch crest the soft rolls of my waist, I tense.

"What's wrong?" he asks, pulling away from our heated kiss.

"Nothing," I reply, quickly covering up my discomfort as I pull him back down.

With a groan, he grinds against me, his hard length pressed to my core. I spread my legs for him, giving him more access as his other hand lifts one of my thighs. Everything in me lights up with need, but a moment later, a car drives by, and I'm reminded that we're basically dry humping in my open garage for everyone to see.

"Inside," I gasp against his mouth. I shove him toward the door, and we barely break contact as he stumbles backward. We only make it into the living room before he picks me up and deposits me on the couch, lying flat on my back as he climbs over me.

"We could have made it upstairs," I say breathlessly as he lifts my shirt over my head and presses his lips to my stomach.

"Nope. Too far," he replies, kissing circles around my belly button.

Chills run up my spine from the way his soft lips feel against my skin. I can't remember the last time anyone even touched my stomach, let alone ran their tongue just above the seam of my pants, which is what he's doing now. And it feels like heaven.

I keep waiting for him to move to a more erogenous

area like between my legs or my breasts, but he doesn't. Instead, he kisses his way up my sternum and along my collarbone.

"I love this spot right here," he whispers, pressing his lips to the divot at the base of my throat. His warm breath against me is making everything so sensitive, and I feel every one of his touches all the way to my core.

When was the last time I let someone just touch and explore me like this? Sex has always been a means to an end, never something I took the time to really enjoy before.

"Beau..." I breathe his name for no particular reason, other than to remind myself that this is really him. Emerson's son.

Reaching for the hem of his shirt, I drag it over his head and stare at the soft planes of his chest, the curve of muscle around his shoulders and the ridges of abs that lead to the perfect V above his shorts.

He's so perfect, so beautiful, and I'm torn between wanting him in a frenzy to fuck me and wanting to savor this moment.

His mouth doesn't stop at my collarbone but travels around my shoulder and down my arms. His wet tongue glides across the tender flesh of my upper arm, sending a warm wave of pleasure through me. I let out a moan, and he doesn't stop, covering my body in exploratory kisses.

"Don't you want to..." My voice trails as he lifts up from my body and stares down in confusion.

"Don't I want to what?"

"You know..."

"I'm doing exactly what I want right now," he replies.

"I...don't understand," I stutter.

Kneeling between my legs, he doesn't reply as he

drags my black pants and underwear down my legs, lifting them up as he tears them off, leaving me almost naked before him. Reaching around my back, he unclasps my bra until I'm at my most vulnerable, fully exposed to him. Every flaw and stretch mark and patch of cellulite on display. But he doesn't look at those.

He lifts one leg and drapes it over his shoulder as he runs his touch gently along the underside from my ankle to my ass, leaving goosebumps in his wake.

My legs are eager to close and I'm itching to cover myself when he gently pulls my hands away from where they're covering my breasts and belly.

"Don't be shy," he teases as his eyes rake over my body.

"I don't like being seen naked," I stammer uncomfortably.

Quickly, his smile is wiped from his face.

"Maggie, you have far more than great tits and a perfect little pussy."

I blush at the words coming out of his mouth.

"But if being your sub has taught me anything, it's that I don't take enough time to worship...the woman I'm with."

I bite my lip, slightly pained at the mention of other women. A slow chill settles in my stomach as I remember that he's doing all of this to be a better boyfriend. I might have him today, but someone else will have him in the future, which hurts to think about.

"And then again," he whispers, massaging my inner thigh. "Maybe I just never found one I was so obsessed with before."

I laugh, rolling my eyes at him as I try to close my legs. "Yeah, right."

Abruptly, he forces them open and looks me in the eye. Then, pressing his erection against my leg, he makes me feel just how aroused he is. "Feel this. *This* is what you do to me. You don't see what I see."

My breath comes out in a rush as that stupid tenderness grows. Why is he doing this? Why can't he just bring me inside and fuck me without affection, so all of this will be easier to end in a month when I go to Phoenix?

"Please, just fuck me," I plead.

A wicked smile grows across his face. "Look who's begging now."

He doesn't tease me for long, easing his shorts down until his cock pops out. Dragging my legs closer, he stares down while aligning himself and slowly inching his way in. His eyes are glued to the place where we're connected, and I'm reveling in the sensation of his impressive size filling me up.

"I love watching it go in," he mutters in a husky tone, and a burst of warmth drips down to my core. He teases me, going torturously slow.

Writhing beneath him, I let him take control. When he finally drapes his body over mine, our lips lock as he starts to pick up speed. Above my head, our fingers intertwine, and we move in sync, his cock slamming into me, my body lighting with pleasure from every thrust.

"Tilt your hips a little," I whisper against his lips, and he does. When he hits my G-spot just right, I let out a high-pitched cry. "Right there. Don't stop."

"I want to see you come first," he moans as he continues to fuck me right where it makes my toes curl and my legs shake.

"Then, keep kissing me," I beg. His soft lips land against mine, and I lose myself in the kiss. Shutting off my brain and all of the fear and doubt, focusing only on his mouth, his cock, and his presence. It's enough to have me shuddering through a full-body climax.

Once I've come down from my orgasm, he pulls his mouth away and smiles down at me. Stilling his hips, he pulls my legs over his forearms and then over his shoulders as he mutters in a sexy, deep tone, "I'm not done with you yet."

Nearly folding me in half, he picks up the intensity of his thrusts, pounding so hard, it has my body lighting up with pleasure again.

"Oh, my God, Beau," I shriek.

He freezes. "I'm not hurting you, am I?" he asks.

I grab his hips and urge him to move again. "No, no. Keep going. Harder."

I can honestly say I've never been fucked this hard, and it's not really something I thought I'd like. But as he nearly drives my body into the couch with force, his already large shaft reaching parts of my body I didn't even know existed, I can now say with confidence, this is definitely my style.

I don't know if my body is climaxing again or if it never truly stopped, but all I do know is sex has *never* felt like this before. I grab onto his arms, my nails digging into his skin as my body pulses with pleasure again. His eyes are glued to my face as I lose myself to the torrent.

"Can I come?" he cries out.

"Yes, yes, yes," I reply.

Two more thrusts and he stills, trembling with his orgasm. His low carnal moan in my ear is decadent, and I commit the sound to memory.

Once we've both stilled and relaxed together on the couch, he rests his head against my chest, and I run my fingers through his hair. It's so intimate and unexpected, but I realize in this moment, that everything I've been trying to avoid has already happened.

I'm falling for my friend's son. And it didn't happen slowly. We collided like two stars moving in the same direction for longer than we knew. There was no changing course or avoiding it. I didn't mean for it to happen. But there's no going back now.

Rule #23: It's good to switch it up from time to time.

Beau

It's some time past midnight and still raining outside. Normally, I'd be home by now, but I can't seem to get off this couch.

I'm facing Maggie, who's scrolling through her phone in nothing but her underwear, while I'm busying my hands with a sketch on my tablet. It's of her, and all the perfect parts of her stretched out before me.

I hate how hard she is on herself. When she's in her Domme mode, she doesn't give a shit and parades herself around proudly—as she should. But I can't stand how easily she slips back into this mindset, where it almost feels like she hates herself. She won't let herself feel pleasure and I can't touch her without her flinching and tensing.

I don't want to be the *only* voice in her head that tells her she's beautiful.

"What are you doing?" she asks, looking over at my tablet. I hold it out for her to see. It's not great. I'm no artist, but I am pretty proud of how well I captured the little crease of her hips and the shape of her tits. Every perfect part of her.

"I'm keeping this for later," I reply with a wink before she grabs it out of my hands.

"Beau..." She's staring down at the messy sketch with a soft expression.

"Do you like it?"

Her lips are slightly parted as I spot the glint of moisture in her eyes, reflected by the light of the tablet in her hands. Fuck, I hope she doesn't see that and start beating herself up again.

She swallows before whispering, "This is beautiful."

"Yeah...well, it's you."

Her head turns in my direction, and I expect her reaction to be warm. Instead, she frowns and looks away, clearly bothered by something.

"You okay?"

With a few quick blinks, she forces a smile, hands back my tablet, and touches my leg. "Yeah. You're a really good artist, Beau."

"Thanks."

After a moment, she adds, "So, I got some news today. At work. Next month, I'll be relocating to Phoenix for a while to open the new club. You'll have to get back on the app and find yourself a new Domme."

I'm frozen, staring at her and trying to piece together what just came out of her mouth. A new Domme? Just last night, she made me promise I belonged to her, and now...she wants me to find someone new?

"You're moving to Phoenix?"

"Temporarily, but at least for six months, if I had to guess."

She looks back down at her phone and her sudden nonchalance regarding this news has me feeling irritable. I want to grab that phone out of her hand and throw it against the wall. I want to yell at her to stop avoiding whatever it is she wants to say, but I don't. If she's going to act like it's nothing, then so will I.

I mean...all the buildup, the trust building, and the things we've learned are just going to be tossed in a month. Just like that.

"I should probably go," I mutter, and her head snaps in my direction as I jump up from the couch.

"In this weather? It's too dangerous. Just stay." She follows me, and I try not to read too much into the way she sounds as she asks me to stay. It's just my safety she's worried about.

"I'll be fine. I'll drive slow," I argue as I grab my keys from the table.

"Beau, stay," she replies, more harshly this time.

When I spin to her, I feel the tension. "Are you asking me or are you telling me?"

She hesitates. "I'm..." The words stop and I watch as she realizes the difference. If she's telling me to stay then we are nothing more than a Domme and her sub. Even if she just implied it with that statement about me needing to find someone new after she abruptly moves away next month. But if she's asking, then it means she wants me here.

"Beau," she says with a sigh as her shoulders sag, "I *want* you to stay. I'm asking you to stay."

"Yes, ma'am," I mutter in response, my tone laced with bitterness.

She reaches for my arm, tenderly running her fingers down my bicep. "You're mad about Phoenix."

I shake my head. "No, I'm not. I don't give a shit. But I'm not finding another Domme. I only did this as an experiment, remember? I'm not my dad. This lifestyle isn't for me."

Her brow folds inward as her shoulders soften even more. "If I told you to kneel right now, you'd do it."

"No, I wouldn't," I snap back. "You think I'm just gonna be your bitch all the time. I just do it for the sex, Maggie."

She pushes her chest out and lifts her chin. "Bullshit. You're just being defensive. You love being a sub, and I don't understand why you can't just admit that."

"Because I'm not. I told you. It was an experiment."

She grabs my shirt and pulls me toward her. "Fine. I'll be submissive tonight."

As she drops to her knees in front of me, I stare at her in surprise. It's odd to see her like this, and I don't like it.

"Stand up. I don't want this."

When I try to pull her up by her elbows, she shakes her arm free. "No. It's good to switch roles every once in a while. To get another perspective."

"Maggie...I don't want you to be submissive to me."

"Why not?" she asks, gazing up at me with those big blue eyes.

"Because I just...don't. I don't even know what to say."

"Tell me what you want me to do."

I let out a sigh. "No. I don't want to use you like that."

She furrows her brow. "But I want you to. I want to please you."

"Not like this. I'm not in the mood. You're just trying to prove a point." When I turn my back to her and pace into the kitchen, I hear her rise onto her feet and follow after me.

"Tell me why. Why don't you want me to be submissive to you when you can be so submissive to me?"

Her hands slide around my waist from behind, settling on my stomach, and I feel her forehead against my spine. Something about feeling her arms around me brings me comfort.

"Because I just don't want to. I'm not...like him."

"What is that supposed to mean?" she asks.

"I'm not..."

"Not what?" She's prying, and I know she won't let it go. I'm glad she's behind me because the more frustrated I get, the more emotional I get, and I couldn't stand for her to see that. "Not what, Beau?" she presses.

"Not good enough." Those three words feel like knives. I hate admitting this. It makes me feel like a kid, like a small version of the man I'm supposed to be.

"Beau," she snaps, turning me around, and I don't fight her as she spins me until we're facing each other. "What do you mean not good enough?"

"I'm not worth it. Not worthy of you or Charlie or any of the other relationships I've fucked up over the years. I'm not the kind of guy women worship. I'm not worth it—"

She slams her hand over my mouth, halting my words before I'm able to speak them. "Don't you say that. Don't you *ever* say that. How can you sit here and blame me for being hard on my body when you talk about yourself like this? You clearly don't see what I see."

"You don't want me as your boyfriend and I get it. I suck at that, but being your sub, that I can do."

"Is this why you want to be submissive, Beau? Because you think you're not worthy of being dominant? Is that what you think this is?"

"No. I just...I feel better about myself when I'm with you. When I can do exactly what you want."

Her soft hands wrap around my neck, pulling me down until our mouths are almost touching. I've never been so comfortable with another person in all my life. Things with Maggie are easy, like she was made just for me, to make being *me* a little easier.

"For what it's worth, I *do* want you for more than my sub. I don't think you'd suck as a boyfriend at all..."

"But..." I reply, staring down at her.

"But...you're too young for me, and I'd be risking so much if anyone found out about us."

I roll my eyes and try to pull away, but she holds me in place. "One month, Beau. We have one month together, and while we have this time, and we're alone in my house, then we can be whatever we want. You'll see how good of a boyfriend you can be. You'll see how worthy you are."

She presses her lips to mine, and I try to absorb her words and make them feel true.

Then, she's dropping to her knees again, and I try in vain to keep her on her feet.

"I want you to see things from my perspective. You should feel what it's like from up there."

My heart hammers in my chest as I watch her gaze up at me with a lust-filled haze in her eyes. Her face is just inches away from my cock, which is hardening quickly behind my boxers at the sight of her kneeling in front of me.

I wish I could say the thoughts in my head were as pure and controlled as hers probably are when she's in this role. She wants to use me. What I want when I stare at her like this, with power so visceral it scares me...is to degrade her.

I can't explain why, but I see this perfect, beautiful thing and I want to ruin it. Immediately, I feel sick with myself.

"I can't do this, Maggie." I stroke her hair away from her face. "You don't want me to do this."

"Yes, I do," she whispers, but she has no idea. She thinks I'm something I'm not. The faith she has in me is unearned, and it's infuriating to watch. Maggie deserves better than this—better than me. Why on earth would she trust me so blindly? "Mercy, remember? Same rules apply. I'm yours, and I'll do whatever you want. If it's too much, I have my safe word."

"Whatever I want?"

She looks like heaven—if heaven was a filthy sin. With that, she nods.

Something in me snaps and I let myself go, running my hands into her hair, gripping it hard at the scalp as I press her head down until she's on all fours, her face just inches away from the floor. She lets out a gentle yelp as I feel something carnal and potent creep its way down my spine.

"Are you sure this is what you want? You want a taste of what I really like, Maggie?"

"Yes," she murmurs, her lips near the floor.

"Because I want to make you feel like a dirty slut. I want to ruin you. I'm not like you. I don't just want to use you, Maggie. I want to hurt you while I do it."

"I can take it," she replies, not even a hitch in her breath as she says it. What the fuck is this woman doing to me?

As I drag her face up toward my cock, I stop seeing

Maggie. When I growl at her to take it out, I see a nameless, faceless woman I don't care about. And the vision is so convincing that when I pry open her lips with my dick, it snuffs out all of those feelings of attachment and hope I was feeling for her before. She gags loudly as I stuff my cock down her throat, fucking her mouth with her hair still in my tight clutches.

I'm free, liberated to do whatever I want, finally letting this monster run the show.

It should feel good. And my cock certainly isn't complaining as I hit the back of her throat with each thrust, saliva dripping from her open mouth. But it's bittersweet. Like I'm seeing myself for the first time, and I hate it even more than I thought I would.

When I pull her mouth off my cock, she gags, and I watch tears stream down her face.

I want to stop, but then I hear her words again—*I can take it.* Suddenly, I want to see just how much she can take.

If she wanted to call mercy she could now, but she doesn't. Instead, she grips my thighs in her hands and stares up at me with red eyes and an expectant expression.

"You liked that, didn't you?" I mutter through clenched teeth.

With tears still pouring, she nods. "Yes, sir."

I grip her hair tighter. "Don't call me that."

When her mouth falls open from the pain, I let that primal, evil part of me take over again, and I spit right down her throat. She flinches but barely reacts.

And I know she probably wants to draw this out a little longer, but I can't help myself. I need to fuck her now. Or maybe I just need to get to the end of this because as much as a part of me is enjoying it, the rest of me hates it.

Dragging her across the floor, I take her to the plush rug in the middle of her living room. Seeing her crawl under my control is intoxicating. Without emotion, I deposit her on all fours as I fall onto my knees behind her.

"You want to be my slut? Well, here you go," I growl as I rip her panties down her thighs and shove my cock into her wet heat. She lets out a scream as her fingers clutch the rug, holding her in place against my relentless pounding.

My mind is blank. I'm not thinking—just feeling. Nothing but filth and shame.

Her hips are pinched in my grasp as I thrust hard, and it's so loud, it drowns out the sound of my grunts and her moans. I'm lost to the motion, and I should be coming soon, but I feel no closer to my climax.

Reaching down, I wrap my hand around her throat and drag her upward, so I can fuck her harder, but with each pounding thrust, I feel something breaking inside me. The hard, unfeeling monster currently behind the wheel is growing weaker.

She lets out a scream, and I watch her skin break out in goosebumps, shivering from the top of her spine to the base. When I finally come, it's unsatisfying and followed up quickly by a crippling sensation of shame and regret.

Then, my quiet brain suddenly wakes up, drowning out the evil emotions coursing through me.

You don't see what I see.

Those words replay in my head, the look on her face as she gazed up at me, touching my face as she uttered them accompanying the memory. Then I see her tears, gagging as I spit in her mouth, degrading her and treating her like something disgusting after she was so kind to me.

What the fuck is wrong with me?

My hand drops from her throat, and I nearly stop breathing.

"Mercy."

In a rush, I pull out. "Mercy. I'm calling mercy," I stammer as I fall to my ass, leaning back against the couch. My fingers dig into my hair as I let my head hang forward.

Without another word, she's there, pulling my face up and putting hers within inches of my own.

"It's okay. I'm okay."

She invades my space, settling my face against her shoulder as she drowns out all the thoughts in my head with her touch.

"Talk to me. What happened?" she whispers.

"What do you mean what happened? Aren't you disgusted by me?" I gape at her in shock.

"No," she replies, stroking my cheek, "I actually liked seeing you take control like that."

I scoff. "Well, I didn't. I don't feel good about myself right now...if you couldn't tell."

"Why? If I gave you consent to do it, then why do you feel so bad?"

I shrug. "I don't know. I wish I knew."

She lifts my face and gazes into my eyes. "Beau, you have some warped perceptions about sex. The shame you feel isn't your fault. Someone else put that there."

I can't pinpoint in the moment if it was my mother talking shit about my dad for so long that I believed her lies or if it was society brainwashing me into believing that sex came with a side order of shame, but Maggie's right, and I'm seeing it now for the first time. My perception is warped.

"You don't have to feel bad about degrading me if that's what gets you off," she says with a shrug. "I got off on it too."

"You did?"

With a wicked-looking half-smile, she nods. "Could you not tell how wet I was?"

"I don't want to do that again. I just want you to be in control."

"Okay, I will. But I think you need to do that more often, until you learn to stop feeling so bad about it."

"I wanted to hurt you, Maggie. I wanted to treat you like garbage." I say this to her like it's common sense how wrong it is, but her facial expression doesn't look convinced.

"Are you saying there's something wrong with me if I get off on being treated like garbage?"

My brow furrows, and I try to ignore how turned on that makes me, knowing how aroused she was by that. On the bright side, some of that shame I was just drowning in has started to fade away. "Nothing makes sense anymore."

"Tell me about it," she replies, stroking my hair out of my face.

Then, without warning, everything bubbles to the top, like I've just opened a wound that won't stop bleeding. "I'm not supposed to show emotion or anger. I'm expected to just accept shit I don't like. I accepted my parents splitting. I accepted when my dad started dating my ex-girlfriend. And now I have to accept them getting married. On the outside, I let them believe I was okay, but I still feel so..."

She nestles closer, touching my shoulder and leaning

against my arm as she listens. I can feel her encouraging me to continue.

"I'm still fucking angry." The moment those words are out, it feels like a weight is lifted from my chest. I think I've been holding that in longer than I realized.

She kisses my cheek. "It's okay to be angry, Beau. What matters is how you let that anger out. You need an outlet, or at the very least, someone to talk to."

I focus on her touch, the calming movement of her hand over the skin of my arm.

"And you know you're safe with me."

Exhaustion washes over me, like I've just run an emotional marathon. But I'm not just tired, I'm also refreshed in a weird way, like I've just put down something I've been carrying for a long time.

"Beau, you got royally fucked by life," she says, and I let a laugh slip through as I lift my eyes to gaze at her. "We all do, but usually when you get royally fucked, you're supposed to get a little aftercare, too."

A smile creeps across my face as I stare at her. Every day I see her, something changes in my perception. I've stopped just seeing her as my dad's friend or a Domme, but with every passing moment, I see her as something far more intimate and familiar. I see her as mine.

Suddenly, she stands, pulling me up by the hand. "Now, come on. It just so happens that aftercare is my favorite part."

I know this is the part where I just get to hold her, touch her, talk to her, and treat her like I know she's supposed to be treated. And even after everything I just did, she's right. It is my favorite part too.

Rule #24: Beating up jerks won't make anything better.

Beau

Hey loser. D&D tonight?

I read the incoming text through one half-opened eye before looking at the time. It's almost noon. Maggie and I were up until three in the morning, and I feel like I have a hangover after that heavy conversation.

God, why did I admit all of that about not feeling good enough?

Next to me, Maggie is sleeping soundly, looking adorable with her messy brown hair covering half her face. She sleeps with her lips slightly parted, and I really want to kiss them. But I don't.

Instead, I toss my phone on the nightstand and peel back the blanket covering Maggie's body. She flinches when the cool air touches her breasts, but doesn't fully wake up. When I pull the blankets lower, revealing her naked body, I lick my lips and feel a twitch in my quickly growing cock.

I press my lips to her bare stomach, and she flinches again. Trailing my mouth upward, I find her nipple with my tongue and lap hungrily as it starts to form a tight bud.

She lets out a soft moan, her body giving a little fidget from the sensation. When I climb over her, I peel her legs apart to settle myself between them, kissing my way down to her belly. Her fingers find my hair, clutching it in a tight grip like she often does. Her hips rise to meet me and just the sight of her abs constricting beneath me as she squirms with need has my cock throbbing for her.

With her hand in my hair, she steers my face to the apex of her thighs, and I dive in vigorously. She lets out a loud whimper as I press my open mouth to her warm cunt, licking through her folds as her thighs close around my head. She's already wet and ready for me, like she was dreaming about me.

"Yes, Beau," she gasps. "Don't stop."

I take my time, savoring her arousal as I fuck her with my tongue before sucking with intensity on her clit. She's fully awake now, but her eyes are still closed, the sheets gripped tightly in her fists. After a few moments of sucking, she finally lets out a raspy scream, her back arched and thighs clenched. When she goes silent, I know she's deep under the waves of her climax.

I love watching her come. Especially now that I know she's been deprived of orgasms for so long. I meant what I said before. I want to be the one to right her past wrongs.

"Fuck me," she pleads. "Now."

And I don't waste a second. Sitting up on my knees, I grab her by the hips and flip her onto her stomach, pulling her up until her pussy is right where I need it. Then I plunge in. With one hard thrust, I'm seated as far in as I can go. She lets out a cry, forcing her hips back as I pull out and pound in again.

Like last night, the soft flesh of her hips fills my grasp as I fuck her. But unlike last night, I don't feel like shit about this. She *liked* the way I treated her. She's basically begging for it now. So I squeeze her tighter, hoping I leave bruises. Not because I want to hurt her, but because I want to mark her. I want everyone who ever considers touching her to know this perfect woman is mine—or rather, I'm hers. It's irrational and ridiculous, but I love the idea of knowing no man can be what I am for Maggie. No more assholes, who just want to take from her. No more fumbling idiots, who don't know how to give my woman pleasure.

Only me.

Forever.

My cock tremors and twitches inside her as I come. We stay like that for a while before I reluctantly pull out and collapse against the mattress. She curls into my arms as I kiss the back of her neck.

"I just decided I want you to stay over more often," she says with a smile.

"Yes, ma'am," I reply.

The day goes by in a blur of sex. Suddenly, Maggie and I are fucking like we're making up for something. Neither of us check our phones all day, and she takes the whole day off without a single minute of work.

I don't even know what time it is when I'm strapped to her mattress and she's riding me like a bull.

"Remind me again who this cock belongs to," she says in her confident, sensuous tone.

I'm wearing a shameless grin as I reply, "You, ma'am. It's all yours."

"That's what I thought," she replies as she picks up the speed of her grinding. I can't move a muscle. My body is laid out like a starfish on her mattress, using these new straps she must have found at the club. I am nothing but a body with a hard dick for her to use, and I couldn't be happier.

I love being at her mercy, watching her come on my dick for the tenth time today. It's fucking amazing. Best sex of my life, and I'm a little afraid of how addicted I'm quickly becoming to this arrangement.

As we're both recovering, her collapsing against my chest, my phone starts ringing from the nightstand.

"Should I untie you so you can answer that?" she asks, reaching across the bed to grab my phone.

"I don't even care," I mumble, struggling to stay awake.

When she goes silent, I peel my eyes open and see that the playful expression on her face is gone.

"It's Charlie," she mutters coldly.

"What?" I struggle against the restraints to get my phone, but not because I give a shit about it being Charlie. Although I can see the look of hurt on Maggie's face. "It must be about my dad. I don't talk to Charlie anymore," I say in my defense. I can't tell by her blank expression if she believes me.

Without answering it, she drops it on the bed and unties my hands. I'm staring at her face, wishing she didn't look so offended by my ex-girlfriend calling, but I can't say I blame her.

As soon as my hands are free, I swipe the screen to answer the call.

"Hello?"

"Why are you ignoring Sophie?" Charlie snaps without a greeting.

"What? I'm not."

"She's been texting you all day. Now she's in her room crying and won't come out. She's sensitive, Beau. I know she's just a kid, but she was just starting to get close to you, and she doesn't need another man in her life to let her down."

"Charlie, I'm not ignoring her. I just haven't been around my phone much." I glance up at Maggie, who's biting her bottom lip with a look of guilt on her face. "Is she really crying?"

The feeling that settles in my gut with that image is worse than guilt. Much worse. It's shame, regret, self-deprecation, and remorse all rolled into one, and I have never hated myself more than I do in this moment.

"Yes. But she's been really moody lately. I think she started seeing that boy from the D&D club, and it's been rocky."

That little fucker.

"All right, I'm coming over."

"Don't bother. It's too late, Beau."

"Fine, then I'm calling her." Without waiting for an answer, I hit End Call and immediately find Sophie's contact in my phone. Before calling her, I glance up at Maggie.

"Is she okay?" she whispers.

"Yeah, I just...fucked up."

Her brow furrows as the call starts to go through to Sophie. It only rings twice before her sniffly voice picks up on the other end. "What?" she says as a greeting, but not a warm one.

"Hey, kid, I'm sorry. I was just busy today."

"Forget about it. I don't care," she mumbles in reply.

"Let's go to D&D now. I'm ready."

"It's almost over by now, Beau. It's too late."

"Then let's go get ice cream or something. Come on. We haven't hung out in a long time." I'm frantically pulling my clothes on as I talk.

"I'm not in the mood," she mutters quietly.

"I don't care. I'll be there in fifteen. Be ready." With that, I hang up, and rush toward the door.

Maggie is sitting on the bed as she watches me. Before leaving, I spin and look at her. She's staring at me with a tense, uncomfortable-looking smile.

"I'm sorry. I have to—"

"Go," she replies.

"Come with me," I say before really thinking about it.

She tilts her head. "We can't be seen together like that, Beau. Charlie would know and then your dad would know."

Fuck, she's right. God, I hate this. Maggie is not some dirty secret, and I don't give a shit about my dad knowing anymore, but I still can't seem to work up the guts to let it out of the bag just yet.

"I'm sorry," I mumble again.

"Don't be. Just go."

Before I can leave, I rush back to the bed and plant a kiss on her lips, pulling her close and feeling her hum against my chest.

Then, I run down to my car and leave.

Sophie is standing outside and I can tell by her posture that she's in a bad mood. Her shoulders are slumped and her hands are tucked inside her sweatshirt.

As I pull up, she climbs in without a word and won't look at me as she buckles up.

"Hey, kid. Why so glum?"

She shrugs. "I'm fine."

"Look, I'm sorry for missing game night lately. I've been busy." When she glances up at me, I feel a wave of guilt wash over me. Getting bossed around by my Domme hardly seems like a good enough reason for not responding to her messages.

"I'm quitting D&D," she replies.

"What? Why?"

"Because I think Kyle is going to break up with me," she mutters into the sleeve of her sweatshirt. My fingers tighten around the steering wheel and my blood starts to boil. If that little asshole gave her any shit or treated her different than he would other girls, I swear to God, I'll kick his ass.

"I didn't know you were dating him. Fuck, I didn't know you were dating at all. Are you sure you're ready for that?"

"Why? Because I'm trans I can't date?"

Well, that felt like a straight slap across my face. My brow furrows as I shake my head. "I didn't say that. Of course you can. I just know how guys are, okay? And they're all selfish dickheads."

"Takes one to know one," she retorts with a smug expression.

"I deserve that," I reply, nudging her shoulder. "Okay, so wait a second. What makes you think Kyle wants to break up with you?"

She shrugs, sadly chewing on her nails. "He just doesn't respond to my texts."

"That little asshole. Let's go to that game night and kick his ass."

With a roll of her eyes, she shakes her head. "No."

"I'll cast a Ray of Douche-ness on him. Make him roll a restitution check."

"A *constitution* check," she corrects me with a laugh.

"I'll sic my imaginary dragon on him and burn his stupid douchey castle down."

She's giggling into her hands now, and it makes me feel a fuck-ton better to see her smile.

"You're a child," she replies with a laugh.

"Yeah, I know. Come on. Let's go get ice-cream wasted." I throw the car into drive and take off toward the DQ we usually stop at after game night. It's packed when we pull up. Teenagers with nothing better to do on a Friday night are lingering around the tables outside. It's not normally so crowded, and I tense as we get out of the car, but I quickly follow Sophie's lead as she confidently crosses the parking lot and heads inside.

"So, what's her name?" she asks after I pay for our chocolate cones and find a seat at one of the tables inside.

"What?" I ask with a mouthful of ice cream.

"The reason you couldn't check your phone all day. What's her name?"

"I was *working*," I reply, and she shakes her head.

"Bullshit."

"I'm telling your mom you said that," I reply.

"No, you're not. So, do I know her? I saw you flirting with my cousin at the shower. Is it her?"

"No," I snap. "You're nosey."

She smiles at me before I notice the way her eyes

travel to the window behind me. Suddenly, her face falls. "Let's go," she mutters quickly.

"What? Why?" I ask, turning to see what she saw when I spot Kyle sitting at one of the tables with a spiky-haired girl in a black goth outfit.

"Come on. Let's just go." Sophie stands up in a rush, tossing what's left of her ice cream in the trash, and heads toward the door.

"Is that Kyle? Is he with another girl?" I shout. My blood starts to boil, seeing the hurt wash over her.

"I don't care," she mumbles as she rushes out the door and to the car.

As I follow behind her, I notice the little fucker's face turn to shock as he spots Sophie crossing the parking lot. "Sophie?"

"Come on, Beau," she calls after me, ignoring the dickhead.

"No. Fuck that." As I march toward the guy, his eyes fill with fear. When he stands up, holding his hands in surrender, I realize this kid, who can't be older than sixteen, is easily as tall as me and almost as wide.

"I'm sorry!" he stammers as I grab the collar of his shirt. Rage boils inside me as his eyes track Sophie. The cotton of his T-shirt tears in my grasp as I drag him closer. I'm not sure where this switch was flipped inside me, but it's like last night all over again. I'm hovering out of the frame, watching this all unfold, and I have no power to stop it. I'm not exactly sure why I hate this guy so much, why I want to hurt him so badly, or why I can't seem to recognize myself anymore.

All I see is red.

"Beau, stop it!" Sophie screams from the parking lot.

"Take your hands off me, man," Kyle argues as he struggles to get out of my hold.

"You're a slimy piece of shit," I say with a sneer. "You don't treat people like this. You don't hurt the girls who are good to you, you fucking asshole. You think you can treat them like they mean nothing, like they don't matter, but *she* matters." When I release his collar, freeing one hand to point at Sophie, I freeze as I notice the tears streaming down her face. Her eyes are on me, pleading with me to stop, and I briefly remember what she said to me just a few weeks ago.

I know you think you're being chivalrous, and I appreciate you looking out for me, but beating up jerks isn't going to make anything better.

She literally asked me not to do this. She *knew* this was what it would come to, how I would react. I'm no better than her dad...always on the attack. Throwing punches and shouting insults instead of listening.

My grip loosens on Kyle's shirt as the regret takes hold. When I look back at him, his face is red and his chest is heaving rapidly with his own anger.

And I'll gladly take whatever he's about to give me, which I genuinely expect to be some colorful language—not a mean right hook. I did *not* see that coming. And as his fist pummels me into motion, and the pain knocks me to the ground, breaking the fall with my own face, the last thought in my head is—*I deserve this.*

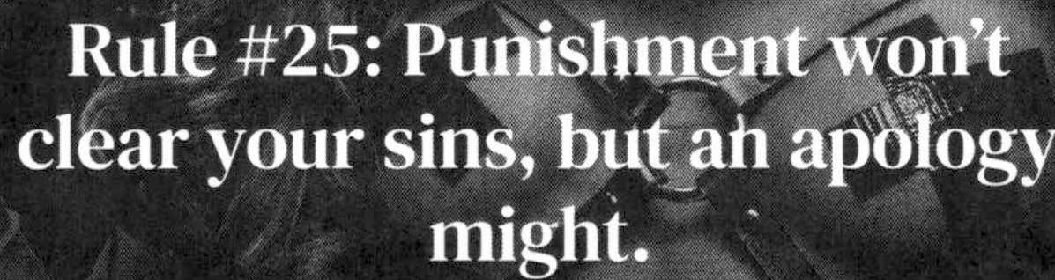

Rule #25: Punishment won't clear your sins, but an apology might.

Maggie

I've scrolled through the rental properties in Phoenix for so long, I keep expecting there to be some answers in these photos. Am I making the right choice? Is it really a good time for me to leave Briar Point, even if it's only for six months? Especially with everything going on between me and Beau.

I mean, maybe a fresh start is good. Maybe dating again in a new city with new co-workers and a new club is what I need. I could start over and find another sub, still exploring this new Domme version of myself.

Or maybe he could come visit. I could see us there, free from all of the judgment of our friends and family, free to live the life we want. Together. Would he want that? Would he really come visit me? Would he stay?

These are dangerous ideas. Getting attached to a life like this could be beyond harmful, but I can't help it. It's too tempting. A fantasy of days like today every day.

But realistically, it's only been a month. We're moving too fast, aren't we?

There's a knock on the door, and I freeze in fear as Ringo starts barking wildly. As I descend the stairs, the knock is back. My first thought is that it's the same people who were responsible for vandalizing Beau's car. But it's after ten at night. Would they really come to my house and knock on my door? I pull out my phone, ready to call Emerson or 9-1-1 or do something when I hear a voice.

"Maggie, it's me."

Beau.

In a rush, I run across the foyer and tear open the door. He's standing on my doormat, an ugly red scrape running from his cheek to his forehead on one side of his head and a large purple bruise forming under the other eye.

"Oh my God, Beau!" I say with a gasp as I pull him inside. "What happened to you?"

He groans as he holds his head. I pull him into the kitchen and rush to the sink to grab a towel, running it under the warm water of the faucet.

"I fucked up," he mumbles.

"What do you mean you fucked up? Weren't you taking Sophie out for ice cream?"

"I did. Her boyfriend was there with another girl."

As I rest the wet cloth against the bloody gash on his face, he winces. "Tell me you didn't start a fight with a teenager."

He doesn't reply, only grimaces. There is remorse dripping from his expression as he stares at the ground.

"Oh my God, Beau. Is he okay?" I ask.

"I didn't even get a punch in. I was just...so mad at him. I hated him."

"Well, you care about Sophie a lot, but you can't beat up every guy who breaks her heart."

His sullen eyes lift to my face, and my heart skips in my chest. The vulnerability he's expressing, the pain, fear, anger, all of it, is somehow as beautiful as much as it is haunting.

"I'm no better than *him*." His expression is pleading, and I hate to hear him talk about himself like this. I hate it. So I turn my back and head toward the freezer for ice.

"No, you're not. Don't say that," I reply with my back turned. As I pile ice cubes in the towel, I hear him standing up from the stool and walking toward me.

"Yes, I am, Maggie. I've cheated on almost every girl I've been with. I cheated on Charlie *twice* and she only knows about one. I fucked the other girl and Charlie in the *same* fucking day."

My hand freezes in the ice bin as his words impale me with fear. Every perfect vision I have of him and any future we may have had evaporates into thin air.

I feel so stupid.

When I turn toward him, ice in my hand, I can't hide the contempt on my face. I don't know what to say. I don't know why he is telling me this or what I'm supposed to do with this information. Does he want me to regret opening my heart to a selfish twenty-two-year-old man? Because at the moment, I do.

"That's terrible, Beau," I whisper.

"I know," he replies, moisture springing to his eyes, "I've been trying to tell you this. I'm terrible. I don't respect any of the women I'm with—I just want to hurt them. I fuck it up every single fucking time. You don't have to hate me. I hate myself enough."

"Don't say that. I don't hate you. I could *never* hate you."

"I get the slightest attention from a woman and I don't care who I hurt to get it. I don't care about anyone but myself. Sooner or later, I'll cheat on you too."

I shake my head, trying to press the ice pack to his forehead. I just want him to stop talking, stop trying to convince me that I shouldn't care about him. It's not working. It's alarming how much it's not working, because everything Beau is saying should have me pushing him out the door, out of my life, out of my heart. But I'm not. The more he deprives himself of love, the more I want to make up for it.

"No, you won't."

"Yes." He grabs my hand and stares into my eyes. "Yes, I will. I will find a way to fuck this up too. It doesn't matter how much I care about you or how this is the best relationship I've ever been in. The second I get a chance to sabotage it, I will."

"Stop it," I snap, trying to put the ice against his face again. Emotion is building behind my eyes, and I'm holding back the urge to cry, scream, kiss him, and hit him, all at the same time.

He swats my hand away as I try to tend to his wound. "Punish me."

"What?" I ask, staring up at him in confusion.

"I don't want this tenderness, this affection. I want you to punish me."

I lift the ice to his head again. "That's not how it works, Beau."

"I don't care. It's the only thing that makes me feel better."

I shake my head as I step away from him. "I *don't want to*, and what I want matters."

"You'd deprive me of what I need?"

"This isn't what you need," I reply. "This is about trying to purge your sins with punishment that will not make any of it go away. This isn't a game, Beau. If you want to feel better about what you've done, try apologizing."

"Fuck this," he mutters angrily as he spins away from me. "I thought you understood me. I thought you wanted to help me."

I grab his arm, stopping him before he can rush out the door. "I do, but not like this."

"Why?" he replies, turning toward me in desperation.

"Because I don't want to hurt you."

"I'm literally asking you to," he pleads with his hands to his chest.

"I'm not ready, and I won't risk it."

"I have a safe word, remember? If it's too much, I'll use it."

I shake my head again. "I said no. And I meant it."

The look of contempt on his face sends chills down my spine. I've never seen so much displeasure in his eyes before and to be on the receiving end of it literally makes me want to crumble.

"Then, you're a shitty fucking Domme. This was all about fucking a young hot guy for you, wasn't it? You're so fucking dense, Maggie. You think trying to see the best in me will make me want to be good for you, but you're fucking stupid to think that."

Tears brim in my eyes as my cheeks burn. "Why are you treating me like this?"

"Me? You're the one being a bitch. Fucking lame-ass

BDSM shit. I'm so done," he shouts. With that, he spins on his feet and rushes out the door, slamming it behind him. I stand in shock as the ice-filled towel falls to the floor, his words raking over me like a harsh wave, again and again.

A sob shakes its way out of my chest, and I collapse on the stairs by the door, letting my tears flow. They fall over my cheeks and onto the hardwood floor as I cry silently with my head against the banister.

This is what I wanted. I thought I could fix him. Just like he said, I thought I could love the good into him, but he's too broken. He will always make it difficult to love him because that's the only defense he has, and I'm the idiot who went and fell anyway.

Not even five minutes pass before there's a weak tap against the front door. Somehow, I knew he'd come back. I could just tell he wouldn't make it far before his own behavior slapped him in the face.

For a moment, I consider not opening it. He wants to be punished, so making him endure this alone and rejecting his attempt at recourse would be punishment enough. But I don't. I *can't*.

Slowly, I rise from the stairs. When I open the door, I don't say a word.

He closes the space between us, hugging his arms around my waist and burying his face in my neck as he lifts me just a few inches from the floor.

"I'm sorry," he whispers. Moisture drips down my neck, and I don't reply as he cries into our embrace, repeating those words over and over. "I'm sorry, I'm sorry, I'm sorry."

As I hold him, I realize I was wrong. Beau isn't broken. He was just never whole to begin with. He fills the cracks with other people's feelings, never considering what it costs those he loves.

It's not an excuse. It's an observation.

And it only makes me care about him more. That tenderness in my chest is growing to the point of being painful.

When he pulls away, anguish still on his face, I delicately touch his cheek.

"Why am I like this?" he cries. "I don't want to hurt you."

"I know," I whisper.

"I won't really cheat on you. I was just saying that—"

"I know."

"You're not stupid, Maggie. You're so fucking smart, and I don't understand why—"

"Shhh..." I quiet him with a kiss, our tears mingled on our lips, and we stay like that for a while with our foreheads pressed together in silence. After I feel him start to relax, I take his hand in mine. "You hold it all in for so long that you explode."

"I don't know what's wrong with me."

I stroke his hair, feeling him shiver from the adrenaline. "There's nothing wrong with you."

"Just tell me what to do," he whispers, pleading for help.

If this was still an experiment or just something casual, I'd turn him away. I'd send him home and let him handle this on his own, but our relationship has become so much more and we both know it. To even talk about cheating means what we have is serious. And I can't send him away. He needs me. I feel that need seeping through the way he looks at me. It's a Domme's job to take care of her sub, so that's exactly what I want to do.

"Come on."

I pull him up the stairs, his fingers intertwined with mine as we reach the shower. "Take your clothes off." My tone is cold and assertive because I realize that's what he needs. When Beau is desperate and afraid, he feeds off the emotions of others, so I won't give him mine. Not right now. Instead, I turn the water to cold and watch him shed his clothes until he's naked.

As he steps into the frigid water, he sucks air in through his teeth, and jerks his foot back out.

"Get in," I say in a detached command.

It's not a punishment, not the way he wants, but it's enough to wash away the regret he's feeling.

As he submerges his body in the cold water, he starts to shiver, breathing heavily, in and out, through tight lips. When he finally submits to the temperature, I watch every muscle in his body relax. With his hands on the wall, he ducks his head and lets the cold rinse away everything.

His breathing is still labored, but he's surrendering to the sensation.

After a while, when he seems at peace, I reach in and turn the dial to Off. Just like the day with the plug, I towel him off with affectionate detail while he shivers. And he lets me take care of him, patting off his arms and legs.

Then, I take him to bed, crawling under the sheets with him after removing my own clothes. It's not about sex tonight. It's about feeling the things that need to be felt, no matter how uncomfortable they are.

His body is still cold when I press mine against it.

"Why didn't you hit Sophie's boyfriend?" I ask. "You wanted to."

"She was upset. I didn't want to make her more mad at me."

"So, even if you lost your cool for a moment, you put her needs first."

"She's just a kid. She takes enough heat as it is."

I sit up, leaning on my elbow as I look down at him. "Exactly. She just needs you. Not your defense. Not your protection. Just your friendship."

He doesn't respond, the moment growing heavy as we stare into each other's eyes. The *what now* question lingers between us. After what he's admitted to me tonight, I'd be stupid to put my trust in him. Irresponsible to let my heart get attached to a serial cheater, knowing that he will only break it and tarnish all of the good feelings I have toward him if I give him the chance.

At what point does unconditional love become...conditional?

I don't know what he's thinking and I almost don't want to. The future is lingering in the distance like an ominous storm cloud, and there's nothing we can do to stop it. And with all of the red flags and signs telling me this move and separation from Beau is the smart thing to do, my heart still can't accept that decision without feeling an immense amount of regret.

Everything about our relationship is doomed, but for some reason, I'm still hanging on.

Rule #26: Nobody will boost your confidence like your closest friends.

Maggie

"Something like this would look amazing on you." Mia is holding up a red corset with black embroidery designs along the bodice.

I give her a shrug. "I like the color, but I'm not sure how a corset would fit me.

She throws it in the basket regardless. "There's only one way to find out."

When I decided I needed lingerie, for some reason, it was Mia who came to mind when looking for a shopping friend. Obviously, I'm not disclosing everything about my dating situation, but she knows that I've started seeing someone and that I'm fulfilling the Domme role she helped me discover with the kink quiz. And seeing as how she and Garrett had to hide their own relationship for a while due to them being stepsiblings, I know she understands the importance of discretion. Not that I've expressed that I have anything to hide.

I pick up a black nightie with fur around the top

before putting it back. I want to find something that makes me feel fierce—not soft and sweet. The whole point of this is to help me harness all of that dominant energy that seems to take some internal coaching to bring out.

Of course, it's also intended to drive Beau crazy, and that sweet little see-through dress is not it.

No, not Beau. Men in general. Beau and I are down to only a few more weeks, so I need to get that idea out of my head.

After his admission of guilt last night, I've finally come to terms with what we really are. A temporary fling. Something fun and experimental, that no one will ever find out about. I should be happy he told me about the cheating. It made this decision so much easier.

But something is still not settling right in my heart. Even though I know it's the smart option, it's not what I want.

Mia is throwing lingerie into her basket like she's trying to clear the racks. When she hands me one that is literally more hanger than fabric, I glare at her skeptically.

"What is that even going to cover?"

"Babe, the idea is to *not* cover," she replies with a dimpled grin.

"That's easy for you to say. You're twenty-three. I have stretch marks to hide, and let's just say...my boobs aren't where they used to be." I skim through the racks as she lets out a frustrated sounding groan. Then, without notice, she latches onto my arm and drags me toward the back of the store, where the red curtain fitting rooms wait for us.

"Get in there," she says in a cute but commanding tone.

"Excuse me?"

"Try these on so you can see just how hot and delusional you are," she snaps with a sassy head tilt. Then she throws the basket in the dressing room and slides the curtain closed around me.

"I'm not delusional," I reply through the curtain as I pick up the first corset from the pile. "I'm realistic. I can pretend I'm blind to those things, but society will never be."

"Fuck society," she barks. I smile at the sound. Mia is curvy and gorgeous. She has the confidence in her own skin I never had. While she was flaunting her perfect body to men on the internet for money, I was still covering up and hiding mine because—and I quote—*boys would get the wrong idea.*

I learned to be ashamed of my body before she was out of diapers. I never had the chance to appreciate it or know how to flaunt it proudly. I have never once seen myself as sexy, because it was drilled into my head at an early age that sexy bodies are sinful.

"Do you know why I started camming?" she asks, taking me by surprise.

Because of the money sounds like an offensive answer, so I don't respond. Although I'm sure that was a big part of it.

"No, why?"

"Because I *love* my body. I saw the way girls on my gymnastic team would whisper about me. I heard so many fucking derogatory remarks and tips about dieting and working out. It didn't matter how I felt about my own body. People honestly thought I should be unhappy with myself. They thought they were helping.

"But men liked me. Men appreciated my body. And I

don't care if that makes me sound like a slut or an attention whore. I was, and am, proud of my curves, and I was tired of hearing how I should change them. So, stop talking about yourself like that. You are beautiful, and any man who gets to touch you is very fucking lucky. And if he doesn't know it, drop him like a bad habit."

As I stand in front of the mirror in nothing but my underwear, I try to let her words penetrate the negative voices in my head that want to criticize every stupid little thing. I picture that drawing Beau did of me on his tablet.

You don't see what I see.

It's obvious I don't see what he sees because the woman in that drawing was radiant. I do my best to see the reflection in the mirror through his eyes. Then I look down at the pile of lingerie and force myself to take a deep breath. I'm completely expecting to hate myself in all of these, but I do my best to go into it with an open mind.

The corset on the top of the pile is sleek and black. It's simple, but I'm still afraid of how it's going to look as it cinches my waist and hugs my hips.

Like she said—there's only one way to find out. So I slide it around my torso, hooking the clasps in the front before spinning it around. The heart-shape edge pushes my bust up, creating cleavage like I've never had before.

Before I can even let my eyes pinpoint things like the soft pillow of skin under my arm, I take a step back and look at the woman in the mirror.

I almost don't recognize her. She's fierce, sexy, fearless. She's me. This is what Beau sees.

"Show me," Mia whines from outside the dressing area. Timidly, I peel open the curtain and watch her reaction as her eyes and mouth both pop open.

"Holy shit! Maggie, you look fucking hot."

I bite my lip as I catch another glimpse of myself in the wall of mirrors behind her.

"I've never worn anything like this before."

"Your tits look phenomenal," she replies. "Your man is going to go nuts for you."

My cheeks warm up at the thought of Beau seeing me in this. It's not even revealing and once I complete the look with some thigh-highs and garter straps, it's going to be even better.

"You want to try on more, don't you?" she asks when she reads the excitement on my face.

I nod eagerly.

"Go, go, go," she says, ushering me back behind the curtain.

The next hour flies by as I slip on every piece of lingerie, some nothing more than strings and small patches of fabric. I don't love them all, but I do love how I feel in them. By the end of the shopping trip, I have two corsets (including the first one), thongs, bras, a garter belt, fishnet stockings, and a new sense of anticipation.

When I walk out of the store, I feel as if I've shed a layer of the person I used to be, and it's not just the sex and lingerie; I'm not just changing in the bedroom. I'm finally proudly and unapologetically wearing my own skin. The way I always should have been.

"I NEED HELP," I WHISPER TO EDEN WHEN I FIND HER standing alone at the bar, reading a worn-looking paperback that I've seen make its rounds at the club, starting with Isabel, of course.

"Jesus, woman. You scared the shit out of me," she replies with a gasp as she shoves a bar napkin between the pages to save her spot.

"Sorry. I was just trying to be discreet."

"Sit," she replies, gesturing to the barstool next to her. "No one's around, and Geo's too busy flirting with that rich guy over there to hear anything you say."

Feeling a little nervous, I decide to just suck it up and take the seat. No one has to know it's Beau I'm talking about and I'm no longer worried about anyone knowing that I'm in a Domme/sub relationship. If they can all live out in the open, then so can I.

"What can I help you with? How's it going with your brat?"

Oh, he's a brat all right, but I don't tell her everything he's done lately. Plus, the brattiness she's referring to is most definitely more playful than what Beau and I have been through the past couple days.

"He wants me to...punish him."

Her eyebrows shoot up. "You're talking about real pain, aren't you?"

With a gulp, I nod. "Yes."

"Is that what you want?"

I drag in a heavy breath and close my eyes for a moment. The image of hurting Beau crosses my mind, not just torturing him with multiple orgasms or orgasm denial, but really hurting him.

"Yes," I reply, and the admission feels both freeing and heavy at the same time. Does this make me a bad person?

"Good..." she replies as if she's waiting for me to expand on this answer.

"I want to make him feel pain, real pain. I want to watch him squirm and hear him scream. Is that bad?"

She gives me a devilish grin. "Not at all."

"I just want to...see how much he can take. Then I want to...kiss it all better."

"Very good," she adds. "So, what are you waiting for?"

With wide eyes, I lean closer to her. "Eden, I have no clue what I'm doing. What if I hurt him? Like *really* hurt him."

Her shoulders melt as she rolls her eyes. "Maggie."

"What?"

"How many of the impact-play demonstrations have you sat through at the club?"

My brow furrows. "Tons, but that's not the same."

"You know the basics. You guys have a safe word. You have his safety in mind and everything is consensual. I think you're waiting for permission to do what you really want, but you have all the permission you need."

My spine is still tense as I stare at her. She's right, but I still feel as if I'm missing something.

After sipping down more of her ice water, she heaves a sigh. "Okay...I have an idea. Do you trust me?"

"Umm...what is it?" I ask, staring at her with concern.

"Let me show you. You can feel everything before you do it to him."

My eyes nearly bug out of my head. I swear to God, most days it feels like I am not cut out for this business at all.

"You want to..." I point to my own chest.

With a laugh, she squeezes my shoulder. "I'm not trying to have sex with you, Maggie. Relax. But I think if you experience it from his perspective, it will make you feel better."

"I'm nervous," I admit, which makes her smile fade.

"Good. You should be. Now, come on."

As she climbs off her barstool and heads down toward room fourteen, I start to feel nauseous. Glancing around the room, I watch for anyone that could see me heading off into one of our most intimidating rooms, with the most fearsome woman at Salacious.

I should really just be glad it's not a voyeur room because no one can watch as Madame Kink herself spanks me with God knows what.

Am I really doing this?

Using my universal key, I unlock the door and quickly slip inside before anyone can see us. Immediately, she starts pulling things off the walls as if she's done this a million times, which honestly, I wouldn't be surprised if she has.

Without a word, I start disrobing, shedding my shirt first and then my skirt, until I'm in nothing but my bra and underwear. I've seen her in far less. In fact, there's not a single friend of mine that I haven't seen naked at Salacious. I'm really the only one holding back. It makes me feel like such an outsider, but I've been doing this to myself the whole time. Letting all of those judgmental voices from my youth ruin my sex life.

When Eden turns around to find me ready, she nods approvingly. "I'll start slow, okay? We're going to use the green, yellow, red safe word system. Green is good to go. Yellow means slow down or you need a break. Red means stop. Deal?"

"Yep."

She winks before holding a hand up toward the ring and cuffs fixed to the wall. "Let's just stick to standing since we don't need the bed. Unless you change your mind about the sex..."

I can't help the heat that spreads across my cheeks.

"Oh, you're so cute when you blush. Make sure your man gets to see that sometimes. I bet he'd love it too."

Leaving her second invitation for sex behind, I step up to the cuffs. "I'm flattered," I stammer. "But I made him promise to be exclusive, so I have to be too."

She laughs as she clips one hand in the harsh metal cuff. "Oh, it's serious, then?"

"For now," I reply, letting the tender affection I feel for him warm the center of my chest at the thought.

"Just for now?"

"Well, I'm going to Phoenix to open the new club. It's just temporary, but long-distance relationships are hard, and he's young. I couldn't bear the thought of him cheating on me. So I figure it's just best to break it off."

She slumps against the wall, giving me a soft expression of concern. "Is that what you want to do?"

"Do I have a choice?"

Her brow furrows. "Have you ever put your personal life before your work, Maggie?"

"Work is my life, and I don't feel bad about that."

"I'm not saying you should feel bad, but you're trying to live two separate lives."

"So, what do I do?" I ask. It's only slightly weird that we're having this deep conversation while I'm cuffed to the wall in my underwear.

"Take him with you. Don't you think he'd go?"

I do think he would, but that's half the problem. Am I ready to have that much control over Beau's life? What if it doesn't work out? What if he really does cheat on me or starts to resent me for taking him so far from his home?

"I think he would."

"Then, you must be a good Domme. He trusts you."

"We'll see about that after this," I reply, gesturing to the whips and paddles along the wall.

"Oh yes. Let's get to it. Okay, I'll do six of each, and you need to count."

"Okay," I reply.

Chills run down my spine as she presses herself to my back, her lips next to my ear as she whispers, "Yes, Madame."

"Yes, Madame," I reply with a gulp.

"Let's get started then."

It's quiet for a while, a little too long, as I wait for her to do something. My body tenses, anticipating the first slap of the paddle. I struggle against the restraints, trying to see what she's doing.

"Deep breath," she says, and goosebumps erupt across my body. Then I force in a deep inhale. As soon as it releases from my chest, the paddle lands hard against my ass.

Holy shit.

That was worse than I expected, but I do my best to put on a brave face and keep in the scream that's begging to come out.

"Count," she barks.

"One," I mutter through clenched teeth.

"Very good."

Without warning, she delivers the second blow, and this time, I let out a squeal. My skin starts to prick with heat.

I don't think I can do this.

"Two..." I say with a hint of fear.

As she inflicts the third, fourth, fifth, and sixth, I

slowly start to lose my composure. She holds my attention by giving me little tips as the Domme in between the blows, but I struggle to focus because the pain is blinding. By the time she's done with the paddle and asks for a color, I quietly whisper, "Yellow."

"Very good," she says, gently rubbing my back.

After a few minutes, she comes back and strokes my hair as I rest my forehead against the wall. "How are you feeling?"

"I hate it," I groan, and she responds with a light chuckle.

"Do you think he'll hate it?" she asks, and I consider Beau for a moment.

"No." The word comes out without much thought. He's so desperate for punishment, and whether or not he gets off on the pain, he seems to crave it. "I think he'll love it."

"I'll do three hits with the flogger, so you can feel it, and one with the riding crop. How are you feeling now?"

I let out a moan. God, I hate pain, but if I want to do this to him, it's only fair that I feel it for myself first. Swallowing down my fear, I lift my head.

"I can take it. Give me six of each."

She laughs again. "You know you're not supposed to be giving me orders, right? But you're learning, so I'll let it slide. And three of each will be plenty."

As it turns out, three of each is *more* than enough. This pain is different and more intense each time. With each new device she uses, the blows are concentrated and sting about ten times more than the one before.

The entire time I'm thinking about him, how he would react to them. And when I'm done, Eden unfastens my cuffs and rubs something across the tender flesh of my ass and upper thighs. An hour ago, I might have been uncomfortable with her touching my butt, but right now... I don't even care.

"So, what do you think now?" she asks. We're sitting on the platform bed, both of us leaning against the headboard and sipping cold waters from the mini fridge. "Are you more or less nervous?"

I think about it for a moment. "Honestly...I'm excited."

Her brows rise as she smiles. "Good."

"I can't wait to see how he breaks."

She smiles wickedly at that response. But I can't stop thinking about what it's going to be like for him. He needs this, something to help him shatter that emotional wall he's built around himself. The pain was bad, but this could be the thing that makes him stronger.

Rule #27: Don't be too cocky. It hurts more than you think.

Beau

"Holy shit, Maggie!" I snap as she shows off her bruised ass and legs.

"It looks worse than it is," she replies.

"Liar," I say with a laugh.

"Okay, yeah. It hurt like a bitch. Are you sure you want to do this?"

"Yes, ma'am." I pull the mask down over my face before cornering her against the bathroom counter and grinding myself between her legs. She lifts it up, finding my mouth with her own. With a hum, she slides her tongue against mine.

I've been looking forward to tonight all week: the club's weekly masquerade night. It's the only opportunity for us to go in there together, without being noticed. Maggie's more nervous than last time because there's a chance my dad and the other owners will actually be there tonight.

But our plan is to go in there disguised and head

straight to a room where we can be alone. We just have to enter separately and do our best not to draw any attention.

I can't explain why I need this; I truly have no clue. I just know I want to feel the worst that Maggie can give me because the thought of her hurting me sends blood coursing straight to my cock. I've never found pain to be a turn-on before, but like everything else, her power over me pushes all the right buttons.

"Come on. Let's go," she replies. "We're gonna be late."

On the entire drive over, I can't stop smiling. After that stupid night when I lost my shit, things have been different between us. The comfort I feel from every moment I kneel for her is addicting, and as much as I know things between us will have to end, I still feel changed. Maggie just calms me. She makes it easier to be me.

So I'm going to soak up every moment I can.

After parking at the lot across the street, I slip on my mask and walk alone toward the club. She's meeting me inside, so we aren't seen entering together.

When I hear what sounds like a crowd standing outside, I pause. Getting closer, I let out a groan when I realize there is a small mob of protesters, harassing people trying to enter Salacious. They're carrying large signs with Bible verses painted across them, spouting hate at each person rushing past them.

There are two security guards helping people cross the street and putting themselves between the members and the protesters.

"Aren't you going to get rid of these assholes?" I ask

one of the guards. He looks frustrated as he opens a door to usher members through.

"We can't touch them. They'll sue the pants off this place."

When one of the jerks holding a sign gets in my face, I clench my fists, ready to throw him across the street, but before I can move, a strong hand yanks me back by the shoulder.

"Don't even think about it," the security guard bellows before shoving me toward the door and away from the protester with a death wish.

As I enter Salacious, I'm still fuming. It pisses me off that my dad puts up with this shit. If he really cared about his club and its members, he wouldn't make them have to go through shit like that.

"What's wrong?"

I don't even see Maggie approach, but as she takes my arm and steers us off to the right and away from the crowd —she can clearly tell something is up. We pause in front of the small shop, where it's quieter and less crowded, so we can talk.

"There's a fucking parade of protestors outside that everyone has to walk past to get in."

I can just make out her eyes as she rolls them. "Assholes," she mutters.

"Why can't you guys do something about them? Have that beefy bouncer pound their asses into the cement."

"Because then they'd sue. That's all they really want anyway. To trigger us enough to act on our anger, so they can take us to court and get every dime this place is worth. We're doing the best we can to avoid them for now."

My teeth clench. It's not enough. "Well, I don't work

for the club. There's no reason I can't give those fuckers exactly what they deserve."

She snatches my collar and pulls me closer. "You promised, remember?"

My shoulders slide away from my ears, remembering that day, a few weeks ago, when I gave her my word that I wouldn't engage with those jerks. "I remember. I won't."

"You better not, Beau. I'm serious."

A smile lifts one side of my mouth. "You're so cute when you're bossy."

Her hand drifts down from my collar to my junk, cupping my dick and balls in one firm grip. "Don't test me, brat."

I walk her backward until we're pressed against the glass counter of the store. "I fucking love testing you."

"I'm going to make this hurt so much," she replies in a dark, sexy tone.

"Promises, promises."

"Can I help you find anything?" An unfamiliar voice pulls us apart as I snap my attention to the woman behind the counter. She must be the shop attendant and she's staring right at me. Even though I don't know her, so she probably doesn't know me, it still feels like too much exposure. Quickly, I look down at the items in the display case.

"No thanks. Just browsing."

"Okay. Let me know if I can answer any questions for you."

"Thanks," I mutter as she walks away. When I glance over at Maggie, she's staring straight down at the case too, and at the same time, we both break out in quiet laughter.

Then my eyes start to focus on the items on display.

"Hey, I recognize that," I say softly, pointing to the black silicone plug.

Maggie laughs. "You should. I made you wear it for eight hours."

"They have one in pink," I reply, pointing to the next one.

"I was looking at this," she says, and I follow her gaze to a mannequin display. But it's what the mannequin is wearing that makes me pause. It's a black leather harness around the hips with a small black ribbed dildo attached to the front.

"What the hell do we need that for?" I ask with a laugh. "I already have a cock."

She's biting her lip as she gazes up at me. "Yeah, well, I don't."

My smile fades as my eyes dance back and forth from the strap-on to her and back. Before I have a chance to respond, she breaks out in laughter.

"Your face. Beau, relax. I'm kidding."

I don't think she is, and I'm not sure how I even want to respond to this. It's not something that ever really crossed my mind, and it's way too much to digest at the moment. So I force a smile, pinching her around the waist as we move through the rest of the store, keeping our faces down and away from the clerk.

We browse through other toys, including some vibrators I'd love to use on her and lingerie I'd give my right arm to see her in.

When we reach the display of leather collars, my eyes linger. When she keeps moving, I grab her arm to hold her in place. I read a lot about collars on the sites she gave me. What they represent to a sub and how some people express the feeling they get when they wear one for their Dom.

I know exactly why she never bought me one, and it doesn't feel good to remember that this thing between us has an expiration date, which is quickly approaching. Only a week after my dad's wedding, this thing between us is over and Maggie will be gone.

"The room is ready," she whispers while I stare down at the simple black collars. This time, when she tugs me away, I let her. I'm so distracted by the things we saw in the store, I don't register much until we're standing together in one of the rooms, and Maggie's pulling off her mask.

"You seem tense. Are you okay?" She runs her hands over my chest and loops them around my neck, pulling my mouth down to hers.

I nod. "Yeah. I'm fine."

After a quick kiss, I lift my gaze up to scan the room. The sight is a bit intimidating. Cuffs on the wall, paddles, floggers, and other painful-looking things on display. There are even restraints on the bed and a bench along the wall.

When I turn around, Maggie has removed her black silk robe, and I freeze in my tracks as I take in the sight of what she's wearing now.

"Holy fucking shit," I mutter in surprise.

Her tits are flowing out of the top of a black corset that is cinched around her waist, giving her a full hourglass figure. Below the corset, she has on black lace panties with little clips that are holding up black stockings. On her feet are black stiletto heels that I would gladly let her step on my face with. And I'd still say *thank you.*

Without a word, I sink to my knees in front of her. She bites her lip as she forces back a smile, while I just gape up at her in wonder.

This is the woman of my dreams. I never fucking knew it until now, but I literally couldn't imagine anything hotter than the sight before me at this very second.

"Maggie, you look...fucking hot."

As she steps toward me, her heels click across the floor, making my dick twitch in my pants.

"I'm glad you like it." She runs her fingers through my hair, tilting back my head before leaning in to kiss my mouth. "The panties are crotchless," she whispers against my lips, and I let out a growl in response. My cock is so hard already, and the night has only just begun.

"Now, get on the bed." Her tone is cold and commanding, and I fucking love it.

"Yes, ma'am."

Crawling to the bed, like the obedient little fuck boy I am, I do as she says when she tells me to lie on my stomach and hold still as she binds my wrists and legs to the bedposts so that I'm sprawled out and completely exposed for her.

I can't see much, but I hear the click of her heels as she crosses the room, and I give her a polite *yes, ma'am* for every bit of instruction she gives me: about how she's going to warm me up first and start slow, what she'll use on me, and how I have to count out loud with each hit.

It reminds me of that feeling you get when you're about to get on a roller coaster. My stomach is tight with anticipation, fear laced with thrill. The unknown looming ahead with both the promise of fun and the threat of danger.

I'm not an idiot—I know this is going to hurt, but pain has always enticed me. I want to feel it in the same way most people fear it. Like a fuse about to reach the dynamite, I need the pain to give me the release I'm looking for. I crave the explosion.

"Ready?" she asks.

Pressing my forehead against the mattress, I nod. "Yes, ma'am."

The first smack of the paddle is easy. It stings, but goes away quickly, leaving only a subtle throb behind.

"One," I call. There's a moment of nothing before the second blow, this one a little harder. It's like the click-click-click of the coaster as it carries me up to the peak of the ride. Torturous anticipation.

"Two," I announce.

The third smack is even harder, but I'm hyped up with confidence. I can handle this.

With each hit of the paddle, my cock stirs and my body tingles with excitement. It hurts, but it's also erotic as fuck.

By the time the dozen paddle smacks are over, I'm *overly* confident. Maybe my pain tolerance is too high for this. But I'm in my sub role, which means I can't ask her for anything, including to hit me harder.

"How are you feeling?" she asks as I hear her put the paddle down.

"Good, ma'am."

"Can I get a color?"

"A color?"

"Green, yellow, or red, Beau? Or were you not paying attention when I was giving you the rules?" I was definitely not paying attention, so it's a good thing I've read up on the traffic light safeword system.

"Oh, green. Sorry, Ma'am."

She fists my hair and pulls it back, so my head is level with her face. "Good boy."

I smile against the mattress after she releases me, a feeling of pride washing over me when I hear her pick something else up.

"This is what you wanted, wasn't it? You wanted me to punish you."

"Yes, ma'am."

"Keep that in mind. We'll do twelve this time," she replies. Moments later, a widespread pain throbs at the back of my right thigh. It aches, causing my muscles to tense along my legs and back.

"Oh, fuck!" I howl as I fight against the restraints. That was unexpected.

"I think you should thank me as you count, since I'm giving you what you wanted."

"Thank you, ma'am," I growl against the mattress.

It strikes again at my left thigh, just under my ass, and I let out a long grunt again.

"Don't forget to count."

"Two. Thank you, ma'am." I groan.

This pain is more exhausting than the sting of the paddle. I never know where it's going to hit as she swings in a figure eight pattern, striking up and then down. The wide reach of the flogger means it hurts *everywhere*. My forehead is starting to sweat, and the only thing my mind can focus on is counting, each accompanied by a *thank you, ma'am*.

After each hit, I feel her hand stroke my thighs and ass, and the physical contact is welcome, but it almost breaks me harder than the hits. It's a gentle reminder that she's here, and I'm safe—even if the pain is fucking excruciating.

When we get to twelve, I'm tempted to say yellow. At the beginning of this, I was so cocky and sure I could take it. But now, my whole body is pain personified. If my dick is still hard, I don't even know it.

"I love watching you take this pain," she says closer to my ear. I didn't even feel her climbing over me, but as she straddles my sore back, I breathe in her nearness.

The strangest thing about this is how close I feel to her as she hurts me. Like it's just her and me, the only two people in the whole world. I *want* her to hurt me, and I've never wanted that before. I was a little worried going into this that feeling her strike me would be humiliating and make me mad at her, but it's actually the opposite. I'm somehow craving more. I want to make her proud.

"You should feel how wet I am, Beau. Hurting you turns me on so much. Tell me I can ride your cock after you're done with your punishment."

My heart is hammering in my chest, and my breathing is labored, but now I know for sure, I'm ready to take the rest. If it turns her on and makes her talk to me like that, then I'll take a hundred more of her worst hits.

"Yes, ma'am. Please."

"God, I love to hear you beg. Do it again."

The plea slips out easily like it's already so natural for me to beg her. "Please touch my cock. Just a little. I'll do anything."

She smiles against my cheek, and I feel the moisture of her pussy against my back. "Give me a color."

"Green," I reply enthusiastically.

"Are you sure about that?"

"Yes, ma'am."

"Mmm..." she hums against my ear. "We'll see how you feel after the next round. But for now, you've earned this."

She snakes her hand between my body and the bed, seeking out my cock and giving it a tight stroke. The sensation is so intense, I squirm against the cuffs, chasing the pleasure before she pulls her hand out.

"I love hearing you beg so much, I want to hear you plead for another hit. I'm warning you now. These are going to hurt. We're only doing six."

"I can take it," I reply, eager to get them over with, so I can feel her on my cock again.

"Ask nicely," she says, just before she swings the crop in the air, letting me hear the whoosh.

"Please, ma'am. Please."

"As you wish."

The crop lands with intensity against my ass, and the sting is so violently concentrated, it's like a hot poker lancing my flesh. I try to speak, but the sound gets caught in my throat. The acute shock of it practically knocks me out, and I forget how to breathe.

I was so cocky a minute ago, sure that I could get through all of this without a struggle, but now the pain is on another level.

"Let me hear you count, Beau."

"One," I say with a gasp, my voice splintered.

When she smacks the other side, I scream into the mattress. It's more than pain. It's being tied up and defenseless with fear and anticipation so I am no longer connected to my own body. I'm hovering again, but instead of watching myself make another bad decision, I'm forced to watch myself suffer the consequences.

"Two," I manage to stutter.

The next smack is on my upper thigh, and it's so intense, I've convinced myself that it really is a hot poker she's stabbing into my leg.

"Beau?" she asks.

"Th-three."

"Color?"

"Green," I scream into the bed. I want to say yellow so bad, but I don't. I don't want breaks, and I refuse to show weakness. It's just a smack on my ass. Why am I acting like such a pussy about this? Why can't I just take it?

"Are you sure? We can take a break."

"Green, ma-ma'am."

The next one is harder. And it's higher, causing me to scream again. The sheets are wet—drool, sweat, or tears, I'm not sure. I just know, I'm falling apart.

"F-four," I stammer.

"You're doing so good," she says with gentle praise, and it's like warm water dripping down my spine, but the pleasantries end there because, a moment later, she lands blow number five, and everything that was holding me together, shatters like glass hitting the floor.

How can one stinging sensation on my ass feel so intense? I must be fucking weaker than I thought. In my head, I'm chanting to myself, *be like Emerson.*

Be strong like him. Be brave like him. Be dominant like him.

Every stupid thing I've done replays in my mind like highlights from the worst moments of my life. Treating Charlie like shit. Cheating. Torturing my dad by withholding contact just because I could. Judging every single person who came to this club or lived a life different than mine.

I deserve this, but bearing the brunt of my punishment isn't making me feel any better.

"Five!" I shout, squirming against the bindings. The bedsheets are clutched in my fists so tightly, my knuckles are aching.

"Color?"

"Green, ma'am," I grunt. Clearly, I'm losing it. It's obvious now, and I hate myself for the way this is affecting me. I can feel the tears streaming through my tightly-closed lids, and I can't bear the thought of her seeing me like this now. We were supposed to have sex after this, and now I'm bawling like a child.

"One more. If you really want it, beg me for it." Her tone is so cruel. I almost don't recognize her voice.

I really don't want another one. I want her to leave me alone, so I can recover without the embarrassment of her seeing me like this. But I have to take the full six. I have to.

"Please, ma'am," I say with a wheeze. "One more, please."

The last one is the worst one. On already tender flesh, it feels like a knife, and I have to bite down on the bedsheets as I drag out the longest painful sounding moan.

I don't hear her set the crop down, and I don't even feel her untie my legs, but suddenly, I can move, and I use the new mobility to try and hide my face from her. But she won't let me.

Once my hands are untied, I wipe at my tears, and she quickly brings a soft cloth to my eyes, tenderly wiping them away.

"You did so good, Beau. I'm so proud of you."

"I'm fine," I lie, turning away from her. And I wish I

could get up and move away, but my limbs are heavy, and I feel like I've just smoked a whole joint by myself. My body sinks into the mattress as her touch surrounds me. I bury my face into her neck as she holds me, stroking my back and whispering words that make me want to cry even more.

"You did so well. You're so perfect. I'm so proud of you." Over and over and over.

And I might be high or in shock, but this time, I let them sink in until I start to believe them.

Rule #28: Aftercare is not the time to make promises.

Maggie

Nothing will ever compare to this moment, his shivering body in my arms, seeking me out for comfort. I knew the pain would take him by surprise. Eden only gave me three hits with the crop and it felt like a hundred.

But I'm not going to lie...that felt good. It felt *really* good. And not because I want to hurt Beau or because I don't care about him. If anything, it made me care about him more. It was all about both of us scratching an itch we needed. It was like sex. Finding the sensation we both craved in each other. And watching him take the pain, trying to hide it and fight it, only to succumb to it, was actually sort of...beautiful.

His fight was strong. *He* was strong. But letting himself really go was even more so.

"I'll be right back," I whisper as I ease myself out from under him. His eyes are bloodshot and red-rimmed, but at least he's finally looking at me.

I don't leave him on the bed for long, seeking out the

aloe balm and ice pack from the aftercare station in the lower cupboards. When I return, I straddle his backside again, this time sitting just above his knees as I squeeze the lotion onto his bright red ass. He winces from the coolness before I gently massage his tender flesh.

He doesn't say anything as I take care of him, and when I return with a bottle of water, he takes it in his tired hands.

"Sit up," I whisper. When he does, I open the bottle and gently pour the water into his mouth. His face is still blotchy and swollen around the eyes.

Moments like these, I remember this is Emerson's son. Even if he is a grown man, this is still his kid. And I should feel bad for the things I've done to him, but I don't. Somewhere along the way, my shame turned into pride. I'm not sorry for making my friend's son my sub—I'm honored.

This man is *mine*.

After his bottle is empty, he collapses against my chest again, and I hold him in my arms, brushing back his hair and kissing his head.

"How are you feeling?" I ask.

He shrugs.

"Beau, talk to me."

"I'm fine," he mutters. And that's how I know he's not.

"You really did do so well," I tell him.

"I know, but I just...wasn't expecting that."

"The pain?" I ask.

"No. It was like I lost control. I thought I could handle it," he says in a low, lazy tone.

"You did handle it. Your reaction was normal."

"It was humiliating," he replies with a grunt.

"Even with me?" I ask, touching his face again.

When he looks up, the nothingness in his eyes is better than the guard he usually keeps up. Because at least Beau can have his guard down around me. He trusts me enough for that.

"No. You're the exception."

My heart soars, but I try not to let it show in my expression. Pulling his face closer, I let my lips graze his before I softly whisper, "You're my exception too."

"I don't want you to leave," he says as he pulls away from my kiss.

"What?"

"I'm not ready to let this go. We're still learning so much, and it would ruin everything if you just leave."

"Beau..." I'm ready to remind him it's just temporary, but that's just an excuse. Even six months is too long to be apart. Especially if we expect this to still be here when I get back. There's really only one solution, and I may be crazy bringing this up, but we're both still high on the moment, so I have no filter. "Come with me," I whisper.

He's staring at me with surprise in his eyes. "What?"

"Come to Phoenix with me. Even if it's only for six months. We can keep doing this."

"Are you serious?"

Chills run through me as the excitement sets in. This is crazy, but I don't care. I want this. Biting my lip with a big smile, I nod my head. "Yes. I'm serious."

I watch as goosebumps erupt along his skin and his face morphs into the same look of excitement. I keep waiting for him to back out, make some excuse and politely let me down. Instead, he nods. "Okay."

"Really?" I ask as I pull him closer.

"Fuck yes."

His mouth crashes against mine as he drapes his body between my legs. Our tongues tangle as we lose ourselves to the frenzy. Breathing the same air, he presses himself even closer.

He's so eager to touch me, as if he just came back to life. His fingers are in my hair and cascading down my neck. His lips follow his touch, licking his way down from my ear to my cleavage.

"Beau, fuck me," I say with a hitch in my voice.

Our bodies are impossibly close as his cock finds its way, thrusting in slowly. We let out a groan together. He lays his weight on top of me as he thrusts, my legs wrapping around his middle.

We are one, connected in every way.

"I love being inside you," he grunts into my neck, and just when I expect him to pick up speed, he pulls out. I watch in surprise as he hops off the bed, snatching me up and pulling me across the room. When we reach the large cabinet on the other side, he lifts me up like I weigh nothing, depositing me on the surface, so he can look down and watch himself sliding home again.

His cock hits that perfect spot inside me that has my body tingling with pleasure. My head hangs back as he fucks me. This is so much better than I ever expected. Better than with anyone else. The connection between us isn't something you can replicate. It can't be forced or faked. It's time we face the truth—we are the real thing.

With a hand behind my neck, he drags my face toward his, but instead of kissing me, he holds our foreheads together, and he breathes in my moans of pleasure as he thrusts.

"I can't get enough of you," he mumbles against my

mouth. "I'd do anything for you, Maggie. Anything. Whatever you want...I'll do it. I'm yours."

I'm barely hanging on, my climax creeping up, so his words are infiltrating my mind without making any sense. He must sense my approaching orgasm because he reaches between us and fiercely strokes my clit, making me scream as he pounds harder.

"Come for me, baby. Give it to me."

Squirming against his relentless assault on my clit, my body betrays me and comes so hard, I nearly levitate off the counter. With my thighs clutched tightly around his waist, I ride out my orgasm on his dick, just as he shudders inside me.

My climax lasts and lasts and lasts, wiggling against him as I ride out every second of the pleasure his body gives me. Before I can fully breathe again, his mouth is on mine in a devouring kiss. His tongue is in my mouth, owning me until I can barely remember my own name.

When we finally come down, he stays buried inside me as he pulls his mouth away. With his intoxicating gaze on my face, he whispers, "I meant what I said. I'm yours. I'll do whatever you want."

"What are you talking about?" I ask, feeling so confused as to what he's referring to. He always does what I say. It's never been a question before. But while he's still staring at me with that vulnerable, enticing gaze, I finally understand.

He's telling me what he wants...in bed. He doesn't just want me to control him. He wants me to...fuck him. The ultimate act of submission. The one thing that takes the most trust, the most vulnerability. And right now, in his post-scene haze, I shouldn't hold him to it. And I won't. This is the worst time to make commitments or promises; I won't even hold him to the Phoenix arrangement if he decides it's too soon, but I can't deny the fact that this could be amazing.

Truly making him mine, having this piece of him no one else gets. I want it more than anything.

Without committing, I just nod, pulling his head to my chest as I hold him close. That tenderness is burning brighter than ever now. Maybe this is the ultimate submission. Because he may give me his body, but what I'm giving him is even more terrifying.

But if he trusts me enough to give his body to me, then I can trust him enough to give him my heart. I hope.

Rule #29: Don't sass your Domme and expect to come.

Beau

"Done." I'm standing in the doorway to her office as she holds up a finger, gesturing to her earbud, meaning she's currently on a call. I lean against the doorjamb and wait for her to finish, wearing only a pair of jeans and no shirt. I watch as her eyes rake over my body, and I'm not the least bit surprised when she curls her finger at me in a summoning motion.

Quietly, I cross the room, standing in front of her as she silently smiles up at me. Her fingers reach out to brush my abs before glancing back at the computer screen. "I've already signed those in the portal," she says to whoever is on the other line.

Then she turns her attention back to me, running her fingers above the seam of my pants, sending shivers across my stomach. With her eyes forward, she slowly unbuttons my jeans, and my breath hitches as I wait. Tugging them down, she gets them low enough to pull out my cock, which is still mostly soft. I love when she gets me hard with her touch, taking me by surprise, so I never even see it coming.

"If the sellers need to close on the first, then we'll have to sign them by proxy. I won't get there until the third," she says.

My eyes widen when I realize she could be talking to my dad. I swallow as I stare down at her, watching her stroke my quickly growing dick. I'm studying her face for any sign that it's him or not, but it's clearly not having any effect on my arousal.

Fuck, do I want it to be him? Or do I not? On one hand, it'd be a killer act of rebellion, but on the other... thinking about my dad doesn't exactly help me get in the mood.

It's been a week since I told Maggie I'd go to Phoenix with her, and I meant it. I still really want to, but...what the fuck am I going to say to my dad? It's too suspicious to move to Phoenix at the same time she does...and for no real reason. We have to tell everyone the truth, and the clock is ticking.

She's leaving in ten days. *We're* leaving in ten days.

I've spent the last week repacking the things she's going to need, but right now, her plan is to rent out the new house while she's gone and find something furnished in Phoenix that will work short term. As for me, I don't have much to pack. I've moved so many times in the past couple years that I purged my crap down to almost nothing. I had that place with Charlie before moving in with Dash for a while and then back in with my mom. I could literally fit my belongings into a single fucking box.

It's moments like these I want to remind Maggie that I'm a loser. She has this beautiful house, a great paying job, owns a fucking company, takes care of a dog, and I'm a homeless, jobless loser.

But it's hard to think about any of that when she brings the tip of my now hard cock to her tongue, licking a torturous circle around the head. I'd enjoy this a lot more if I thought for a second, she was going to let me come at the end of it. But I know better. Edging me to the point of pain is her favorite thing to do. She'll do this shit all day, and if she's really feeling evil, she'll send me home and make me promise not to touch myself.

And I don't. I've learned my lesson. Being a brat is only fun for so long because sometimes the punishment really fucking sucks.

My ass is still sore and bruised with the proof of that fact.

I have to bite the knuckle of my middle finger to keep from groaning when she takes my cock all the way into her mouth, coating it with saliva. After pulling off, it's wet enough that she can stroke me through the rest of her call.

When I reach the verge of coming, she slowly shakes her head as she stares up at me.

Just after she hangs up with, who I assume now is the realtor in Phoenix, I'm ready to start begging.

"Please..."

"You've been so good," she whispers before licking a circle around the head again. Her free hand reaches between my legs, massaging the space between my ass and balls, making me whimper. Then, she takes my sac in her palm, pulling it down enough to cause a little pain.

"I'm so close," I cry. "Maggie, please."

"Maggie?" she asks after she pops her mouth off my throbbing cock.

Fuck. I blew it. "Ma'am, I mean. I'm sorry. Ma'am, please."

She makes a tsking sound as she stuffs my aching erection back in my tight black briefs. "I almost gave in, but I need to learn to be more strict with you. I can't be spoiling you. No matter how much I want to."

The idea of being trained and spoiled isn't so weird to me anymore. Two months ago, I would have thought this was the strangest relationship in the world—in fact, I did, but now? I get it. Everything between me and Maggie is natural, easier than a regular relationship. With other women, I had no boundaries, no rules, no consequences. I was a bratty kid alone in a candy shop, and I wreaked so much havoc.

So I don't complain *much* when she denies me my orgasm again. If she wants to keep me under control, then I'll let her.

She glances down at her watch. "We have to start getting ready. The rehearsal starts in an hour."

I slump against her desk. I've been dreading this weekend all month.

"Before you get dressed, I bought you something."

Pausing with a mix of fear and curiosity, I watch as she spins in her chair and pulls a small box out of a discreet black bag. "Open it," she says as she drops the box on the desk between us.

Getting a strange black box from your Domme is never really a good sign because you never know if it's a reward or a punishment, but I'm too curious to resist. When I peel back the top, I stare down at a silver wire-shaped dick that's hollow inside and has a ring at the end of it. "What is it?"

She lifts it from the box. "It's a cage."

"For my dick?"

A devilish grin pulls one side of her mouth up into a crooked smile. "Since I can't exactly be your Domme this weekend, I needed something to remind you that you belong to me. Hopefully, this will keep you in line, so you behave."

"I did behave," I argue.

She tilts her head to the side. "You made a fool of yourself at the engagement party, and you flirted with Charlie's cousin at the bridal shower. Tonight, you will be nothing but obedient and well behaved. The cage is there to remind you."

"I can't get hard with this on," I point out. To which she laughs.

"Sort of the point, babe."

"Are you still hard?" she asks, peering down at my cock. It's almost fully deflated, and thinking about putting this thing on isn't really helping. Why does any mention of the kinky shit she wants to do to me make me instantly aroused?

It takes me a few minutes of deep breathing and clearing my mind to get it to go away, but the minute she tries pulling my briefs down, the blood starts flowing again.

"I can't do this if you keep touching me," I say with a moan. She laughs again.

"Better figure it out."

"Well, if you let me finish..." I reply, but she gives me a harsh glare in response.

"Sounds like someone doesn't want to come today at all." It's a warning, because I'm being mouthy. And I know better, but I can't help it. She puts me in these situations, and my natural instinct is to talk back.

The first thing to go on is the ring. It sits snugly behind my balls and over my finally flaccid dick. After that, the front part slides around my shaft, locking it into place with the ring so that my balls are hanging free between the ring and the cage. It's constricting, and I'm not quite sure how I'm going to function normally with this thing on. I'm so *aware* of it.

"Everyone is going to see this thing," I complain.

"No, they won't," she replies. "Now go get dressed."

She reaches up on her tiptoes and kisses my mouth sweetly, before dangling the tiny key in my face and disappearing out of her office and heading up to her room.

"Evil fucking woman," I mumble to myself, unable to keep the grin off my face as I do.

We have to drive separately to the event, of course. Maggie is one of Charlie's bridesmaids, right next to Mia and Isabel, with Sophie as her maid of honor. My dad picked Garrett for his best man—for obvious reasons. Under any other circumstance, I think he would have chosen me, but in this case, I'm just a groomsman, and even that is awkward as fuck.

When I arrive at the venue, a beachfront gazebo not far from his house with a large green garden and plenty of seating, I spot Maggie already in conversation with Charlie and the girls by the makeshift altar. My dad spots me with a smile and waves me over.

He's by himself for now, Garrett and the other guys congregating by the entrance. Being alone with my dad makes me instantly uncomfortable—made even worse by the metal cage currently secured around my dick.

He claps a hand on my shoulder. "Glad you could make it."

I nod with a tight-lipped smile. "Of course. It's your wedding. Well...the rehearsal."

"Yeah, but I understand this is uncomfortable for you," he replies, and just like that, we've treaded over casual and right into awkward and heavy.

"I'm really past that. Seriously. I'm happy for you," I mutter, without looking him in the eye. I'm staring down at my shoes as I kick the grass with my toe.

"I'm so glad, Beau. That means a lot."

When I look up, I pray that someone, anyone, will join us to break the tension. Hell, at this point, I'm praying for a hurricane to randomly hit the California coast and wipe us all out.

"You know..." His hand is back on my shoulder, and he squeezes it in a way that lets me know he's about to say something serious.

Come on, hurricane.

"I only asked Garrett to be my best man because I knew it would be too hard for you. But you're—"

"I know, Dad," I say, cutting him off. "I know. It's fine."

He lets out a heavy breath before releasing my shoulder. "I just want you to be happy, Beau."

"I am happy," I say, and for the first time in a long time, I mean it. I just wish I could tell him that part.

"You seem it. Something's changed," he replies. "Are you seeing someone?"

"No," I answer quickly, "I just...don't bother caring so much anymore."

"About me?" he asks.

"About the things that used to piss me off. The club,

Charlie, you and Mom breaking up. Being mad was so exhausting. It's nice to just...not care anymore."

"What *do* you care about?" he asks, and I genuinely didn't see that question coming. It catches me off guard. I swallow, thinking about the things that have been taking priority in my life lately.

"The people...that make me want to be better." Well, that was a whole lot more insightful than I intended it to be.

My dad freezes, his brow furrowing as he stares at me. Just as he's about to open his mouth to respond, Charlie approaches us. "Hey, guys. The officiant is ready to get started."

He wraps an arm around her waist before kissing her temple. "Okay. We're coming."

She smiles up at him before turning to me. I notice the way her joy fades, just a little, when she looks at me. Without a word, we head toward the altar together.

It makes me wonder if Charlie ever once thought her and I would be here. Did she envision forever with me? We were together for a year and a half. A long time for a couple of twenty-year-olds. I almost want to tell her how much better off she is now.

My gaze catches on Maggie on the other side of the venue with the women, and she glances up at me for only a moment. Just one look and it clears away the fog from the talk with my dad and the look from Charlie.

Does *she* ever see us getting here?

Fuck, do I?

Not exactly. At least, not like this. I see something, though. And that's the most I've honestly ever thought about a woman I'm dating. I can see a future with her, and that sounds amazing.

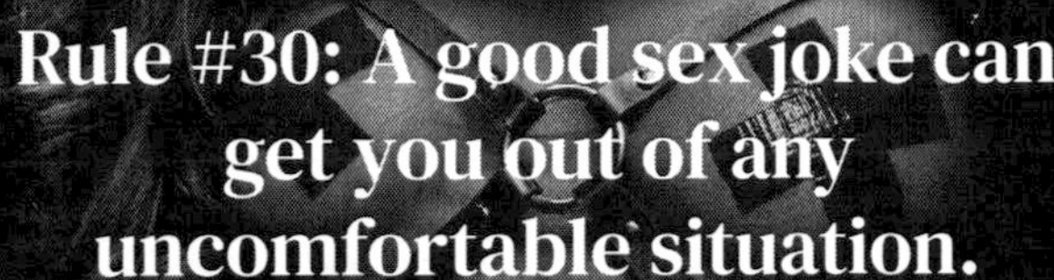

Rule #30: A good sex joke can get you out of any uncomfortable situation.

Maggie

Weddings aren't really my thing. The whole dressed in white with all of your friends in matching gowns just feels so cliché to me, but it's hard to hate it all when Charlie looks so freaking happy. I didn't take her for a traditional wedding kind of girl either, but I think a lot of her preferences changed when she met Emerson—at least that's how it appears to me.

Luckily, she's letting the bridesmaids wear black, and for that, I love her.

As the wedding planner starts arranging us into our places, I'm suddenly whisked back to about ten years in the past. This used to be me, not a wedding planner, but an event coordinator. I loved the control and all of the frantic energy that went along with it. It was like the more stressful it became, the bossier I could be, and now that makes so much sense. It's amazing I never figured this about myself sooner.

When the wedding planner places me with Drake, I

breathe a sigh of relief. Hunter is next to Isabel and Mia is with Beau. It's better this way. I'm too afraid of what I'll reveal if I have to walk down the aisle next to him. Besides, he's still wearing that contraption, and I'd hate for anything between us to make that painful for him—meaning he starts to get hard against his will.

Okay, I guess I do, sort of want to see him squirm a little with the cage on. That's why I put it on him in the first place, wasn't it? Giving Beau just a hint of torture gets me more excited than I ever expected.

When the event coordinator gets the men lined up, I immediately see the problem. Drake is too tall to stand in the middle, so she shuffles them around so he's at the end. My breath hitches as Beau is placed at my side.

I force myself not to react as his familiar scent makes its way to my nose. Just standing next to him has me feeling as if we're exposed, as if *everyone* can tell that I had his dick in my mouth an hour ago.

"Okay, we'll do one simple walk-through," the woman announces, and the entire group heads toward the staging area. Beau walks next to me in silence and we only glance up at each other once, our gazes meeting for one charged second.

We stood next to each other at parties, and it never felt as forbidden as this feels right now. And in just ten days, he's supposedly moving with me to Phoenix. What were we thinking? How on earth are we going to pull this off without letting everyone in on our secret?

I know the mature thing to do would be to just come out of hiding, but I'll be honest—the secrecy is so appealing. I love having Beau to myself. I don't want to share him or our lives with anyone. I just want to have him in my bed and in my home without the entanglements of anyone's opinions. What we have is sacred and it's ours.

Not to mention, I'm the one who will feel the judgment from others. I'm too old for him or I'm not pretty enough, so I must be manipulating him to be in this relationship. It's irrational to think that way, but I can't help it. It's exactly where my paranoid brain goes.

An hour later, we're sitting around the table in a fancy Italian restaurant. The mood is light and happy. Across from me, Isabel is looking more and more uncomfortable as she adjusts herself around the bulging swell of her belly while Hunter and Drake both dote on her constantly. Next to me, Mia is clinging to the side of Garrett's arm. On the other side, Beau sits in silence, clearly feeling uncomfortable in the current group of his father's friends.

Whenever Charlie and Emerson break into anything remotely *coupley*, Beau looks away or down at his menu. The urge to comfort him is too much, and I find myself nudging my foot against his, where no one can see.

When no one is looking at us, I glance up at him for only a second, our eyes meeting like some sort of secret language that no one else can hear or understand. With one look alone, we can say so much.

His leg brushes mine in return. Then I feel his fingers brush the back of my arm, and suddenly, I've never wanted to be home and away from people more than I do right now.

"Maggie!" a high-pitched voice calls from across the table, and I jump in shock, tearing myself away from the one person I want to be with at the moment. Charlotte is staring at me with an expectant smile, and I wait for her to clarify why she just screamed my name.

"What?" I ask.

"You're coming out with us tonight, right? For my bachelorette party!"

I immediately shake my head. "Oh, no. I'm sorry, but...I really have to get home."

"Oh, I know why she won't join us..." Mia teases with a wink.

Fuck.

"Why?" Isabel asks before looking at me.

"Maggie's got a beau," Mia replies, and my face drops, the blood draining all the way down to my feet as my skin goes cold. Next to me, Beau starts choking on his water.

"What? No!" I stammer, trying to look nearly everyone in the eyes as I defend my secret, but no one seems to be appalled. Instead, they're all smiling.

"Is that true?" Charlie asks with eagerness, leaning her elbows on the table. "Maggie's seeing someone?"

Mia nudges my shoulder. "Come on. Tell us about him."

"Does he work at the club?" Emerson asks, and I meet his scrutinizing gaze.

"No," I say, shaking my head.

"Does he *go* to the club?" Charlie asks with a wicked smile.

I shake my head again. "You don't know him. It's... nothing, really. It was...a fling." I'm stammering uncomfortably, feeling all of their eyes on me.

"Hey," Beau announces, drawing the attention of the table. I stare wide-eyed, expecting him to say something I'm not ready for. To my surprise, he loudly asks, "How can you tell the difference between a nerd and someone into BDSM?"

Wait...what?

My brow furrows as I stare at him. In fact, *everyone* is staring at him with the same look of confusion. The tension is growing uncomfortable as we collectively wait for him to explain what the hell he's talking about.

Leaning one arm on the back of my chair, he looks up at the group with a proud smile as he says, "Ask them what a Dungeon Master is."

A joke. He was telling a dirty joke...to take the attention off of me.

Garrett is the first to laugh. He claps hard as he howls in delight, the rest of the table following his lead. Everyone is cracking up and Beau looks pleased with himself as his left hand brushes my back casually before he pulls it back into his lap.

My heart is swelling as I bite my lip, wishing I could pull him into a kiss right now.

No one asks about my secret boyfriend again.

After dinner, I excuse myself to the bathroom. While I'm washing my hands, my phone buzzes on the counter with a text message.

Just a fling?

I smile, composing a response after drying my hands.

Dungeon Master?

Sophie told me that joke.

How is that cage feeling?

Uncomfortable as fuck. I'm ready to go home and take it off.

Okay. Leave before me. Go to the house and be naked by the time I get there.

Leave the cage on.

There's a long silence before his response pops up.

Yes, ma'am.

When I get back to the table, Beau is already saying his goodbyes. I take my seat, resisting the urge to follow him, not wanting to attract suspicion. After Charlie asks me again to go out with them, and I decline, I spot Emerson watching me skeptically. My skin starts to crawl as I quickly look away to avoid his curious stare. There's no way he would suspect the truth. It's just my paranoia making me think he knows.

I've done nothing to make them suspect. While they all sat around the table in their happy little couples, I kept my hands to myself, even when it killed me. But in ten days I won't have to worry about that anymore.

Thirty minutes later, I walk through the garage and into the house. The lights are off, but there is a trail of clothes from the door, and I shake my head as I pick them up, carrying them to the couch where I toss them. How many times have I told him to fold his clothes when he takes them off? For that, I'll tease him a little extra tonight.

As I walk toward the living room, I find him kneeling on the pillow, completely naked as he stares at the floor. For a moment, I pause just to stare at him like this, appreciating the sight.

I tousle his hair as I pass by him headed to my office, pulling off my own clothes and draping them casually over the large armchair before flipping on the lamp. In nothing but my underwear, I sit on my office chair and call him over.

"Beau, come here."

He crawls over, and when he does, I think again about the collar we saw at the club. Just thinking about how good it would look around his neck and how amazing it would feel to snap it on him has goosebumps erupting on my skin.

When he kneels in front of me, I wrap one hand around his neck, just imagining my collar there.

"Mine," I whisper, and he leans into my touch.

Gripping him by the throat, I guide him to his feet, so he's standing in front of me. His cock is straining against the cage, so I release his neck and move to unclasp it from his straining length.

"You were good tonight," I say as I click the cage from the ring. He winces as I pull it free. "Should I let you come?"

"Yes, ma'am," he rasps.

"Tell me why I should let you," I ask, easing the ring over his scrotum and down the length of his cock. Without it constricting the blood flow, his erection starts growing even faster.

He swallows. "Because I behaved. I told that stupid joke to stop everyone from bothering you."

"You did good," I reply, making him grunt as I stroke him in my open fist.

"I don't like the way they treat you," he says, and my hand freezes.

"What do you mean by that?"

"They made you uncomfortable. You deserve respect."

A smile creeps onto my face. Just those words coming out of his mouth have me feeling needy to touch him. My hand releases his cock and travels up his body. Pulling him down, I bring his mouth to mine. Pressing our lips together, I ease my tongue into his mouth, and he melts into the kiss. As our lips part, I whisper to him, "It means a lot to hear you say that, but they don't mean any harm. They just don't know me like you do."

His perfect blue eyes bore into mine as he kneels between my legs.

"What are you doing?" I ask.

"Can I please..." His hands drift up my thighs as he leans closer.

"Please what?" I ask, running my fingers through his wavy auburn brown hair.

"Make you come."

My breath hitches in my chest as I stare at him, forcing myself to swallow as I nod. "Yes, you can."

Without another word, he hooks both arms under my legs and tugs me to the edge of the chair. His fingers slide under the elastic of my panties, and I lift up as he drags them down my legs. Once I'm naked, he lunges, devouring my sex like a starving man. I let out a yelp as his mouth closes in on my clit, sucking hard with a hungry groan.

After a few minutes of his relentless licking, my spine begins to arch as he continues lapping at my folds.

To go from almost never getting oral from a man, and *never* getting an orgasm out of sex in general, Beau feels like a miracle. He *wants* to see my pleasure, and I don't feel the need to hide it anymore. I know these moments make him proud, to see me coming from his touch alone, but I don't know if he understands it from my perspective. He might think they are just orgasms, and it's no big deal, but he'll never truly grasp how powerful and liberating this is for me.

"Oh my God, Beau," I cry out, digging my hands into his hair to pull him closer. "More," I plead.

His deep humming grows louder, adding more vibration to my sensitive clit, using his mouth to bring me more pleasure than my body has ever known.

"Right there," I scream, but just before I reach a quick and intense orgasm, he plunges two fingers inside, curling them against my G-spot as my body spins out of control.

"Yes, yes, yes!" My voice is strained and weak as I'm sent flying into pleasure as it quakes through me from my head to my toes.

I love this man.

It's a naive thing to think when he's got his face buried between my legs, but I'm suddenly reminded that no man has ever accomplished what Beau has. It's like *he's* reminding me. As if I could forget.

He rubs his wet mouth against the inside of my thigh as I start to come down.

"Beau," I say, drawing his attention to me.

"Yes?" he responds.

"Fuck me now."

He doesn't hesitate. Taking me by surprise, he stands up in a rush, hooking his arms under my legs as he hoists me off the chair and into his arms. The next thing I know, I'm being slammed against the wall, my leg lifted high over his forearm as he plunges himself inside me.

With heavy grunts, he pounds me into the wall, and I cling to his neck for support. The pleasure of being pierced by his impressive length sends me careening toward another violent orgasm.

"Don't stop," I cry out. He answers my request by picking up the intensity of his thrusts until it feels as if we are soaring together, caught in a passionate storm of pleasure and desire. I will never have my fill of him—never.

With every movement of his body, I meet him halfway. Like we are two halves, only whole together. Like nothing made sense before we had each other, but now we know why. No one could ever fill the hole in my life the way Beau can. Together, we are complete.

Sweat drips from his brow as he keeps up his steady cadence, but before he finishes, I'm torn away from the wall and tossed onto the desk, immediately missing the way he fills me. Suddenly, he flips me, so I'm bent over the surface.

I don't even mind that he's taking charge. Technically, I told him to do this. And when he enters me from behind, I'm too blinded by how good it feels that I don't bother putting up a fight. My fingers grip the edge of my desk to keep me tethered to the surface. I press back into him, meeting his violent thrusts.

"Let me hear you," he begs, so I make my cries even louder, practically screaming against the wood of my desk.

There is nothing but ecstasy between us, our bodies meeting in perfect harmony as we come together. My walls pulse around him as he tremors inside me.

Somewhere during the recovery of my climax, I want to tell him how I feel. I want to utter those three words so he knows. This isn't an experiment to me. It's not about control or dominance. It's real. It's love. But the fear holds me back.

What if this intensity between us is different for him? What if the connection I think I feel is just about sex to him? He agreed to come to Phoenix, but that was during the high of his aftercare. At some point, we need to have a serious conversation about this, but I admit, I'm too afraid. If there is any risk of losing him, I'm not willing to take it.

Rule #31: Punishment won't clear your conscience, but an apology might.

Beau

There are a few things I expected to do on the day my ex-girlfriend marries my dad. Drink heavily. Cuss some people out. Get stoned out of my mind and post those nude photos of her I still have on my phone.

The old me might have done all three.

What I did not see coming is this—sitting outside her house, in my car, at nine in the morning, psyching myself up to go in there and say what I need to say. But it's hard to do the things you know are going to suck hard, even if you know you'll feel better afterward.

And no amount of crop smacks or vibrating butt plugs are going to punish me enough to undo everything I've done. How's that for self-reflection? Who even am I anymore?

Since I can't put this shit off anymore, I jump out of the car and march up the walkway to her house. Before shoving my hands in my pockets, I quickly rap on the front door. I hear voices on the other side, and a moment later, it opens to reveal Sophie with a face full of makeup.

"What are you doing here?" she snaps playfully.

"Thanks, kid. I'm here to talk to your sister. Is she around?"

She squints at me. "Of course, she is. But you're aware it's her wedding day, right?" she asks like an adorable little guard dog.

With a smile, I reply, "I come in peace."

"All right, fine," she says, slowly opening the door. "She's in the living room, getting her hair done."

"Thanks," I mutter as I slide past. "You look pretty, by the way," I add, catching the blushing smile on her face before I disappear into the house.

The living room is buzzing with excitement, and I almost back out. I might be here to do a good thing, but I'm a little worried at the moment that I'm still bringing down the mood by just being here.

Everyone quiets down as my presence is made known with the clearing of my throat. Charlie's mom, Gwen, is the first to talk.

"Hey, Beau...everything okay?"

"Yep," I reply with a tense smile. "I just...came to talk to Charlie for a second. If that's okay."

"Now?" Charlie asks. Like Sophie, her face is already covered in makeup. There's a woman standing behind her, curling her hair with a round iron. She gives it a quick douse of spray before backing away.

"It'll only take a minute," I reply.

Her face softens before she turns to her mother. "We'll step out back for a second. Is that okay?"

"Of course," Gwen answers. "We'll go have another round of mimosas in the kitchen." I smile at the women as they pass by me. Then I follow Charlie out to the back patio.

Standing by the pool, I gaze out at the pool house where she used to live. I can't imagine she goes in there much anymore since she moved in with my dad, but that pool house still holds a lot of memories for me. Trying to get her back when I was at my lowest. Watching her asshole of a dad berate her and Sophie when he found out about the club. And seeing my dad come to the rescue, remembering how everything changed for me that day.

"What's going on?" Charlie asks, crossing her arms skeptically. She immediately takes the defense, and I only have myself to blame for that. The sooner I get this over with, the better.

"Charlie, I'm here to apologize."

Her arms relax. "What? Why?"

"Because I was an asshole to you. A terrible boyfriend. I used you, didn't treat you the way you deserved to be treated. I, uh..."

Fuck, this is hard.

Without looking her in the eye, I quickly mutter the worst part. "I cheated on you...twice."

When I finally look up at her, she's staring back in confusion. Brow furrowed and head tilted, she looks completely lost.

"Why are you doing this now?" she asks.

"Because...you're getting married today, and before you do...I want everything between us to be forgiven, forgotten, and in the past."

"Beau..." She says my name with a sigh, letting her crossed arms drop. "I've already forgiven you. I'm not mad..."

"But I never apologized."

"Well, I appreciate it, but you didn't have to do this—"

"Yes, I did," I say with conviction. "I should have done it a year ago. Fuck, I never should have done any of that crap in the first place, but to be honest...if me being a dick to you...brought you two together, then I'm not mad about that."

She gives me a confused squint.

"What I mean is...I'm sorry, but I'm glad..."

"You're glad you were a terrible boyfriend?"

"No," I stammer, "I'm glad you found him. I'm glad you're marrying my dad, I guess. Fuck, this is weird."

I let out an exasperated sigh, and a moment later, Charlie lets out a lighthearted laugh that turns into a heavy cackle. It softens the hard, uncomfortable exterior I was wearing when I walked into this conversation.

"This *is* weird, but I think it's really sweet that you came here to say this to me. You've changed, Beau. I hope you find as much happiness as I have. I really do."

"Thanks," I reply, my mind instantly going to Maggie.

"And thanks for sticking up for Sophie that night at the ice cream shop. I'm sorry you got hurt, but I bet it felt good to shake that little asshole up first."

I smile as I rub the new scar above my brow. "Yeah, it did." It felt even better to get the punch I deserved, but I don't tell her that part.

"You wanna stay for mimosas?" she asks with an awkward smile.

Shaking my head, I shove my hands back in my pockets. "Tempting, but no. I gotta get going. I'll...uh, see you later."

"See you later," she replies with a wave.

I leave through the side gate instead of facing the swarm of women inside. Once I'm in my car, I let out the heavy breath I was holding. It almost feels like the first real deep breath I've taken in a long time. I feel free.

I GET READY FOR THE WEDDING AT MAGGIE'S HOUSE to avoid my mother. She has nothing nice to say about today, and I'm tired of hearing about it. Standing in the kitchen, I scroll through my phone in my uncomfortable tux as I wait for Maggie to come down. We have to drive separately—again—but I don't want to get there that much earlier than her.

When I hear her heels click against the stairs, I head toward the sound, staring down at my phone as I wander mindlessly through her house.

"I'm ready," she announces, and I look up from my phone, frozen in place, gaping at her. She's in a tight, black strapless gown. It hugs her hips and shows off the fullness of her tits. Instinctively, I lick my lips, biting the lower one as I think about peeling that dress off her later.

"God damn," I mutter as I close the distance between us, wrapping my hands around her waist. She lets out a sweet giggle as my lips find her neck and I bury my face against her soft skin. She smells like perfume and shampoo.

"Don't you dare mess up my hair or makeup," she warns, without sounding all that serious.

"Oh, I want to mess it up." My hands clench the satin as I drag it up her legs, but before I can reach beneath and find her ass, she shoves me away.

"Behave," she scolds.

"I don't want to," I whine, reaching for her again.

Taking her hand in mine, I run my thumb over her

knuckles, pressing my lips to each one. Seeing her dressed up like this is doing things to me. Like making me feel like her boyfriend instead of her sub. Something territorial creeps up my spine when I think about other men seeing her in this dress.

"I was thinking..." she says, biting her red-stained lip.

"Whatever you want, I'll do it," I reply.

"We could go to the club after the wedding."

My eyes lift up to her face. "It's not Masquerade night."

"I know," she replies. "But I could sneak you in."

"And do what?" I ask, a little afraid she has plans to punish me again—not that I don't enjoy the pain element of our relationship. I'd just rather not end the evening in tears and an emotional breakdown.

When she doesn't answer, I study her expression, trying to understand. As she smiles, pulling me closer, realization dawns.

"You want to fuck me."

I swallow, my cheeks starting to heat up.

"If you're not ready—"

"I'm ready," I say, cutting her off.

Her eyes light up with excitement. "Really?"

With our gazes locked, I nod. My hands travel across her jaw, grasping her by the back of the neck as I pull her mouth to mine. She clings to my arms as I take her lips in a fierce kiss. I can feel her lipstick smearing, and I love it. My cock twitches in my pants, so I grind it against her tight dress.

When we finally come up for air, panting together, she smiles. "I told you not to mess up my makeup."

"I never listen."

Pulling back, she laughs when she sees my lipstick-covered mouth. Then, she drags me upstairs and wipes my face clean with a soft wet cloth. The whole time I don't say a word, even as I watch her fix her own, meticulously reapplying the red color. It's sexy as fuck.

Call it reckless, but I am excited for tonight. Maybe I should think this through more, but at the end of the day, I trust her, and I'm more than willing to throw caution to the wind and put everything in her hands. I can't get over how good that feels, letting her have control. Especially since she wants it. And not just during sex, but for my entire future.

The pressure of having to decide what to do with my life has just evaporated. All of that weight is just gone. Putting my trust in her is liberating.

"Ready?" she asks as she throws her red lipstick in her tiny purse.

With a deep sigh, I nod. "Lead the way."

Rule #32: When an opportunity arises, don't miss it.

Maggie

The entire day is a blur. The moment we get to the venue, it's a frenzy of *stand here, where's the bouquet, fix my makeup, is the officiant ready, someone get Charlie a shot.* I'm too busy running around being helpful that I hardly get a free moment to admire how handsome Beau looks in that tux.

I also notice for the first time just how much he looks like Emerson, especially as they wear the same tux and stand next to each other. That's something I'm going to have to unpack later. I've certainly never been attracted to Emerson. He's handsome, sure. But I never wanted to drag him into the bathroom and drop down to my knees for him like I do his son.

Geez, Maggie. Did you seriously just think that?

We're standing in the staging area as Beau saunters toward me to stand by my side, giving me one of those private looks before putting out his elbow for me to wrap my arm through. The moment I can touch him, I'm comfortable.

I never understood the idea of *your person* until now. That one other person who can make you feel comfortable, at peace, loved, and appreciated all at the same time. This whole time I thought my friends were crazy, but now I get it. Charlie is Emerson's person.

Beau is mine.

It feels as if we blink and we're suddenly walking down the aisle to the string quartet playing at the back of the garden. After Hunter and Isabel make their way down, Beau and I walk casually together. People smile at us from their seats, and I do my best to keep myself composed. Oh, if they only knew.

When I catch Charlie's cousin gazing a little too long at Beau, I clutch him a little closer, *mine* echoing in my mind. If I could scream it right here, I would. Is it stupid to imagine that someday I might be able to? If Beau even wants me for that long. And if I get over the fear of telling his father about us.

When we reach the front, we separate. He takes his place across the aisle, wedged between Garrett and Hunter. As the officiant starts the wedding, going through the sappy quotes and all that, I silently start to wonder how the hell we got here. How is the man I've been sleeping with for the past two months Emerson's bratty, self-centered, ill-tempered son?

As Emerson and Charlie say their vows, my eyes find Beau's and I smile as I realize he's already looking at me. Our gazes meet for a long, charged glance. Everyone's looking at the bride and groom anyway.

So for one quiet moment, I let myself exist in his eyes. And I'm struck by how much it feels like *us*, even if we're around everyone else. My house has become our private place, the only space I feel genuinely happy anymore, and to find that same feeling exists, when I can freely stare into his eyes, is like heaven.

When I feel another pair of eyes on me, I glance next to him to see Hunter watching me, subtle curiosity on his face, and I quickly glance away, my blood pressure starting to spike. God, did he pick up on any of that? It's weird for me to be staring at Beau that way.

I quickly swallow down my paranoia and make a mental note to avoid talking to Hunter alone anytime soon.

"I now pronounce you husband and wife," the officiant announces as the small crowd cheers. "You may now kiss your bride."

This time, I do look at Beau, because no matter how much he's grown to accept this awkward situation, watching your dad kiss your ex still has to feel weird. His eyes widen as he stares back at me because his dad isn't just kissing his ex...he's fully making out with her in front of everyone. I let out a little laugh, trying to hide it behind my bouquet.

Beside me, Mia makes a loud *woo hoo* yell, and the crowd's cheers grow louder.

AFTER THE CEREMONY, WE HEAD TO EMERSON'S house, where he is hosting a small reception in the backyard. Beau is standing with Sophie near the edge of the party, while I'm stuck in conversation with Ronan Kade, the club's wealthiest member, Garrett, Mia, and Fitz. Nearly every regular and major club employee is here tonight, which means the club is in the hands of our floor managers and most trustworthy staff. It's an all hands-on deck sort of evening, which makes me nervous about smuggling the groom's son in unnoticed.

My plan is to bring him in the back, since there are no security guards at the employee entrance. From there, we'll go straight to the room. I personally blocked out room twenty-three tonight, a VIP room on the second floor that I think will be the most comfortable for Beau. It has a low platform bed with bedding nicer than what's in my house. There's something masculine about the room that I love. Dark gray bedding, a mix of sandalwood and sage oils in the diffuser, special lubricants specifically for first-timers, and the best aftercare station our club has to offer. It's been unofficially donned the *first-timers'* room, and from what I can tell, that's what it's been used for. Not first-timers in the sense of losing your virginity—as far as I know, that honor belongs only to Mia. But first-timers for anything, really, but mostly, first time trying anal.

And this is the only reason I'm doing this at the club and not at home. I have more confidence at the club. I feel more comfortable there, and tonight, I need all the comfort and confidence I can get. I'm not worried about hurting him. I trust him to communicate with me enough before that happens.

I *am* worried about losing him. This could very well be too much for him. This could be the wake-up call, the moment he realizes we've passed his kink-tolerance threshold, and pegging is just a little *too* far out of the realm of vanilla, where he's spent all of his life.

Watching him from across the yard, I think back to the man I knew before the quiz and the app threw him into my life. I try to mentally put myself in those memories, when I thought he was nothing but a brat—and not the kinky kind. I vividly remember the day Emerson came crying to me because his son stopped taking his calls after he found out his dad owned a kink club. I recall how much I...despised Beau for that. But I didn't even know him.

Beau said it himself—we judge what we don't understand. And I didn't understand Beau. Hell, he didn't even understand himself, which would explain why he came to me so broken and self-deprecating. He hated himself because he didn't understand his submissive side.

Look at how far he's come. How is this even the same person? I wasn't even aware a person's mind could open as much as Beau's has. Even now as he slings an arm around Charlie's little sister, a smile as wide as the sun on his face—and twice as bright—I shove away the misguided memories of the man I thought I knew. And I let that tender feeling, which I know now was the slowly building roots of what would become love, fill every crevice of my body, swimming through my veins as tears fill my eyes.

I love him *so much*, and I hate that I can't tell a soul.

But none of that matters because, soon, he'll be with me in Phoenix, and no one here will matter anymore. We can stay there, not just for six months. If he's really happy with me there, then we have a chance to make a real life. The forever kind.

"They shouldn't be bothering you guys anymore," Fitz says, and something about it draws my attention back to the company I'm standing with.

"What?" I ask.

Garrett smiles. "Fitz took care of those protestor

assholes. Found enough dirt on them to scare them away for now."

"Dirt on them?"

"Yeah. Even the tiniest smudge on their record can be used against them when they think they have the legal upper hand," Fitz elaborates.

"That won't backfire, will it?" I ask.

He shakes his head with smug confidence. "Like I said, you should be good for a while."

"Thank God," Mia replies, hugging closer to Garrett's side.

I see the concern etched on Garrett's face. Having his loved one passing them every day, knowing they could hurt her, fueled only by the ignorant hatred in their hearts, is terrifying. No one should have to feel that way. If it was Beau...I know how I'd feel.

"Thank you for that, Fitz. Really..."

"I'm happy to help," he replies with a warm, lopsided grin. Such a handsome man. Makes me wonder how often he loosens that tie of his.

Then, of course, I have Ronan next to me, who loosens his tie every chance he gets. Even at fifty-six, he shows no signs of slowing down. I have no doubt that man will be at the club, still drawing a crowd of ladies until the day he dies. And it has nothing to do with the money. The confidence and swagger he exudes, with every subtle movement, is the world's most potent aphrodisiac.

Suddenly, the sound of metal gently clinking against glass draws our attention to the newly married couple standing by the quartet of musicians stationed near the patio. White string lights illuminate the party overhead, giving the large yard a romantic ambiance.

"If you don't mind, I'd like to lead my new wife in our

first dance," Emerson says, holding her hand in his and gently pressing his lips to her knuckles. She beams up at him with love and adoration shining in her eyes. The crowd softly applauds, and the quartet begins to play an instrumental rendition of "Can't Help Falling in Love."

We watch in silence as they hold each other impossibly close on the makeshift dance floor, staring into each other's eyes as they slowly turn to the music.

When I search for Beau across the yard, I can't find him. He probably ditched this part, and I wouldn't blame him. A man can only take so much.

After the song ends, other couples begin to join the bride and groom. First, Mia and Garrett. Then, Isabel and Drake, him towering over her so much, it almost looks funny to see them together, especially with that round basketball of a belly she's sporting in that tight dress. I can tell by the way he's holding her that he's literally taking some of her weight off her feet, and she beams up at him before pulling his mouth down to hers for a loving kiss. I thought it would be weird to see them together after knowing her as Hunter's wife for so long, but it's not. It's as if they were in a poly relationship this whole time and nothing's changed.

"Can I have this dance?" a deep familiar voice rumbles in my ear from behind me.

I spin around and stare at Beau with his perfectly coiffed locks, disarming bright blue eyes and skin tone so perfectly sun-kissed, it looks good enough to taste.

"I think that's a little risky, don't you?"

He's wearing a smug, tight-lipped smile as he shakes his head. "Dancing with you is not a risk. Letting a beautiful woman stand alone at the edge of a dance floor, that's a risk. Letting people think you're available...also a risk.

Wasting this opportunity, risk. None of which I'm willing to take."

He curves his fingers around my wrist, gently pulling me toward the dance floor. Quietly, so no one can hear, he whispers, "Ma'am, please don't make me beg."

Finally, to avoid causing a scene, I relent, letting him take me to the middle of the floor and wrapping my arms around his neck. I feel too vulnerable, too exposed. But his warm eyes settle me, and I stare into them, finding that comfort of *us* I enjoyed earlier. Then, I simply drown out the party around us and let him lead me into a gentle turn around the dance floor.

"But I do enjoy you begging," I whisper.

"I know you do," he replies with a smile. For the most part, we look friendly. We aren't kissing like Drake and Isabel. We aren't pressed hard against each other like Charlie and Emerson, and Beau's hand is nowhere near my ass like Garrett's is to Mia's.

"Is it bad that I want to drag you inside and bury my face up that dress of yours?"

With wide eyes, I quickly glance around to be sure no one heard us. Luckily, everyone is too engrossed in their own partners to care about the filthy words coming from Beau's mouth.

"Stop it," I reply, but he only grins. My resolve starts to crumble when he looks at me like that. "Meet me in the office in ten minutes," I reply, just as the song ends. He laughs to himself as we resume our charade of just being barely friends. With polite smiles, we part, each going in different directions. Then I watch as he heads toward the house. When one of the caterers passes by with a tray of champagne flutes, I quickly snatch one and throw it back in a rush.

I have a nice little buzz as I go in the same path Beau took, only a few minutes ago. The only people inside are the caterers and a few people in line for the bathroom. Quickly, I evade them as I make my way to Emerson's office on the other side of the house.

Am I being reckless and stupid...and maybe a bit petty too? Yes. Very much so. But I don't care. If Beau wants to rebel against his father on his wedding day...and he'd like to make me come in the process, then I approve of this plan.

Tiptoeing into the dark recesses of the house, I feel a hand drag me to the secluded corner of the office. Beau presses me against the wall as his mouth finds mine, warm lips sending a wave of heat to my core.

Silently, he drops to his knees in front of me. When he lifts my dress, it feels so dirty, only making me want it more. He places his lips against my thigh, gently parting my legs as he trails his mouth upward.

He begins peppering kisses all over my belly, my hips, my thighs. My legs grow weak from the heat of his mouth. When he licks his way through my sex and across my clit, I clap a hand over my mouth to keep from crying out.

He doesn't stop. His lips suck eagerly at the sensitive spot, and I clutch a handful of his hair as I press his face there for more pressure.

The closer he brings my body to climax, the more I fight against it. His mouth is like heaven, and the way he's sucking at my clit is sending me in a pleasure spiral. Using his fingers, he spreads me wide, licking his way inside me before replacing his tongue with two fingers, which he thrusts hard against my G-spot.

This is so wrong, and I should really feel bad about letting Beau tongue-fuck me in his dad's office, but the wrongness is what drives me to the crest of my pleasure. I ride his face for as long as I can before I finally lose control. Clutching my thighs around his head, I come with a silent shudder, my body trembling with the need to express how good this feels.

I'm left gasping against the wall as I stare down at Beau who wipes his mouth with a devious smile on his face.

"We're going to hell for that," I whisper.

"Worth it," he replies as he stands. "Now when I think about my dad's wedding, I'm going to remember the delicious taste of your cunt."

Biting my lip, I blush. With a smile, he leans down to kiss me.

"When are we getting out of here?" he whispers.

"It'd be too suspicious if we leave before they cut the cake."

"After cake, then."

"We have to stop by my house for my bag," I say.

"I figured. What if I leave my car at your house and we take yours to the club?"

I smile. I think I'll miss all of these logistics of a secret relationship. In Phoenix, there will be no sneaking in or separate cars. And as nice as that will be, I think I'll miss the excitement of having to keep it a secret. So we might as well enjoy it one last time.

"Yeah, that's a good plan."

"I'm excited," he mutters cautiously. I feel as if I can read something more in his words as if he's saying he's excited but really means something else. Something...*more.*

"I'm excited too," I reply.

But what I really mean is *I really fucking love you.*

Rule #33: Show him who he belongs to.

Maggie

"Wear that dress to the club," he says from my garage as I climb out of my car.

"Wear that tux," I reply.

I left the reception about fifteen minutes after him, both of us anxious to get out of there once the cake was cut. The party seemed to just be getting started, and they all faked their enthusiasm for me to stay, but everyone knows I'm the last one to prolong the party, so they didn't put up much of a fight. We hugged, I wished them congratulations again, and they sent me on my way.

The moment Beau and I are finally alone in my garage feels like the first time I've actually taken a full breath all day. I practically fall into his arms, inhaling his kiss like it's oxygen. He smells and tastes like him, and the familiarity of it is like a drug to me now.

He moans into our kiss and I feel him starting to harden behind his pants.

"I should have put you in another cage today," I tease

him, running my hand down to his crotch and cupping his erection.

"Would have been wildly unfair with you in that dress. I've been hiding this boner all day."

I laugh at his language—the dirty vernacular of a twenty-two-year-old man, something I find endearing now and not as annoying as I once did.

"Well, then we should hurry to the club because you're not coming until I fuck you."

He shivers deep in his bones, and I can feel it. I bite my lip as I grin up at him. "God, I love it when you talk like that." Reaching down, he squeezes my ass hard, using it as leverage to grind himself against me.

Pulling away feels almost impossible, but I really do need to get him to the club. And I'm too excited to let this opportunity pass us by. In a frenzy, I run upstairs to pack the bag I readied for tonight with the necessary...supplies. Then, we're out the door, both of us buzzing with excitement, our hands clasped over the center console as I drive.

When we pass the front of the club, I'm relieved to see not a protester in sight. All of the stars are aligned tonight, and I'm feeling on top of the world. We park behind the club in the employee parking area, and my hands are trembling with nerves.

I'm sneaking Emerson's son into the club.

I mean, obviously, he's been here before, but this is the first time he's walking in with me and no mask. If someone sees us, the jig is up, but maybe that's okay now. Maybe that's why we're taking the risk. Just to be caught.

Using my key, I open the brightly lit back entrance, and check to make sure no one is in the employee hall that runs behind the club. It's empty, since everyone is at the wedding anyway. Taking Beau's hand, I lead him in behind me. There's a service stairwell to the right that leads up to the VIP floor. Again, I check to make sure it's empty before dragging him up.

Thankfully, the VIP area is dark, but it's also...open play. Which might be a little much for Beau, something I forgot to warn him about. Too late now. As I lead him quickly through the large room, the moaning and cries of pleasure barely resonate over the music playing, I turn around to find him staring wide-eyed at the display around him.

Room twenty-three is just on the other side of the room, and I'm fast with my keycard, dragging him in and closing the door before he can gawk anymore. Once we're inside, I stare at him, gauging his reaction.

"Holy shit," he mutters quietly.

"Sorry, I should have warned you about that," I reply.

"Yeah...you probably should have." He's wearing a contemplative expression, and I see the wheels turning in his head.

"What are you thinking about?"

"Is that how it's going to be at the new club?" he asks. My spine tenses as I ready my answer, afraid this may turn into a discussion I don't want to have right now.

"Is that a problem?" I ask carefully.

He thinks some more. "No. It's just...a big leap for me."

"I understand. But everything we do is safe, sane, and consensual. You know that."

With a nod, he replies, "Yeah."

Something about it still feels unfinished, and I can tell there's worry gnawing at him, so I gently pull him deeper into the room. Placing my bag on the chair, I reach for him. Eagerly, he steps into my arms, leaning down to take my mouth in a sensual kiss.

I didn't have much of a plan for tonight. I figured we'd get to this point and let our bodies lead the way, so when he reaches for the bottom of my dress, I let him. Our hands take over from here, peeling back each layer as the electricity between us grows hotter. Anticipation and excitement color every emotion flowing through me. And when he peels down my panties, kneeling before me, I let out a small whimper of appreciation.

He looks so good on his knees for me.

"Maggie..." he says, drawing my attention to his face.

"What is it?" I ask, afraid he's about to back out.

"Before we do this, I just need to say something."

I wait expectantly as he runs his hands along the backs of my legs, drawing me closer.

The words that finally come out of his mouth have my knees buckling.

"I'm not perfect, by any means. But I want to be...for you. I've never been in love before," he says, and my breath hitches. "I thought I was. But it never felt like this. I never wanted to be better for anyone. Maggie...my heart is yours. Do whatever you want with it."

He leaves those words hanging between us, and I swear my heart has not beat for a full minute. Reaching down, I wrap my hands around the back of his head, curling myself around him as he clings to my legs.

Gently into our embrace, I whisper, "To me, you are perfect. You have my heart, too." His hands around my legs squeeze a little tighter. We are so melted into one, I almost don't want to part.

But I'm too excited for what comes next. Before I come all the way down from this high, I pull his mouth away with a tight grip of his hair. He winces as I mutter, "Now get on the bed."

He swallows nervously before I release him and watch him crawl onto the mattress. He sits in the middle, as if he's waiting for me to bind him to the bedposts. He knows that's not what's about to happen, but old habits die hard, I guess.

Before I join him, I grab the bag I left on the chair. Bringing it over to the bed, I set it down and stare at him gently. "We're going to use *mercy* again, okay? But I'm serious, Beau. I need to trust that you'll use it if you need it."

"I will," he replies.

After a deep breath, I put myself in the right mindset. I'm his Domme, and his body is *mine*. To possess. To command.

First, I pull out the black blindfold and let it hang from my index finger. "On all fours," I command, and instinctively, he falls in line, turning until he's perched on his hands and knees. Coming up behind him, I place the blindfold across his eyes and tie it around the back. Then, I pull him upright and kiss his mouth, taking the lead on the kiss by pressing my tongue into his mouth until I feel him surrender control to me.

Breaking the kiss, I run my hand along his spine, pressing him back down to all fours. Once there, I shove a little harder between his shoulder blades until he's down on his elbows, leaving his ass in the air for me.

"Lower," I say, forcing him even farther into the mattress. "Show me how much you want this," I tease him.

Leaning back, I lick my lips as I appreciate how amazingly hot his body is in this bent position. The delicious curve of his ass and the way this position exposes each delicious muscle in his back, elongated across the bed, is so good I wish I could stare at him like this forever. He is totally at my will, and it's actually really beautiful. His body is large and strong and could easily overpower me, but he's not. He's submitting, willfully.

"Say it, Beau. Tell me how bad you want this." I rub my hips across his backside, teasing him as I feel his hips shift toward me.

"I want this, ma'am. I want it so bad."

Heat tingles its way down to my core at his dirty pleas.

Next, I take out the belt I bought here at the club and the small black attachment that I did *a lot* of research on to be sure it was the right size to start with for a beginner. I let him hear me putting it on, belting it around my waist and thighs until it's tight. I notice the way he quivers with every sound.

I realize, in this moment, this isn't just about Beau submitting or doing something that other *men* could judge him for, but it's also about him experiencing something new and scary. Which is something I can definitely relate to. So as much as I want to be his Domme in this moment, I also want to treat him the way I wish I was treated in my most vulnerable moments.

Before attaching the black silicone to the strap, I lean over him and glide my hand down his abs. "Are you hard for me?" I whisper. When my hand meets the steel length hanging between his legs, I get my answer. He lets out a groan as I stroke him.

"Oh...yes, you are. Don't worry...I'm wet too." At that, he moans into the bed linens.

"The good news is that I'm going to let you come, and

I want you to do it while I fuck you. So when I say so, I want you to stroke yourself."

"Yes, ma'am," he grunts with his face buried.

Finally, I let go of his cock and rise from the bed. The lube is in a bottle on the shelves next to the bed. Standing with the strap-on wrapped around my hips, I catch a glimpse of my reflection. Like that first time I took control, I wear this power like a second skin. It doesn't feel foreign anymore—it feels like the real me.

After choosing one of the lubes off the shelf, I bring it over and uncap the lid, so he can hear what I'm doing. Then I drizzle a little right over the tight round muscle of his backside. When I run my thumb over the hole, he clenches. But I keep up the gentle massaging, waiting for him to relax. I'm in no rush. We have all the time in the world tonight.

My other hand softly runs along his lower back, and I watch as his shoulders start to ease further into the bed. His face is still buried between his forearms, but he's looking more and more at peace, even as I'm slowly breaching his tight hole.

When he does finally relax, letting me prep him properly with a second finger, I notice subtle moans emitting from his chest. His body begins to open up for me and it's something that both chokes me up and turns me on. Of all the things I want to do to him, this moment has to be the biggest. All of the desire and need I've felt for three months has led to this. I've already punished him, humiliated him, tortured him, controlled him, but now, this is the big one. Now I get to own him.

My body is on fire with anticipation, my legs clenching together, delicately rubbing as I get warmer and warmer with arousal. My breathing is becoming labored as I work him more and more, his sounds provoking my own.

When he's finally ready, I drizzle more lube onto the dildo, after securing it in place. Then, I appreciate him again. How erotic and amazing he looks in his position. Open and ready. Vulnerable and *mine*. He wouldn't do this for anyone else. No one on earth could have gotten Beau Grant to this point, but I did.

A sense of pride washes over me.

"Remind me...who do you belong to?" I ask.

His chest moves faster with his breaths as he turns his head in my direction. Unable to see me through the blindfold and looking preciously at my mercy, he proclaims, "I'm yours."

"Good boy," I reply, stroking his ass. With those words, I ease my way in, inch by delicate inch.

Watching the way his body takes everything I'm giving him is something that will stay etched in my memory forever. The trembles, gasps, moans, and finally, the shudder of pleasure when I reach farther inside him.

"Oh fuck..." He grunts into the bed, unable to keep himself quiet.

"That's okay, baby. I want you to be loud. Make as much noise as you want. Yell, scream, cuss. Give it all to me."

He doesn't respond, only gasps into the sandalwood-scented air.

"How are you?" I ask once I'm seated in as far as I can go. My hips are pressed against his backside.

"Good," he mumbles with a shaky breath. "Fuck, it's different, but good. Just go slow. Please, ma'am."

"Since you asked nicely," I reply playfully. Not that

he had to ask nicely. I wouldn't fuck him hard right away even if he hadn't said please. I'm not a monster.

Slowly, I ease out just a few inches before sliding back in. It's a foreign feeling to be the one doing the fucking, but a vigorous feeling of carnal energy runs through me too. I want to let loose on him, go wild and rough, demanding pleasure from his body. I want to take him to his breaking point without going over.

But we're not there yet, so I go easy.

After a while, I sense his hips moving back to meet my thrusts, so I pick up a little speed, pulling out more each time, striking at different angles. His groans get louder, and his language gets more colorful, and I know the exact moment I find his prostate.

"Jesus, fuck me. God, Maggie...ugh." I'm not sure if that was a prayer or a request for more, but I take it as the latter. Grabbing on tight to his hips, I slam into him harder. Seeing the way his body reacts to the powerful thrusts makes my clit pulse and my thighs grow even more moist.

"You're taking me so well, Beau. You should see how good this looks," I say in a raspy tone.

This is the hottest thing I've ever seen in my entire life. With each thrust, the strap between my legs rubs against my clit, making me more and more keyed in and turned on. As much as I want to tear this thing off and ride his cock until I come, I am more interested in seeing this part through first, because it's so, *so* good.

"Are you ready to come yet?" I ask.

"Yes, please," he groans.

"Not yet," I reply. "Don't you even think about touching your dick until I say so. Do *not* come yet. Understand?"

"Yes, ma'am," he replies tightly with a dirty sounding grunt.

Squeezing his hips tighter, I finally let go of everything else. Every thought in my head is gone until it's just him and me and this insane, intense, unbelievable moment. All of the power he's handed me is burning like a fire between us. The only sound in the room is of the pounding of our bodies and the noises it's eliciting with each thrust. Cries of pleasure and need and desire. He's desperate to touch himself, I know it. But I want to wait until the very last minute.

The strap is rubbing my clit raw, and I'm probably going just as insane as he is. But I don't stop. I drive him to the very edge, where pleasure becomes pain. Want turns to need. Where our bodies don't feel like our bodies anymore but just vessels of raw, filthy, breathtaking sex.

Once we've reached that point, and I notice his fists are turning white with the way they've clutched the bedsheets, I let him have what he wants. "Do it, Beau. Stroke yourself. Come all over this bed and show me how much you love this."

The sound that comes out of him at that moment is part cry, part moan, and part animalistic roar. It's enough to make me let out a high-pitched cry of my own, and as I watch him fist his aching cock, reflected in the mirror on the wall, I keep up my thrusting.

I'm so turned on I can barely breathe, but I don't quite expect my own orgasm to slam into me with the force that it does. I use his body for leverage, grinding into him as every nerve ending in my body lights up with pleasure.

Then I watch with satisfaction as he paints the bed white, spraying his pleasure where I can see it. I'm buried to the hilt as he comes, and I love the way his body shudders against mine.

"Good boy," I mumble again and again. "So, *so* good."

It feels like it takes us both forever to catch our breaths. When he's finally emptied himself of his cum, I gently ease out of him, working to remove the strap-on in a rush. Once it's unfastened, I toss it to the floor and focus on him. My hands run along the sweat-soaked planes of his back and the erratic cadence of his breathing.

"Talk to me. How are you?"

"So fucking good," he replies breathlessly. He's blindfolded, but he still turns his head toward me.

"Lie down."

Without another word, he collapses against the mattress, clearly not caring that he landed in his own mess. Spreading out behind him, I rub his back and kiss his shoulder. When he turns toward me, I gently remove his blindfold and pull him into my arms, loving the way the quick pulse in his neck feels against my chest.

His hand slides down my body, reaching between my legs to find me wet and sensitive. "What about you?" he asks, and I smile at the thought of him being so focused on my pleasure.

"I'm good," I reply, kissing his head. "I came."

"You did?" he asks, looking up at me.

A chuckle escapes my lips. "Yeah, it surprised me too, but that was so hot, it didn't take much."

He groans, burying his face in my neck. Apparently, the thought of me being turned on never fails to have an effect on him.

We stay like that for a while, just breathing in the silence and caressing each other. Finally, I get out of bed and use the sink to wash my hands and gather him some things. I glance back to find him watching me with an adoring expression. With a blush in my cheeks, I carry a cold bottle of water and the prepackaged fruit tray from the small fridge over to the bed, climbing up to sit next to him.

"Do I really need grapes right now?" he says with a scowl as he stares at the plastic container I'm holding in front of him. I can't help but laugh as I pop one into his mouth.

"Just let me take care of you, please. You know I like this part," I say as I unscrew the cap to an ice-cold water bottle.

With a smug grin, he lets me pamper him for a while, forcing cheese and fruit while he sips the water. We don't say much, letting the delicate moment linger for a while. It seems with everything we do, we grow closer. Silently, I drag a warm, wet washcloth across his body, enjoying each inch of his perfect skin.

"So?" I ask, finally.

"So what?" he asks, looking both drunk and in a euphoric daze as he leans against the headboard with his eyes barely open.

"So, how did you feel about that?" I'm dying to know that he's not ready to run for the hills, but I don't want to come off as desperate.

"Maggie." He states my name very clearly as his eyes open. "I just came so hard I think that comforter will have to be trashed. And I've never made so much noise during sex before. I think you might have actually fucked me senseless. So how did I feel about that? I'd say pretty fucking good."

With a laugh, I feed him another grape. "Okay, good."

"Were you worried?" he asks.

"A little."

"Why?"

With a shrug, I shake my head.

"Did you think if I didn't like that then I would...leave you?"

As my gaze travels back up to his face, I bite my lower lip. I guess it was a little crazy, wasn't it? He simply shakes his head at me.

When he holds out a slice of strawberry, I open my mouth, letting him rest it on my tongue. Then he drags me toward him, planting a kiss on my mouth before nudging me down to lie in his arms.

"You're crazy," he whispers against my head. "And I'm not going anywhere."

With a sigh, I close my eyes as relief swims through me. We're still us.

Somehow, I drift off without meaning to. I guess I didn't realize how exhausting this whole thing was for me. But the comfort of his arms and the peace of having him to myself is enough to send me into a deep, restful sleep.

Rule #34: It's good to see things from another perspective.

Beau

My body is wrecked in the best way possible. I'm sore, of course, but it's like the soreness after her punishment. I wear it like a badge of honor. The pain is well worth it, and I would gladly endure it again.

Staring down at her while she sleeps, I replay the last few hours and then the last few weeks. How the fuck did I get here? I can't believe I just did that. If you told me two months ago I'd be getting railed by *anyone*, let alone my dad's co-worker at Salacious on his wedding day, I'd tell you that you smoked a bad batch.

But it wasn't really a slow transition to this point, was it? It was more like a deep dive, and I'm clearly the one who jumped. And I gotta say...I'm pretty happy with where I've landed. Having the best sex of my life, giving my partner the best sex of hers, all while being a good fucking boyfriend for once. Maggie makes it all so easy, though.

After a few minutes, I start to grow restless. She's so

peaceful and I don't want to wake her up. But I also can't just sit in this room either. It's two in the morning, and I've never been more awake.

A bad idea brews in my mind. I'm definitely going to be punished for this, but I can't help myself. I mean...all of the people I know that my dad works with are probably home asleep or drunk off their asses, definitely not here. No one would recognize me. So why can't I peek around a little bit?

Quietly pulling my clothes back on, skipping the jacket, so I'm only in the now wrinkled white shirt and black pants, I quickly roll up the sleeves, button it halfway and tuck in the messy bottom. It's good enough to blend in, I hope.

I have to take Maggie's keycard to get back into the room, something else I'll surely get punished for. Once I have it, I delicately open the door and slide out into the dark hallway, without waking her. I'm a dead man when she wakes up, so I guess it's a good thing I love punishment so much.

I am a brat, after all. Aren't I?

I don't even know anymore. I've been so good lately, and I sort of miss the way it felt that night to purposefully disobey her. I loved the thrill of it. Maybe my penance will be unlimited orgasms again. Can't complain too much about that.

The hallway only has three doors down one side, ours being the first. Instead of heading back toward the service stairwell that she brought me up, I head in the other direction. It brings me out into a bar area on the second floor. There's a bartender and a few people mingling around private tables.

They're not openly screwing like they were behind

that black curtain. That was a real eye-opener, and I surprised myself a little with how much I didn't hate it. I reserved so much judgment for this place, but now that I see it, I feel differently.

Hell, maybe I have been corrupted. Maybe this is just how you feel when you've been brainwashed by deviants, as my mother would put it, but you don't see me complaining. Sort of feels like the opposite of brainwashing, if you ask me.

The second-floor bar has a balcony that overlooks the bottom floor, which I recognize from our nights here during the masquerade parties. It's not as dark tonight and no one is wearing masks. They're just meandering through the space, and no one looks ashamed or embarrassed that they're all here to be kinky, to have sex and to get off.

There's another bar down there that Maggie would never let me get close to, probably because we would be recognized, but again...the bartender doesn't look familiar to me, so I shouldn't look familiar to him. I also notice another doorway on the other side, this one guarded by a red rope and a mean-looking bouncer.

Deciding to try my luck, I walk down the stairs and across the large space, glancing up at the stage where a DJ is playing and women are dancing in cages. Once I reach the red rope, I duck my head a little, still paranoid that someone is going to point out that the owner's son has been smuggled into the club and should definitely not be here. Instead, he simply nods his head and lifts the barrier, gesturing for me to enter.

With a curt nod in his direction, I step into the darkness. The first thing I notice is the windows. Large, floor-to-ceiling glass that opens into what appears to be separate rooms on either side.

A smile curls one half of my mouth as I realize there is a couple watching another couple fucking behind the glass. It's erotic and intimate and strangely...wonderful. Each room is filled, people hovering around to watch, but not in a gross way. In an appreciative way.

I don't linger too long near any window. I just pass by the voyeurs as I make my way down the dark space. Once I reach the end, I can't fight the grin on my face. This is the coolest fucking thing I've ever seen. But it's not for me. Not right now. I'd rather come back with Maggie, where we can enjoy it together.

I hope we have something like this at our club.

When that thought makes its way through my head, I pause. *Our* club. How long have I been seeing it that way? What would she think about that? Instinct tells me she'd love it. The idea of running our own club, having it be *our* thing gives me more excitement than anything has in a very long time.

My whole life I've been searching for purpose, and nothing ever felt as good as this idea does. I almost want to go wake her up right now to tell her. But I'm not done exploring yet.

After coming out of the hallway, I meander my way through every corner of the club, seeing as much as I'm allowed. Counting rooms and checking out the store again.

My dad did this. Not alone, of course, but he built this place, and I spent so long hating him for it when I should have been proud of him. I *am* proud of him. Now I almost want people to figure out who I am. Know that I'm Emerson Grant's son.

When I finally make my way back to the bar, I must be wearing my emotions all over my face because the large man seated at the corner laughs when I sit down three seats away from him.

"First time?" he asks.

When I glance up, I stutter out my answer. "Um...not really. But sort of."

He laughs. "Okay, then."

After a moment, I recognize him as the bouncer who stopped me from handing that protester's ass to him on the second masquerade night I attended. I guess I owe him for that. If I had ended up in jail, I wouldn't have experienced the mind-bending power of the riding crop.

"So...what do you think?" he asks, taking a sip of his clear drink. Just then a bartender walks up to take my order and I politely ask for a Jack and Coke.

Turning toward the bouncer, I answer him, "I think it's great." Then for some reason, I feel the need to spill my secrets to a complete stranger. "I used to not think it was so great. In fact, I used to think it was terrible. But that was before I ever actually came here."

He looks almost offended before I clarify, "I was an idiot. I only saw what I wanted to see and that was enough to feed all of my anger. But then I met someone. And she opened my eyes, so I see things very differently now."

The bartender places my drink on the table and I slip him some cash to avoid having to hand over my credit card with my name on it. The bouncer nods at me before finishing his own drink and asking for another.

"You know...so did I, once," he says, and that surprises me. "But people change. Minds change. Courses change. Don't beat yourself up."

I smile as I sip my drink. "I'm not. Not anymore."

Suddenly, a hand latches onto my arm and spins me until I'm facing a shocked and angry-looking Maggie. "What are you doing?" she mutters quietly.

"Having a drink," I reply, looking back at the man at the end of the bar. He smiles up at us before taking another sip.

"Hey, Maggie," he says before looking forward.

"Hi, Hank," she replies politely before tugging on my arm. "Come on. We have to go."

"Am I in trouble?" I ask with a mischievous grin.

"So much trouble," she whispers. As we make our way back upstairs, her eyes are traveling back and forth around the club, waiting to see someone call her out, but no one moves.

"Did you have a nice little tour of the club," she asks in a teasing tone before we reach our room.

"I did," I reply as I hand her the keycard.

"Good." As she reaches for the door, I grab her hand, drawing her attention to me.

"I was thinking...about Phoenix."

Her mouth falls open as she stares up at me. She almost looks worried. "Okay..."

"What if I help you?" I ask, and her face instantly changes from worry to confusion. Brows pinched inward and mouth closed.

"Help me?"

"Run the club."

There's a moment of hesitation before she continues, "You want to help me run the club?"

Her fingers are intertwined with mine, and I tug her closer so she has to stare up at me. "Yes, I do. I want to be a part of it. Help you manage everything and come up with new ideas...and test stuff." I add in that last part with a wink, which makes her roll her eyes.

"But...if we do that, then we have to tell everyone about us."

"I'm ready," I reply, placing a soft kiss on her pouty lips.

She looks less than sure about that, still struggling to admit whether she wants people to know about us.

"Okay," she mumbles against my mouth, and I pull back, staring down at her in surprise.

"Really?"

"Yeah." She nods. "Fuck it. Let's tell them. And then immediately move away so they can't kill us."

With a laugh, I wrap my arms around her waist, hoisting her off the floor. She squeals into my neck, and I feel on top of the world. Setting her back down, I drag her lips to mine, kissing her hard and tasting the moan on her lips as our bodies slam against the closed door.

"Let's go home," I mutter into our kiss.

"You really think I'm gonna let you come after that little escape you just pulled?"

"That's okay. I came so hard tonight, I don't think I need to do it again for a week."

She laughs as she unlocks the door. We quickly gather our things and lock up as she intertwines her fingers with mine. I guess she's not worried about being seen together anymore.

As we reach the back door of the club, I hold open the door for her, letting her walk in front of me into the dimly lit parking lot behind the building.

My eyes are on her as I let the door close behind me, so as we cross the space toward her car, I almost don't see the man approaching. At first, I think he's just another employee, but when I glance up and see the seething look on his face as he approaches us, the hairs on the back of my neck rise in alarm. Instinctively, I grab Maggie and place her behind me.

"What's up, man?" I ask, figuring we're probably about to get mugged.

Maggie gasps behind me when she notices him walking toward us.

"I know who you are," he says in a low growl, stopping just a couple feet away.

"Oh yeah? Well, I don't know you," I reply.

He lets out an evil sounding snicker, coming a little closer into the light. It's then that I place his face. This is the guy who holds the signs out front protesting and probably the same guy who painted the hell out of my car.

I hold up my hands in surrender, even though I'm not too worried. He's harmless. Much older than me, he's probably in his late fifties, withered away and scrawny in oversized clothes and a worn pair of shoes. Just a misguided asshole who's spent too long in his own ways that he won't see anything outside of the tiny box he lives in.

Still, the sooner I get Maggie in her car and safe from this confrontation, the better. We're already too far across the lot to try and make it back to the club now anyway.

"Listen, we don't want any trouble. We're just heading home," I say. Then he steps in front of me, blocking my path.

"Let's go back inside," she mumbles quietly, pulling me by the arm.

"Mr. Grant, right?" the man says, and my brow furrows. Something about bringing my last name into it makes my spine straighten. "I know what you two were doing in there. In that house of sin. You make me sick," he snarls with a face full of hatred. "I raised my kids in this town, and now I have grandkids and I won't stand by while heathens like you tarnish our home with your filth."

"Beau, come on," Maggie says with a shake in her voice, pulling me away, but my feet are glued in place.

I know she's afraid I'll fight with him, but that's not what I want at all. I just want him to understand. I want him to stop giving so much hate to my family, when this place offers anything but.

"You don't know what you're talking about," I argue, placing a hand out toward the man, hoping he'll realize I mean him no harm. "I know you think it's sinful and bad, but the people in that building are happy and safe and free. No one is threatening your family, just because of one private club."

"The perverts will come far and wide, and soon, this city will be overrun by pedophiles and deviants...all because of *your* father."

When he mentions my dad, the blood drains from my face. "Leave my dad out of this. He's a good man."

"A good man? He's a sinner, worse than the rest of them. He's the one responsible for this abomination, and I want him to know what it's like." He's wearing a hate-filled sneer that chills me to the bone as he inches closer with one hand held behind his back. This man *hates* me, and he doesn't even know me.

"Beau, *now*," Maggie says in a fierce command, and instinct is telling me to listen to her, but I'm not all that great at making good decisions. In my defense, I don't want to hurt this guy. Even after he's threatened my family, my girlfriend, her business, and me. The problem is that I see a man who looks a little too familiar, like

Sophie's boyfriend at the ice cream shop. I see a piece of myself.

And maybe I should have listened to Maggie's commands. Instead, I feel the need to reach this stranger, almost like penance for my sins. Be the bigger man and all that.

"I promise it's not as bad as you think," I say as I step toward him with both hands raised in front of my chest.

"I want Emerson Grant to know what it's like when someone else puts his kids in danger."

He takes a threatening step toward me, just as I mutter in confusion, "Huh?"

The man pounces on me in a quick violent motion. I hear Maggie scream before I feel any pain or register that blood is dripping over my eyes. My hand feels heavy as I reach it up toward my head, where a sharp pain is starting to throb. Then, the sky starts to tumble with the ground before I land on the pavement. Another pain strikes my shoulder and then my stomach.

I'm lying there, defenseless and confused, as Maggie screams and the pain continues. The problem is that I figured this guy was harmless. I figured if he wanted a fight, I could take him. I thought I was tough. I thought I was invincible.

But just before it all goes black, I spot the crowbar in his hands.

Rule #35: Don't back down from a fight!

Maggie

My hands are still covered in blood as I sit on the cement curb behind the club, watching the blue and red lights of the ambulance as they speed away, headed toward the hospital. Beside me, Hank rubs my back with his jacket draped over my shoulders, trying to keep me warm—as if my shivering is because I'm cold.

No. I'm shivering because my body is in shock. Because I'm replaying the last horrifying fifteen minutes of watching that monster bash the man I love over the head before running away like a coward. Then holding Beau in my arms as I screamed for help, too shaken to call 9-1-1 myself.

They dragged me away from him, threw him on the stretcher and took off before I could do anything. It all happened so fast.

"Someone's called the owner already," Hank says while he rubs my back.

The owner. *Emerson.*

My eyes widen as I stare at him in shock. Oh, God. *Emerson.*

"It's okay, Maggie. They told him you're okay. You don't have to do anything. But maybe we should call your friend's family or something?"

He doesn't know that was Beau. No one knows.

I'm responsible for this. I brought him here. I put him in danger. I'm the reason he's...

"Is...Emerson coming...here?" I stutter.

"I think so," he replies.

"I need to go to the hospital," I say in a rush as I rise from the curb. "Now."

"You shouldn't drive," he argues, but I simply toss his jacket down as I grab my keys out of my purse.

"I have to." As I storm off toward my car, my hands still shaking and covered in blood, Hank grabs me hard by the arms, putting his face in front of mine as he shakes me.

"Oh, I don't think so. Go inside and wash up. When you get back, I'll drive you to the hospital. Understand?"

My mind is in a fog, and the distance between me and Beau starts to ache. As much as I want to shove this two-hundred-pound linebacker out of the way and get to my man, he's right. I can't drive. I couldn't even handle getting the key in the ignition in this state. With a passive nod, I quickly rush back to the club to do as he said.

The frigid water in the bathroom helps to shake away the shock. So I douse a little on my face once my hands are clean. Then reality sinks in like a penetrating wind. Two harsh, debilitating facts that make it hard to pull air into my lungs.

One: I don't know if Beau is okay. I keep telling myself he is, but even that feels like a convenient lie. From the second he hit the ground, he was unconscious, and there was *so* much blood. My bones begin to shake with this realization. He *has to be* okay. He just has to. I can't live—

The second thing I know to be true has bile rising in my throat. I have to call Emerson. He thinks his son is safe at home in his bed. Instead, he was with *me* and that's why he's hurt.

Shoving the cruel thoughts away, I spring into action and race out of the club. The bright lights of the police cars outside illuminate the dark parking lot, projecting blue and red on the buildings around us, so it feels like I'm walking into an actual nightmare. I see Hank behind the wheel of my car and I sprint toward him and jump into the passenger seat.

"Please drive fast," I beg as I clip my seat belt into place.

And he does. He zips through the city and along the shore until he reaches St. Francis by the harbor.

"Just take my car back to the club," I tell him, but he only shakes his head. Parking in a spot near the emergency room entrance, he quickly pulls my keys out and hands them to me.

"You keep your car. I'm grabbing a lift."

When I look up at him, those kind, dark brown eyes gazing back at me, I want to hug him.

"Thank you," I mumble, hoping it conveys just how much I appreciate this. Someone who stepped up when no one else I knew was around. If it had been any other night, I would have been swarmed by friends at the club to help me, but I had to bring Beau tonight.

Shame engulfs me as I realize just how wrongly I've treated him this whole time. Keeping him like a dirty secret, too ashamed to own up to *my own* actions. Too afraid of facing confrontation and proudly proclaiming Beau as mine, like I should have so many times. I smuggled him into the club and put him in danger.

"Go, go," Hank urges me on after I climb out of my car and swiftly lock it. Maybe later, when I'm not so fucked up by shock and shame, I'll express just how much I appreciate him. But for now, I need to go to Beau.

When I bolt into the emergency room, I practically slam into the reception desk. The nurse stares up at me in a panic as I start spouting off demands like I'm her boss.

"The ambulance brought my friend in. He was hit over the head. I need to know how he is. I need to go up there *now*."

"Ma'am," she replies in a voice a little too sweet for how harshly I'm speaking to her.

"Don't *ma'am* me!" I shout.

"You'll have to calm down. Give me your friend's name."

"Beau Grant," I say loudly. My head turns toward the full waiting room as I realize everyone heard me. Of course, I don't know anyone here, but still. It's strange to say his name out loud like that without cowering in embarrassment.

The nurse types on her computer for a moment, and I'm trying to read her face like we're in a poker game. When her eyes widen just slightly, I almost snatch the computer off the desk to see for myself.

"He's been admitted. They still have him in the ER. Have a seat, and I'll have them check in with you. Are you family?"

"He's mine," I snap in a rush, and her brow furrows in response.

"He's *yours?*"

"My boyfriend," I add, squaring my shoulders as I proudly proclaim it.

"Okay, well, if he has any family to contact, you might want to do that. As soon as we have any answers, we'll let you know. Please have a seat."

Have a seat? Impossible.

Leaning forward, I'm about ready to drop to my knees and beg. For him, I would. I'd crawl all the way across the California coastline if I had to. I just can't...have a seat.

"Please," I whisper, hoping she has the slightest amount of pity in her tonight. "Can you at least tell me if he's okay?"

I fold my hands together, leaning hard against the counter. "Please." The word is heavy on my tongue. "I'm desperate. If you've ever loved anyone, I'm begging you to please, *please* help me."

Her head tilts to the side as she lets out a sigh.

"They brought him in fifteen minutes ago. There's no update in the system, but I'll poke around to see what I can find out, but no promises." She adds that last part with a sternness as if to indicate she's not showing me *too* much mercy.

"Thank you," I reply, grabbing her hand on the counter and giving it a tight squeeze.

"You're welcome." As she gets up from the desk, I stand there like a statue.

I know what I need to do now, but there's not a bone in my body that wants to pick up my phone.

Shakily, I walk outside, standing just near the doors as I hold my phone in my hands. As I think about Beau, I try to muster all of the courage and strength he's shown me in the last two months. The things he's had to face about himself and the guts it took to make those changes within himself were far scarier than what I'm about to do.

So, with that, I pull up Emerson's contact.

My hands are trembling as I hit the phone icon to call, and when it starts ringing, I want to throw up. All of the tears held back by shock have finally burst through the dam and start flowing across my face. By the time I hear his tired and scared sounding voice on the line, I'm sobbing.

"Maggie," he says with concern, "I heard what happened. I'm on my way. Are you all right?"

I suck in a wet, shaky breath. He's on his way to the club. He thinks I'm there.

"You need to come to the hospital," I mutter as I wipe at my wet face.

"Hospital? Are you hurt?"

"No...I'm okay," I whisper.

"They told me you were with someone. Is he okay? Are you at the hospital now?"

"Emerson." I say his name to stop his questions. To prepare myself for the next, horrifying words that are about to come out of my mouth. There is no going back from this. There is no way for me to remove the terror I'm about to cause him. It's easily the cruelest, most evil thing I'm about to do, to tell one of my closest friends that his son is hurt and his life is at risk. It's deeply harrowing and god-awful.

"Maggie, what's going on?"

I sob again, the pain in my chest unbearable.

"It's Beau," I mumble, my heart starting to splinter with those two words.

There's silence on the line before he replies in a cold, lifeless response. "What about Beau?"

"I was with Beau. That's who..."

"*My* Beau? Is he okay?" The frantic fear in his voice sends chills down my spine.

"They brought him in. I'm waiting for answers. I just..."

"Tell me he's okay," he demands, and I cry a little louder into the receiver. "Why was he there? Was he... What the fuck, Maggie?"

"I'm sorry," I whisper, crying into my hand as I wish all of this away.

"I'm on my way," he barks in a cold, emotionless declaration. A moment later, the line goes dead, and I stare down at my phone. I want to scream. I want to hurl my phone into the street for *all* of the things out of my control. My helpless, futile hands clutch hard to the unbreakable device as I squeeze it so hard, my bones start to ache.

I want to march into that hospital and find Beau, hold him, demand they fix him. But I can't. I'm useless to him now. Two months ago, Beau meant almost nothing to me. I was *fine* without him. I felt useful. I had a purpose. Now...I'm sitting on the concrete of a hospital parking lot, feeling entirely worthless, because he's in there and there's not a damn thing I can do to help him. My entire identity has been completely altered *by him*, all of my worth reprogrammed *for him*.

And as long as he walks out of that hospital, I won't regret a thing.

But if he doesn't...

"Ma'am," a soft voice says, pulling me from my pathetic mess of tears as I cry into this stupid satin gown I'm still wearing. When I look up into the eyes of the reception desk nurse, I take in a hopeful breath. I stand in a rush, waiting for her to speak.

For some reason, I'm bracing myself for her to utter the words that will end me. Just a simple, "I'm sorry," out of her mouth, and I will shatter into a million pieces.

"They just put him in a triage room."

I force in a breath. "What does that mean?"

"It means they've finished with him, and they're monitoring him."

"That's a good sign," I say excitedly as my spine straightens, and I look to her for confirmation.

She shrugs. "He is alive."

My breath shudders out of me. "When can I see him?"

"Not for a while. Not until he gets into a room, but I'll send the doctor out to check in with you, okay?"

I grab her hand, clutching to it as I force a sad smile on my face. "Thank you."

She doesn't respond. Only nods before pulling away from my grip and heading back inside. As I sit alone on the cement bench outside, my mind is mostly blank. Makeup is smeared across my face, and I realize it will be morning soon. My bones ache with exhaustion, but I can't sleep. Not anytime soon.

When I see a familiar man crossing the parking lot toward me, his walk rushed and enraged, I sit up and brace myself.

As he charges up to meet me, I stand, squaring my shoulders and preparing myself for what's about to happen.

"How is he?"

"They put him in a triage room. I think that's a good sign, but I'm still waiting for an update."

"Tell me exactly what happened."

"We were coming out through the back and the guy just ambushed us. He had...a crowbar."

Emerson winces, clearly mustering his courage to hear this.

"I want to kill that motherfucker," he grits through his clenched teeth.

"We have security footage. We can give it to the police and get an ID on this guy. He's one of the protestors—"

"I know it's one of the protestors," he snaps, cutting me off. He's so tense and unhinged, nothing like the calm and collected man I've known for over a decade.

He stares at me with wild, tired-looking eyes, before running his hands through his hair and pacing in a circle before coming back toward me.

I ready myself for what I know is coming next.

"So let me get this straight. You and Beau were at the club *together*?"

Solemnly, I nod.

"*What the fuck*, Maggie?" he barks. I flinch from the anger in his voice. "My *son*?"

"It just happened, Emerson—"

He holds up a hand to stop me. "No. You crossed a line and you know it. You don't fuck your friend's kid."

"He's not a kid," I reply calmly, feeling my blood starting to boil. I can respect that Emerson is going through a lot as a father, fearing for his child's life, but he's wrong. And I'm itching to tell him.

"You fucking knew him as a kid," he growls, and my brow furrows.

"It's not like that and you know it."

"No, I don't know it," he says, his voice an octave

lower than normal from his fierce temper. "Turns out I don't know you at all."

"That was meant to hurt me, and that's unfair," I reply, standing tall.

"Unfair? You think that was unfair? You brought my son to our club. You've been..." He lets out a frustrated sound. "Behind my back?"

All of the will and discipline to bite my tongue is gone now as the need to fight back builds inside me. "You're being such a hypocrite!"

He looks up stunned before I continue.

"You *fucked* his ex girlfriend. You just married her! You pretend like Beau is so delicate and breakable, but you didn't hesitate to stomp all over his heart a year ago."

"Maggie," he says in a warning. But I'm too riled up now. Maybe it's exhaustion and adrenaline, but I can't stop. He started it.

"I don't blame you for what happened with Charlie, but don't stand there and act like you have his best interests at heart and I don't."

"I would do anything for my son, and you know it."

"Everyone knows it!" I shout. "But what are you trying to protect him from, Emerson? Me? The club? Do you really think your son would be hurt by kink? Are you really that much of a fraud?"

"You wouldn't understand," he growls as he turns away.

"Why? Because I'm not a parent? Well, I love him. I would do anything for him too. And I'm sorry if that's hard for you to understand."

He's fuming silently as he stares out at the dark parking lot.

"If you're not ashamed of it, then why did you keep it a secret?" he mutters quietly.

"I'm not ashamed of anything," I reply with my fists clenched.

"Then why lie to me?" he bellows.

"Because you're Emerson *fucking* Grant and what you say goes. You want to control *everything* and I knew that you'd try to control us. Well, you might be Charlotte's Dom, but you're not mine."

My teeth are clenched as I glare at him, heat and anger mixed with adrenaline, creating a lethal combination of *no fucks given*. I'm tired of tiptoeing. I'm tired of asking for permission or forgiveness. The days of making myself as small and as quiet as possible are over.

When he doesn't respond to my outrage, I take it as a good sign.

"It was on your app, you know? That's how we found each other. Beau took the quiz—"

"He did?" His head snaps up with a look of shock.

Slowly, I nod. His gaze is practically burning a hole through me as I watch him work out the rest. Beau's sex life is none of Emerson's business, but it doesn't take a genius to piece together that puzzle. Now that everyone and their mother knows my quiz results, it's not hard to imagine what his were if it paired us together.

"Is it serious? Between you two?" he asks with a soft gaze on my face.

"Yes," I reply proudly. Then, because it feels like a rip the bandage off kind of night, I add in the kicker. "He's coming with me to Phoenix...permanently."

I might as well have knocked all the air out of him. His nostrils flare as he forces a swallow and looks away. Then I watch with pity as he crumbles, dropping his ass to the curb with his back to me. I have to swallow the emotion building like needles in my throat.

"Emerson?" I ask after a few minutes.

"I just need a minute, Maggie. It's a lot to absorb."

"I understand," I whisper.

We sit in silence for a while, and after almost an hour goes by, I start to feel like I might die of impatience. Just as I'm about to walk back in and ask for more answers, a man in scrubs finds us outside.

"You're here for the man with the head wound?" he asks.

Emerson and I jump up at the same time and stare at him with matching hopeful expressions on our faces.

"Yes, how is he?"

"He's stable," he says, and we both let out heavy sighs. "He's awake and in recovery. He suffered a severe concussion and will need to stay for at least the next twenty-four hours for observation. They're taking him back now for a CT scan to rule out a TBI."

"Can we see him?" I ask.

"I can let one of you back there for now. We can move him upstairs in the morning, where he'll be allowed to have visitors."

My head snaps toward Emerson and my heart falls because I know he's going to fight me on this. My heart is *aching* to see Beau, just to rid my mind of that awful vision of him bleeding on the concrete. I need to replace that image with one of him lying peacefully in a bed, awake and alive.

"Would you mind giving us a minute?" Emerson asks the doctor, who nods politely.

"Let the nurse at the desk know and she can take one

of you back for just a few minutes. He really needs his rest."

"We understand. Thank you."

We watch in silence as the doctor disappears through the sliding glass doors. The moment he's gone, I work up the courage to fight this battle.

I can't only wear my dominance when it's convenient, when Beau and I are in a scene or sex is involved. I'm tired of being passive and compliant when it suits someone else. And right now, Beau needs me to fight for him.

Before Emerson can get a word in, I grit my teeth and mutter, "I have to see him, Emerson. He's mine."

His reaction isn't as surprised as I expected. Instead, he nods as our eyes meet. "Just go. But tell him I'm here. As soon as they move him upstairs, I'll go see him."

"I will," I reply, and I'm itching to run through those doors.

When he drops onto the bench next to the hospital doors, I pause. I should apologize or say something, but I'm not sorry and what I said was true. I wish I had a moment to appreciate how lighter my shoulders feel without all of the weight of this secret and all of my guilt.

But instead, I sprint through the automatic glass doors and straight into the hospital.

Rule #36: Listen to your Domme—and your nurse.

Beau

Normally, I like getting bossed around by a woman in bed, but it turns out the exception to that is hospital beds and mean nurses who won't let me fall back to sleep.

"Until those results come back from radiology, your eyes better stay open," she snaps, after fussing with my IV.

"Yes, ma'am," I mutter with attitude, side-eyeing her with a scowl. I notice the way she tsks in response. Whatever they wiped my face with smells terrible, and these pain meds aren't doing shit for the itch in my scalp.

This is fucking miserable.

And to make things worse, these assholes won't give me any answers. I don't know if Maggie is okay or if that waste of human flesh hurt her, too, after he knocked me out with that fucking crowbar.

I'm about to throw a royal fit when a familiar face appears through a crack in the door like an angel. As soon as our eyes meet, Maggie's expression contorts into anguish before she rushes into the room, right past the mean nurse and directly up to my bedside.

"Oh my God," she cries as she wraps her arms around me, burying her face in my neck. "Are you okay?"

Her touch is like heaven. She's all warm hands and sweet perfume, but most importantly, she seems perfectly fine. Her embrace is strong and desperate, and the weight is lifted from my shoulders when I feel her in my arms.

I'm in a hospital gown to cover my chest, since they had to cut my shirt off to put in my IV. I'm still covered in crusty blood and dirt. I look like shit and feel like shit, but Maggie doesn't care about any of that. She's just here to see *me*.

"Are you okay?" I reply.

"I'm fine." When she pulls back, she inspects my head, giving me a grimace as she notices the nasty-looking stitches and swelling above my left eye.

"I'm lucky that dickhead didn't bash my skull in."

Tears fill her eyes as she winces. I shouldn't have said that. Although it's true.

"Are you sure you're okay?" I ask. She looks rough. Her hair is a mess, makeup smeared across her face, and there are heavy bags under her eyes, which means she must have spent a lot of time crying.

She still looks beautiful, though.

"I'm okay now," she says, sitting on the edge of my bed. I don't want to let her go. My hands cling to hers, and I wish this mean nurse would fuck off, so I can pull Maggie into this bed with me. Just to have her close.

"They're not letting me go home," I say with a huff. Then I glare angrily at the nurse again.

"You need to be monitored and get better. Don't worry about going home." Her fingers are stroking my knuckles as the conversation grows quiet. The air gets thick and I realize just how tense she is.

She's not telling me something.

We wait a few moments, not saying anything, until the mean nurse finally ducks out of the room. As soon as we're alone, Maggie squeezes my hand tighter.

"What's going on?" I ask, demanding to know what she's not telling me.

"Your dad is here."

My eyes search her face for more. My doped-up brain is taking too long to connect any dots. What the hell happened while I was out?

"He knows?" I ask.

"He knows." She still has tears in her eyes. Part of me *really* wants to go to sleep now. I don't want to face the truth, and I definitely don't want him coming in here and asking me a million questions or lecturing me about this.

"What did he say? Was he mad?"

Her eyes widen, and I take that to mean yes. "He was very mad."

"He'll get over it," I reply bluntly.

"Beau..."

"I'm serious. He will. I had to get over him and Charlie. He'll get over me and you. He doesn't have a choice."

She forces a smile, and a tear slips over her lashes, plunging to the bed and landing on the scratchy white sheet. The sight of her crying is all wrong. I hate it, so I quickly wipe it away from her face and pull her against me again, using her body to keep me warm.

When she feels me shiver, she snaps upward. "You're freezing. You need a blanket."

"I'm fine," I reply, tugging on her again, but she doesn't budge. Instead, she stands up in a rush. Marching over to the door in her black gown and someone else's black jacket, she tears open the door and starts barking orders at anyone who will listen.

"Excuse me," she yells, "my boyfriend is in here freezing. He needs a blanket."

I hear voices out in the hospital answering her, and I smile as I watch Maggie scowl at the nurses who left me lying in here cold as hell. When she returns and notices me grinning at her, she pauses.

"What?" She perches back on the edge of my bed.

"It's hot as fuck watching you boss people around like that."

She rolls her eyes and takes my hand again. "Well, don't start thinking I'm bossing you around anytime soon. You're getting a nice long break from being bossed around."

"You're going to dote on me and shit, aren't you?" I ask as I squeeze her fingers.

"Yep. And you're going to let me." With her other hand, she strokes my cheek, sending a buzz of warmth down my spine. Then I bring her fingers to my mouth and kiss her knuckles.

My brow furrows. "Did you tell him about Phoenix?"

With a nod, her lips tighten into a thin line. "Yeah. I think it was a lot for him to take in at once. But when you're ready...you'll need to have a talk with him."

"Can't wait," I groan. My head is starting to hurt again. Just then, the mean nurse returns, covering me with a warm blanket like it's fresh out of the dryer.

"Well, I've got good news and bad news," she announces as she tosses the blanket over my legs. "Your scan came back clear."

"What's the bad news?" Maggie asks as she stands.

"Visiting hours are over, and he needs to rest. Once we get him to his room, you can visit him there, but for now, you gotta go."

I shift in my seat. "I'll rest better if she's here."

Maggie looks down at me with a stern expression. "No, you need to sleep." When she leans down to press her lips to mine, she softly pulls back and adds, "Behave."

With a scoff, my brow tightens. "Yes, ma'am."

Then, she kisses me again. As she stands up, she glances at the nurse. "Don't let him give you any sass. He can be a real brat."

"Oh, I've noticed," the nurse replies with a laugh.

"What the hell..." I groan.

"When he woke up, he was shouting at everyone. He wanted to know where *you* were," the nurse says, nodding toward Maggie, whose expression softens as she hears it. "He barely let the doctors stitch him up. He wouldn't listen to anyone."

I barely remember that. I was so out of it. All I remember was waking up in an ambulance and her not being there.

As Maggie turns away, she wipes at her face, hiding the emotion she's showing. She's always so calm and collected that it's strange to see her expressing such vulnerability. When she lets go of my hand, my stomach turns. I hate watching her leave, and I really don't want to be here alone. When she reaches the door, I call her name. As she turns, I swallow the emotion building in my throat.

"I love you."

She pauses halfway out the door, staring at me with tenderness in her eyes that are starting to fill with tears again. In a quick stride, she crosses the room and practically climbs onto my bed, pulling me in for a hungry kiss.

Her teeth pinch my bottom lip in a fierce bite that doesn't hurt, but is really fucking reassuring. Then her tongue brushes against mine, and I almost forget I'm in a hospital bed and that today has easily been the longest day of my life.

"I love you too," she mumbles against my lips.

"Aw, ain't that sweet. Now, get out," the nurse replies, and I grimace as Maggie smiles.

"I'm going," she says, before climbing off my lap and wiping her tears away.

"You're coming back later, right?"

"I'll be here when you wake up," she replies, and I believe it. When Maggie makes promises, I trust her. There's just something really fucking comforting about that. I've never been able to rely on someone like that before. I never knew I needed to learn to trust so badly.

"Tell my dad I'll see him later," I say before she leaves. As she looks back with a tight smile, she nods.

"I will."

When she's gone, my eyes start to feel heavy, and I'm relieved that I can finally close my eyes and rest. My head still hurts like a bitch, but everything feels a little lighter now. No more secrets. No more lies. Without the heavy weight on my shoulders, I fall into a restful sleep.

Rule #37: People let you see what they want you to see.

Beau

My face is pressed against the warmth of Maggie's bare chest, her tits like perfect pillows cradling my head. I'm not sure when we took our clothes off or where the fuck we are, but when I wake up, she's lying beneath me, naked and ready. Suddenly, I'm hard and grinding against her, torn between the desire just to sleep in her arms or muster the energy to bury myself deep inside her, where it's safe and warm.

I'd honestly be happy with either, but unfortunately, someone is currently drilling screws into my skull and pulling me from the serenity of my dream.

When I peel my eyes open, the blinding light of the room only makes the drilling worse. Which, as it turns out, isn't actually drilling. It's just the pain meds wearing off and the throbbing reminder that crowbars and skulls don't mix.

When I let out a groan, shifting in my bed, a deep, familiar voice takes me by surprise.

"Beau?" my father asks. My lids crack open enough to notice my dad jumping up from the chair next to my bed, his facial features tense with concern. "Are you in pain? Nurse!" He calls as he rushes across the room to the door.

Considering that my father and I have a very awkward conversation on deck, I might actually consider letting the stabbing pain stay. It's actually a nice distraction from the fact that my dad now knows that not only am I screwing one of his oldest friends, but I'm also doing it in his club, and oh yeah...she's my Domme.

Can't wait to bask in the glow of that disappointment.

I must start to drift off again because when I hear a woman's voice and instantly recognize that it's *not* Maggie, I open my eyes to find a nurse, not the mean one, plugging something into my IV. Whatever it is, I hope it's strong.

What's a guy gotta do to get a morphine drip around here?

Within a few minutes, the drilling is gone, and I can actually open my eyes without wanting to gouge out my eyeballs. My dad must have pulled the curtains closed because it's peaceful and dim when I finally do make eye contact with him.

He looks tired as fuck. Dark circles under his eyes, messy hair, wrinkled clothes.

"What time is it?" I ask, my voice dry and raspy. He quickly grabs a pitcher of water off the table next to me and fills a small plastic cup with it.

"It's just after two. You slept all day, which is good."

"Where's Maggie?" I ask as I lift the water to my lips. I watch his reaction as I say her name, and I only notice the most subtle hitch in his breath before he replies,

"She's on her way back. I sent her home to get some rest and food."

"Good," I reply as I finish the cup. Food sounds fucking amazing right now.

"Your mom was here too. She'll be back in a couple hours."

"Okay," I reply dryly.

When I hand him back the empty cup, the room grows thick with tension. It's like we're not the same two people we were last night. Last night, he existed in blissful ignorance. Today, he has to face the truth that I'm not who he thought I was.

Welcome to the fucking club.

My back is aching, so I try to sit up, and once he notices me struggling, he jumps into action, trying to help. Grabbing the bed's remote panel to adjust the angle, he presses the button that has me slowly sitting up.

"I got it," I snap, taking the remote from him. "I'm not useless."

"I'm just trying to help," he replies.

"Why? Because you think I'm too weak to do anything on my own?"

"I didn't say that," he argues as he takes a step back, crossing his large arms in front of his chest. Something about his presence has me on edge. Maybe it's the painkillers kicking in or the fact that I am fucking starving, but there are no filters in place to stop me from revving up the attitude and starting this argument.

"Yeah, well, I know what you're thinking," I snap.

"What am I thinking, Beau? Because if it's anything other than how relieved I am that you're alive and healthy, you're wrong."

I scoff. "You're thinking what a disappointment I am. Or maybe you're pissed that I'm a hypocrite and gave you shit for years, but ended up in your club anyway, which makes me fucking stupid."

"Stop it," he barks, but I don't listen. Not to him.

"Are you? Disappointed? That I'm not more like you."

"What does that even mean?" he replies with his brows pinched together in confusion.

"That I can't just be a real man. I know you know the truth now. Maggie is my Domme. I'm her sub."

"Your relationship with Maggie is your business," he replies calmly.

He's being passive and agreeable, and it just pisses me off more. I want him to fight with me. I wish, for once, my father would just say the things to me that I see him thinking.

"Bullshit," I bark at him. "It bugs you, doesn't it? To find out I'm not as masculine as you thought."

"Beau, stop it," he bellows, loud enough to send his voice echoing through the room. My mouth shuts in a tight clench as I glare at him. "The only thing that bugs me is you thinking that my love and support for you has anything to do with masculinity. You think I care about how submissive you are to your partner? You think a *real* man can't be submissive? Then I've failed you as a father, and *that* bugs me."

I don't have a quippy response to that, but I'm still heated, still angry for no fucking reason. My nostrils flare as I stare ahead, replaying his words because, even though everything he said should make me feel better, it doesn't. He's being too fucking nice to me.

Why do I hate that so much?

I've been nothing but an asshole to him. I've spewed resentment and bitter jealousy at my father like poison for so long, I forget where it even started or why.

When he finally takes a seat in the chair by the window, I see the way his shoulders sag, his large frame starting to crumble, and for the first time I see Emerson Grant for what he really is.

Just a man.

He looks as lost and frustrated and confused as I feel all the fucking time.

"I just wish you'd be honest with me. Tell me what a fuck-up I am," I mutter, already knowing what he's about to say.

"You're not a fuck-up, Beau. You think I had my shit figured out at twenty-two? No. I had a shitty job and a loveless marriage. But I also had you, so don't tell me about feeling like a fuck-up, because, trust me, I know."

As my eyes shift up to his face, all of the anger and frustration and desperation I was feeling suddenly congregates right in my throat, and not even the painkillers can make that shit not hurt.

"You weren't a fuck-up," I say quietly as I search my memory for any reminder of what Emerson, the twenty-two-year-old mess of a dad, looked like, but I can't place a single instance. He's always seemed put together, controlled, confident. He's had it all figured out my entire life. I've never seen him struggle with anything.

At that, he laughs. Leaning back in his chair, he smiles. "Do you remember when you were six and we went on that last-minute road trip, just me and you, and we stayed at that motel by the ocean? We dumped our coin jars on the bed and rolled quarters all night while watching movies until the middle of the night?"

"Yeah..." I say, remembering that trip very well. He picked me up from school before I caught the bus and surprised me with a road trip. "We went surfing at the ass crack of dawn."

He nods. "Yeah, well...we were homeless."

I freeze. "What are you talking about?"

"I got evicted that day from the apartment I was renting because I couldn't make a payment. But it was my weekend with you, so instead of canceling, I maxed out my credit card and took you on a trip."

I sit up a little straighter. "But...no, you..." I stammer, trying to remember the details to prove him wrong. His expression is flat as he waits for me to figure it out.

"It took me a couple more months to find a place, so we stayed with friends for a while, but my point is that you think I had my shit together because I let you think that. I felt like a fuck-up, a *royal* one that weekend, but I figured it out. Eventually. It took some time, but five years later, I started working with Garrett, and four years after that, we started a company. I still mess up, Beau. I don't always have it together, and if you ever think I'm so confident or perfect, just remember that trip. I'm letting you see what I want you to see."

As I stare at him in surprise, suddenly all the pieces click into place. "That day when they vandalized my car... why did they come to Mom's house?" I ask, although I already know the answer.

"It must still show my name for the residence," he replies.

"But you gave that house to Mom."

He doesn't respond.

"Because you own the deed, don't you? You gave her the house, but you paid for it, didn't you?"

"When I had the opportunity, I did."

I can't exactly put into words how this news makes me feel. Weirdly irritated with him. And strangely proud at the same time. I've looked up to my dad my entire life, and I've spent the entire time comparing myself to him. Who could live up to that?

Maybe he should have let me see him fuck up. If I ever got the chance to see my dad as a real person and not as the hero he tried to be, I wouldn't feel like the letdown of the century.

Thank fuck the doctor walks in, dissipating the tension with her presence. She gives us the basic rundown of my injuries—severe concussion, stitches, no bleeding on the brain or anything on the CT scan. With any luck, I can go home tomorrow.

And I notice his eyes track my way when the doctor says that. Because he's probably thinking exactly what I'm thinking. I'm sure as fuck not going back to *my* home with my mom. She doesn't have a nurturing bone in her body, and as much as I love her, I think I'd rather stay with the newlyweds than listen to whatever guilt trip bullshit my mother wants to spin about this.

But let's face it. We all know where I'm going when I get out of here tomorrow. And it's a fucking relief that we don't have to lie about it anymore.

My mom is acting weird. After I woke up, she and my dad coexisted peacefully in this room for twenty awkward minutes. Then, he finally relented and went home for a while to rest and freshen up.

Now, it's just me and my mom and this lingering tension between us. I don't know exactly what's going on in her head, but I do know that the club she's been slandering for over a year is the reason I'm in the hospital right now. And I'm just waiting for her to say something.

"I told you that place was trouble," she mutters bitterly, staring out the window.

"Mom," I reply, letting out a groan. "The club is not trouble."

Her mouth hangs open in shock. "You were nearly killed there!"

"You're overreacting," I argue, but she's already revved up and there's no stopping her now.

"I'm *overreacting*? Beau, I got a call in the middle of the night that my son's head was nearly bashed in outside his *father's* club. Now, you tell me how I should react to that."

As my eyes track up toward her face, noticing the tears welling in her lashes, I'm ambushed by guilt. She quickly blinks them away as her jaw clenches and she looks away.

"Mom, sit down."

She's restless, clearly not wanting to settle, almost like if she does then she'll really break. I notice as I get older how much my mother resembles a cornered animal, anxious and aggressive because it's her only option left.

After a few minutes, she finally gives in and takes the seat in the chair next to my bed. I sit up a little straighter to look at her.

"The man who attacked me wasn't a member of the club," I say, but when I see her starting to argue already, I hold up a hand. "I know you think that place is terrible, but that's only because you've never been there. You don't understand it."

"I'm *never* going there," she bites back.

"That's fine. You don't have to, but just because you don't like it doesn't make it as bad and evil as you think it is."

She's studying my face now, looking at me as if I'm a stranger. And I guess in some way, I am. My mother is realizing at this moment that I'm not a kid anymore. I'm a man with my own life that she knows nothing about. And she never will.

"I don't think I can ever change your mind about Dad or the club or...me. But I don't want you to push me away, too, just because I live the same lifestyle as him."

At the word *lifestyle* her eyes widen, but she quickly shuts it down, hiding her shock as she takes my hand. "I would never push you away. I just want you to be safe."

"I am safe, Mom," I reply, and it's clear she doesn't quite agree by the way her lips tighten into a thin line, but at least she doesn't reply. It's a miracle my mom learned to listen without arguing. "I'm also happy," I continue, "a lot happier than I've ever been."

"Because of this new girlfriend..." she adds, lifting her brow and giving me a questioning glance.

An unexpected smile creeps across my mouth. I never really talk about my girlfriends much with my mom, especially this one.

"Yes, because of her."

"I've met her, you know," she adds, and I force myself to swallow down how weird that is. "And I still think she's too old for you..."

"But...?" I ask, hoping there's a but coming.

She looks down at her hands as she shrugs. "But she's nice."

I bite my lip as my smile grows. If only my mom knew just how *nice* Maggie is, especially when she was turning my ass red with that riding crop. "Yeah, she is nice."

"I think she could be good for you. Maybe help you get a good job so you can finally get a place of your own." She's joking with me about still living in her house at twenty-two, and I wish I could laugh but I'm suddenly reminded that I'm moving out of state next week and my mother should know that by now, but she doesn't.

I reach for her hand, and when she sees my smile fade, hers does too. "Mom, I have to tell you something."

She rests her fingers in my hand, and I give them a comforting squeeze. "Maggie is going to Phoenix in a few days to open the new club they bought there."

My mother's brow pinches inward as she waits for me to elaborate.

"And I'm going with her. To stay."

The expression melts off her face, and I'm pierced by shame that I'm bringing my mother so much pain. I don't say anything for a few minutes as she contemplates this news, her eyes dancing from my face to a blank spot against the wall and back.

"Mom, say something," I plead when it feels like a full minute has gone by.

"I'm...happy for you."

My body tenses at that response. "What?"

"Baby, you've been stuck since you graduated high school, and I've been wishing you would do something big like move or get married or go to college. Something to get you out of this rut, so I can ignore the part about there being another *club* involved. I just want your life to begin."

I'm speechless. I expected an all-out fight over this, and she's basically giving me an *about damn time* response. I'm not complaining, but still...it's weird.

"Thanks, Mom," I reply, and she squeezes my hand.

"I'm gonna miss you, though." A tear slips over her lashes and she quickly swipes it away.

"I'll miss you too."

I notice someone pop their head into the room, and I turn to see Maggie standing in the doorway, waiting to see if it's safe to enter. She looks at my mom with a guarded expression.

"I brought you some of your things," she says carefully.

"Come in, Maggie," I say, releasing my mom's hand. To our surprise, my mom moves from her chair next to my bed and gestures for Maggie to sit.

"Yeah, come in," my mom adds. "I think I'll head out anyway and let you get some rest." As she leans over to kiss my forehead, I pull her in for a quick hug. "Just keep me updated when they discharge you. I assume you're going to..."

"Yeah, I'll stay at Maggie's," I reply quickly.

My mom only nods, kissing my forehead again. After saying a quick and awkward goodbye to Maggie, she slips out of the room, and I feel as if I can finally breathe easily.

"How did that go?" Maggie asks as she sits on the edge of my bed instead of the plastic chair.

Letting out a sigh, I nod. "It went a hell of a lot better than I expected."

"Good," she replies, leaning forward to kiss me, and I

use the opportunity to drag her down until she's lying on the bed next to me, her head using my shoulder as a pillow. If the mean nurse comes back and tries to yell at me for it, I don't care. There's only one woman I listen to anyway.

Rule #38: A good Domme knows exactly what her brat needs.

Maggie

"The club has been really quiet all week," Hank says. He's sitting in my living room, our temporary boardroom while I'm here with Beau during his recovery. Everyone is here—Emerson, Charlie, Garrett, Mia, Hunter, and Drake. Even Isabel is nestled into the corner of my couch, rubbing her belly as we all listen to Hank, who dropped by to check on Beau.

"Yeah, there's definitely some concern among members. People are still coming, but the vibes feel off," Mia says with a contemplative look on her face.

"We've increased security, made a public statement to members, and handed over all the security footage. What more can we do?" Garrett asks.

"It'll get better with time," I say.

"She's right," Emerson adds. "We stand our ground. We're not going to close our doors or scare easily."

"Besides, he messed up when he resorted to violence.

No legal action against the club will stand in court now," I reply.

Emerson nods in my direction. Next to him, I feel Charlie's eyes on my face. I haven't officially spoken to her since the news broke about me and Beau. The attack sort of drowned out that scandal, which I guess is a silver lining. But I do catch her studying me like she is now.

I wonder if she's curious about our relationship, knowing what she knows about me and my kink results. Perhaps she's imagining me whipping him in the BDSM room. More than likely she's realizing why the two of them never really worked, two subs looking for guidance. Either way, I'll never know because that would be far too awkward of a conversation to have.

Suddenly, my phone rings in my pocket, pulling me from my deep thoughts. I glance down to see Fitz's name on the caller ID. It's weird that he'd call me and not Emerson, but I quickly excuse myself to answer it.

"Hello?" I say as I enter the kitchen.

"Hi, Maggie. I'm calling to let you know there's been arrest made on the man who attacked Beau."

"Oh, thank God," I reply, dropping onto the chair in relief. "Emerson's here. I'll let him know."

"Okay," Fitz replies, "I appreciate it. I wanted you to know first."

I smile down at my coffee as I stir in the creamer. "That means a lot. Thanks for everything."

I feel Emerson's presence behind me. The look on his face is confident as I spin around and nod. "They got him."

His doesn't look as surprised or as relieved as I expected. He calmly replies, "Thank God."

There's an audible celebration in the living room when they overhear the news.

"Yeah. He turned himself in," Fitz adds, and I freeze.

"He did?"

"Yeah. Just between you and me, someone must have gotten to him first. He looked pretty roughed up when he came into the station."

"What?" I ask in confusion. Who would have...

Then, as I lift my eyes, I stare across the kitchen at the man leaning calmly against the countertop. He's wearing a knowing expression, and I nearly drop the phone out of my hand.

I'm assaulted by guilt when I remember attacking him the other night and judging his love for his son. I should have known better, and I will never doubt it again.

"It was nothing serious," Fitz adds. "A guy like that causes problems, so he should expect to receive them too. He won't press charges against whoever it was. I'm almost sure of it."

"I hope not..." I reply softly.

A moment later, I hear footsteps on the stairs, and I know it's Beau coming down when he should be sleeping. I rush into the front room to greet him.

"I'm sorry, were we being too loud?"

He shakes his head. "No, I'm just not tired. I hate lying up there alone when everyone's here. Plus, I've been in bed for three days. I can't do it anymore."

"Take it easy, please," I say in warning, but he tilts his head at me.

"Stop babying me."

As he reaches the bottom of the stairs, I take a look at his bandage, checking that it doesn't need to be changed.

Then I grab his arms and pull him closer. "Don't get bossy with me. I'm taking care of you, now get over it."

His eyes move from my face to something behind me, and I turn to see Emerson watching us uncomfortably. I jerk my hand away from Beau. This is really going to take some getting used to. Since everyone found out about us, no one has really seen us together or said anything. It's the giant elephant in every room.

"She's right, Beau. You need to rest," Emerson adds, agreeing with me. Which I'd appreciate, if I didn't have to worry about how Beau feels about this.

"Oh great," he snaps. "Now I have two people bossing me around." He's in a bad mood, and not a cute bad mood. Normally when he gets like this, I can get tough with him, but with everyone around, it's a little hard to step into that role. Emerson's still getting used to us being together. I don't think he's ready to see me force his son into submission.

Beau brushes past me as Emerson gives me a concerned expression.

I shrug and follow Beau into the kitchen. "I heard the news," he grumbles, reaching for a glass and filling it with water.

"Let me get your painkillers," I say when I notice him wincing.

"I can do it!" he snaps, and my eyes widen as I stare at him. Oh no, we're not going back to the way it was that day he lost his temper on me. He knows that's a road we don't travel down anymore. My fists clench as I fight the urge to be firm with him.

"Watch your tone," Emerson says in a warning, and I spin on him, giving him a rage-filled glare. I'm about two seconds from screaming at everyone in my house.

Having him here is throwing everything off and I hate it.

"I can handle it," I mutter with my teeth clenched. I mean, how would he feel if I went over to his house and started barking orders at Charlie? Can't imagine that would go over well.

Tensions are high and I can see the way that affects Beau. He looks miserable, tired, frustrated and ready to burst. Maybe the painkillers will help, so I bite my tongue and take my coffee into the living room with the others. They're discussing increased security and the possibility of having to offer public escorts for members to and from their cars.

I hate this. I hate that our members feel like they're risking their safety by coming to our club. A moment ago, we seemed confident that the problem would pass. But suddenly, Beau's here, and his injury is a harsh reminder that things can get serious very fast. And lives aren't something we can gamble with.

"That's a great idea," Emerson says to Hank, who offers the suggestion. Emerson has been carrying a look of guilt since the night it happened, and I don't know how much he knows about what happened, if Beau ever told him what the attacker said before he hit him. He knew Beau was Emerson's son; the attack was targeted. It's important information, but I know it has to be hard for Emerson to hear.

"If the protesters come back, we have the option for support from the police, if we feel it will get violent again," he adds.

On the couch, I see Beau growing more tense and frustrated.

"At what point do we consider closing down?" The

words come out of my mouth, but I immediately regret them. The room grows silent as everyone stares at me with expressions of disbelief.

But it's Beau who speaks up.

"Fuck that," he snaps with a scowl.

"Beau..." I say, staring at him with a harsh look in my eyes.

"No. You can't cower to these ignorant fuckers. And your members won't either."

"We're not risking another attack," I reply, raising my voice a little over his.

"So you're going to let them win? Once they see you escorting people to their cars or closing your doors, you'll let them see they got to you," he fights.

"They did get to us." Emerson growls. The entire room is tense as they watch the argument unfold.

"Bullshit." Beau stands, staring down at his father across the room. "That's not the dad I know. We don't let the bullies win. If you want to show that asshole who's in control, you don't change a fucking thing. In fact, throw a goddamn party. Invite the whole fucking town. Send a personal invitation to that fucking idiot's family. But if you close down that club because one person hates it, then you're not who I thought you were."

With that, he storms out of the room and stomps his way up the stairs.

We sit in silence for a while before I finally make eye contact with Emerson. He wants to follow him, I know it. But he has to know that's not a good idea.

"We should probably get going," Garrett says first, and everyone follows suit, until I'm sending most of the team out the door. Of course, Emerson is the last to go.

"I'll talk to him," I say, but I sense his hesitation. His

eyes keep glancing upstairs and he's not moving to the door the way he should.

"I hate it when he's mad at me." It's a fairly vulnerable thing for Emerson to say to me and I'm a little surprised by it.

"He's not mad at you. Beau has big feelings, and if I've learned anything recently, it's that I'd rather feel his anger than nothing at all. Anger is better than indifference."

"And he listens to you?" he asks carefully. We're bordering on inappropriate. But I guess if he wants to know, then I'm willing to share.

"Yes, he does, and he knows what he needs." And that's all I say. It's enough to get the point across. When Beau gets so angry he can't control his own emotions, he needs me to put him in his place, and that's exactly what I'm going to do.

Emerson gives me one more uncomfortable expression before finally letting out a surrendering sigh and reaching for the doorknob. I feel his pain in that moment; letting Beau go isn't something I could imagine doing. But it's exactly what Emerson is forced to do. Sometimes letting go is a show of love, and it's probably the hardest one.

"Emerson," I say, stopping him before he disappears. As he turns to me, waiting to hear what I have to say, I give him a tight smile. "The night of the attack, he called you a good man. Your son thinks you're a good man. I just thought you should know that."

His expression softens and I almost spot a smile as he thanks me and turns to leave. I hope Emerson never truly learns about how that attack was meant to hurt him because that doesn't matter. The attacker will never matter to him as much as what his son said about him. So I hope that little bit of information offers him some relief.

"Take care of him," he adds after walking out my door. I suspect it'll be the last thing we really say about this, or at least I hope it is.

"I will," I reply.

Once he's gone, I walk up the stairs to find Beau lying on the bed, gazing up at the ceiling, almost as if he's waiting for me. Without stopping, I walk up to the bed and stare at him as I reach under my knee-length skirt and slide down my simple black lace panties.

He's watching with confusion as I climb on top of him, straddling his waist, and then shove my underwear in his mouth. To his credit, he doesn't put up a fight, just lets me gag him as I put my face near his.

"You don't get to talk anymore. Now, you listen. Nod if you understand."

There's a sense of anger laced in his expression as he furrows his brow and nods.

Then I take his jaw in my hands roughly as I stare down at him. "Salacious Players' Club is just a fucking club. It's the greatest fucking sex club in the country, sure, but it's *just a club*. I hope you never know the fear I felt that night, but I wish for one second, you could see things from my perspective. Your life and safety come first. Not just to me and not just to your dad, but to everyone who fucking loves you, and there are a lot of people."

Then I lean forward, putting my forehead against his. "I love you for your bravery and conviction, Beau, but if it comes down to letting those assholes win, so we don't lose you, then I'd let them win every *fucking* time."

I watch his throat move as he swallows, and the hard wrinkle in his forehead is gone.

"I'm going to take my underwear out of your mouth now, but you don't get to speak for the rest of the day after that outburst downstairs, understand?"

With his blue eyes on me, he nods. After I pull my panties from his mouth, I toss them on the floor and kiss his soft lips with tenderness.

Then I rest my body alongside his, using his shoulder as a pillow when his arms wrap around me, holding me tight. We're entangled in my bed when I feel the muscles in his body start to melt.

"Now, get better, so I can punish you for real," I say as I close my eyes against him, letting the steady beat of his heart lull me to sleep.

Rule #39: Bad boys don't get what they want.

Maggie

Just as I press a piece of packing tape over the box, I feel a hand slide across my ass, making me jump with a yelp. As I spin on Beau, I give him a scowl. "You're supposed to be resting."

His head hangs back with a sigh. "I've been resting for days, and I'm going crazy. I can't *do* anything. I can't stare at my tablet for too long. Can't help you pack. Can't drive. Can't fuck. What *can* I do?"

Turning to him, I stroke his cheek with my hand. He leans into my touch. "You can rest and heal. The doctor said two weeks, and it's only been five days."

"But I feel fine." His hands wind around my waist, tugging me closer, and I'll admit, the temptation is getting too strong to pass up. After we brought him home from the hospital, it's been a whirlwind, and we've had almost no time alone. Emerson stationed himself in my box-filled living room for a whole day before I had to call Charlie and beg her to take him home. He and I have worked together for over a decade and never once butted heads. But it turns out when we're watching over the same person, two dominant energies are a bit too much.

Beau's mom has been coming and going, which has been...awkward, to say the least. It might be a saving grace since I think it was that awkwardness that made her leave early and show up rarely. I've met Marie before. It's not like we don't know each other, but suddenly, I'm the thirty-four-year-old woman currently dating her twenty-two-year-old son and things feel a little—or a lot—different.

Not to mention, this move is hanging in the air like a threat. We've swept it under the rug all week, but now I'm supposed to drive to Arizona in three days to see the club and meet with the sellers, and I have no idea if he's still coming with me or not.

He presses his lips to my neck and kisses his way up to my ear, making my thoughts turn to mush in my head.

"Beau..." I say in warning, but it does nothing to stop him.

His hands grip my sides as he crushes his hips against me. "Come on. I'll lie there and do nothing. I promise if you just come to bed with me and ride my dick, I'll relax for the rest of the day without complaint."

"You're not listening to me." I groan as his hand cups my breast through my shirt, giving my nipple a gentle pinch.

"I don't even have to come. I'll be so good."

One hand digs into my hair as he pulls my mouth to his, tangling his soft lips with mine, and I nearly melt into the floor.

"Beau," I gasp as I drop the tape and kiss him back. Right now, the idea of hauling him to the bedroom and dragging orgasms out of his body until he's a gooey mess of pleasure sounds like the greatest thing in the world. At least then I'd know we're still us and everything is going to be okay.

But that's no guarantee. The rug we're trying to sweep this issue under isn't big enough to hide it anymore. So even after he drags his finger between my legs to feel how I'm soaking my leggings, I know I have to pull away from him.

It's not easy, but I need to know.

He lets out a groan as I push his chest away, putting distance between our bodies.

"Come on..." he whines.

"We need to talk," I say, and he tenses at those words, staring at me like I've just insulted him.

"About what?"

"About Phoenix," I reply.

"What about it?" When he reaches for me again, I hold a hand up to stop him.

"This is getting serious. We're taking a big step, and after what happened, I just need to know if this is still—"

"Are you backing out?" he snaps.

"No. I'm not backing out. I'm just..."

He ambushes me. Grabbing the back of my neck, he heaves me against him, putting our faces within inches as he glares at me. "I thought I was going to die. And all I kept thinking when they put me through that stupid CT scan machine was that if I made it through this without fucking brain damage, then I was never going to waste a stupid day of my life ever again. Because that would just be my luck. To finally find happiness and then lose it that fast. So tell me, Maggie. Why the fuck would I stay here when I could have the life I always wanted with you there?"

"I don't know..." I argue. "I was afraid it was too intense or dangerous..."

"My life is boring as hell!" he replies. "Playing video games and working at some shit job is not a life worth getting knocked over the head for. But the life we could have in Phoenix..."

"Are you sure?" I ask again.

"Fuck. Please stop asking me that."

I don't bother responding, at least not with words. Instead, I kiss him. And that's answer enough. Just because he *likes* me to make choices for him doesn't mean he's not capable of doing it himself.

"I wasn't doubting you," I say, pulling away.

"Good," he replies, diving back in for a kiss. As he shoves me against the boxes, I let out a groan. His body is like heaven in my hands. He feels strong and alive, and that thought alone has my core warming with desire.

"Maggie," he breathes into my mouth, "I *need* you."

I know I shouldn't give in. I'm not supposed to be spoiling him, but dammit, I want this too. And the doctor never said anything about sex, just no strenuous activities.

Wrapping my hand around the collar of his T-shirt, I keep his lips against mine as I pull him toward the stairs. He follows like a hungry puppy, all the way to my room. I'm practically walking him like he's on a leash, and it reminds me of something.

When we reach my room, I freeze. Sensing my hesitation, he pulls back and asks, "What's wrong?"

"I bought you something."

When his face falls into a mix of dread and worry, I laugh. "It's not bad, I promise."

"Your gifts usually hurt."

I kiss him on the cheek as I head over to my bedside table, where I stashed it away. It looks more like a necklace box than anything, but as soon as I hold it out to him, his eyes stare at it as if he knows.

"I guess this is proof that I was never doubting you."

I hand it to him, and he slides it open before running his fingers over the sleek black leather collar.

"This is a symbol of commitment, a promise that I will always take care of you. That I will always have your best interests at heart. This...means you're mine."

His eyes dance up toward my face as he swallows. I wait for his confirmation before I take it out of its box.

"You never have to wear it outside of the house or in public. It's just for us."

He nods, and his eyes don't leave the collar.

"Is that...something you want? You can say no."

"Of course, it is," he replies warmly. "I couldn't imagine saying this to anyone else, but with you, I want this."

I can't put into words what it feels like to hear him say those words, to know how much he genuinely wants me, and not just for sex or kink or convenience, but *me*. This thing between us is real, and with any luck, it will last forever.

With a tremble, I take the collar in my hands and toss the box on the bed. As I unclasp the buckle, I stare at him with a fierce level of excitement in my eyes. "On your knees."

Without a word, he drops down to the floor, gazing up at me as I wrap the collar around his neck. The audible click of the buckle feels significant, like a declaration. And just the sight of this beautiful man collared for me is the most amazing thing I've ever seen.

I stroke his hair, being careful not to get near his stitches. Seeing that wound reminds me just how recently it was that I held him cradled in my arms in the parking lot, how scared I was of losing him. It has me wanting to be gentle with him and show him another side of my dominance.

"Stand."

He does, his eyes on me the entire time. My fingers grip the bottom of his T-shirt and I gently pull it over his head, careful of his stitches. Once his shirt is off, he reaches for me, but I grab his wrists and place them behind his back.

"Hands to yourself," I whisper into his ear, and I feel him shudder against me. "I want to play with what's mine." His eyes dilate with arousal as I run my fingers under the elastic waistline of his joggers. His cock is straining against the gray cotton, creating a large print in the fabric. My core is hit with a burst of electric warmth as I rub my palm over the surface, feeling just how hard he is for me. The deep hum vibrating from his chest only makes me hotter for him

Gently, I ease his pants down, over his cock, as I lower to my knees. His mouth falls open as he watches me bring my lips torturously slow toward the aching length of him jutting out just inches from my mouth. As my tongue extends to lick the bead of pre-cum leaking from the tip, he groans.

The saltiness hits my tongue and my thighs clench in response. Taking this slow is going to be hard on me. But I don't rush. Instead, I lick around the head and then down the shaft, teasing him to the point where he starts begging.

I lick and kiss every inch of him, before finally pulling him into my mouth, but I don't let him get anywhere near coming.

"Please, don't stop." He groans, his hands staying obediently clasped behind his back.

But I do stop. Gazing up at him with a smile, I say, "Go lie down on the bed."

With a sigh, he walks over to the bed and lies his head on the pillow while I begin peeling my clothes off. He watches me, biting his lip as I unclasp my bra, letting my breasts fall free. As I drag my pants down, he fidgets.

His cock looks painfully hard as I crawl up his body, settling my weight against his stiff length. Grinding myself against him, I notice his hands aching to move.

"I want to touch you so bad," he whines.

Leaning over him, I press my mouth to his ear as I whisper, "But you've been bad, and bad boys don't get what they want." He groans in response.

I soak his cock with my arousal, rubbing myself all over him until I feel my body starting to reach the peak. Lifting my hips up slightly, I dock him at my entrance and pause there, just as he closes his eyes.

"Open them, Beau."

His eyes shoot open as I start to lower my hips, pulling him into my body. His brows fold upward with delight as I swallow him to the hilt. God, I missed this. It's been less than a week since we had sex, but it's painfully clear now we would have been miserable if we tried to do the long-distance thing. We need each other in a way that makes it impossible to imagine life without the other now.

My body is illuminated with a deep aching pleasure as he reaches far inside me. Biting my lip, I tease my clit with one hand, while pinching my left nipple with the other, and I start to grind on him. Using his body as my source of ecstasy, I move fast, chasing my orgasm. It doesn't take long. His grunts mingled with my moans are filthy and erotic, like my own personal sex soundtrack.

"I want you to come when I tell you to," I cry as I pinch my nipple harder, bringing myself enough pain to intensify the pleasure. My eyes stay fixed to that collar around his neck, the cadence of *mine, mine, mine* echoing through my mind.

"Yes, ma'am," he replies, his voice strained.

"Come. Now," I say in a breathless command, just as I'm about to crest the height of my own climax. His body tenses beneath me as he gasps for air, euphoria written all over his face. His head hangs back as he moans his way through his orgasm.

As we both start to come down together, I drape my body over his, burying my face in his neck.

"Can I touch you now?" he whispers.

"Yes."

With that, he wraps his arms around me, squeezing me tightly against him. My heart practically stutters in my chest, and when I lift up to smile down at him, he kisses my lips.

If you had told me three months ago this would happen, I would have told you, you were crazy. I never saw love in the cards for me. I couldn't imagine fitting with someone the way I fit with Beau. We're an unlikely and ridiculous couple, but that's what makes us all the more perfect for each other.

Beau doesn't just let me be myself, but he loves me for it.

Rule #40: Don't be afraid of goodbyes.

Beau

My dad loads the suitcases in the back of Maggie's car and the trunk closes with a finality that I've been waiting for all week. This is it. We had to move everything back a few days after the attack, even though I would have been ready the day after. I can't remember the last time I was so anxiously awaiting something like this move.

The moving company already took off with the boxes of stuff we're taking, but since the apartment we're moving into is furnished, we're leaving her furniture here with the house. It's a big downsize for her, to move from this giant house to an apartment in the downtown Phoenix area, but she seems ecstatic about it.

I don't see it as a downsize, she said, and I can see what she means. This house always seemed like the thing she was supposed to do, but it never quite fit her, or us.

"That's everything," my dad says with one hand on the back of her car, almost as if he doesn't want to let it go.

When his eyes drift up toward my face, I see a hint of dread in his expression.

I clap a hand on his shoulder. "We'll see you guys in two weeks, right?"

"We'll be there," he replies. Charlie approaches, wrapping her arms around his waist and nuzzling up against his side.

"Can't wait to see it," she adds with a smile.

"Yeah, me too," I say, awkwardly scratching the back of my head. We're just gonna talk about the sex clubs we own like it's no big deal now. Weird how things come around. This is definitely going to take some getting used to.

When Maggie and Gwen walk outside with Sophie between them, my heart sinks. Sophie won't look up, her hair hanging in her face to hide her expression from me.

"Let us know when you get there," my dad says, and I swallow the emotion building in my throat as I nod toward him.

"We will," Maggie replies for me.

"Hey, kid," I call toward Sophie. "Come inside with me. I got something for you."

When she looks up at me with interest on her face, I smile. Then I throw my arm around her and drag her toward the house. Sitting on the kitchen counter is a large white envelope, so I pick it up and hand it to her.

"It's kind of stupid, but I had it made last week and thought you'd like it."

"What is it?" she asks in that awkward fifteen-year-old way she often talks.

"Open it," I say, shoving her shoulder.

As she rips open the top and pulls out the colorful eight-by-ten print inside, my spine straightens with anticipation. Her eyes focus on the character on the page, pink and blue cotton candy hair, longer on one side than the other, with elf ears, a sparkling sage green robe, and a staff in her hand with a shimmering crystal at the top.

"Holy shit," she stutters as her fingers glide over the print. "Is this me?"

"Well, it's you as your badass D&D character. I drew it when I was bored in the hospital, but I had to do the original on a notepad with a pen since Maggie wouldn't let me use my tablet because it was bad for my head."

She laughs at that, but her eyes stay down on the picture in her hands. That emotion building in my throat is getting worse. Fuck, I didn't think this would be so hard. She's just a kid, and to be totally honest, I only started hanging out with her because I felt bad for the way things went down with Charlie. I hated the idea of Sophie hating me.

That may have been why I started taking her to game night and ice cream, but that's not why I kept doing it. I kept hanging out with Sophie because, while I was a pissy, bitter, self-absorbed man-child, who never had the guts to admit when I was wrong, Sophie gave me a chance to change her first impression of me. I actually started to like myself when I was around her.

While my dad was busy protecting me from the truth, Sophie didn't sugarcoat shit. She wasn't afraid to give it to me straight. If I was being a dick, she'd tell me. If I was wrong, she'd tell me. And since I wanted to be the kind of guy she felt safe with, I wasn't afraid to change for the better.

"You're my best friend, kid."

She stares at me with a skeptical expression. "That's really sad for you," she replies, and I laugh.

"Probably, but that's okay."

We grow quiet for a moment before she ambushes me, wrapping her arms around my waist and hugging me hard, her head coming up to my chin. After a couple of seconds, she pulls away and wipes her eyes quickly to hide her tears.

"You're such a jerk," she mutters before slugging me in the arm, a little too hard, but I laugh anyway. "I can't believe you're moving to Arizona. It's, like, a million degrees there and they have scorpions."

"Does that mean you're not going to visit me?" I ask, slinging an arm over her shoulder as I guide her back outside.

"Hell no. We have the ocean and better comic book stores. You should just come visit here."

"Okay, I will. Promise."

For a girl who doesn't take promises lightly, I know how serious it is for me to say that. When we approach the group outside, I notice how tense my dad is, guarding his expression as he talks to Maggie.

This is it. There's nothing left to do. The car is packed and the moving truck is gone. The only thing left to do is say our goodbyes.

And when my dad turns toward me with an emotionless expression, I think about the motel story again and how hard he worked to protect me from feeling anything at all. How it only taught me to bottle up my emotions for so long I became a ticking time bomb. So instead of bottling it up anymore, I break the cycle.

It takes him completely by surprise as I step up to him, throwing an arm out for a hug and pulling him tight against my chest. He squeezes me back, and I have to clench my jaw to keep from getting choked up.

Then the asshole has to quietly mumble, "You're a good man, and I'm so proud of you," and it all goes to hell.

There's a tremble in my chest that I know he can feel because he squeezes tighter.

Then we finally break apart and, believe it or not, there are tears in his eyes. Mr. Tough Guy himself. I don't have any room to talk because they clearly mirror mine, but who the fuck cares? I don't. I'm not afraid of crying in front of my dad or our family. Not anymore.

"Thanks," I mutter quietly before blinking away any moisture. Behind us, Maggie and the rest of them are saying their goodbyes too. When I come around to Charlie, I feel the need to pause.

"Bring Sophie out sometime, please," I say, and she nods in agreement.

"I will."

"And don't let my dad get all bummed out about me leaving."

"I won't. Just be sure to call."

I nod, knowing that, deep down, she's referring to the six months I spent giving him the silent treatment, ironically because he owned a sex club, and I thought that was some sort of moral offense.

Then, Charlie opens her arms, and I step in to give her a quick hug. It's not as awkward as it used to be, but I mean...she is still my ex-girlfriend.

Technically, now my stepmom, but I'm not ever, ever going to revisit that thought or even dare to say it out loud. Although I'm aware Sophie will make a joke out of it for the rest of our lives.

And that's it. All the hugs have been had, and the goodbyes have been said.

I look at Maggie, just as she looks back at me. I'm so

ready to get into the car and go, as if the rest of our lives is somewhere on that highway. There's not a thread of uncertainty there anymore.

I spent the past five years wishing I knew who I was or what I wanted in my life, but I was too busy shutting doors without opening any. Sure, there's a lot more to my life than just being *hers* and I'm the one responsible for paving my own path, but knowing she'll be at my side, for whatever we face, means I'm not alone anymore. I have someone who sees the good *and* the bad. Someone capable of tough love *and* mercy.

Someone who will punish me when I need it.

And I look forward to every single second.

Rule #41: Remind him who he belongs to.

Maggie's epilogue

One year later

"Oh, I know it's not a competition, Emerson. I'm just calling to point out that the Fire Palace now officially has more members than Salacious."

"You're gloating," he replies dryly on the other end of the call. "Besides, you started with a pre-established market, so technically, you had a head start."

I laugh. "Oh, you're scrambling for excuses, Mr. Grant. I know it's hard to admit I'm doing better than you, but you always were a sucker for praise. You're doing a very good job running your club," I say in a teasing tone.

"I'm hanging up now," he replies, and I hear the smile in his voice.

"All right, all right. I'm done teasing you. I'll see you next week."

"See you next week," he adds. "Tell my son to text me back."

Just then, I turn the corner, heading toward the office when I spot Beau standing there, staring down at his phone in his tight black-on-black suit with his auburn locks perfectly styled with just the right amount hanging over his brow. It points like an arrow to the vertical scar on his forehead. He looks too good for words, and I pause as I watch him for a moment.

"I will," I reply quietly to Emerson. When the line goes dead, I slip the earbud out and slide it into the pocket of my pants before crossing the long hall. When he hears the click of my heels, Beau looks up and smiles at me as he watches me approach.

"Enjoy that?" he asks with a coy smile.

"What are you talking about?"

"Rubbing it in my dad's face. I know what you've been up to."

As I step up to him, his hands wrap around my waist and he pulls me tightly against him. Sandwiching me between him and the wall, he lays a hungry kiss on my lips, making my knees go weak. I let him kiss me for a while, grinding himself against me just as a door opens down the hall and a couple walk out.

Beau pulls his mouth away as we watch them disappear around the corner. Then he looks back down at me, biting his bottom lip before dropping his lips back to mine.

"Are we still on for our date tonight?" he whispers into our kiss.

"Oh, you're not getting out of this one."

"I wasn't trying to," he replies.

We finally separate, and he adjusts the tie around his neck as I reach out to help him, tightening it just a hair. Then, I open the boardroom door and walk in. Our four team members are already waiting for us as I take my seat at the head of the table. Beau walks in behind me and takes the one to my right.

I feel his gaze on me during the entire meeting, watching me with lust-filled eyes as I delegate tasks and ask for updates from the team. Toward the end, when we're discussing the mural design we've hired a talented young artist from California to do in the main hall, Beau picks up his phone, and I know, without even looking, that he's up to no good. He's looking for punishment today.

When my phone pings on the table, I don't even open it. Chances are it's a filthy picture he's taken this week to distract me. He's being a brat, and he knows it. I allow it because later tonight, I'm going to make him pay.

Room fifteen is *our* room. I mean, obviously it's open to the public, but we charge extra for it, and use it for ourselves whenever we have the chance. At midnight on the dot, I open the door with my private key to find my man kneeling naked on his pillow, waiting for me. His eyes are cast down and his hands are folded obediently in his lap.

When I lock the door behind me, he doesn't move, but when I pull off my robe I wore in the hallway and hang it on the hook, I wait for him to glance up.

As his eyes finally lift and cast a hungry gaze over my tight black leather corset, thong, and garter straps, I watch him force down a gulp. Then I step closer to him, standing in my black heels.

Reaching down, I wrap the collar around his neck, clasping it with a resounding click. The sound of it sends a shudder down his spine that I can visibly track. As I stand back up, I smile.

"Go ahead," I whisper. Without a word, he bends forward, pressing his lips to the leather of my shoes. "Good boy."

As he lifts back up, I notice a pleased expression on his face. Then I raise my foot and press the sharp stiletto heel against his shoulder. He slowly falls backward until he's lying on the floor, staring up at me with a devilish grin. He *looks* like a brat right now, and I fucking love it.

I press my heel down a little harder until he winces, finally giving up that smug look on his face.

"What did you do wrong today?"

"I sent you a video during the meeting."

"A video of what?"

He smiles again, so I press down harder, careful not to let my weight settle too hard on the foot currently in position to puncture his pecs.

"Me in the shower, stroking my dick for you."

"Why did you send me that video?"

When he smiles again, I move my foot from his shoulder to his throat, now being vigilant to balance carefully. His smile fades quickly. "Because I want your attention on me."

"Hmm..." I reply. "I think you did it because you're a filthy slut. Is that it?"

His mouth twitches. "Yes, ma'am."

"Thought so. Now get up."

After I remove my shoe from his windpipe, he stands. With a nod, I gesture toward the St. Andrew's cross against the wall, and he walks obediently over to it, so I can affix the cuffs to his wrists and ankles.

I take it a little easy on him tonight, only giving him

three lashes with the crop because I know any more than that will have him in a weeping mess on the floor by the time we're done. And I still have plans for him after this.

He takes the twelve paddle slaps and six rounds with the flogger extremely well. He's shivering, sweaty, and beet red by the time I uncuff him. His cock is leaking at the tip as I guide him by his collar to the bed, where I make him sit and then climb over him, kissing his mouth as I straddle his lap.

"Remind me again what you are," I whisper against his lips.

"A filthy slut," he replies as I lower myself over his hard length. He slides in with a groan, and I feel a shiver run through me when I have him as deep as he can go.

"*My* filthy slut," I reply before kissing him.

Our cries and groans echo through the room, and I know he has an extra sting of pain on his backside as I grind him into the bed, riding his cock until I come with a scream.

"Please, ma'am," he gasps when he feels my body constricting around him. "Can I please come?"

"Yes," I reply, grabbing his face in a fierce kiss. "You can come, Beau."

On command, he shudders inside me, grunting through his orgasm.

"Good boy," I whisper against his temple as he gasps for air, coming down from his climax.

We stay that way for a while, and after I feel his body slump against mine, I find the clasp of his collar and press it with a click until it releases from his neck.

After putting it away, I rub his back with some aloe balm, and let him rest between my bare legs with his head against my stomach. With my back against the headboard,

I stroke my fingers through his hair while he sips his drink. It's comfortable in the silence together.

The last year has felt like a dream. It took us three months to fix the mess the previous owners of the club left us. It was nothing like Salacious, but Beau and I were able to make it our own. Being a pair of reformed vanillas gave us a unique perspective for our members, and within nine months, membership was booming.

As for him and me, it's been a journey. It's never perfect, but I never expected it to be. No matter what, we're always us.

"Are you going to tell him your ideas for the club when he comes to visit next week?" I ask.

He shrugs. "Yeah, I don't see why not."

"Well, you two still act weird talking about the club."

"*He* acts weird," Beau argues, and I smile down at him.

"You are his son," I reply.

"Why they're choosing to come in the dead of summer, when it's fucking two hundred degrees outside, is beyond me."

"It is not two hundred degrees." I laugh.

"It feels like it," he says, making a disgruntled sound.

"Well, if you don't like it here, you can go back to California," I say in a teasing tone.

He freezes as he's screwing the cap on his protein drink. As he slowly looks up at me, I bite back the smile creeping across my face because I know exactly what's coming. I like to push his buttons on purpose.

"Ma'am, are you trying to get rid of me?"

I let out a squeal as he drags me down and pins my hands above my head, burying his face in my neck. His facial hair scratches my sensitive skin, and I giggle hard in his hold, his other hand pinching my backside.

"Oh, I know what you need," he says with a laugh, flipping me over.

"Beau!" I scream with a laugh before his large hand lands with a smack against my ass. I gasp, staring back in shock. He's frozen in place with a wicked grin stretched across his perfect face.

"You're in so much trouble for that," I say in a low whisper.

"Am I? Because I think you liked it."

With that, he spanks my ass again, and I can't help the whimper that comes out of my mouth.

His brows rise in interest, and I find myself blushing, but before he can do it again, I flip onto my back. He covers my body with his, and I stare up into his eyes.

"I would never try to get rid of you," I whisper, brushing his hair out of his face. "I love you too much."

His lips brush softly along my jawline. "I know you wouldn't. I'm yours."

"Yes, you are. Mine forever."

Rule #42: Play fair.

Beau's epilogue
Three years later

"Roll a constitution check," I say with a smug smile, crossing my arms.

"We're playing Yahtzee," Sophie replies with a sassy scowl.

Maggie giggles from the kitchen. Ever since Sophie moved here for college, choosing ASU over a school across the country so she'd have family if she needs it, she comes over for dinner and game night every week. We promised Charlie we'd keep an eye on her, like I wouldn't anyway.

As Sophie picks up two of the dice, she shuts her eyes and shakes them in her fist before tossing them out on the table. They both land on two, matching the other three dice.

"Yahtzee, asshole!" she yells with her arms in the air.

"I'm telling your mom you said that," I tease her as I mark her scorecard.

"I'm nineteen, you doofus."

Maggie laughs again as she sits in the chair next to me. Reaching under the table, I clasp her hand, and she squeezes back. I play with the simple silver band around her finger as I read out the scores.

Once I settle the scores on the sheet, I scowl at the teenager across from me who is wearing a proud smile as she shoves a handful of popcorn into her mouth.

"You beat us again," Maggie says to Sophie with a smile.

"You let him win," Sophie replies as we start putting the game away.

"Oh, she's never easy on me," I joke, giving Mags a sly wink.

"It's true."

"Same time next week?" Maggie asks as she hands Sophie a bag full of leftovers from dinner, along with whatever else a college student could possibly need from our pantry.

"Yep. Thanks for dinner. It was delicious," Sophie replies, pulling Maggie in for a hug.

"You know you're welcome anytime. Drive safe."

"I'll walk you out," I say to Soph after she slips on her shoes. She pats Ringo on the head before opening the front door and slipping out into the warm Arizona night.

Walking down the sidewalk to her car, she glances at me with a curious expression. "When are you two gonna get married?"

I laugh loudly. "Why should we get married?"

"Because you've been living together for, like, four years. You own a house together. Normal people get married."

"We're not normal," I reply as I open her car door. I

can't exactly add the part about how Maggie and I make commitments to each other that feel just as serious and binding as a marriage certificate.

"Well, *you're* not normal. But maybe she wants to get married."

I consider it for a moment as Sophie stuffs the big bag of food in the passenger side. Mags and I have had this conversation before. She was fine without a ceremony, but what if Sophie is right? What if I'm depriving Maggie of something she secretly wants?

"Are you worried that we're going to break up just because we're not married?"

Sophie laughs. "Not at all. I just keep wondering when you're going to grow up and do the adult thing."

"Hey," I reply, appearing offended, "I am grown up." But even as I say it, I hear how funny it sounds. I'm nearly twenty-six and I don't feel any older than eighteen most days. Running the club has given my life more purpose, but I still don't quite feel adult enough. "My point is that as long as you're happy, who cares if you follow convention. What other people think doesn't matter."

"I know," she replies with a genuine nod of her head. "I didn't mean anything by it. I was just curious. Seriously, you two are couple goals."

"Good," I reply, feeling a bit proud of that. Who knew I'd end up in a relationship that was considered *couple goals*.

Then she leans in for a hug, and I squeeze her tight under one arm before putting her in her car and watching her drive away. While I wait for her taillights to disappear, I shoot a quick response to the group chat I have with Gwen and Charlie, reassuring them that Sophie is doing well, not too thin or showing signs that she's getting into trouble. Honestly, it feels ridiculous. Sophie might as well be the most mature one out of all of us. She should be looking after us.

When I walk back into the house, the living room is dark and quiet, and I follow the dim light until I find Maggie sitting on the bed in nothing but a lacy bra, underwear, and her confidence-laced Domme face. My mouth waters at the sight.

"Well, hello, ma'am," I say as I drop slowly to my knees.

She hooks her finger at me, so I crawl toward her, just like I have hundreds of times before. A warm sense of comfort washes over me as she leans down, clipping the collar into place.

As it clicks, I furrow my brow. Sophie's words are stuck in my head. When Maggie senses the subtle hesitation on my face, she pauses.

"What's wrong?"

Kneeling between her legs, I gaze up and try to remember what it felt like the first time we were in this position. It was all so new and exciting back then. But now I'm so used to it, it's become second nature. This is who I am and she is what I need.

But is it still enough for her?

Is this promise around my neck enough to show Maggie that I'm hers, forever?

"Do you want to get married?" I ask, seemingly out of nowhere.

Her eyebrows lift as she stares down at me. "What?"

"Is this enough for you? Are you happy?"

"I'm very happy. Where is this coming from?" she asks.

"Sophie asked why we're not married. She said maybe

you would want to be and it had me worried. I would marry you, you know? I'd do it right now. If that's what you want."

Sensing the concern in my tone, she reaches down and wraps her hands around my neck.

"No, Beau. I don't want to get married." It doesn't exactly quell my worries.

"Why not? Don't you want a wedding? Some sort of show of commitment from me?" I ask.

When a gentle smile stretches across her lips, she kisses me. "Every day you give me love, you submit to me, you trust me with your body and your heart, and you stay faithful to me. *That* shows me your commitment. You choose me every single day. I'd rather have that than a legally binding contract any day. This collar around your neck is my wedding ring, and nothing in the world could mean more to me."

My shoulders relax as I let out a deep breath. I never thought about it like that. I do choose her every day, and she chooses me too. But when you find something perfect, you don't throw that away. "I love you," I whisper.

She pulls me up toward her for a kiss. Burying my hands in her hair, I let her deepen it. As she pulls away with a smile, I drop my hands.

"Can I make you come now?" I ask as I skate my fingers down her thighs.

"Only if you ask nicely."

"Please, ma'am. Can I make you feel good?"

She strokes my head with a smile.

"You've been so good today. Yes, you can."

I smile up at her before burying my face between her legs, loving the way she lets out a sweet whimper when I do. Making her feel good makes *me* feel good. And that's not something I ever thought I'd say before. But now that I know who I really am, it's not so weird to me anymore. This is what I was always meant to be—*hers*.

Want to hear news about the next Salacious Players Club news? Join the newsletter! geni.us/SaraCateNewsletter

---

If you liked Salacious Players Club, try The Wilde Boys! Start with Gravity: geni.us/GravityKindle

---

Want to read another older woman romance? Download Burn for Me on Kindle: geni.us/BurnForMe

Thank you

Well, that was something.

If you were blushing while reading Mercy, I promise I was blushing ten times as much writing it. If you were surprised to find your inner Domme, trust me, I was a hundred times more surprised.

Why? Well, you know that lecture Maggie got from her mother with the ripped up piece of paper? That was verbatim the same lecture I got as a young woman (Not from my mother, though. She would never.)

I grew up in the same world Maggie did, and I'm willing to bet a lot of you did too. If even one word in this novel helps to change that even a little bit, then it's worth it.

If the world wants to tell you you should be ashamed of your sexuality, then I will be louder. You have nothing to be ashamed of.

A year ago, I had an idea that I thought was just a good smutty story my readers would love. That idea became four stories, then an entire series, a whole world, a family, a movement.

We deserve better than the world we were born into, and I hope for one second you found an ounce of empowerment from these stories. Thank you so much to everyone who has reached out over the past few months to share your stories. You have no idea how encouraging that is for me.

I didn't do any of this alone, so I need to thank the amazing team I have by my side.

Amanda Anderson—look at what we did. None of this would have happened without you. Thank you for the support, encouragement, laughs, and friendship. Beau is yours.

Behind every good book is a beautiful team of beta readers. Adrian, Amanda, Brittni, and Claudia.

Tasha, thank you so much for your expertise and tough love. I hope Maggie has made you proud.

My editor, Rebecca's Fairest Reviews. Your dedication to this series does not go unnoticed. Thank you so much for everything!

My proofreader, Rumi Khan. I'm so blessed to have you on my team.

Lori, the hardest working PA in the business. I love you so much.

Misty—Thank you for joining me on this journey. Your love and support gets me through.

My business bishes—thank you for all of the advice, camaraderie, and friendship.

My Corn Star sisters—Rachel, Tits, Katie, Ashton, Gail, and Lori. The best thing to come from all of this craziness is our friendship.

And last, to my readers. Thank you for breathing life into this world and these characters.

We're not done. Not even close.

If you're still in, I'm still in.

And you better fucking believe we're coming back to Salacious. No way are we done now.

You think I would leave characters like Ronan Kade and Eden St. Claire without a story??

Also by Sara Cate

Salacious Players' Club

Praise

Eyes on Me

Give Me More

Mercy

Wilde Boys duet

Gravity

Freefall

Age-gap romance

Beautiful Monster

Beautiful Sinner

Reverse Age Gap romance

Burn for Me

Black Heart Duet

Four

Five

Cocky Hero Club

Handsome Devil

Wicked Hearts Series

Delicate

Dangerous

Defiant

About Sara Cate

Sara Cate writes forbidden romance with lots of angst, a little age gap, and heaps of steam. Living in Arizona with her husband and kids, Sara spends most of her time reading, writing, or baking.

You can find more information about her at www.saracatebooks.com

Made in United States
North Haven, CT
02 May 2023

36165687R00240